The Scientific Marvel Fiction
of the French H.-G. Wells

THE MASTER OF LIGHT

The Scientific Marvel Fiction
of the French H.-G. Wells

THE MASTER OF LIGHT

by
Maurice Renard

translated, annotated and introduced by
Brian Stableford

A Black Coat Press Book

Visit our website at www.blackcoatpress.com

ISBN 978-1-935558-19-4. First Printing. June 2010. Published
by Black Coat Press, an imprint of Hollywood Comics.com,
LLC, P.O. Box 17270, Encino, CA 91416. All rights reserved.
Except for review purposes, no part of this book may be reproduced or transmitted in any form or by any means, elec-
tronic or mechanical, including photocopying, recording, or by
any information storage and retrieval system, without permission in writing from the publisher. The stories and characters
depicted in this novel are entirely fictional. Printed in the
United States of America.

Introduction

This is the fifth volume of a set of five, which includes most of the "scientific marvel fiction" of Maurice Renard, and some related works. It comprises a translation of the novel *Le Maître de la lumière*, which first appeared as a *feuilleton* serial in *L'Intransigeant* between March 8 and May 2 1933.

The first volume of the series, *Doctor Lerne*, includes translations of the novella "Les Vacances de Monsieur Dupont," first published in *Fantômes et Fantoches* [Phantoms and Marionettes] (Plon, 1905), the novel *Le Docteur Lerne, sous-dieu* (Mercure de France, 1908) and the essay "Du Roman merveilleux-scientifique et de son action sur l'intelligence du progrès," first published in the sixth issue of *Le Spectateur* in October 1909.

The second volume, *A Man Among the Microbes and Other Stories*, includes translations of the novel *Un Home chez les microbes*, the first version of which was written in 1907-08, although no version was actually published until Crès released one in 1928, and the entire contents of the collection *Le Voyage Immobile suivi d'autres histoires singulières* (Mercure de France, 1909).

The third volume, *The Blue Peril*, comprises a translation of the novel *Le Péril bleu* (Louis Michaud, 1911).

The fourth volume, *The Doctored Man and Other Stories*, includes translations of four stories from the collection *Monsieur d'Outremort et autres histoires singulières* (Louis Michaud, 1913), the novella "L'Homme truqué," first published in *Je Sais Tout* in March 1921, and a miscellany of later short stories taken from various sources.

The introduction to the first of the five volumes includes a general overview of Renard's life and career in relation to his scientific marvel fiction, which I shall not reiterate here, confining the remainder of this brief introduction to the specif-

5

ic work featured in this volume. I shall, however, reserve discussion of the novel's central speculative motif until an afterword, in order not to give too much of the plot away in advance.

Renard's intention to write a novel entitled *Le Maître de la lumière*, the 1933 version of which is here translated as *The Master of Light*, was first registered in the preliminary matter to the 1920 reprint of *Le Péril bleu* (tr. as *The Blue Peril* in volume three of the series). The title was included there in a list of four works "*à paraître*" [forthcoming] and explicitly labeled as a *roman* [novel].

Whether Renard had actually done any work on the novel in question at that stage, or whether it was merely an idea he hoped and intended to develop, there is no way of knowing. All possibilities are open to conjecture, including the possibility that the novel he had in mind in 1920 actually had no connection other than its projected title with the one that was serialized in 1933, and the possibility that he had already produced of a version of the novel before or during the Great War. The likelihood is, however, that in 1920 he had already written at least part of a draft of the novel that was eventually revised for publication in 1933, the specific role played by a key event of the year 1930 in the published version being an artifact of the revision.

It seems probable that Renard came up with the idea of the central speculative motif of *Le Maître de la lumière* after writing an earlier story, "Le Brouillard du 26 Octobre," which was published in *Monsieur d'Outremort et autres histoires singulières* in 1913 and is translated in volume four of this series as "The Fog of October 26." That story, which is set in 1907 and might have been written some years before its appearance in the collection, describes what its characters interpret as a sort of "mirage," which allows scenes from the remote past to be seen in the present. Although that vision eventually turns out to be a conventional time-slip rather than an optical effect, the character's attempts to reason it out in that fashion presumably reflected mental effort that Renard put in himself, in the hope of rationalizing the phenomenon he wanted to describe, and that mental effort was presumably not bounded by the story. The idea for *Le Maître de la lumière* might easily have resulted therefrom.

Renard grew disillusioned with the possibility of publishing any more scientific marvel fiction within a year of placing that advertisement in *Le Péril bleu*, and shelved any work he had already done on the version of *Le Maître de la lumière* that he had previously hoped to complete. His eventual decision to resume work on it was probably prompted by the fact that a work that had been on the shelf even longer, *Un Homme chez les microbes* (tr. in volume two as *A Man Among the Microbes*), had finally reached print in 1928 thanks to Georges Crès, who had, by then, been his regular publisher for some years.

Renard probably did not have Crès solely or immediately in mind when he planned the revised version of *Le Maître de la lumière*, because that publisher had also reprinted another work with a scientific marvel component, which had first appeared as a feuilleton serial in *L'Intransigeant*: *Le Singe* (1924; tr. as *Blind Circle*), written in collaboration with Albert Jean—who was probably the original author of a manuscript that Renard was commissioned to revise. The new version of *Le Maître de la lumière* was almost certainly written with a view to similar double publication, and designed with that in mind—although Crès did not, in fact, reprint it after its serialization and did not publish anything else by Renard after 1933, when he issued another work that the author had shelved before the Great War, the historical study *Notre Dame Royale*. It was left to Tallandier to reprint the serial in book form, but that did not happen until 1947, 14 years after the serialization and eight years after Renard's death.

Feuilleton serials were on their last legs in the 1930s, although Renard was to publish several more after *Le Maître de la lumière*—none of them in *L'Intransigeant* and none of them having any scientific marvel content—and the fundamental method of their construction had long been formularized. Newspapers had readers of both sexes, and it was widely believed that female readers were slightly more likely than their male counterparts to be interested in serial fiction, so that fiction had to be careful to appeal to both sexes. In practical terms, editorial wisdom specified that "appealing to both sexes" consisted of cleverly amalgamating the mystery/thriller fiction that male readers were generally supposed to prefer with the syrupy love stories to which female readers were held to be devoted, both components being liberally seasoned with melodrama and suspense in order to prevent reader interest from flagging. In effect, feuilletons had to do exactly the same sort of narrative labor as modern television soap operas.

Renard had bent these rules and stretched these limits in the past, but he must have become keenly aware by 1933 of the hazards of so doing, and he obviously set out to plan the revised version of *Le Maître de la lumière* as a work that would tick all the feuilleton boxes—because if it did not, the unconventional move of adding a scientific marvel component to the mix would probably guarantee its rejection. Indeed, he apparently went further than the requirements of the day by adding in some components that harked all the way back to the heyday of feuilleton fiction, deliberately recalling some of its classic but long-obsolete clichés.

Renard had long been a loyal member of the Société des Gens de Lettres—he was to be elected as its vice-president in 1935—and knew full well that a leading role in the early history of that organization had been taken by Paul Féval, the great pioneer of *feuilleton* crime fiction, in such works as *Jean Diable* (1861; tr. in a Black Coat Press edition as *John Devil*) and the *Habits Noirs* series (launched 1863; currently appearing in translation in Black Coat Press editions as *The Blackcoats* at the rate of one volume per year). *Le Maître de la lumière* reproduces several of the key components of Féval's works in this vein, including a Corsican vendetta, a key setting in the Boulevard du Temple, and the hoariest cliché of them all, which even Féval satirized in *Les Habits Noirs* as a "cardboard baby:" an ex-foundling whose true ancestry will ultimately be revealed in the course of the plot by virtue of meager relics found along with him.

It is highly unlikely that Renard wrote *Le Maître de la lumière* in the same way that Féval other renowned *feuilletonistes* wrote their serials, making it up as they went along and delivering their copy on the eve of publication, often having written it that morning; it is much too intricately-plotted for that to have been the case. There are however, signs that he inserted extra explanations in response to editorial request, and sometimes stretched his copy in order to spin it out (by the time-honored method of inserting gratuitous sequences of terse dialogue), so he might well have been rewriting on a near-daily basis as he put narrative flesh on the bones of a detailed pre-existent plan.

However the composition was orchestrated, though, there is no doubt that *Le Maître de la lumière* is a *bravura* performance of the *feuilletoniste*'s slightly-dubious art, featuring everything but the kitchen sink (*L'Intransigeant* was an ultra-conservative "family newspaper;" it had once serialized a reprint of *Le Péril bleu*, but would never have played host to the kind of scandalous eroticism paraded in *Le Docteur Lerne*). As an example of what it actually aspires to be—which is not at all the same as what the novel that Renard advertised in 1920 would presumably have aspired to be—it is carried off with consummate skill and not a little flair, and is therefore fully entitled to take its place as a significant addendum to the chronicle of Renard's magnificent, but ultimately ill-fated, endeavors as a writer of scientific marvel fiction.

This translation has been taken from the version of the novel reprinted in *Maurice Renard: Romans et Contes Fantastiques*, the omnibus published in 1990 by Robert Laffont. I have not been able to check it against any earlier addition, but the text appears to be quite clean, with only a few trivial typos.

Brian Stableford

THE MASTER OF LIGHT

I. The Tender and Romantic Adventure

This extraordinary story begins in a very ordinary manner.

At the end of September 1929 the young historian Charles Christiani decided to spend a few days in La Rochelle. A historian specializing in the study of the Restoration and the reign of Louis-Philippe, at that time he had already published a well-regarded little book on *Les Quatre Sergents de La Rochelle*;[1] he was writing another on the same subject and thought it necessary to return to the location in order to consult certain documents.

---

[1] The four sergeants of La Rochelle, who had been soldiers stationed there, were guillotined in Paris in September 1822, having been denounced as participants in a plot to assassinate Louis XVIII. They were also alleged to be members of a Bonapartist secret society allied or affiliated to the Italian Carbonari. Their refusal to name any co-conspirators or fellow Carbonari members won them a reputation for heroism among admiring Republicans—no one seems to have considered the alternative hypothesis that there were no names to reveal, because the plot and the secret organization were illusory—and the publicity attached to their case provided an enormous, and presumably very welcome, boost to the popularity and notoriety of the Carbonari. As Renard was undoubtedly aware, the incident had a considerable influence on French popular fiction; the allegations and rumors associated with it provided Paul Féval with a significant model for the secret societies that feature so extensively in his work.

It seems irrelevant to us to ask why the Christiani family had already returned to the Rue de Tournon in Paris at a time of year when the fortunate members of that society were still at the seaside, traveling or in the country. Autumn had begun morosely, and we believe that was the only reason for their slightly premature return—for Madame Christiani, her daughter and her son did not lack the means to lead the most expansive existence, and had rural retreats at their disposal in which more or less active vacations might be enjoyed. Two beautiful family properties, in fact, were available to their choice: the old Château de Silaz in Savoy, which they had forsaken completely, and a pleasant country house situated near Meaux, where they had spent the entire summer.

For the moment, the noble and spacious apartment in the Rue de Tournon accommodated, in the Christianis, three people in perfect harmony. Madame Louise Christiani, *née* Bernardi, aged 50 years old, was the widow of Adrien Christiani, who had died for France in 1915. Her son Charles was 26. Her charming daughter Colomba, who was not yet 20, was responsible for the adjunction of a fourth character: Bertrand Valois, the darling of our dramatic authors and the happiest fiancé on the terrestrial globe.

It ought to be noted that Madame Christiani attempted—without, however, insisting—to persuade her son to delay his departure for La Rochelle. That same morning, she had received a letter that seemed to require Charles to spend some time in Savoy, at the Château de Silaz, which they never visited except to take care of matters of farm-rents or repairs. This letter came from an old and devoted steward, Claude—pronounced Glaude if you wish to respect local usage. He spoke therein of various matters related to the management of the estate, saying that the presence of Monsieur Charles would be very useful in that respect, and that, in addition, he desired that presence for another reason, which he did not wish to explain because "Madame would laugh at him"—and yet, things were happening at Silaz that disturbed him and old Péronne:

extraordinary things with which it was absolutely necessary to deal.

"He sounds a little crazy," said Madame Christiani. "Perhaps you'd do better, Charles, to go to Silaz first."

"No, Mama. You know Claude and Péronne. They're worthy old souls, but simple and superstitious. I'll wager that it concerns another story of some revenant, or *sarvant*,[2] as they say. Believe me, it can wait—I'm certain of it. As I've notified the librarian at La Rochelle of my arrival, you'll appreciate that I don't want to make a bad impression on him because of these excellent but simple old folks. As for the business affairs—the *real* affairs—there's obviously nothing urgent.

"As you wish, my child. I leave it up to you. How long will you stay in La Rochelle?"

"In La Rochelle itself, exactly two days—but my intention is to make a small detour as I return to the Ile d'Oléron, with which I'm unfamiliar. I've just learned from the concierge that Luc de Certeuil is there. He's competing in a tennis tournament at Saint-Trojan; it's a good opportunity for me..."

"Luc de Certeuil..." Madame Christiani pronounced, without the slightest enthusiasm—with a rather marked reprobation, in fact.

---

[2] The Laffont edition renders this word as "*servant*," presumably following the Tallandier text, although the version of *Le Péril bleu* in the same omnibus follows the previous editions of that novel in rendering it as "*sarvant*" and the present text subsequently offers that spelling as an alternative. I thought it best to unify the spelling between the two volumes of the present set, especially in view of the awkward double meaning of "servant," which does not have the same range in English as it does in French. *Servant* is used more often as an adjective than a noun in French, although its use as a noun had become more common between 1911 and 1933 because of its application to members of artillery gun-crews in the Great War.

"Oh, don't worry, Mama. I don't have any excessive affection for him—but let's not exaggerate. He's like many others, neither better nor worse; I'll be happy to find someone I know on that unknown isle, and I know that he'll be very happy to see me."

"Of course!" said Madame Christiani, while a gleam of irritation shone in her dark eyes—and, with a gesture that revealed her annoyance, she smoothed the blue-tinted hatbands that framed her suntanned Mediterranean visage. She did not like Luc de Certeuil. He had a three-room apartment in the building overlooking the courtyard. Charles, who did not go out much, would doubtless never had met him save for that circumstance, of which the other had taken advantage to cultivate his friendship. Luc was a good-looking man devoid of scruples, a sportsman and a dancer. He was attractive to women in spite of his disconcerting gaze. Madame Christiani, being mistrustful and resolute, had kept him at a distance until her daughter Colomba was engaged.

"At any rate," she said, "do you think you can be in Silaz within a week?"

"Certainly."

"Good. I'll write to tell Claude that."

This dialogue took place on a Monday. The following Thursday, at 2 p.m., Charles Christiani, accompanied by the librarian—who had greatly facilitated his investigations— came into La Rochelle harbor looking for the steam-yacht *Boyardville*, which was about to depart for the Ile d'Oléron.

His companion, Monsieur Palanque, the municipal librarian, pointed it out to him: a steamship of more imposing dimensions than Charles had imagined. The vessel, lying alongside the quay, was animated by that human effervescence which always precedes crossings, however insignificant they might be. With a racket of unraveling chains, derricks were lowering cargo through the hatchways of the hold. Passengers were going across the gangplank.

For many years, the *Boyardville* had been making a daily voyage from La Rochelle to Boyardville on the Ile d'Oléron and back, stopping off at the Ile d'Aix when the sea permitted—which is to say, usually. The timetable of departures varied according to the tide. The duration of the voyage, in either direction, was about two hours, sometimes more.

Monsieur Palanque accompanied the young historian on to the deck. The latter deposited his suitcase against the wall of the first-class lounge and reserved one of those pliant armchairs known as "transatlantic."

The weather, without being splendid, left nothing to be desired. Although the sky lacked purity, the Sun was bright enough to cast shadows and to bathe the incomparable scene of La Rochelle harbor, with its ancient walls and historic towers, in warm light.

"In Boyardville," said Monsieur Palanque, "you'll easily find a cab that will get you to Saint-Trojan in less than half an hour. In summer, there's probably a coach-service as well."

"I could have notified the friend I'm going to meet of my arrival. He never goes anywhere except by automobile—and at top speed, moreover!—but he would have felt obliged to come and collect me in Boyardville, and I always try not to put people out."

Monsieur Palanque, who was looking at Charles Christiani in the most ordinary fashion imaginable, caught sight of an abrupt change in his interlocutor's expression: a momentary disturbance, immediately suppressed, and a glint in the eyes of the sort produced by suddenly-awakened attention. Involuntarily, Monsieur Palanque followed the direction of the other's gaze as it was drawn to some unexpected and undoubtedly more interesting particularity—and thus discovered the object of that intensified curiosity.

Two young women, discreetly but perfectly elegant, were just setting foot on deck, having crossed the gangplank.

Two young women? A momentary examination modified the initial judgment. The blonde, yes, that one was a woman—but the brunette could not be any more than a girl; she bore the exquisite hallmarks of juvenile splendor in her beauty.

"Here are some pleasant traveling companions!" said the worthy Monsieur Palanque, as if he were congratulating the fortunate passenger.

"Indeed!" Charles murmured. "Are they local? Do you know them?"

"I don't have that honor, and I regret it! I've never seen them before."

"She's lovely, isn't she?"

"Which one?" asked Monsieur Palanque, smiling.

"Oh, the brunette, of course!" said Charles, reproachfully.

A porter carrying their baggage was following the two female travelers. On their instructions, he deposited his burden not far from Charles Christiani's suitcase.

The *Boyardville*'s siren whistled three times, amid a jet of white vapor. The vessel was about to cast off.

"I'll leave you to it!" said Monsieur Palanque, hurriedly. "Have a pleasant stay in Oléron and a safe journey back to Paris!"

A few minutes later the *Boyardville*, exiting from La Rochelle harbor, left behind the celebrated scene of keeps and lanterns and set a course southwards.

The two women had installed themselves in their armchair on deck. In order to get closer to them, Charles had only to sit down in the one that he had reserved. The passengers were not very numerous. Sheltered in a sort of alcove, the three first-class passengers were relatively isolated.

Charles listened to his neighbors' conversation. They were speaking quite freely, and there was no need for him to strain his ears to hear them. The blonde woman—who was a very pale blonde—was making almost all of the conversation by herself. Her quavering and languid voice was indefatigable. Charles found its soft inflexions irritating. As for the brunette, she limited herself to replying soberly, in order not to be impolite, whenever she was forced to do so by a "Don't you think so?" or a "Wouldn't you say, Rita?" She spoke calmly, in a low-pitched and musical voice.

So her name was Rita—and her friend was Geneviève. There was nothing to inform Charles of their surnames, but the manner in which they talked about La Rochelle made it easy for him to understand that they had just spent 48 hours visiting the town. Then certain phrases revealed to him that they were returning to Oléron, where they had already been staying for some time, following that instructive excursion. There was mention of tennis matches. The words "Saint-Trojan" recurred several times; that was where they were returning, and where they were staying. There was mention on the blonde side of "my uncle," "my cousins" and "my brother," and on the brunette side of "my mother" and "my parents." Names were mentioned in familiar terms—including, among others, Luc de Certeuil.

Singularly satisfied, as a man always is when a man finds the connivance of chance in his favor, Charles Christiani considered introducing himself immediately. It seemed more appropriate, though, to be patient and to await some opportunity that would doubtless crop up to furnish him with an admissible pretext. He resolved that, if necessary, he would contrive that pretext.

Chance, however, continued to favor to him—so strangely that the young man began to it as the marvelous assurance of a providential hand steering events to the benefit of his desires and happiness.

The conversation of Madame Geneviève X and Mademoiselle Rita Z faded away. Its initial impetus exhausted, the chatter became sparse, all the more so because Rita never made any contribution to its alimentation. The large boat rocked gently at the whim of a tranquil sea. A pleasantly fresh breeze ran through the air. The girl picked up a bag, took a book out of it, and opened it, saying: "I have to finish this."

Now that book was none other than Charles Christiani's latest work: *Les Quatre Sergents de La Rochelle*—the short but substantial account he had written on the request of an editor, which evidently constituted a handy little book for the use of tourists.

He saw—with what delight!—the beautiful unknown absorb herself in reading his work, devouring the pages that remained to be read. It was a profound joy for him, of a rare quality. Rita, this mysterious Rita, did not know that he was there, close by, and she was providing him with the feast of an undeniably sincere admiration—a girl who had subjugated him at first glance, and whom he had suddenly placed in advance of all the women in the world.

Eventually, Rita closed the book and, placing it mechanically against her cheek, lost herself in thought.

"Finished?" asked Geneviève. "Still entranced?"

The low-pitched voice pronounced: "It's really very, very good"—upon which Charles estimated that if he were going to intervene, the moment had come. The praise that Rita had already conferred rendered the situation a trifle embarrassing for him, for her and for Geneviève, who had revealed the "entrancement" of the reader. To let the young women proceed any further with the eulogy might stupidly compromise the continuation of the adventure. His delicacy, moreover, protested.

He got to his feet, took off his hat and said, with a politeness mingled with confusion: "Pardon me, Madame, and you too, Mademoiselle, but I have quite unwittingly discovered coincidences that enchant me: that you are bound, as I am, for Saint-Trojan; that we have a friend in common, Luc de Certeuil; and, to cap it all, Mademoiselle, the book that you have just finished reading is by an author to whom I am very attached. Permit me, therefore to introduce myself to you: Charles Christiani."

As he had anticipated and feared, his intrusion caused a considerable disturbance. They had begun by staring at him in astonishment; then, as his explanation continued, their cheeks had colored brightly; and now he could see them in front of him, as red as two red roses, their young bosoms heaving.

"Monsieur," said Rita, "I'm charmed…"

Charles immediately began speaking again. He feared the embarrassed silence that might otherwise have left both of them speechless. He had also had an idea—an idea that would surely acquaint him with the name of his adorable admirer. "It would be a genuine pleasure for me," he said, taking out his pen, "to inscribe this little volume for you, since it has not displeased you. Will you give me your authorization?"

Rita, smiling, shook her head. "I would be flattered by that, Monsieur, but the book doesn't belong to me. It belongs to my friend here, Madame Le Tourneur, who will doubtless be very happy for you to inscribe it to her."

The historian for the *Quatre Sergents* bowed, constraining his smile to remain on his lips, even though the smile was not disposed to do so. For Madame Le Tourneur, instead of protesting and immediately offering the volume to Rita, maintained an exasperating silence.

"I shall, therefore, be glad to send you a copy of your own," he said, turning to the girl. He was on the point of asking her for her name and address, for this purpose, but he stopped himself; the bad taste of the device restrained him from employing it, in violation of the rules of etiquette that were still observed, thank God, in his family and his society.

He wrote a few lines of classic gallantry on the title page, beneath the name of Geneviève Le Tourneur—after which the latter, charmed, read the dedication, made Rita read it, and finally replaced it in the bag from which it had emerged, whose tan leather bore her initials: *G. L. T.* None of the other bags and cases was marked with any identification.

It's truly inexcusable for me to show myself so rarely at salons, Charles thought. *It's quite idiotic. Otherwise, I'd have made* her *acquaintance a long time ago. No matter! She's exquisite; she admires me a little; she is, indubitably, from an excellent family. The weather's fine! God, how fine it is!*

It was, as is evident, the "thunderbolt" in all its magnificence. This time, though, in complete contrast to the most common cases, everything seemed to prove that the thunderbolt had fallen in both directions at the same time. Two flashes of lightning, sprung from two inner beings, had intersected—so neatly that the exchange of sparks had struck both of them

19

simultaneously with a powerful, unexpected and delightful commotion. That is very rare.

Poor Geneviève Le Tourneur, having assumed the responsibility of chaperoning Rita, quickly perceived the truth. She made that obvious by fidgeting, moving her fingers over the keyboard of an imaginary piano, and assuming a fearful expression in her features. But Rita did not notice that at all, or did not care. It seemed that Geneviève no longer existed, so far as she was concerned, as she abandoned herself to the joys of a dialogue that was admirably banal, but in which she and Charles took great pleasure in listening to one another talk, by turns.

Charles could not doubt Rita's sentiments. To tell the truth, given the condition of his heart, he would not have doubted them even if those sentiments had not been those he desired.

Geneviève, being a woman and a disinterested observer, was not deceived in that regard—so she made her anxiety and reprobation manifest, albeit in vain. Neglected, she ended up getting to her feet and, darting a glance full of warnings at Rita, drew away at a nonchalant pace—only to come back almost immediately to say: "We're arriving at the Ile d'Aix."

She seemed glad to break up the intimacy of that sweet conversation, to which the Greeks would have given the musical name *oaristys*.[3]

---

[3] Actually, this variant of the Greek *oaristis* [familiar conversation] is entirely French, the variant spelling having been improvised by André Chénier in 1794 as a title for his translation of an idyll by Theocritus. The title was then adopted as a label for a subgenre of poetry comprising poems cast as intimate dialogues of an affectionate and erotic character, production of which was sparse until the formula was adopted by the Symbolists—where Renard undoubtedly came across it while he was a Symbolist fellow-traveler before the outbreak of the Great War.

Charles and Rita seemed to wake up. "Already!" the exclaimed, in unison.

The boat changed direction. The Ile d'Aix appeared to them. A sailor circulated among the groups of passengers and told them that the stopover, unusually, would be half an hour rather than a few minutes, because an exceptionally important cargo had to be unloaded. Any tourists who wanted to disembark there were authorized to do so.

"I know the Ile d'Aix," said Rita. "I visited it last year with my parents—but I'd gladly see it again."

"I don't know it myself," said Geneviève, "but do you think that half an hour is time enough…"

"It's very tiny. One can easily take account of its general aspect. Monsieur Christiani has never been there either. Would you like to go with us, Monsieur?"

"At your disposal!" the man in question accepted, joyfully. He admired Rita's decisiveness, the contained ardor that emanated from her slender person, the dark fire in her eyes and—when he looked her full in the face—all the honesty, will-power and occasional enigmatic shadows of profound thought that those eyes revealed: a consciousness of actions, their importance and consequences. This young girl was "someone:" a force, an intelligence, an energy. A true woman, above all, to whom he felt himself drawn by a thousand influences: to her adventurous spirit; to the feminine mystery he divined within her. There was also something else acting to draw him magnetically toward so much grace and beauty: the muffled conviction—perhaps illusory—that they were both, in some unknown fashion, from the same sentimental country; that the same climate regulated their temperament; and that, speaking the same language, their hearts had a common fatherland in the Europe of love.

"Let's go!" she said.

The *Boyardville* came about, its engines reversing, then going forwards, with bells ringing and the rudder-chain grinding. Mooring-ropes were thrown ashore. A crowd of passengers formed at the cutaway, ready to disembark.

They were able to study the walls of the fortifications and, higher up, in front of the distant semaphore-station, two harshly white twin towers, one surmounted by a lantern-light, the other by a screen of red glass.

The gangplank linked the steamship to the extremity of a pier.

"Come on, quickly!" said Rita. "We'll go through the village and take a look at the fields..."

They accelerated their steps and rapidly drew ahead of the bulk of the tourists.

Deserted drawbridges. Unmanned sentry-posts. A verdant and shady parade-ground framed by geometrically-sloped embankments. Beyond that, a white and silent village, where they breathed an air that was no longer that of the present day.

Addressing herself to Charles, Geneviève said: "It was from here, wasn't it, that Napoleon departed for Saint Helena?"

The young historian summarized that tragic chapter of the imperial epic in a few words. He did so briefly, careful not to make any ostentatious display of his knowledge. The subject was, however, of some personal interest—not because he had the slightest inclination to write about Napoléon I, but because the Emperor's history was linked to that of his ancestor, the corsair captain César Christiani. Like Napoléon, César had been born at Ajaccio, and on the same day—with the result that "the other" had always protected him, in memory of what seemed to him to be a fateful conjunction.

There could be no question of visiting the Napoleonic museum installed in the building known as "the Emperor's House;" there was not enough time. They contented themselves with walking less rapidly as they passed before its time-worn door, with its worn steps and its humble columns, by which one might say that the man of Waterloo had left France never to return—alive, at least.

More drawbridges, or rather bridges that had once been capable of being raised. Moats full of stagnant water. And, before the three visitors, bordered to the right by a graceful cove, in the background by fleecy woods and to the left by military earthworks covered in grass, a little sunlit plain.

The entire island, or very nearly, was there.

"There's no point going any further," Rita declared. "We don't have time. It's regrettable, because over there, on the far side of the woods, one has the most beautiful view over the straits of Antioch, the Ile de Ré, La Rochelle and so on. Let's not think about it."

"We have to go back to the harbor," Geneviève decided. "We only have 13 minutes."

"I know a short cut. Going that way, to our left, and along the shore, we'll arrive very quickly—and on the way we'll see the beach, which is pleasant. Last year, we stayed here for three days, my parents and I; I could have stayed for weeks! But Papa was bored…"

"And he wouldn't hide it!" joked Madame Le Tourneur. "What a bear!"

Rita frowned almost imperceptibly, and her expression darkened again. She walked beside Charles, elbow to elbow, along the narrow and shady street. Few women walk along the by-ways of life with such a harmonious stride.

Charles, already sensitive to everything that the slender young girl felt, enveloped her with a gaze as loving as it was attentive, but without daring to question her on the subject of the father who was "a bear."

She raised her head again and smiled gaily. "Look!" she said. "You see: the Ile d'Oléron!"

They had passed through an archway that pierced an embankment, and they found themselves confronted by the sea.

On the horizon, a solid line terminated by the vertical streak of a lighthouse, separated the vast luminous sky from the green extent of the waves.

"Are you sure this is a short cut?" asked Charles, consulting his watch.

"Let's hurry!" said Madame Le Tourneur.

Rita had made no reply. To begin with, she followed a winding path which snaked between stone blocks not far from the shore, through a wilderness of grass that was growing tall and dry. It seemed to be zigzagging at will.

Suddenly, behind the mass of outcrops beyond which the summits of the semaphore and the twin lighthouses could be seen, the siren of the *Boyardville* was heard three times—the signal of an imminent departure.

"There it goes!" grumbled Geneviève. "I was certain of it. We're in trouble now!"

Charles assumed that the boat would whistle again before putting to sea. Was that not the custom?

Rita continued on her way silently. Her companions, moving in Indian file, could not see her face.

As they arrived on the beach, where several bathers were frolicking, the bow of a great steamship was displayed, drawing away, seeming to emerge from a mass of trees and rocks that had hidden it until then.

"Oh well!" said Charles, placidly. "It's the *Boyardville*."

"Oh, Rita! Really!" groaned Madame Le Tourneur.

"I'm extremely sorry, my dear Geneviève."

"Ah!" said the young woman, annoyed. "What are we going to do now? Yes, it's funny—you can laugh!"

"But I'm not laughing, Geneviève. What can I do about it, though? We've missed the boat—it happens to everyone..."

"We're expected at Saint-Trojan," complained the young woman, reproachfully. "They'll be waiting for us, for sure, in Boyardville..." She lowered her eyelids before Rita's gaze; the latter was still smiling, but her eyes had taken on a certain fixity. Their softness, without any deception, revealed such profound and absolute calmness that she had become imperious.

"And there's our luggage!" Geneviève recriminated, in a defeated tone.

Charles said nothing. An immense joy overwhelmed him. He was certain that Rita had just executed a preconceived plan. She was not the sort of person to make that kind of mistake, and she knew exactly what she wanted. What had she wanted? To spend 24 hours with him, in the retreat of this silent and restful isle. For all three of them knew full well that the *Boyardville* would not come back until the following afternoon, heading for Oléron. For what reason had she decided upon this somewhat romantic subterfuge?

Was she romantic? Charles hesitated to believe it. No, no, if she had done it, it was because she had understood that such a good opportunity might not reappear for a long time and that, once back in Saint-Trojan, she would not be in control of the situation to the extent she was today, reclaimed as she would be by the obligations of society—curious, malicious, gossipy society—under the authority of a father who was not indulgent. Did she want to study Charles at her leisure, better than she could in any other circumstances? Had she simply yielded to a desire to prolong a tender intimacy that Geneviève's presence sanctioned without inconveniencing it unduly? What did it matter? There was so much independence in that undoubtedly-premeditated action, put so firmly at the service of such an inclination, that the dazzled Charles was bowled over by it. He waited for his throat to unclench so that he might speak. In any case, they had started walking again, and the village was suddenly very close, as they rounded a knoll.

"I'll send telegrams to Boyardville and Saint-Trojan," Rita said. "The hotelier in Boyardville will hold on to our luggage until tomorrow."

"It might perhaps be possible to get there by motorboat?" suggested Geneviève.

Ignoring her proposal, Rita took her by the arm. "Come with me to the Post Office. In the meantime, Monsieur Christiani will be good enough to find rooms for us. There are two hotels next door to one another, Monsieur, at the corner of the main street and the parade-ground. Would you care to go there?"

He was able to understand that she wanted an opportunity to talk to her friend in private. She doubtless wanted to complete the task of wining her over, which could only be done while Charles was present by means of glances and notoriously insufficient sign language.

In fact, when they met up again he found Madame Le Tourneur much more cheerful and entirely ready, it seemed, to play the role of complaisant young duenna to the end. What followed demonstrated, moreover, that she could do so with abundant aptitude.

The Ile d'Aix's two hoteliers were almost full. Of the few rooms they contained, only one was free; a supplementary camp-bed was introduced therein, enabling the young women to pass the night tolerably. As for Charles, he had to be content, in the other establishment, with a sofa, to which some bedclothes would be added. The holiday season had not finished, and the isle's regulars were taking advantage of the restfulness that they found there until the end.

Madame Le Tourneur seemed to be satisfied by an arrangement that separated Rita's and Charles's sleeping arrangements under different roofs. Reassured on this point and perhaps confirming to instructions she had just received, she declared herself to be rather tired, inclined to go to bed until dinner...

Her companions in misfortune went out again, alone at last, and were not long delayed in discovering, not far from the village, a blanket of grass that seemed to be waiting for them, beneath lovely trees. From there, between the bushy terraces of an artillery-emplacement, they could see an expanse of sea in the shape of a trapezium. Dusk was beginning to fall. The Sun was setting in a reddening sky, increasingly fiery...

And as they chatted, Charles heart became increasingly heated. To an ever-greater extend he savored the delights of the marvelous adventure, seasoned by a mystery that Rita continued to maintain. Who was she? At the end of the day, that was not importance, since they pleased one another mutually, and she gave evidence of a faultless education and an elevated mind. So Charles meekly accepted the piquant game of secrecy and made no effort to violate his companion's incognito.

The atmosphere emitted by such an accord exhaled a special, curious and amusing perfume: that of intrigues and fairy tales. Chasing away the word "romantic" again—which returned nevertheless with significant insistence—Charles thought that she wanted to test him, to assure herself of his conscience and his sentiments, to acquire the certainty that she was loved for herself, outside of any consideration foreign to the mind, the soul and the heart. Was she, for example, very poor? Everything belied that: her dress and the clothes that she wore; her charming and pure hands; the indefinable confidence imprinted in her features, whose serene lines had never been crumpled by any anguish. Was she very rich, then? Too rich? Did she fear that Charles, moved by omnipotent scruples, might recoil before millions? Did she want, first of all, to attach him by bonds so solid that nothing in the world could release them?

In all of that, Charles could only discern, wisely, one more reason to love her—since all of it, whatever its cause, proved that she loved him.

They were in love with one another! The evidence of it leapt to the eye while, as night fell, they went back to one of the hotels for dinner. They were in love with one another! That prodigious, unimaginable thing had occurred, as abrupt as an impact, as violent and stunning as a kind of divinely morbid stroke—a sort of voluptuous transport of the brain that had modified the regime of their blood in an exquisite manner.

Madame Le Tourneur, sitting by the door on the terrace of the hotel, watched them coming back. She could not help being alarmed by their approach—as if, in the shades of dusk, they were made of light. All through dinner, which manly consisted of fish and cockles, she had the same impression, and tried to hide the embarrassment of being a third party between two such palpitant and radiant victims of the god of Love. She was, however, unable to hide that embarrassment, or the anxiety that gradually overtook her as she was bathed in the quivering radiation of which they were, so to speak, the blissful emitters.

The worst thing about that was that the evening extended indefinitely. Rita was obstinately determined to prolong it well into the night. Charles, who would have followed her to the ends of space and time, surrendered to that nocturnal fantasy delightedly. Finally, though, they gave in to the imploring objurgations of Madame Le Tourneur, and the separation was accepted at about 2 a.m.

The daylight had not yet acquired its full force when Charles came out into the street. Silence weighed upon the dead village. Nevertheless, light footsteps resonated on wooden steps in the depths of the other hotel. It was Rita. She had sworn not to lose a minute of the hours that she had won.

At the sight of her, Charles felt a doubt—to which the solitude and the matinal lucidity had given birth in him—die away. What doubt? This one: that he had perhaps, been mistaken. Perhaps he had mistaken his desires for realities; perhaps Rita had not had any intention of missing that boat...

The young woman had only to appear within the frame of the doorway and everything became quite simple and favorable again. She was as fresh as if she had just emerged from a bathroom lacking none of the refinements of luxury. Her suntanned complexion, without make-up, warmed in the cheeks like a crimson reflection of the dawn. Her dark shiny hair had blue tints. The air around her was scented with the morning in the midst of the morning.

But shutters clattered on the second floor of the building. Disheveled, with her hair in her eyes, still heavy with sleep, and her bare arms raised, Geneviève cried out in anguish: "Rita!"

"What is it?" was the response, with a tranquil and cheerful irony.

"Oh, my God! There you are! I've just woken up. I didn't see you. So..."

They began to laugh.

"Come on, hurry up and come down," Rita advised. "I've got an idea. We'll organize something. You'll thank me for it!"

Lifting her blonde curls in one hand and veiling her bosom with the other, Geneviève beat a modest retreat, lamenting: "Yes, I'm coming. What thing? What is it now?"

As soon as she came down she received an explanation. It was a matter of going to eat lunch in the spot that Rita had mentioned the day before, on the edge of the woods facing north. The day promised to be particularly fine. The grocer's shop and inn cuisine would furnish the elements of a perfectly suitable meal. Geneviève agreed, relieved. She had anticipated more fearful possibilities than a picnic.

The preparations for the little feast took all morning. They disrupted an idleness that it was still necessary to avoid. Slender as it was, that cooperation was nevertheless of value in establishing that Charles and Rita had similar tastes—or, at least, that they took pleasure in adopting one another's views and predilections.

A donkey was found to transport the provisions baskets slung over its back. They walked behind it along the shore of the admirably convex bay. Then a shallow slope led up to the edge of a wood, through which they went.

Soon—for the island was small—they reached the goal of their expedition. In a corner of the wood, at the top of a rocky cliff, there was what might be called a kiosk of verdure. The soil was mossy and flexible. Hospitable shade filleted crystalline light. The shelter, though natural, offered a comfortable interior and a poetic character that was indefinable, reminiscent of the "boscages" of outdated romances.

At the foot of the cliff, however, the ocean was white with foam; an immense gulf, it climbed half way up the sky, limited by the thin blanched or foamy streaks, struck here and there by sunlight, that were the Ile de Ré and the coast of France. We assert that this is one of the most charming viewpoints on the Atlantic coast. Rita, who remembered it very well, had the joy of knowing that Charles would remember it too.

The lunch left nothing to be desired, except that it seemed brief. The day was wearing on, and Rita suddenly became melancholy—which is to say that a moment came when she lost the strength to master her increasing sadness.

Charles drew nearer to her as she sat on a bed of moss, staring into infinity. Oh, what he would have given to restore her beautiful gaiety! But a deference, an imperious delicacy, prevented him from intervening in that melancholy, either with words or the gesture that his hand attempted to make, inviting him to extend it tenderly toward Rita's. In addition, he too was anticipating, without pleasure, the end of this fantasy-filled prologue. Both of them were seriously in need of a distraction.

Madame Le Tourneur was picking heather some distance away. Charles and Rita, following the inclination of their thoughts, were chatting gravely—and still they were falling into agreement. Still, in everything, their opinions coincided. Instructed in the rigid principles of an uncompromising education, Charles set above everything else the religion of the family: irreducible fidelity to ancestral traditions, filial love and respect for the institutions, beliefs and domestic laws that are the sole foundation of durable hearths. Rita, far from being frightened by such a profession of faith, listened to it approvingly. And each of them was profoundly moved to discover in the other such a harmony of judgment, whether in respect of the smallest or the largest questions.

Thus the time ran by, enriched by their unity, impoverished by a reparation that Charles assumed would be temporary, but which was drawing nearer all the same—and which suddenly took on a material aspect, a visible and moving form: that of a plume of grey smoke above a black dot visible in the distance in the direction of La Rochelle, growing in size and seemingly descending toward them.

"There it is!" sighed the young woman.

"Bah!" he said, in an intentionally off-hand manner.

And they watched, without saying anything more and without moving, with a gleam in their eyes and an almost-painful smile on lips that had not even brushed one another.

"Let's be off!" she said. "Geneviève! The *Boyardville*."

Charles, thinking that he would be obliged, in three days, to leave her for a while, knew the misery of a child-like distress.

Two hours later, the *Boyardville* went through the entrance canal of Oléron's harbor. Hearts racing, Charles and Rita watched the sands of the shore, its thickets of young pines, its houses and the quay file by.

Various carriages, rustic or sumptuous, were grouped there. On the bank of the canal, a middle-aged gentleman was waving his hat. Beside him, with his hands in the pocket of his broad culottes, a tall bare-headed young man raked the assembly of the arriving passengers with his eyes.

"Ah!" said Madame Le Tourneur, dolefully. "Look, Rita—my uncle has come to look for us with Monsieur de Certeuil."

She waved her scarf. Charles' handkerchief was deployed. Rita raised her left hand—but her right hand, hidden by the bulwark, grabbed her neighbor's wrist, and they embraced in that manner, secretly and passionately.

II. A Cyclone in a Heart

A keen astonishment had been painted on Luc de Certeuil's face when he suddenly perceived Charles Christiani on
the deck of the *Boyardville*. Immediately thereafter, he had
taken care to give his surprise an expression of superlative joy,
which it had perhaps not offered initially. Charles saw that
quite clearly, but it made him neither hot nor cold. He knew
the man, knew his temperament, and accepted him for what he
was. From his comrade's attitude, he deduced that Rita, when
she had telegraphed from the Ile d'Aix, had abstained from
advertising the arrival of her unexpected companion—a perfectly natural abstention, since Charles had confided his desire
not to put anyone out, and, in consequence, not to forewarn
anyone.

The three travelers set foot, along with the others, on the
soil of Oléron.

"Well!" cried Madame Le Tourneur's uncle, laughing.
"You've made a fine mess! What an escapade!"

Geneviève adopted her shrillest voice and her most insi-
nuating intonations. "Uncle, may I introduce Monsieur
Charles Christiani, the historian, who shared our suffering."

Luc de Certeuil had not yet realized that Charles and the
two women comprised a group within the crowd. "What!" he
exclaimed, in amazement. "You know one another! Now
there's a thing!" And he displayed a prodigious amusement,
while handshakes, bows and polite greetings were exchanged
all round.

Rita, unexcited, smiled without merriment.

"Will all five of us fit into your car?" the uncle asked
Luc de Certeuil. "I'd have brought mine if I'd known."

"Don't worry," said the sportsman distractedly, not having recovered yet from his astonishment. "My old banger has
taken more! It'll be a bit cramped in the back, that's all. You
get in the front, Monsieur, next to me." He had taken Charles'

arm in a familiar fashion, and while they all headed toward the carriages he said: "What a pleasant surprise, Christiani! What a nice idea! You couldn't have given me more pleasure! So, if I understand correctly, you too missed the boat on the Ile d'Aix! That's hilarious!"

Charles did not much like the joyful grimace that accompanied Luc's appreciation. Rita was walking beside them; he tried to interrogate the young woman's face, but only encountered an impenetrable scowling mask. In any case, Luc de Certeuil's opinion of the matter was, deep down, a matter of total indifference to him.

"I hope you've brought your racket," the latter went on. "Where's your luggage?"

They had forgotten it. They sent for it. In the meantime Charles explained that he was only making a rapid stopover in Saint-Trojan—four or five days at the most.

"Bah! We'll see about that!" affirmed Luc de Certeuil, who had recovered all his composure. "Never swear to anything!"

In fact, the traveler was thinking of prolonging his voyage. All things considered, he was free! Nothing was calling him back to Paris imperatively. There was only that business at the Château de Silaz, and the promise he had made his mother to go to Savoy within a week...

At the thought of his mother, a smile crossed his lips. When she found out why her son had not kept his word, Madame Christiani would be the happiest of mothers!

One question, however, was burning his lips. He would have liked to find himself alone for a moment with Luc in order to put it to him—but he understood that he would still have to have a little patience. They had reached the car, and Luc set out to make arrangements designed to permit the accommodation of five human beings and several bags and suitcases within that elegant vehicle.

"Very chic, your automobile," said Charles.

"A hundred notes," said the other, negligently.

Well, thought Charles, *this aristocrat will never become a gentleman. On the other hand, I'd very much like to know where he found the "hundred notes" in question...*

He made himself very slender, though, for Geneviève and Rita, drawing apart, had left a rather narrow but enviable space between them. Luc, behind the steering-wheel, turned round to assure himself, with a mocking expression, that they were ready. At the same time, the machine-gun sound of the liberated exhaust, so dear to sportsmen, began to explode. The car took off like a wild mustang trying to throw off the grip of a cowboy.

Two sharp turns at the entrance and exit of a bridge, and in a few seconds they were speeding alongside the canal at more than 100 kph. Soon, though, it was necessary to slow down, the uneven road describing numerous curves across a charmless plain divided up by watery ditches.

Everything always works out better than one fears, Charles said to himself. *I assumed we'd be separated immediately, but...just the opposite.*

He felt that infinitely precious form pressed against him now by the narrowness of the seat, as if all its "lines of force" were converging toward some inconceivable magnet. His heart was racing at the contact of an individual who seemed to him to be chosen among all individuals, in the same way that there are things that are supremely rare, delicate, rich and pure; things made of gold, lace, and diamond. And, for the first time, Charles understood the meaning of the ancient words *idol, goddess*, and *divinity*; they lost every vestige of the ridiculous for him, and he was compelled to recognize that those ancient words described what they meant with an adorable exactitude. Could there ever be enough attentions, kindnesses, considerations for that young enchantress? What sanctified arms might carry her, in moments of fatigue, over the fords of life? In what pious caresses would his hands have to take wing, in order to touch her?

The automobile went through white villages with ancient pink roofs and brightly colored shutters. Luc announced, successively, "Les Allards" and "Dolus." They cut across a straight road rimmed by a double line of trees. The causeway became more extensively ornamented. Cool woodlands deepened. They came out of them to run alongside others, through a succession of hamlets as neat as linen in a cupboard. After a quarter of an hour, the little red car straightened its roaring course, along the edge of a forest. Its speed surpassed 125 kph. They saw the sea again on the left, beyond a marsh.

Finally, Rita said: "Saint-Trojan."

The hotel rose up in front of the beach. To reach it, they traversed the town from end to end and sped along a large avenue in the midst of pine-trees. Luc brought the car to a halt, level with a passage between two trimmed hedges. At the far end was a series of rose-gardens with tennis-players running hither and yon, leaping after invisible balls.

"Further on, because of the luggage!" implored Geneviève.

"Your wish is my command," said Luc. And he went further on, to pull up facing a perron. The vestibule and the lounges were empty.

"Everyone's outside," said the uncle.

Rita and Madame Le Tourneur slipped away hurriedly. Luc de Certeuil took Charles to the office and requested a nice room with a sea view for him.

"Do me the kindness of accompanying me," Charles said. "I'm eager to ask you a question."

"Willingly," said the other, intrigued.

They went upstairs together.

The room was spacious. Through the open window, equipped with two shutters, the Couraux channel—the beginning of the straits of Maumusson—was visible, and further away, at the limit of vision, the continental coast, with the keep of Fort Chapus in front of it. Against the immense, already darkening sky, seagulls were flying back and forth with powerful wing-beats. Children could be heard shouting on the beach.

When the door had closed after the departure of the chambermaid, Charles said: "My dear Certeuil, the manner of my arrival must seem a trifle bizarre to you. Forgive me...you see before you a rather emotional man. Here it is: that young woman, Mademoiselle Rita...she's made a profound impression on me..."

Without saying anything, Luc was looking at him with an expression so indecipherable that Charles paused momentarily, and stared in his turn at the eyes that were staring at him. "What is it?" Charles asked, slightly disconcerted.

"Nothing. I'm listening to you with great interest."

"Nothing, really? I would have thought..."

"That is to say...you'll understand, of course, my dear friend, that I won't be the only one to experience some surprise..."

"What!" said Charles, cheerfully. "Because I don't dance, because I don't go out into society, because I'm an explorer of archives and libraries, do people assume I've taken holy vows and take me for a monk? Tell me?"

Luc de Certeuil affected to blink his eyes precipitately, to manifest his incomprehension. "You'll have to excuse me," he said. I don't get it. I'm missing something—not to say several things..."

"What are they, if you please?"

"Firstly...well, my dear chap, let's see, are you really talking to me? Come on, you're having me on!"

"I beg your pardon," said Charles, anxious now and speaking in a changed voice. "I'm not dreaming, though. Isn't she charming? Full of intelligence? Irreproachable?"

"Certainly!" Luc confirmed, without losing his ironic rictus.

"I assume that there's nothing to be said against her parents? Honest, eh?"

"Agreed!"

"On her side, therefore, not a shadow in the picture. Then...is it on my side that...? But I don't see anything, myself, on that side..."

"One second, my dear chap. I thought I knew you, and even now, in fact, I'm convinced that I know you quite well—but we're certainly talking at cross-purposes. It's not possible that you—*you*—would speak as you have just done. In those conditions….oh, I'd be choked if anyone were playing with you, if anyone were deceiving you…and yet, unbelievable as that is, I can't think of any other explanation…"

"What!" said Charles, indignantly.

"No other! Someone, my dear chap, must have given you a false name."

"No one has given me any name! And that's exactly what I wanted to ask you. Who is she?"

A silence.

"Who is she?"

Charles gripped Luc's shoulders. The latter's closed lips were smiling, with a malevolent expression. "Marguerite Ortofieri," he said, finally. "Rita to her friends."

Frightfully pale, Charles stepped away from him.

Silence had fallen again. Standing in front of the window, stunned by the revelation, the unfortunate individual watched the flight of the seagulls without seeing them. Accentuating the syllables, he repeated: "Marguerite Ortofieri!" And he sat down slowly, with his face in his hands.

Long moments passed during his prostration.

Luc de Certeuil was profoundly thoughtful. With his eyebrows furrowed and his eyes restless, he looked back and forth from the man sunk in his own mediation to the birds, the sky, the sea, the distant coast: a vast luminous landscape that attracted the gaze. His attitude testified to an extremely intense internal turmoil, of hesitations, uncertainties and ignorance. Then, his features easing, he went to Charles and gently and fraternally placed a hand on his shoulder. "Come on!" he said, benevolently.

Charles, seeming to emerge from a profound slumber, unmasked his face. "I beg your pardon," he said. "I'm nothing but an idiot—a fool with no excuses, at the very least."

"One always has excuses. It's certain that if Mademoiselle Ortofieri had given you her name, as she should have done…in sum, she tricked you. Perhaps not maliciously, but tricked all the same. In this context, hiding her real name from you was tantamount to giving you a false name. It's regrettable."

"You're mistaken," Charles said. "I'm putting myself in her shoes, and I think that I would have acted exactly as she did. Suddenly finding herself in the presence of a polite man, who has no other fault in her eyes than being named Christiani, while she is named Ortofieri, she preferred, out of courtesy and delicacy, not to rebuff him brutally by hurling the name of Ortofieri at him, as one might slam a door in the face of a lout."

"Perhaps so," Luc accepted. "But just now, on seeing you so heated, I had the very clear impression that this…courtesy did not stop there."

"What do you mean?"

"I'm trying to demonstrate to you that you're not the only one responsible for your discomfort. Be just with yourself. An admiration does not develop so quickly and so extravagantly when it is not encouraged. Knowing who you are, knowing that this masked ball intrigue was fated to have no tomorrow, Mademoiselle Ortofieri is reproachable for having pushed politeness as far as amiability. That was extrapolating playfulness to the point of temerity."

"Mademoiselle Ortofieri has done nothing to encourage my sympathy," Charles declared, dryly. "She simply showed herself as she is: pretty and natural, intelligent and good."

"That's fine! Don't get annoyed! I had no intention of attacking her."

"I should think so!" said Charles. And he buried in the most inaccessible depths of his memory the resplendent and dolorous truth: the unforgettable secret of which Rita, Geneviève and he were the only custodians. For he knew now, alas, why that name—a Corsican name, like his own—had not been revealed to him, and why, above all, the young woman had seized the opportunity to remain with him for an entire day: a day magnificently stolen from destiny, bravely snatched from the ancient hatred of their families; a day that would be the first and last of their love! And he desperately reviewed every minute of those 24 hours of dream, cradled on the waves and caressed by the gentle breezes of a blissful isle, from the moment when he had perceived the little book in Rita's hands—which she could only read without the knowledge of her parents, and which she did not have the right to own—until the supreme moment of the exceedingly chaste embrace when their fingers had joined together behind the *Boyardville*'s bulwark. The idyll with no possible future had ended there. A Christiani and an Ortofieri could not love one another.

"Let's forget it!" Charles said, resolutely.

"From you, the contrary would have surprised me—but I confess that I asked myself, momentarily, whether love was not about to transform many things…"

"I've let you see my sentiments; I shall not deny them. Only be assured that tomorrow, I will have forgotten them, as I beg you now to forget them yourself."

Luc de Certeuil bowed. An indefinable incredulity floated in his gaze. "You can rely on me," he said. "It's done—and I admire you, my friend. That haughty fidelity to the rancor of your race isn't lacking in grandeur, or nobility…"

"I'm a Corsican, and I submit to the laws of my family."

"Personally, you've never had any complaint against an Ortofieri?"

"Never. I've heard mention of the present head of the family, the banker, but I've never met him. Oh, if I were alone in the world, perhaps I'd think next to nothing of an ancestral hatred of which I have merely accepted the succession—but there's my family; one cannot conduct oneself in the same fashion for oneself and for others. Then again, at the head of my family there's my mother. She's more Corsican than all my compatriots put together—remember that she baptized my sister Colomba. That says it all! I've had numerous ancestors

39

originating from various provinces: one was Champenoise, another Norman, yet another Savoyard, but my mother, born Bernardi, first saw the light of day in Bastia. She's unshakable on the chapter of aversions. In marrying my father and becoming a Christiani, she espoused all the family's hereditary quarrels. I know too that, even if we were disposed to make peace, the banker Ortofieri, for his part, would refuse."

"So it's a matter of a very grave offence? The hostility of the Christianis and the Ortofieris is known to many people, but how many could specify the reasons? I've heard mention of a murder dating from the last century..."

"Yes, there's certainly that," said Charles, loosening his cravat and unbuttoning the collar of his short with a nervous hand. "The murder of my great-great-great-grandfather[4] César Christiani, the mariner, by Fabius Ortofieri, an ancestor of Mademoiselle Rita's..."

"I fear that I'm overstaying my welcome—you seem rather tired. Would you like me to leave you in peace?"

"No—on the contrary. I prefer to talk. It keeps me occupied, and soothes me—and I'm grateful to you for giving me the opportunity, Certeuil.

"Out there in Corsica, since the sixteenth century, the two families have been prey to all sorts of disputes, over forests, livestock, boundaries. Until the murder of César Christiani, though, no vendetta had led to a man's death. Note, however, that Fabius Ortofieri always denied his culpability and there was never anything against him but presumptions—no irrefutable proofs."

"Did he go into hiding?"

"Not at all. It was in Paris that the murder was committed, on July 28, 1835, nearly 100 years ago. Fabius Ortofieri

---

[4] At this point in the text Charles takes care to specify that César is his "*quadrisaïeul*" [great-great-great-grandfather], but at other points the designation is conventionally shortened to "*grandpère*" [grandfather]—a convention I have followed, although it is not commonplace in English.

was arrested the following day, still in Paris, and died a natural death in prison before coming to trial. His conviction was anticipated; everything weighed against him and the opinion of the Christianis has never wavered: he was guilty."

"If I may—I can easily understand that the Christianis have retained a resentment against the Ortofieris, but it's more difficult to understand why the Ortofieris hold a grudge against the Christianis. That the relatives of a murderer should conceive a detestation for the relatives of his victim seems to me to be implausible, at first glance.

"You'll grasp it. To begin with, there was a long history of disputes between the two clans, as I've told you: legal wrangles, brawls, bad turns—two centuries of enmity, not counting previous eras that have left us no documents on the subject. Because of that, undoubtedly, the opinion of the Ortofieris regarding the crime of 1835, although it has varied between individuals, has always remained unfavorable— hatefully unfavorable—to the Christianis."

"Because?"

"Because certain Ortofieris, convinced of Fabius' innocence, never forgave my forefathers for having accused him of a crime that, according to them, he did not commit. And because certain other Ortofieris—persuaded, on the contrary, of Fabius' guilt—maintained that so just and calm a man could only have killed one of his peers to avenge an even greater crime. What crime? A mystery. Fabius, they said, did not wish to reveal it, either by virtue of magnanimity and moral elegance, or because, in revealing it, he would have articulated a crushing charge against himself that would have convicted him of César's murder."

"That's rather curious, psychologically."

"Bah! For the latter, it was a means of reconciling two rather contradictory sentiments: the desire to continue to detest us and a more honorable need to admit that the king's prosecutor was right, and that Fabius really was César's murderer. I know that Ortofieri the banker is convinced to this day that his ancestor took revenge on mine for some vile outrage—which

41

is indefensible when one knows the character of César Christiani well, having studied it objectively. He was rectitude itself—and a remarkable intelligence. I thought about him as recently as yesterday, on the Ile d'Aix. Napoléon loved him dearly..."

That evocation of the Ile d'Aix brought the clouds back to Charles Christiani's brow. He made a valiant effort to master himself. *Forget it! Forget it!* he said to himself, in a frenzied manner. And he went on talking, in order to stun himself, in order that Luc de Certeuil might be fully convinced of his detachment and that nothing would betray the wound in his soul that he was suppressing with all his spiritual strength.

Behind that façade of bravery, however, in the wings of his inner being, mute thoughts were unfolding, including one that was down to earth and increasing in magnitude: to leave as soon as possible; to go very rapidly to Chapus, which was visible in the distance, with its railway station; to be in Paris the following morning. But he knew that he had to execute that plan promptly; his flight was subordinate to the timetable of the boat, which he remembered having consulted in advance when he was anticipating such a happy return!

Another thought too, somewhat vaguer, persisted while he chatted—an interrogative thought. Luc de Certeuil, while listening with an undeniable interest, seemed nevertheless to be preoccupied with his own secret cogitations. Why?

Luc doubtless divined, from some hesitation by Charles, the fear that he had of being unwelcome, for every time that the historian appeared to be about to stop, he started him off again by means of a question—and the result of that was that Luc de Certeuil became, for Charles Christiani, a little more than an everyday acquaintance: a chance confidant.

"In the final account," Charles continued, "César is the great man of my family. He was born on August 15, 1769, at the same time as Madame Bonaparte was giving birth to her second son, not far away. Thus, little César with the imperial name became the childhood friend of little Napoléon, whose name meant nothing. Now, the amity of the future emperor was never belied. He made my ancestor a corsair captain, whose reputation almost matched the glory of Surcouf.[5] He enriched him and received him at the Tuileries every time the old sea-dog returned to France, Napoléon delighted in reminding him of their time in Ajaccio and mocking his thick accent, as gladly as he chided himself for having lost his own—which was not entirely true.

"Unfortunately, there was Waterloo. The Restoration was not propitious for César Christiani, Faithful to his god Napoléon, he was in disgrace. Louis XVIII and Charles X affected to ignore him, along with all the other impenitent Bonapartists.

"He retired in 1816. Corsica did not tempt him. I firmly believe that, after a life of combat and naval engagements, he wanted to rest, far away from quarrels, vendettas and Ortofieris. That's why we find him living thereafter in a petty Savoyard domain that his wife had brought him as a dowry, and which was the cradle of her family, He had married Hélène de Silaz in 1791. She was dead when he installed himself in that property, at the age of 47, having provided him with a son, Horace, my ancestor, and a daughter, Lucile, who has one very old descendant still alive.

"Why, 13 years later, did he come to live in Paris at 53 Boulevard du Temple? Why, without hope of return, did he forsake his retreat at Silaz? His papers—his *Memoirs*, which I have consulted—lack precision on this point. It may be assumed, quite simply, that he had had enough of the country and solitude, as happens to many men when they turn 60. Perhaps, too—although this is an even more gratuitous hypothesis—he had always missed France and made haste to return

---

[5] Robert Surcouf (1773-1827) was a corsair captain—a French corsair being the equivalent of an English privateer rather than a mere pirate—who distinguished himself in the war against the English by capturing several ships; he was rewarded with a Barony in Napoleon's Empire and became a rich ship-owner.

there, having been secretly alerted to the imminent fall of the Bourbons.

"It was there, in the Boulevard du Temple, that he was assassinated, by a pistol bullet fired by Ortofieri, who invaded his home while he was at his window watching King Louis-Philippe review the National Guard on July 28, 1835. He was 66 years old."

"The review of July 28, 1835?" said Luc de Certeuil. "I'm not strong on history, but I think I remember something in that regard. What was it? Hold on…"

"Fieschi's assassination attempt against the King," said Charles. "The infernal machine that had so many victims in the crowd. Fieschi fired on the Louis-Philippe and his followers by means of a machine of his own invention. He had taken aim from the window of his small apartment at 50 Boulevard du Temple, almost directly opposite César's house. It was even thought that the explosion of the machine, analogous to a firing squad, had masked the pistol-shot that killed César, no one having remembered hearing any detonation inside the house bearing the number 53."

"That's an extraordinary coincidence!"

"I know of others," Charles observed, with sad irony. "Life, Certeuil—even the most banal life—is littered with extraordinary coincidences…except that we don't always perceive them…"

"According to what you've told me about the pistol shot, then, César Christiani was alone in his apartment when he was murdered?"

"Alone, with his animals."

"What animals? All this is very exciting."

"He had brought various curious animals back from his voyages, especially birds and monkeys. His portraits always represent him with a parrot on his shoulder, and sometimes with a marmoset on the other, or a chimpanzee hanging from his waistcoat."

"And…it's certain that it really was a man who killed him?" Luc Certeuil risked, laughing.

"Perfectly certain."

"To the extent that things can be certain, in this world!"

Charles thought for a second, then retorted: "The depositions made against Ortofieri really left no doubt about his guilt. The policeman on duty in that part of the Boulevard saw him prowling around the vicinity and going into César's house a few minutes before the presumed time of the murder."

"Which was?"

"The moment when Fieschi's machine exploded on the other sides of the road, since there was a presumption of simultaneity—synchrony, as one says nowadays. Besides, César's corpse, when it was discovered a few hours later, confirmed that presumption in the opinion of experts. The death had to have occurred at midday."

"You're marvelously knowledgeable about the affair!"

"It's my vocation as a historian and my duty as a great-grandson. I've made a careful study of Fieschi's assassination attempt. At the Palais de Justice, no less minutely, I've gone through the entire dossier of the Ortofieri case, item by item, and have taken on the task of completing it for myself, with all that remains to us of César's papers—his correspondence, his memoirs, and so on."

"Is there mention of the Ortofieris therein?"

"From time to time. He still had property in Corsica, of course—land and farms—which gave rise to disputes with the eternal neighbors, the eternal enemies. I found scattered traces of their disentanglement everywhere, not only in our family archives but those of court clerks and notaries.

"It's quite evident that César distrusted Fabius, just as Fabius surely distrusted César. The bushes,[6] for them, were

---

[6] The word I have translated as "bushes"—*maquis*—carries considerable metaphorical weight in France, beyond its literal reference to scrubland. *Prendre le maquis* means "to go into hiding" or to work mischief covertly, as the French resistance to German occupation did during the two world wars. *Les Mystères de Paris* by Eugène Sue was the archetypal *roman*

those of legal procedure. They were also—and in a more dangerous fashion—the Paris of 100 years ago, with its narrow streets and dark passages: the Paris of barricades and ambushes; the Paris of *Les Mystères de Paris*—which was to appear seven years later."

"Fabius had also settled permanently in the capital, then?"

"In the Rue Saint-Honoré. He was a financier. That was the origin of their prosperity. It's said that the banker is extremely well-off."

"So it's said."

At that point, the reverie took over. Charles mechanically lit a cigarette that Luc had just offered him and leaned his elbows on the window-sill. He leaned back almost immediately, to avoid the gaze of some passing bathers who had looked up at his appearance. He tried to interest himself as much as possible in the capers of swimmers of both sexes mounted on absurd inflatable rubber steeds. Those childish antics seemed utterly pitiful, given that his heart was grieving; and, turning his attention away from the seaside games, he perceived the dim reflection in the pane of the inwardly-opened widow of Luc de Certeuil, plunged in the bosom of reflections so arduous that they strongly resembled perplexities.

Charles did not say a word, and watched the young man's expression curiously, from the corner of his eye. He saw him in profile, sitting down and leaning forward, with his elbows on his thighs, his head lowered and his hands set flat, one against the other, finger to finger—and those fingers were drumming. He saw that snub-nosed profile, that face inces-

---

feuilleton, some of whose themes and methods became the foundation-stone on which Féval built his own mythology of criminality, which Renard seems to be consciously echoing here in a respectfully nostalgic fashion. Féval's *Habits Noirs* series (tr. as *The Blackcoats*), which also uses the Boulevard du Temple as one of its key settings, often refers to "la forêt de Paris" [the Parisian jungle].

santly animated by a conceited boldness that imposed itself powerfully—and he was not favorably impressed thereby. What the Devil could Certeuil be thinking about so ardently?

"Pardon?" said Charles. "Oh—I thought you were about to say something."

"It's true—it was on the tip of my tongue, and then…I no longer know whether I should…"

"Come on—spit it out!"

"Yes, that would perhaps be best. We're both honest men, aren't we? You're going to leave, I assume…"

"In exactly half an hour."

"It's possible that I won't see you again for several weeks. Between now and then, gossip might tell you…things that I'd definitely rather tell you myself."

"That's very solemn! Speak, my dear Certeuil."

"If it's reported to you that here, in Saint-Trojan, and then elsewhere, I am very assiduous in keeping company with Mademoiselle Ortofieri, do me the kindness of remembering that I was the first to tell you that."

Charles was obliged to summon up all his strength to remain impassive as he resisted the brutal blow.

"I beg your pardon," he said, "but is it an engagement you're announcing to me?"

"Almost."

"My congratulations." He extended his hand. Luc de Certeuil shook it energetically.

"Now I'll leave you," Luc declared, in an uncertain vice. "I'll find you again at the boat, when you board…"

"Yes…that's preferable…"

By his frankness—or his cynicism—Luc had just created an intolerably false situation. Dumbfounded, Charles, once he was alone, had some difficulty pulling himself together. A new light had been cast on things. In the first place, he congratulated himself immeasurably for having moderated his confidences, already excessively indiscreet! Had he really not let slip the affection that Rita had evidenced for him? No, nothing. What luck! Oh, that was not Luc's doing! He had done everything possible to find out more about it! His fit of sincerity had come very late...in fact, one might easily believe—pending more ample information—that he had yielded it reluctantly.

Anyway, what did Luc de Certeuil matter! What mattered most of all, what obliterated everything else with its glare, was the ineffable revelation that he had just made to Charles, on the assumption that someone else would make it. It was the joy that he had given him, thinking that he would give him nothing but pain. A sad joy, certainly, since nothing had changed in matters of inevitable necessity, but an immense joy nevertheless—for, in Rita's life, Charles was therefore not merely the one who delights because he is the first and sole emergence, aureoled by mystery and adventure, of the forbidden fruit of love. He was the one who is more than loved—not, in fact, the one who is loved but, far better, the one who is *preferred*: the chosen one.

Oh, that beautiful day! Even more madly beautiful that he had dreamed. And what a sparkling wake it left behind it!

Almost afraid to feel a memory alive within him with such vibrant force that could not be accompanied by any hope, Charles surprised himself by making a trenchant gesture and saying aloud: "You must forget! You must forget!"

Someone knocked discreetly on the door.

Experiencing some embarrassment at the thought that the domestic had heard him speak and would nevertheless find him alone, Charles blushed in advance. "Come in! Come in!" he repeated—for no one appeared.

He went to the door with the intention of opening it.

A large blue envelope slid along the floor, one of its corners still caught beneath the door. He picked it up and saw his name, traced in elegant, steady feminine handwriting.

Outside, in the corridor, there was no one to be seen.

On the back of the envelope there was a monogram: *M.O.*

The letter read:

You know everything now, since you know who I am. But of what I am, do you know enough?

That is what I want to tell you; or, rather, it is that of which I want to assure you, for I shall not offer you the insult of doubting your judgment—which is to say, your esteem. I am certain that you have not suspected Marguerite Ortofieri, even for a moment, of being that which she is not. No accusation, I am sure, has been raised in your mind against me, my sentiments or my character. In commencing this letter, I want to bring you confirmation of your thoughts, like a sworn statement that is owed to them—along with, perhaps, the hope of reinforcing and affirming them. In writing this letter, I am aware that it would neither be worthy or you nor of me if it were to contain anything resembling a defensive plea or even an attestation. It cannot be anything other than an expression of gratitude.

I shall, therefore, not even say to you: Believe that in all of this I have been the most sincere of women. I simply thank you for that belief, and beg you to pardon me if any of the preceding sentences have led you to mistake my intentions.

The fact is—need I admit it to you?—I don't perceive my intentions very clearly. The fact is that my state of mind is entirely new to me, and I am having some difficulty in coming to terms with it. Finally, the fact is that I have never had to write a letter like this, of which I dare not even pronounce the name! A letter, Monsieur, that I have so much grief, and nevertheless so much joy, in addressing to you.

But it is not to speak to you about my grief and my poor joy that I have taken up my pen, and I do not want to let myself be distracted thereby into filling these four large pages—for I know full well that I shall fill them—instead of simply putting down the words: "Thank you!"

Thank you for having the certainty that I have been, for a day, as happy as can be on a temporary basis.

Thank you for that day.

Thank you for retaining a faithful and stainless memory of it.

Thank you for being who you are—and by that I mean, with everything else that it implies, a gentleman: chivalrous, old France, devoted, as I am myself, to all sorts of ideas that are no longer very fashionable, but which, I imagine, are sufficiently eternal.

Thank you for placing as the highest of duties that of sacrificing nothing, even love, to the religion of race, the cult of the family—for, without anyone informing me, I will swear that you are about to leave without seeing me again. And how can I reproach the sentiments that dictate that course of action, since they are those that I appreciate the most in what you are?

Thank you, therefore, for going far away from me, who would give anything in the world to be close to you, but who would not tell you that if it were not impossible.

Thank you for your love and thank you for your hatred.
Thank you for being Christiani, as I am
Ortofieri.

It was signed, briefly, "*Ortofieri.*" Proudly, "*Ortofieri.*" One might have thought that the entire lineage of the Ortofieris had signed that tender and cruel note via the single small hand of its unique descendant. And, indeed, one sensed that the soul of generations had inspired that valiant confirmation, so dignified and so touching at the same time.

Charles held the blue letter up to the limpid light of the setting sun. He could only distinguish one word, which summarized its entirety and similarly encapsulated the whole tragic situation: the word "impossible."

And Charles thought he could hear the abominable word being repeated by all the Christianis and all the Ortofieris who had succeeded one another since July 28, 1835, including old César, with his southern accent, and old Fabius, raising his pistol—all the way to his mother, who seemed to be standing in front of him, stern and authoritarian, smoothing her bandeaux, like the wings of a crow, with an angry finger, and shouting at him, like all the rest—like Horace Christiani, like

Napoléon Christiani, Eugène and Achille, the two brothers, and Adrien, his father, dead on the field of honor—"Impossible! Impossible! Impossible!" as if all those Corsicans had forgotten that, since Louis XV, Corsica had been French.[7]

---

[7] This sarcastic remark refers to the famous declaration, attributed to Napoléon I, that "the word impossible is not French!"

III. At Home

The train that brought Charles Christiani back did not get in to the Gare Montparnasse until 9 a.m. It was very late and contained far more standing passengers than seated ones. Everyone was coming back from vacation.

In spite of his most sincere efforts, Charles could not drag his thoughts far from the events that had just unfolded so rapidly. He never left off revisiting them, analyzing them and chewing over their bitter yet delightful taste. He was now better able to explain certain details of the sojourn on the Ile d'Aix and the voyage that it had so memorably interrupted. The great confusion into which he had thrown Madame Le Tourneur and Rita by introducing himself now appeared to him with all its causes, which were not slight. He understood poor Geneviève's fearful anxiety when she had seen her friend throw herself into an adventure with a Christiani. He also understood why Rita had refused to bathe in the sea, for all the obscure reasons of foresight, generosity and modesty, in order not to leave Charles with too vivid a memory of the woman he would never see again, whose race and rhythm he had instinctively perceived, that being his own race and the very rhythm of his own Corsican blood.

He numbed himself and hypnotized himself with those memories, incapable of extracting anything from them but a sort of confused and distressing sensuousness. The arrival in Paris produced an almost funereal effect in him. Everything seemed to have changed, without him being able to understand how. He could not have felt more out of place on returning from a very long voyage through strange and distant countries. It was as if his memory had been deformed, in the space of a few days, or that Paris had been mysteriously subjected to modifications that were impossible to specify, in its proportions, in the color of the sky, in its atmosphere, and God knows what other aspects that he sought in vain to define. He saw everything smaller, poorer, darker; there was a silent element in the hubbub of the streets, a dull quality that set a weight of anxiety upon his soul, the cause of which escaped him completely. He was heartbroken, and could not react to anything.

He got a taxi, gave the chauffeur the address in the Rue de Tournon, then changed his mind on the way and had himself taken to the Quai Malaquais, to the home of his future brother-in-law Bertrand Valois. Before confronting his mother again, it seemed to be a good idea to chat with a stalwart friend, a sensible man, full of heart and blessed with a perpetual cheerfulness, who would certainly "restore his morale." He did not admit to himself that he needed to talk, and needed to relive events in talking about them. And he did not imagine that in going to the Quai Malaquais he was surrendering to the impulse that drives us all, when things are "not going well," toward people who are fortunate, who are continually successful in everything, and whose luck takes on the appearance of a contagious power. In the company of those favorites of fate, we have the illusion of being immunized against misfortune and of renewing our provisions of confidence, strength and competence.

No one could represent good fortune better than Bertrand Valois, the cheerful author. His plays were bringing him a sensational success; everyone liked him and rejoiced in his achievements. He was also endowed with an open and buoyant physical appearance that legitimated a great deal of sympathy. Not that he was handsome, strictly speaking—fortunately for him, for handsomeness in a man disadvantages him with many of his fellows—but his joyful friendliness won him the support of the masculine tribe while his spiritual gaiety assured him of all feminine approval, for God knows how our sisters love to laugh.

Why not say that Bernard Valois had required all the prestige of his genteel renown and all the promise of a radiant future to bend Madame Christiani's rigidity and obtain Colomba's hand from her? There was nothing in him to reproach, except being born of very modest parents, but his father had only been a simple ward of poor-law relief, a foundling, and Madame Christiani, infatuated with ancestry and proud of her genealogy, had hesitated for long months before giving her daughter to a fellow who had accumulated nothing from the heritage of past centuries but an old ring and an old walking-stick. They were the only objects that had been discovered, one morning in the year 1872, next to the new-born baby wailing in a corner of the Galerie de la Valois in the Palais-Royal—whence came the name "Valois," which Bertrand bore after his father, who owed that uniquely sonorous patronymic to the place of his abandonment and the thoughtless caprice of the poor-law administrators. After all, "Valois" is a historic name, and it was perhaps audacious to give it to an unknown brat who might subsequently dishonor, as his destiny unfolded, the memory of Louis XII, François I and Henri III, of whom it was very doubtful that he was a descendant.

The ring, in fact—that gold ring enameled in black and provided with a tiny diamond; the ring that Colomba had undertaken to wear on the day of her engagement—did not indicate a royal origin, but one scarcely bourgeois. And the walking-stick—a long rattan cane surmounted by a silver pommel ornamented with meager garlands—was entirely in agreement with the ring on this point. To tell the truth, these two witnesses, each offering the characteristics of Louis XVI style, constituted Bertrand Valois' only ancestors, and we need to note that circumstance in order to make the fashion in which Charles Christiani addressed the young author understandable.

He found him in his study, working on some comedy. The place was arranged for the pleasure of the eyes and the accommodation of necessities. A large bay window looked out upon the Seine and the Louvre. As for Bertrand, who was already carefully shaven, his coppery hair smoothed over the rounded skull one could ever see, he had tightened about his fine figure the belt of a dressing-gown elegant enough to put a cinematic Don Juan to shame. When Charles came in, he hastened to meet him with open arms—and the visitor felt better simple for having seen that welcoming face, ornamented by the very nose of comic genius, a nose molded with malice, with nostrils so flared that they truly warranted the name of wings: the famous nose to the wind with which the late Monsieur Choiseul[8] had sniffed the breezes of Versailles; the nose of great actors never mistaken in their theatrical vocation. A trifle large, no doubt; a trifle turned up, agreed—but, in the final analysis, a famous nose, pleasant, generous, artistic and jolly; one of those that one is delighted to see between two bright eyes.

"What, back already?" said Bertrand. "I thought…but where have you come from? Did you sleep in a doss-house?"

"On the train."

"What brings you here?" asked the other, raising his eyebrows.

"The fact that you don't know how lucky you are."

"What sort of luck? I haven't won that much."

"The luck of having no ancestors," Charles pronounced.

"Unsought!"

"Ah, my friend, when I think that you, an intelligent fellow, a man of spirit, regret your lack of ancestors!"

"That's true," Bertrand admitted. "I have that inexcusable fault."

"Yes, yes, I know. I've only seen you melancholy once—we were talking about the past, ancestors…well, today, my old friend, I'd give anything to have no forebears!"

"Known, at least," observed Bertrand. "For, since Adam, no one has yet found a means of doing without them, in the natural order of things. Come on, tell me—what have your ancestors done to you?"

"I'm talking about César, and those who followed him."

---

[8] Duc Etienne-François de Choiseul (1719-1785) was Louis XV's foreign minister from 1758-70, when he manifested considerable diplomatic skill in settling the fall-out of the Seven Years' War and was responsible for the French acquisition of Corsica.

"Which means?"

"*Romeo and Juliet*. The Capulets and the Montagus—get it?"

"Perfectly. You've met Juliet, you being Romeo, and Juliet is named Ortofieri."

"That's it, exactly. Juliet is named Marguerite Ortofieri. She's the daughter of the banker and the great-great-granddaughter of César Christiani's murderer."

"That complicates matters," said Bertrand. "Forgive the pun—it was unintentional.[9] What are you going to do?"

"Erase. Forget."

"She doesn't like you, then?"

"Yes—very much; I'm certain of it."

"To the Devil with the quarrels of the dead, then!"

Charles looked at him in surprise. "Is it you who's saying that, Bertrand? Think about it. Put yourself in my place. I've heard you say—quite frequently—that, deep down, you're convinced of being the offshoot of an old and noble family..."

"Oh, nonsense!" said Bertrand, with a smile. "Sometimes, you know, one feels things—a thousand things stirring in the shadows of the brain: regrets, inclinations, desires, surges of emotion, intuitions of a sort, false certainties...one takes all that for ready money—I mean, for advertisements of heredity, the voice of atavism—but..."

"Be sincere."

"Well, I admit it! I would take so much pleasure in descending from rich folk that I've ended up believing that it's true, and that one day, as in melodramas, papers will be found in a casket that will cause me to be recognized! The Duc of somewhere or other! The Marquis of this or that!" He burst out laughing.

---

[9] What Bertrand says in French is "*Cela se corse,*" *corser* being a French verb signifying "to complicate"—but Corse is also the French term for Corsica, or a Corsican, so the sentence could almost be construed as "That's Corsica."

"You can laugh," said Charles, shaking his head, "but listen: imagine for a moment, you who are honest, who don't joke about honor, in spite of your indulgent child-like face—who, in sum, conduct yourself as if you belonged to a four-quartered nobility that has come down in the world—imagine that you *really* had dozens of generations behind you infatuated with honor and tradition, to the extent of stupid but superb prejudices! Imagine that you bore the standard and the épée of your race!"

"Damnation!" Bertrand admitted. "That's true…"

"Do you think that I can betray mine?"

"Oh! Colomba wouldn't hold it against you!"

"What about my mother?"

"Oh—yes, that's something else."

"And Mademoiselle Ortofieri is of the same opinion, rigorously."

"Then, indeed, I can't see any way out…"

"I haven't come here seeking your help in finding one, but for your help in forgetting."

"It's a great pity," said Bertrand, "that no Christiani has thought of avenging old César. In almost a century, one proper vendetta, one serious sweep of the broom…today, you'd be quits."

"Our two families have evolved, since then, in a society in which grudges don't manifest themselves in dagger-thrusts or blunderbuss-shots. And it's better that way; one is never finished with vendettas; every act of vengeance calls forth another."

"And the blood of César cries vengeance!" declaimed Bertrand.

"In spite of which the Ortofieris want it from us—as if, by God, it was their Fabius who had been assassinated by his victim!"

"Oh, you really aren't easy-going people! When I think that my own children will be half-Corsican! What defenders I shall have!"

"Who knows?" Charles remarked. "Perhaps you're more Corsican than I am!"

"With a nose like this? A nose...in the Choiseul style?"

"Go on, you aristocrat!" said his friend, smiling affectionately.

"I'll concede that my walking-stick undoubtedly comes from a Parisian boutique—which proves absolutely nothing with respect to the nationality of my forefathers!" He unhooked the object in question, which was suspended lengthways on the wall.

"Ah, if objects could speak. Eh?" said Charles.

"At the rate at which science is progressing, anything's possible. Anyway, that cane has already spoken, although it doesn't say much. This is how: it's long, after the fashion of its time; but, according to its proportions, it must have belonged to someone of my height. The stem is old, contemporary; the handle has the dimensions of a fist like mine. The cane has had a great deal of use—look at the silver pommel, which resembles a little shako without a visor; it's polished by the friction of the palm, the decorative garlands are worn; the iron tip at the other end, however, isn't much eroded by contact with the ground. We may deduce that the possessor of that came must have carried it under his arm most of the time—and, indeed, on the upper third of the rattan, we remark that the varnish is scored, by virtue of having experienced the contact of the arm and the torso while the right hand caressed the pommel."

"Bravo, Sherlock Holmes! Have you taken the handle off, to see whether some clue might be hidden inside?"

"Child! My father did not neglect that operation. There's nothing under the pommel. And I've interrogated my ancestor's cane thoroughly, without it telling me anymore. But let's get back to our business—how can I help you?"

"You've helped me as much as you could, by letting me confide my misery to you. I shan't say anything about it to my mother. What good would it do?"

"Couldn't you get a change of air? That's still the best treatment for depression."

"Exactly. I intend to leave for Silaz this afternoon, Claude's requesting my presence. A few days of calm and solitude will do me good."

"Beware of isolation."

"Bah! I'll take some papers with me, and the four sergeants of La Rochelle will keep me company. If I have a void in my soul, I'll write another chapter of my book."

"Brrr! Stories of conspiracy and the scaffold! You'd do better to write a farce!"

"I have no subject!" Charles replied, in the same bantering tone, shaking his hand.

When he had gone, Bertrand smiled delicately with his fleshy mouth, his mischievous eyes and, if one might put it thus, his excessively expressive nose. *No subject!* he said to himself. *What more does he need? But some "see tragedy" and the others "see comedy", and that's the way it will always be, so long as there are men or anything analogous.*

"You've arrived just in time, Charles—I was about to send a telegram asking you to return, or catch the Geneva train at La Rochelle."

Madame Christiani was sitting at her desk, in front of open letters and domestic account-books. Her sharp profile was silhouetted against the softly sunlit background of large yellowing trees and the apse of the church of Saint-Sulpice. Having no suspicion that her son had been to Oléron, she simply said: "You've renounced that detour you intended to take. I approve. I don't much like your Luc de Certeuil, as you know. I've received this from Claude." She held out a letter in the tips of her swarthy, carefully-manicured fingers.

Charles hastened to take the folded piece of paper, without making any reply but thinking that his mother had just shown him, unknowingly, the best course to follow. That was it: so far as everyone was concerned, *including himself*, he had come directly from La Rochelle. The day before, he had been consulting the dustiest items in the library, guided in his research by the erudite Monsieur Palanque. He had never set foot on the spar-deck of the Boyardville; the Ile d'Aix and the Ile d'Oléron were still unknown to him. And Rita...Rita...

An emotion that made him feel quite ill stopped these vigorous thoughts in their tracks. Meanwhile, he read old Claude's letter, whose style we shall respect, if not its spelling:

Madame,

Madame will be kind enough on excuse us, Péronne and your servant, for sending you a letter hot on the heels, so to speak, of the last one I had the honor of sending Madame, only last Sunday week.

The present is to let you know that the situation here is not tolerable. Things are enough to make your hair stand on end, and it's only because of our devotion to Madame, her demoiselle and our Monsieur Charles that we have stayed at the château until now. Madame may believe me. You say that what is happening—oh, no, I'm only a poor peasant, and I repeat it—is that someone's making fun of us. But this can't go on. Monsieur Charles will certainly be generous enough to come pay us a little visit right away. Otherwise, Madame will excuse me, but we're each going home, as soon as the grape-harvest, me to Virieu, Péronne to Aignoz, until all these frightful phantasmagorias at the château are over and done with.

I beg Madame to accept my respectful salutations, and also the demoiselle and Monsieur Charles. And Péronne sends her respects too.

Claude Cornarel.

"You have to leave immediately, Charles. I don't know what's got into him. You'll have to sort it out."

"You'll have to sort it out" was Madame Christiani's answer to everything pertaining to Silaz. Since her marriage, she had only put in three or four appearances there. She did not

like the mountains—which, she said, overwhelmed and op-
pressed her. The ancient dwelling appeared to her to be
odiously sad. Colomba had scarcely ever seen it, but Charles
went there from time to time to "sort things out." That didn't
displease him, in any case. During his childhood, he had spent
short periods at Silaz with his father. Later, when his vocation
as a historian began to form, he had returned there to study
and file the mass of family papers that were kept there, most
notably the memoirs and correspondence of the corsair César
Christiani. A lover of the past in all its forms, he gladly
breathed in the ancient odors of the manor, which had not
been opened up for a very long time, except to air it or when
Charles came to settle a farmer's lease, check the roofs, inspect the vintage and shake a few callused hands in the neighboring hamlets.

As for Madame Christiani, not content to flee Silaz, she
had conceived an aversion for it, as she took to certain people
even though they had done her no harm. She was not a nasty
woman but, as the domestics put it "she got ideas". Thus, for
example, she had no longer wanted to see, for an indefinite
interval, her old cousin Drouet, the last representative of the
other branch of the Christianis. She had severed all relations
with her. Charles and Colomba did not know what their relative looked like, and when they questioned their mother about
her, the latter invariably replied that cousin Drouet had "behaved badly toward Mélanie" and that she no longer wanted to
hear mention of her, Mélanie—another cousin, but on the Bernardi side—had no memory whatsoever of Madame Drouet
ever having done anything to her, but Madame Christiani never forgot. Oh, she would not have been able to go into detail;
she no longer knew what it was about, but one thing was certain: cousin Drouet had behaved badly toward Mélanie, and
that could not be forgiven.

One can judge by that the execration in which Madame
Christiani held the Ortofieris. Whenever she mentioned Silaz,
her jet-black pupils reflected the hostile and acrimonious aspect of her soul, and all the rancor she nurtured lit up her gaze

61

with sharp gleams. Charles divined that, with respect to Silaz, she was cursing, among others, cousin Drouet and the Ortofieris—and his somber mother's black eyes filled him with a disappointment that he was astonished to experience, because he thought that he had banished all hope.

"It would be pleasant to travel by automobile," he said. "Can I take the cabriolet?"

"Certainly."

"On the Bordeaux-Geneva," he added, "I'd have to suffer a very long railway journey, and I confess that I don't find that tempting."

"What's more," opined his mother, "I don't know how you'd be able to get by without a car in Silaz—that hole!"

"But I'll be depriving you of your car, and that…"

"That's of no importance—Bertrand will lend us his. He'll be delighted to do so—and then again, there are cars just as good as ours for hire."

"Thank you," said Charles. He kissed his mother on the forehead, at the junction of the parting that separated her hair into two flat and dull bangs. Madame Christiani, in return, sniffed against her son's cheek; that was her own manner of kissing; her thin lips never participated under any circumstances, and it was obvious that they were not designed for that usage.

Colomba joined them for lunch. She was the smile of the house—and everything smiled upon her in return: her youth, her beauty, her engagement, her fiancé, and even Madame Christiani, who elevated a corner of her mouth in her favor, smiling on one side only, unable to do any better.

In the presence of his sister, Charles strove even harder than before to hide his melancholy. He mocked Claude's terrors, not without wit, declaring himself convinced that superstitions, aided by some trickster, were responsible for all the trouble out there. He talked a great deal, gaily, without taking anything seriously—with the result that, as they left the table, when he saw Colomba approaching and she drew him to one

62

side, he wondered what request was about to be addressed to him thanks to the joyful disposition he had just exhibited.

What she actually said to him, in a low voice was: "Are you upset?"

The shock he received put him off his stride; he blushed and then went pale, only to blush again.

"Would you like me to ask Mama for permission to go to Silaz with you?" she added.

"What about Bertrand? No, no—stay with him! Stay in Paris. When one's in love, it's best not to be apart. On the other hand, a few days' retreat…"

"*Who is she?*" she demanded, through clenched teeth, her eyes looking sideways, fixed on Madame Christiani.

"No one! There *was* someone; not anymore."

"Colomba—pour the coffee!"

"*Au revoir!*" said Charles, brusquely. "I'm going to get ready."

When the two women were alone, Madame Christiani said: "Do you think there's something wrong with him, then?"

"My God, Mama, perhaps…"

"As if you hadn't noticed it, little faker! Except that I have no need to ask him what's wrong to know what it is. He's in love, my girl, he's in love—and it's not going as he'd wish. A love story! There we are. It was only to be expected, after all! Bah! He's a Christiani; it will all work itself out, and we'll make a second marriage…and I'll be forced to invite that cousin Drouet—who behaved badly towards Mélanie—twice over."

The young woman was amused, but remained thoughtful nevertheless, twisting the little black-enameled ring that Bertrand had given her around her finger. After a pause, she said: "It's sad to be unhappy because one's in love."

"When one loves judiciously, my beauty, it's impossible to be unhappy for long—and I'm sure of my Charles, from that point of view. If he's in love, it's judiciously."

"Judiciously?"

"Yes. A woman worthy of him. And free. So I'm confident, you see. It will all work itself out."

"Of course," said Colomba.

IV. The Phantom of Silaz

The Château de Silaz is situated on the left bank of the Rhône, a few kilometers from Culoz. It rises up in the woods between the broad river and the long straight line of highway that follows its course. The hamlet of Silaz groups a few hearths around the domain at the foot of a small round crag, rocky and isolated, covered with bushes and shrubs, known as the Molard de Silaz. The region is therefore located on the border of the department of Savoy and, as in the ancient Sardinian province, old country people can still be found there who say "in France" when they talk about the right bank of the Rhône, from which extends the département de l'Ain.

The situation of the château is very beautiful, because of the mountains, which can be seen from all parts, and the woods, cut through by fields, vineyards and marshes, which surround it. The buildings are not very tall, and give the impression—falsely—of being constructed at a low level, the huge butte that supports them being dominated by the mass of the Molard and the imposing height of the horizon. It is a secluded spot. The road that goes to the nearby highway stops there, or, at least, only continues beyond Silaz in stony pathways, like all the hill-paths in the region.

The daylight was fading when Charles Christiani's cabriolet, driven by the chauffeur Julien, left the highway and set off along the final stage of the 550-kilometer journey from Paris to Silaz.

They had left the day before in the early afternoon. Charles had instructed the chauffeur not to hurry. That way, the voyage became salutary for him. He had sat beside Julien. The open air entered into his lungs generously. The spectacle of the world paraded its hundred thousand scenes before him, and he had been able to exchange a few words with his neighbor, who was neither stupid nor indiscreetly loquacious.

Charles was not at all worried about the cause that was bringing him to Savoy. He had dined well and slept well in Saulieu; they had been in no hurry to get back on the road. He abandoned himself quietly to pensive pleasure, to the beneficent dream of returning to a region and a house where he knew that his melancholy would not be jarred by any presence, untimely memory, ugliness or pettiness: a beautiful and silent desert.

A profound peace had filtered into him when, at Ambérieu, the car had suddenly gone into the gorges along a level road, following incessant curves at the bottom of the magnificent defile. Personally, he loved the mountain; it gave him physical pleasure to breathe the light and energetic atmosphere, while measuring the summits and the slopes, seeing the peaks stand out against the pure sky high above, or losing sight of them in the moving clouds.

Then, at the mouth of the valleys, in the grandiose enlargement of the land and the sky, in the dazzle of the returning bright light, as the descending road still overlooked the vast panorama, he had perceived the Molard de Silaz in the middle of the plain, and felt an almost-imperceptible quiver in his heart. Then he had thought that there was a little of the past preserved in his heard, a little of the Savoyard great-great-great-grandmother that stirred on approaching Silaz, and that idea charmed him again with a strange secret pleasure when he perceived the slate roofs and square tower of the manor.

All that dissipated within a second. Claude's face reminded him instantly that he had not come to Silaz to enjoy a romantic repose.

The old man had come running in response to the clamor of the horn, as quickly as his age permitted. Properly dressed in his Sunday clothes, he raised his gnarled hands in an almost adoring gesture, coarse and touching. "Oh, Monsieur Charles!"

Joy and anxiety were combined in his face: a joy that was entirely new superimposed on an anterior anxiety, which it had not yet succeeded in effacing. He had his hat in his hand. He was bald. His fine grey moustache accentuated the astonishingly deep suntan of his complexion. The muscles of his neck disappeared into the collar of a shirt of coarse white linen, a vestige of olden times. "I can't tell you, Monsieur Charles, how glad I am that you've come!"

"Because of the *sarvant*?" said Charles, laughing.

"How do you know about that?" asked the astonished guardian of Silaz. "I didn't put anything in my letter."

Péronne had come out in her turn, wearing her white frilly bonnet, wiping her hands on her blue apron. She had a simple, open face, molded by honesty and devotion—and also common sense—and two eyes that expressed a rarely-seen fidelity and respectful submission toward Charles.

An odd household! A bizarre couple, who were not a married couple, but more like a pair of hounds.[10] Claude and Péronne had been living there since their youth, in the service of the Christiani family. No other bond united them, but they had a marvelous mutual understanding as comrades, and nothing had ever disturbed their amity. An old man and an old woman, each having "property" in a native village, they remained at Silaz, content to serve the same masters with the same probity.

"Is Monsieur Charles up to date?" said Péronne, looking up at the traveler plaintively. "Have you explained it to him, Claude?"

"No, but Monsieur knows already that it's the *sarvant*."

They were on the threshold of the garage, sheltered by an arch. The little road continued between the commons and the grounds. Charles, flanked by the two old people, headed for the château. They went in by the kitchen door.

---

[10] This is expressed much more elegantly in French, in which the masculine noun *couple* refers specifically to a man and a woman, while the feminine noun *couple* refers to other sorts of paired individuals, especially in the context of hunting, so Renard only has to say that Claude and Péronne constitute *une couple* rather than *un couple*.

"Come with me," said Charles. "Tell me about it."

The windows of the drawing-room were open, as was the glazed door overlooking the English park. The weather was mild and the light gilded. The great silence of the countryside reigned like a fascination. After a day in a roaring automobile, Charles felt the spaciousness weighing upon him.

"Well?" the young man queried.

"It's in the little top room," said Claude. "Every night, there's a light that appears—and someone can be seen."

Charles smiled.

"Monsieur Charles will see for himself," said Péronne, respectfully. "It's in the evening, when dusk has fallen, that the *sarvant* goes into the little top room. The people in the village have seen it, as we have."

"All right! I believe you. Since when?"

"We first saw it a fortnight ago," Claude said. "That night, we were about to go to bed after supper. I'd just released the dog Milord—which is, as you know, a very good guard-dog—when, all of a sudden, I heard him barking in the grounds, near the château. I went out and made a tour of the buildings…"

"You should know," Péronne added, "that the dog was barking very loudly, more loudly than he does from time to time when animals are on the prowl or people are passing by on the road."

"Yes," Claude confirmed. "So, in consequence, I muffled my footsteps on the gravel. Look, Monsieur Charles, Milord was there." He pointed through the open window at a place outside. "If you wouldn't mind stepping out in front of the château, I'll show you…"

They went out.

The floor of the drawing-room was on a level with the gravel-covered esplanade that preceded the lawns. There was a porch outside the door with a glass canopy. As they passed through it, Charles looked at it critically. That addition dated from 1860; Napoléon Christiani had had it built at the time of the annexation of the Savoy, on which occasion he had splashed out on celebratory parties, moved by patriotism and ambition. The porch, in the Napoléon III style, contrasted strongly with the aspect of the thoroughly Savoyard façade, with its ancient coarse stonework, its little windows and its heavy, steeply-sloped roofs, which overhung it like a firmly pushed-down hat.

Apart from the porch, in fact, the slightly-dilapidated Château de Silaz presented a remarkable example of the regional architecture of the 17th century, unpolished but charming. Charles noticed that once again as he raised his eyes toward the "little top room"—which it seems indispensable to us to situate more precisely for the reader's benefit.

The façade of the château facing the grounds—which still exists, of course, at the time of writing—is not established on a single vertical plane but composed of two parts, one of which extends further forward than the other. For an observer placed in the grounds, it is the section on the right that is set back from the section on the left, to a depth of one room, and it is from that section in retreat that Charles, Claude and Péronne had just emerged beneath the porch.

The other section, on the left, which protrudes by comparison with the one on the right, is similarly provided with a ground floor and a first floor, but it is surmounted, though only on its right-hand part, by a second floor, the side of which forms a right-angle with the façade in retreat. That second story, consisting of only one room, forms a square tower, similarly topped by a tiled roof, whose base is integrated into the advanced construction. This tower is pierced by two windows on each floor, one facing southwards—the orientation of the whole façade—the other facing eastwards and having a view, at right-angles, of the retreating façade.

The ground-floor of the tower is a study.

The first floor is a bathroom connected to the next room.

The second and final floor is the "little top room," a library and work-room.

"It's up there!" said Claude. "I didn't suspect anything when I arrived close to Milord, of course. The night was al-

69

ready dark, with no moon. Immediately, my attention was drawn to that window." He pointed to the eastward-facing window, the one in the sheltered corner formed above the gravel esplanade by the two sections of the building. "The dog had his head raised, barking and turning round and round, growling. And up there, Monsieur, there was a light, as in a room that someone was using. My first impulse was to go fetch my revolver and go up to the little top room, because my first thought was that we were dealing with burglars. But—I don't know why—it suddenly occurred to me that it must be the *sarvant*..."

Charles chided him in a mocking tone. "Come on, Claude! Seriously, do you still believe in ghosts?"

As the two old people lowered their heads, Charles recalled all the ghost stories they had told him when he was young. He knew that both of them were convinced that they had glimpsed the *sarvant* in various forms, indecisive but alarming, at dusk, in moonlight, in darkness, in the gloomy depths of wine-cellars, going along a corridor in a deserted house or disappearing around the corner of a shadowed staircase.

What exactly is a *sarvant*, or *servant*? A shade, a specter, a spirit, a demon, a soul in torment—anything you like. Savoyard and Bugist legends are haunted by them. Simple minds, influenced by the wild solitudes and somber gorges, have not yet abjured the ancient superstition, and they create these nocturnal scarecrows for themselves, before which they shiver all the more because they are imaginatively tailored to their fears, in such a way that nothing could be more frightening.

"So you didn't go up to see what the light was?" Claude went on. "To see what produced it?"

"I wouldn't have gone up there for all the gold in the world!"

"He came to look for me," said Péronne. "He brought the dog back..."

"Yes, I wanted there to be two of us, at first. Afterwards, I tried to shut Milord up, so as to be able to listen without his growling and barking."

"Didn't the racket the dog was making disturb the person with the light?" Charles asked. "You mentioned someone just now—someone who had gone into the little top room, and continues to go into it every night. Is that right?"

"Yes, Monsieur Charles, that's right. But the din that Milord was making hadn't drawn anyone to the window, or caused any sort of movement inside. Perhaps it was that, fundamentally, that seemed bizarre to me, you see! When I came back with Péronne, a few minutes later, without the dog, the light was still there…"

"What sort of light? White? Yellow? Bright?"

"Lamplight," said Péronne, "and not very strong. Yellowish—like a small lamp. We had gone out without making any noise, me in my slippers, Claude in his socks. There was still nothing to be heard. Nothing was moving in the room. We stayed there for three-quarters of an hour, looking up, and looking behind us at the darkness from time to time. We weren't reassured, you know, Monsieur Charles."

"But in the end, you saw someone?"

Claude took up the story. "The *shadow* of someone, at first. On the wall and the ceiling, then on the bookcase. And suddenly—oh, goodnight! I remember it!—a man, or the false semblance of a man, came from the left to stand in front of the window."

Charles examined the window, quite calmly. From below he could indeed see, through the panes, a corner of the ceiling and the edge of the bookcase, which he recognized. He was familiar with the "little top room." He had worked there in the past. The glass-fronted bookcase, in varnished mahogany, contained the great majority of the documents that he had taken the trouble to organize. His memory recalled the other items of furniture: a ridge-backed desk in fruit-tree wood; a nice simply-designed Directory-style chest of drawers. All of that gave an impression of the "good old days," to which no modification had probably been made since the beginning of the 19th century.

The window at which he was looking was not equipped with shutters. He went around the corner to look at the little top room's other window; that one was hermetically sealed by solid shutters. (There is no need to be surprised by such disparities, which are quite common in the older buildings of the region.) Now, anticipating Charles' arrival, Claude had opened the shutters—solid or slatted—of all the other windows in the château. On seeing those closed shutters, Charles knew that the brave man was decidedly not brave enough to have dared to go into the little top room, even in broad daylight.

Claude confessed that he had only opened the door, cast a glance around, and assured himself that everything was in its usual place. "One might have thought that no one had been in there since the last inspection—but a *sarvant* isn't someone!" The old fellow, surprised and annoyed to see his master so incredulous and indifferent, added: "Monsieur Charles hasn't even asked me for the end of my story!"

"Well, go on, my brave Claude. What happened next?"

"What happened, Monsieur, is that the man turned round—and then he started walking around, quickly, like someone deep in thought. And imagine this, Monsieur Charles: *his footsteps didn't make the slightest sound, and the silence was so profound that we would have heard him walking in the room, even if he were wearing carpet-slippers.* There's no carpet up there, on the floor, and we have sharp ears, Péronne and me, thank God!

"Finally, about midnight, we saw him go out of the room. Because of the height, we could only see his head. He took the light away, but we couldn't see whether he was holding a lamp or a lantern, or anything else. Anyway, we saw perfectly clearly that he opened the door—didn't we, Péronne?—and that the door closed behind him, silently, like a phantom door! And everything went dark again in the top room...except that he must have put the light out as soon as he went out, because we didn't see the slightest glimmer in the windows of the loft."

"That's true," said Charles. "The door to the little top room lets out into the loft, via the stairway. He remembered the picturesque disposition that had delighted him when, as a small boy, he had played beneath the roofs of Silaz—too rarely for his liking. The little top room did not entirely occupy the contents of the square tower on the top floor; its door opened on to a light fir-wood stairway which led down to the loft of the section in retreat, by means of a door-less opening. There was no other exit from the little top room.

"What does Monsieur Charles think of all that?" Péronne asked, anxiously. "No noise! Not a whisper! And every night, the *sarvant* comes back at the same time, and goes away at the same time! I don't know if Monsieur can imagine what it's like to lodge under the same roof as such a frightful thing! Not to mention that we don't know where the accursed thing goes when it leaves that room up there!"

"In sum," said Charles, "What have you done? What measures have you taken?"

Claude made a gesture of helplessness. "I've written to Madame. I've moved our beds to the ground floor, because our bedrooms in the attic...you understand! Besides, I've continued to keep a lookout, even with men from the village. They've kept me company and will repeat what I've just told you."

"A lookout? Where? How?"

"But...from here, where we're standing...from nightfall until the disappearance of...the thing."

"What does he look like, your *sarvant*?"

"It's difficult to be sure, Monsieur Charles. The light's weak. You can only make out a dark shape, and you can only see the upper part of the body, of course."

"None of the men from the village thought of going up there while your visitor was there?"

"Oh!" cried Claude, while Péronne expressed the same sentiment. "Not one of them wanted to get mixed up in it!"

"Right. And tell me, Claude: have you suspected anyone of playing a malicious joke on you? That must have occurred to you, mustn't it? Have you any enemies? Have *we*? You've been deceived by a practical joker—I'm sure of it. Think hard. Who? Think of anyone who might have a reason for doing it, who thinks he has a score to settle with you, if not with my family…"

"Honestly, I can't think of anyone. Come on, Monsieur Charles, believe me—it's no good looking for an explanation in that direction. What's happening *isn't natural*, and I'll wager a hundred francs that you'll soon share our opinion, when you've seen with your own eyes…"

"Unless the presumed *sarvant* doesn't do me the honor of putting in an appearance for me!"

The setting sun had just slipped behind the blue chains of the west. The temperature was cooling rapidly. The grounds were full of shadows. Only one sheer slope, quite close by, still benefited from the rays of sunlight, but the shadow was moving up it like a tide and the golden mountain was gradually turning into a mountain of darkness. Soon the very peaks were submerged and extinguished. Bats began their rounds in the crepuscular twilight.

Péronne and Claude followed Charles Christiani back into the drawing-room. The two servants waited expectantly for questions and instructions.

"Where am I to sleep?" he asked.

"I'll prepare whichever room Monsieur wishes," said Péronne.

"The usual one, then."

"Very well, Monsieur," said the servant, meekly. "Has Monsieur taken account…?"

"Of what, my dear?" he said cordially. "Of the fact that the room I usually occupy is next to the tower? That its bathroom is immediately underneath the little top room? I assure you that it's all the same to me." He added: "Ah! I'll have dinner right away, so as not to miss the arrival of the *sarvant*!"

74

"I hope that Monsieur Charles will not be imprudent!" said Péronne, anxiously.

"I suspect that the circumstances will not permit any recklessness," he replied. "I'm convinced, my friends, that someone has been trying to frighten you; I shall try, in the next few days, to find out why and penetrate the secrets of this stage-setting. As for this evening, I'll wager, myself, that all will be tranquil and that your trickster won't come! I regret now having arrived without taking any precautions. I ought to have left the automobile somewhere nearby and slipped in here on foot or by bicycle, without being seen.

"In any case, don't mention my arrival in the village. Try not to make any more movement here than usual. Don't go into the room I'll be staying in until I tell you. I'll only go into it myself at bedtime—and, of course, I'll be ready to go up to the little top room at a moment's notice. In brief, let's do our best not to tip off the joker."

"But what if he comes, Monsieur Charles?" said Claude.

"If he comes, Monsieur Claude, Julien and I are big enough to deprive him of any desire to return!"

"Oh, my God, my God!" groaned Péronne, heading for the kitchen.

"I have my revolver," Claude recalled.

"You'd do better to get your shotgun and load it with coarse salt! Call Julien, then, if you please, and I'll give him his instructions…"

At 9:30 p.m., Charles, the chauffeur Julien and Claude were posted under a chestnut-tree. Through the foliage, they were easily able to observe the suspect window, a casement formed in four squares, two to the left and two to the right. The dog Milord, a rather handsome briard, was keeping Péronne company in the closed kitchen.

The crescent Moon was descending in the south-west, in a clear sky. An autumn chill was emanating from the Rhône, with a rising mist. Odors of grass and moist earth were in the air. Leaves could be heard falling, along with chestnuts, which sometimes tumbled noisily through the branches. In the distance, trains were rumbling along, then leaving the silence of nature to re-establish itself like dormant water that had been momentarily disturbed.

It was in one of these almost absolute silences that the window was softly illuminated. Up there, *someone* was opening the door and coming in. The light spread further. The door having been closed again, a man passed by and disappeared toward the left. The shadows immobilized; doubtless the lamp had now been placed on an item of furniture. Then the window remained illuminated within the dark wall, for the moon no longer struck that wall, although it bathed the façade around the corner to the right, and made the glass in the porch glisten. There had not been the slightest perceptible sound.

"What did I tell you!" said Claude, triumphantly, feeling safe with his companions.

"There's something different about the window," Charles murmured. "It's partly masked; something—perhaps a curtain—has been drawn across the left-hand side; at no time have I seen the light on that side, which leads me to believe that someone has come into the room without a light to block that half of the window, before coming in with a lamp. We'll come back to that later. For the moment, it's necessary to act. We can't see anything from here. I have a plan.

"You, Claude, are going to stay under the chestnut-tree, and you, Julien, are going to come with me. We'll go up to the loft. The small window nearest to the lighted window is no more than three or four meters away, and isn't so far beneath it that one can't easily see from there what's happening in the room. All this is rather curious. We're dealing with an ingenious robber, but there's no evidence that he knows he's being watched tonight by new forces...Julien, I advise you to be silent. Let's get going."

As they set forth on this preliminary operation, Claude, strongly impressed, whispered: "Be careful, Monsieur Charles!"

"Don't worry. Our fists will suffice, but we both have revolvers as well."

Claude shook his head. "Something tells me that a revolver is just as good as nothing, on this occasion."

"Come on!" Charles said to the chauffeur.

The latter, a sturdy fellow in the prime of life, could hardly contain his jubilation. This adventure pleased him enormously.

In the drawing-room, Charles switched on an electric pocket-torch. Preceding his auxiliary, he crossed the room, thus reaching a spiral staircase. They went up stealthily.

The door to the loft was not locked. They went in. Two small windows facing the door cut out two rectangles of moonlit sky. The other windows visible from outside were those of the attic bedrooms.

A bluish milky light filled the lethargic, extraordinarily silent place. There were thick shadows between the beams and in the corners. To the right of the right-hand window, forming a rectangular patch of darkness in the grey wall, was a gap: the opening giving access to the bottom of the little five- or six-step stairway that led to the mysterious room—with the consequence that, in order to leave that room, it was necessary to pass through the loft. And to get out of the loft through the door that good Christians used, it was necessary to go past the widows.

Walking on tiptoe, having put out the little electric torch, Charles reached the right-hand window without meeting any obstacle, followed by Julien. Not a single creak escaped the old floorboards, which were thick and solid.

As he had expected, without being perfect, that observatory offered very appreciable advantages. It did not permit the revelation of the entire little top room, but allowed much more of it to be seen than Charles had hoped. Although the door was no longer visible at all, at least the bookcase appeared in nearly all of its breadth, only the bottom third remaining hidden— for, as we remember, the small window was on a lower level. Finally, to the left of the bookcase, an expanse of wall was visible, clad in the old flowered wallpaper that Charles recognized, and ornamented with engravings no less dear to his memory.

He hoisted himself up on tiptoe. The top of a lamp-glass was reveled—and that lamp was definitely set on the lower shelf of the ridge-backed desk. He cursed the curtain, screen, or whatever it was, though, that blocked the whole left side of the lighted window, preventing an observer from seeing an important part of the little top room. Nothing else could be seen, relative to the intruder, but the top of that lamp-glass. It was necessary to be patient and wait for something to happen. Then they would take action accordingly.

They remained motionless for minutes that seemed to them to be singularly long, their eyes fixed on that feebly-lit half-window—the lamp must be fitted with a shade—careful not to reveal their presence by any distraction.

Suddenly, Charles drew back reflexively into the shadow of the loft. *The man had just got to his feet, unhurriedly.* He had undoubtedly been sitting down at the desk, until that moment. He picked up the lamp, went to the bookcase, opened one of the glass doors, lifted up the light, and began to search for some book or document.

In an almost non-existent whisper, Julien observed: "I don't understand. What's he doing?"

The pressure of Charles' hand imposed silence on him. The latter opened his eyes so extraordinarily wide that the chauffeur, seeing his stupefied face in the moonlight, began to lose confidence.

Charles was, in fact, experiencing an indescribable stupefaction at that moment.

The man with the lamp was of medium height. He wore short graying side-whiskers; his long hair formed an unkempt mass of curls. His features testified to his vigor. His eyes were bright. He was dressed in an ill-fitting, unbuttoned olive-green jacket with a brown velvet collar. The broad collar of his loose-fitting shirt was negligently open, maintained by a silk cravat, tied without much artistry.

He was not a man of our era—and yet, Charles knew him as well as he knew himself. For he had before him, on the other side of the window in the little top room, the individual represented in a certain romantic painting, a paining full of life and charm, hanging in the drawing-room of the house in the Rue de Tournon. The only things lacking in the matter of absolute resemblance, were a rifle in one hand, a telescope in the other, a pistol passed through his red belt and a parrot on his shoulder.

In brief, incredible as it was, on that night in September 1929, Charles was looking at the moving, living—or, rather, re-living—image of...who? You've guessed it: César Christiani, the former corsair captain of His Majesty the Emperor Napoléon I, who had been murdered in Paris at 53 Boulevard du Temple on July 28, 1835, at the age of 66.

Shivering with an indescribable fever, Charles devoured the incredible spectacle with his eyes. Then, abruptly, he returned to a rational conception of things. The trick had been mounted with care, very intelligently, and was, without any doubt, aimed at him, Charles Christiani—for such a reconstruction would not have been able to evoke a *particular* disturbance in Claude, Péronne or any of the neighboring villagers. He therefore observed in a cooler manner the disguised individual and the scene that he was playing for his clandestine spectator.

It was well done, and it was well played: a perfect imitation of the old sea-dog, aged about 60; the coarse gestures, the original clothing, and an unspecifiable air of the obsolete, the outdated, foreign to our time. And the lamp! The old oil-lamp of the first Empire, which was still kept in the cabinet on the ground floor, from which the trickster must have removed it without Claude's knowledge!

Meanwhile, the individual was pursuing his search of the bookcase shelves with an admirable conviction. He made a semblance of finding what he was pretending to look for: a stack of papers. Then he returned to the invisible desk and, once again, nothing more could be seen than the upper part of the bookcase and the wall.

You can imagine how Charles searched for something that would reveal the truth. He went from hypothesis to hypothesis, but nothing caused him to pause at one rather than another. The only clear point in his mind related to the continuation of the operation; he was firmly resolved to lie in wait for the joker to make his exit, in order to find out where he would go and what he would do after quitting the little top room, since he routinely came out of it at midnight.

It was a long wait. The man only showed himself once before his departure, marching back and forth, still in that deceptive silence, which ended up becoming oppressive.

The moment arrived, nevertheless, when he picked up the inefficient old lamp again, ran his fingers through his untidy hair, like a sentry weary of his duty, and, having darting a glance toward the window *which seemed a trifle ironic*, extended his long free arm toward the handle of the invisible door.

"Look out!" said Charles, in a whisper—and they both plastered themselves against the wall.

It was a critical, ambiguous, anxious moment. To tell the truth, they had both lost a sense of reality, to some degree—and, in the depths of their inner being, they were not too sure of the shape of events. Someone was about to come out of the room, come down the steps of the stairway, come into the loft, and pass in front of them, or move away in the direction of the other attic rooms...

It would happen noiselessly, as if in a dream, and it was unpleasant to anticipate that phantasmal march...

While they waited, nothing appeared. Obviously, the mysterious man had put out his lamp, as Claude had predicted; of that there was no doubt. But no one appeared in the opening at the bottom of the stairway. No one passed through the moonlight that picked out the black and white shadows of the cross-sectioned windows on the floor.

When a certain time had gone by, Charles returned to his original observation-post, expecting to see the light in the room again. They must have witnessed a false exit on the part of the night-walker…

No, there was no longer any lamplight in the room—but the moon threw a more intense illumination into it than one would have thought possible; that anomaly was evidently due to the reflection of the façade at right-angles to it.

By virtue of that luminosity, Charles could still see.

There was no movement, either in the room or in the loft; not a tremor was perceptible.

Where had the individual gone, then?

V. The Marvelous Reality

Charles switched on his electric torch. The chauffeur did likewise.

The well of the little stairway to the top room was quite empty. They verified that with as much ease as certainty, the steps being nothing more than planks with slits between them.

They climbed the steps, one after the other. In the lead, Charles reached the narrow landing outside the door of the little top room. There he listened—and there, childishly, he hesitated.

There was no sound.

He pushed the door abruptly, having turned the handle rapidly. The two minuscule pocket searchlights did their work.

The little top room was deserted. Glacially, harshly, gloomily deserted. There was no one behind the door, no one under the sofa. Nothing in the atmosphere testified that a man had recently been there for three hours with his lamp lit.

Charles, who was scanning the room with the dazzling beam of his pocket-torch, uttered an exclamation. "Look at that!" he said, pointing at the bookcase.

"So what? It's a spider's web."

"Doesn't that tell you anything? Think. That spider's web is situated in such a way that it would be torn away if the bookcase were opened. Now, that bookcase was opened a little while ago. We saw the man open and close that glass door! That, without a doubt, is prodigious! I have to let Claude know—I'll go call him."

In order to do that he turned to the window, from which he intended to hail the old steward—but stupefaction petrified him.

"The...the Moon!" he pronounced, hoarsely. "Look at the Moon!"

"Good God, Monsieur Charles. That's a full Moon!"

"Yes, *an entirely round Moon in the east*—a Moon that rose scarcely three-quarters of an hour ago, *although we know that tonight's Moon is a crescent and that it was about to set over there, in the west!* It's a dream! We've been drugged…"

Without any further palaver, Julien ran to the window at the back—the one looking southwards—and shoved the shutters open with a bang…

The nacreous crescent appeared in the south-west.

"Two Moons!" Charles exclaimed, having remained facing the round silver face rising into the clear sky. He moved closer to the window that looked out on that full Moon. "I'm going mad, Julien!" he cried.

"What is it now?"

"Come here—put out your torch and look. Then tell me…the porch…can you see it?"

"No, Monsieur—it's no longer there. It's disappeared."

"That's not all. The grounds…"

It was, in fact, enough to drive one mad. The large chestnut-trees were now small saplings. The lawns, spirited away, had given place to a vineyard pierced by a narrow pathway, at the end of which was a small rustic summer-house. In the bright moonlight, all of that was as visible as in broad daylight.

"Do you understand?" said Charles. "That's the garden as it once was, the château as it once was, the château before the addition of the porch, before 1860! I have drawings, paintings of those times; there's no mistake! That little summer-house out there is unmistakable!"

"What summer-house?" said Julien. "I can't see it! And what's more—am I seeing things?—the porch has come back, Monsieur Charles!"

"No it hasn't!" stammered the young man, anxiously.

"Yes it has!" the other insisted, no less anxiously.

"Ah! I think I understand!"

Charles had noticed that Julien, at present, was not looking through the same window panes as himself, but through the part of the window that had seemed to be blocked a little while ago when seen from without, which was now to their right. The historian, in his turn, stationed himself at that part of the window—which comprised two panes—and saw the modern landscape again, with its tall chestnut-trees, its porch, its lawns, and a sky that was moonless on that side.

"I've got it!" he announced, with a marvelous delight.

Julien waited open-mouthed for the explanation.

At that moment, Claude—having seen the two men gesticulating from down below, heard them speak and seen them open the south-facing window—arrived on the site of the prodigy.

"Here are two very singular window-panes," said Charles, pointing to the left-hand half of the window. When one looks through them from within, one sees the garden as it was before 1860—perhaps many years before 1860. And when one looks through these windows from outside, one sees the little top room as it was then—as it was before 1829, the year when my ancestor César Christiani left Silaz, never to return."

Claude was still unable to see anything in that but confusion—but Julien, who was more intelligent, asked how Charles knew that the vision had shown them a room anterior to 1829 and the departure of "Monsieur his grandfather."

"Because," Charles revealed, "*it was him that we saw.* And it's you who've won your bet, Claude. We really are dealing with a phantom, and absolutely genuine specter, an indisputable *sarvant*. And, as there's no such thing as the supernatural, we must conclude that this phenomenon is perfectly natural, and that our phantom is merely an entirely-explicable image.

"When one places oneself on either side of these surprising windows, what one sees is not what is there *now*, but what *was* there before 1829, or in 1829 but before the autumn, the time of the departure in question, when César Christiani went to Paris."

"But how can that be?"

"I'm trying to figure that out… First of all, I now recall, much more precisely, something I only remembered vaguely a little while ago under the chestnut-tree, at the moment when I observed that half the window seemed blocked—the *left* half, which, now that we're inside the room, is naturally to our *right*.

"That something is that, since my childhood, I've always seen the other half of the window covered with sheets that I took to be wooden panels. Understand me—the other half; not the one that seemed to me to be masked just now, but the other, which is now the left half, in which the phantasmagoria was produced. Yes, dark sheets, which I assumed to be wooden boards. I assumed that, for want of glass, someone had made a provisional repair at some time in the past, but then neglected to follow it up by substituting panes of glass for the boards. The glazed half-window and the south-facing window let sufficient daylight into the room, in any case. If I had remembered that detail when you talked to me about apparitions, I would have asked you immediately when the two opaque panels had been replaced by plates of glass."

"Not at any time!" retorted the old steward. "Personally, I've never paid any great attention to such details. What I can certify is that, in the more than 30 years that I've been in service with your family, Monsieur Charles, no glazier has made any repair in the little top room."

"Hold on!" said Charles, meditatively. "On reflection, therefore, one arrives at the conclusion, in fact, that those panels must have been placed there in the time of César Christiani himself. But then, it's necessary to admit that they suddenly ceased to become opaque, to become what we see now—which is to say, displayers of a bygone era…"

"Retrovisors," ventured the chauffeur Julien. "Like the mirrors mounted on automobiles for seeing behind the car, seeing the road traveled…"

Charles smiled. "It can't be quite like that—for our past doesn't seem to me to be directly observable, at least by us."

"Naturally," said Julien, "since it no longer exists."

85

"Yes it does," said Charles. "The past still exists in the medium of light, in optical form; but until now, our own past—that of the inhabitants of the Earth—has not been available to our own eyes. That doesn't prevent it from being visually eternalized, like all the pasts in which light has reigned. Thus, when we look at the stars, it's their past that we see, for light, in spite of its velocity of 3000 kilometers a second, takes years to reach us from the nearest star—in other words, to bring us the image of that star. With the result that we only see, in the firmament, stars as they shone 10, 20, 50 or 100 years ago, according to the distance that separates us from them, and not as they shine at the moment when we contemplate them."

After a pause, he continued: "In sum, these panes act exactly as if light, in passing through them, took as much time as it takes to cross immense celestial distances. It's exactly as if they were condensates of space, compressing distance. I think that's the direction in which it's necessary to seek the solution of this marvelous enigma, however strange its initial formulation might seem—I don't doubt that another can be found, which will be acceptable, since it will be true.

"At any rate, I understand now why, from outside, once darkness fell and a luminous image was produced by these mysterious panes, the left half of the window seemed to us to be dark, as if covered by some sort of curtain. It's simply because, behind the ordinary panes as behind the other window, there was, in reality, only darkness. But these…retrovisory panes showed us the brightness of the past that they contain."

"My God, Monsieur Charles," said Claude. "All this is beginning to get a little clearer now for me—but how do you explain that these panes suddenly began to mirror time past, since neither you nor I have ever noticed anything before? They've been, so to speak, dead, inanimate, for years and years; then, all of a sudden—bang! Here they are, alive, showing us a cinema film…"

"Give me time to consider that question at leisure," said Charles. "I haven't explained anything yet, whatever you might think. I've simply described the phenomenon, by comparing it with what happens in the starry sky. Let's verify something…"

He opened the window then, not without difficulty—which proved that no one had done that for a very long time. As he had expected, the inexplicable images followed the movement of the batten. However it was positioned, one still perceived the moonlit grounds looking through it one way, and the dark room looking through it the other was—as if the batten still occupied its original position in the closed window.

Charles was thinking unrelentingly. "Fetch me my tools, Claude. I want to take these two panes out; that will make it easier to examine them. And bring us a good kerosene-lamp."

Half an hour later, the two window-panes had been transported to Charles Christiani's bedroom—and Charles Christiani devoted himself to a meticulous investigation of them.

They were relatively heavy and very thick plates. When one examined them along the edge, that edge seemed to be composed of an infinity of very thin layers, some of which were black, others luminous and others of varying brightness. He felt each edge-section; its texture seemed to him to be laminated.

The plates had been fixed in the window-frame with the aid of tacks and mastic, just like ordinary windows, but much too thick.

What caused the person studying them to marvel further was that they were behaving exactly like window-panes and not at all like a projection-screen or the frosted glass of a camera obscura.

We shall explain that immediately.

Where a screen or the back wall of a camera obscura is concerned, you may change your location relative to those planes but it is always the same image that appears to you. You can duck down, raise yourself up, or move to the side, but you will not discover, by doing so, a single inch of supplementary image. By contrast, Charles, who was already amazed to have these live views of another place in his bedroom, perceived that he was able to vary the field and the perspective in accordance with his position, in the same way that, when one looks through a window, whether from the left or the right, looking down, looking up or straight ahead, close up or from a distance, the landscape, by courtesy of these movements, becomes partly invisible there, while being uncovered there, modifying the relationship of its lines, growing or shrinking.

Charles tried to recall what appearance the secret substance had presented before, while it was still opaque and he had noticed it when he went to work in the little top room. He thought that he was not mistaken in evoking a mat surface analogous to polished slate, or rather a hard black—or blackened—wood; it was, moreover, the idea of pear-tree wood or ebony that lingered within him with the greatest tenacity. Now, though, because of the laminated texture, he was inclined to believe that it was a kind of slate, and he speculated: "A natural material? No. More likely a manufactured product."

When he tapped the "slate" with his finger, it made a very dull and muffled sound—which made Charles think of another substance formed of innumerable layers: mica.

What more could he do, for now? The night was getting on. The three servants had gone to bed, much less emotional than such a sensational discovery merited. The full extent of its significance and its strangeness escaped them.

The large bed offered a glimpse of its hospitable white sheets beneath its aged curtains, but Charles had not the slightest desire to lie down. He seemed to have been electrified, as if he had champagne in his blood! He was like the first man to discover the existence of electricity, the power of steam, the possibility of speaking at a distance or the omnipotent properties of a liquid or a gas. And besides, the historian in him experienced an incomparable sensuousness therein. An artisan of the past, loving vanished eras as a musician loves sounds and a sculptor marble, he experienced an acute joy in possessing these things, in his room, in front of him—these two seeming marvels which were, although present, of the past: of the real, palpitating past. They were the extraordinary location in which, at least for the eyes, the life of the world unfolded with a delay of about a century. They were History, not preserved on film, but admirably present, although ancient!

It made him shiver—because, confusedly, but with an increasing vehemence and an anxiety that became sharper, the superstitious conviction was taking hold of him that the apparition of César Christiani was not a matter of chance. That the apparition was scientific was of scant importance—were there any other kind, after all? Could anything happen, even in Heaven, that did not conform to the laws of Creation? The indisputable fact was that César had appeared—a natural revenant, but a revenant all the same—and at which moment among all the billions of moments of duration? At the exact moment when the memory of his tragic death had opposed itself to the happiness of his great-great-grandson. Coincidence? A poet putting the story into verse would rhyme that word with "Providence."

Oh, to be sure, this could do nothing to change the situation directly—but for Charles, it took on a profound and fateful significance. It was a kind of encouragement: a sign, or something even more inexpressible, which, enveloped in mystery, sent forth an obscure appeal to new sentiments, imprecise but salutary.

Nothing makes as much impact on human beings as the unexpected intersection of events at the crossroads of destiny; they are always tempted to call it a pointer rather than chance. Those who do not resist the temptation feel happy.

One might say, moreover, that Rita Ortofieri was party to that solitary celebration. Charles, overflowing with ideas and emotions, exultant with enthusiasm, had perceived that henceforth, in spite of his determination, he would no longer be able to experience either joy or pain, or any other vivid reaction, without associating Rita with his own destiny—even Rita absent, distant, aged, dead! The thought of Rita could never become foreign to him. He had to admit that it had never left

him for an instant. Neither the soothing diversion of the journey not the bewildering bizarrerie of the consecutive adventure had succeeded in driving away that imaginary presence.
And how could it not take on a new sharpness at a time when
Charles, separated from everyone, surrounded by silence and
peace, found himself face to face with a night from another
era, and contemplating—magical, terrible and delightful as it
was!—the bright white face of that Moon, behind which slept
the César Christiani whose future fate, to be murdered by Fabius Ortofieri, he knew!

For the past night wore on within the two window-panes,
peaceful and slow, but neither more slowly nor more rapidly
than the present night. And Charles could not get enough of
the spectacle of those hours fallen into oblivion.

Suddenly, in the background of the scene of yesteryear,
he saw the planet Venus twinkling in a paler darkness, and the
whitening sky cut out the jagged horizon in silhouette. He
turned one of the plates over and saw within its rectangle the
first glimmers of dawn lighting to the little top room, as if,
hanging from the guttering of the tower, he were spying on
that interior through the window—but the spectacle of the
exterior was more interesting, so he returned to it.

The ancient dawn spread its dew, its radiance and its
nuanced tenderness over the garden of yesteryear. Scarcely
had the sun appeared when the peasants headed for the vineyard. Some wore short culottes and thick stockings, others
wore trousers, but all of them—all those people now dead—
were decked out in costumes that resembled disguises. A
horse-drawn cart was brought, and vats unloaded from it. A
dozen men and women went into the vineyard; it was harvest-
time.

Then he saw the door of the château open—the one that
the porch was later to shelter—and the early-rising châtelain
emerged. He was dressed, as on the previous day, in his green
jacket with the brown collar. Large striped mariner's trousers
floated about his legs. His felt hat had broad rims folded back

in rolls. A monkey was gamboling at his side; a magnificent green and yellow parrot was sitting on his shoulder.

Charles, infatuated with all things Historical, had not forgotten anything from the annals of Captain Christiani. He knew the parrot's name: Pitt; and the name of the chimpanzee: Coburg—names facetiously forged by César to caricature the English and Austrian adversaries of the Revolution and Napoléon I. Nothing could have amused him as much as seeing the animals commemorated in his memoirs in company with the former corsair.

He watched the master go into the pathway through the vineyard, his servants bowing to him with an emphatic respect that has disappeared completely from our customs. Then a sturdy fellow who seemed to be authority over the others, summoned an old woman in a bonnet, bent over by the years, and Charles understood that he was explaining something to do with the old woman. Indeed, César handed a well-filled purse to the poor woman, who started kissing his hands, while Pitt and Coburg extended themselves, each in his fashion.

The charitable scene was a flash of enlightenment for Charles, for he remembered quite clearly that César had thought the generous gift he had made to an old grape-picker, when he was on the point of leaving Silaz for Paris, worthy of mention in his writings. It followed that the autumnal day so marvelously conserved and restored by the retrospective plates was one of the last days in the month of September 1829.

At that moment, Charles noticed that the sun had risen in the present, as in the past, and that a new day was beginning in the month of September 1929. A century, exactly, separated the two mornings that he was contemplating at the same time.

VI. A Century

A century. Exactly.

It is easy to imagine Charles's state of mind. The marvel that he had just discovered filled him with a passionate curiosity that had not yet begun to attenuate. Besides, at the moment of which we are speaking, he was still steeped in ignorance; a dense cloud of mystery enveloped the prodigy that he was observing but could not explain—a circumstance that lent an incomparable attraction to the adventure.

All day long he remained in his room, absorbed by the extraordinary contemplation of the haunted windows, and by the examination of the problem that they posed relative to physics—and quite probably to other sciences. He had cleared the mantelpiece and had installed there two window-panes there, one beside the other, instead of the clock and the rococo candelabras. The first showed him the grounds in 1829; the second, because he had set it the other way round, showed him the interior of the little top room. And in the mirror, against which the plates were leaning, the inverse views were reflected, the first plate showing the room and the second the park: outside and inside; inside and outside.

Claude, Péronne and Julien came to keep "Monsieur Charles" company from time to time and marvel with him at the astounding spectacle, almost incredible by virtue of the suddenness and unexpectedness that characterized it—for humankind has seen and will see many others, and this phenomenon, which was astonishing enough to amaze a admirably cultivated young man, was certainly no more prodigious than the effect of X-rays, a manifestation of wireless telegraph waves or television.

At a time when the miracles of science allow our skeletons to be seen through our flesh, transmit words and images through space without wires, and project the living appearance of a person or a place across leagues of distance, in truth, what

92

Charles Christiani saw before him—that phenomenon of special television, of *retrovision*—was not so formidable. Except, of course, that it was totally unexpected.

Charles, however, became accustomed to it. Everything, alas, is subject to the calming and dulling action of habitude, that inexorable de-gilder. He accustomed himself to it to the extent that he desired—and he desired it, knowing that every man must beware of the slightest sentimental or emotional distractions. So he stifled the stirrings of his heart and soul that attempted to agitate him when, by virtue of a an accumulation of undeniably true details, the image of 1829 reminded him that what he saw there was a corner of Savoy that was not yet French, although King Charles X had still to reign in France for a few more months; that he was seeing things, animals and people, trees and clouds, of *100 years ago*!

Doubtless because of the grape-harvest—a traditional festival—the old corsair's family had gathered at Silaz. As the morning advanced, in the bright sunlight of a lovely day, Charles saw César's son mingling with the grape-pickers: Horace, aged 37; and his wife, whom the observer had some difficulty identifying and not confusing with Horace's sister Lucile, aged 34, coiffed in a beribboned capeline and having, like her sister-in-law, vast leg-of-mutton sleeves and a bell-like skirt with flounces. Two children, delightfully dolled-up, were playing tag in front of the château: little Napoléon, Horace's only son, 15 years of age, and little Anselme Leboulard, Lucile's son, who was 14.

Charles was in no doubt about it; it was them. That genteel little squire in the tasseled cap, was really his great-grandfather, who had died in 1899 at the age of 85—only five years before Charles was born. And the other one, with his little English jacket and his shirt so blithely open on his breast, yes, that had to be the future Court Councilor, who had died in Paris in 1883, the father of cousin Drouet "who had behaved badly toward Mélanie." For, as often happens, of the two branches issuing from César Christiani, Charles's counted five generations and that of Cousin Drouet only three.

"So," Charles murmured, "this is my great-grandfather Napoléon, and that's cousin Anselm...unless it's the other way round. Children! One might think that it was a painting by Isabey.[11] Bah! After all, if the cinema had been invented in the time of Charles X, this family scene wouldn't surprise me at all! In 100 years, my grandsons will see me on the screen and not experience the slightest astonishment in consequence.

My grandsons! he thought, as a shadow passed over his thoughts. *My sons!* And Rita, in spite of everything, emerged once more within his reverie, with her luminous gaze, so frank and firm.

Péronne was there; while putting a tablecloth and cutlery on a side-table she never ceased looking at the plates and repeating, enthusiastically, that she did not understand it at all.

Charles touched the surface of the enigmatic substance yet again. Always the same impression: that of caressing frosted glass on the frosted side; no remarkable warmth or coldness. The phenomenon seemed to be exclusively due to the light and the nature of the material in which it produced the effect...

The 100-year-old landscape was slightly darkened by the effect of the means that had conserved it.

The nature of the material... Charles repeated to himself.

On examining the plates sideways, very attentively, an almost-imperceptible fuzz could be felt, furthering the resemblance to frosted glass. There was no reflection.

"The nature of the material..." reasoned the young historian. "Let's see: when light goes through red glass, it becomes red, and we see a red landscape. Analogous results for all the colors."

"That I understand," said Péronne, "but what I don't understand..."

---

[11] The reference is presumably to the famous miniaturist Jean-Baptiste Isabey (1767-1855), although the time-frame would also accommodate his son Eugène (1804-1866), best known for historical paintings and landscapes.

"Wait!" said Charles. "When light passes through crystal lenses or crystal prisms, it's deflected or decomposed. When light travels through water rather than through air, it's slowed down. Yes, Péronne, underwater, for example, the image of objects reaches us less rapidly that on the surface of the ground—*very little* less rapidly, but all the same, mathematically speaking, *less rapidly*."

"These plates, then," said Péronne, "are, so to speak, like plates of water that slow down light 100,000 times more than ordinary water?"

"Evidently!" Charles exclaimed. "These panes are composed of a substance in which light is slowed down in the same way that it is in water, in the same way that sound is slowed down in certain media. You know full well, Péronne, that one hears a sound more quickly through, for example, a metal conduit, or any sort of solid, than through the open air. Well then, Péronne! All of these phenomena belong to the same family!

"This, therefore, is the solution: these kinds of pane slow light down to a remarkable degree, since it only requires a relatively small thickness to retard it by 100 years. It takes 100 years for a ray of light to transpierce this layer of material! It must take one year to transpierce 1/100th of this depth."

It was then that, taking a sudden decision, Charles Christiani picked up one of the two plates and, with abundant precautions, inserted his pocket-knife into the center of the slice, in order to try to split the plate, in the whole of its breadth and length, into two halves, maintaining the same surface area, each of near-equal thickness.

He succeeded without difficulty; nothing was easier than separating one from the other, "cleaving" the innumerable layers of the stratified substance.

Having thus divided one of the two plates into two, he looked at the planes that he had just separated; and he saw what he expected to see—which is to say, on the one hand, the grounds and the façade of Silaz as they had been half way between 1829 and 1929, in 1879, with the porch over the drawing-room door; and on the other, the little top room, always the same through time, since it had not been touched for such a long period.

Charles, continuing his experiments, measured the thicknesses by eye, planted his knife in the striated side of the plate—the side with the thousand luminous and dark stripes—two millimeters from one edge: the edge limiting the view of the little top room. And he detached the micaceous sheets with a dry click.

He saw Claude, less than 20 years of age, going into the depths of the grounds with a wheelbarrow.

Charles repeated the same operation close to the other edge, and then—and then!—as he had sectioned it only a few years from the present day, he perceived a young man leaning over stacks of paper in the little top room, the sight of whom shook him violently in all the fibers of his mental being.

He saw *himself*, three years earlier.

Everything had now been clarified, at least with respect to the optical properties of this marvelous material, natural or composed. It was such that light went through it, in every direction, like a window, but *very slowly*, at the rate of a fraction of a millimeter every 24 hours.

At this point in our story, we shall ask our readers to excuse us for continuing to simplify—perhaps excessively—everything related to the scientific aspect of this story. Everything has its place. There are many reports and technical works on the subject of the material that Charles Christiani had just discovered—or, rather, rediscovered—and which he baptized *luminite*. We shall refer lovers of detail and explanation—who, in any case, might already have derived fecund speculations from the elementary data that we have already furnished—to the scientific works in question. We do not think it necessary to our own concerns to descend any further into the depths of science, for we are merely a scribe charged with telling a curiously-developed love story, and nothing more. That is already, in itself, a sufficiently fine task, and one that enchants us.

Let us, therefore, set aside everything concerning chemistry and mathematics, not to mention the rest; and if any female reader has started sulking as she read the preceding pages, may we simply ask her to remember, for the moment, that *luminite*—as Charles Christiani baptized the retrospective substance—is something that produces the following result: because light passes through this material at an extremely decelerated speed., one sees, in looking through plates of luminite, things as they once were; and the thicker the plate is, the more distant is the past revealed on both sides of the plate.[12]

Having established that, let us take up the thread of events.

The first that offers itself to us for retracing occurred that same evening.

When night fell, Charles Christiani, who had not left his room all day, saw his ancestor César enter the little top room for the second time, as if instead of being in front of his mantelpiece, Charles had been up there watching what happened from outside the second floor of the tower. And with regard to that, he made the rather curious remark to himself that, even if the little top room had been empty of all its furniture in 1929, the luminite window-pane would have shown it to him as it

---

[12] This scrupulous but repetitive summation and the mildly sarcastic apology that precedes it were presumably inserted into the opening sentences of one of the *feuilleton*'s episodes in response to editorial demand, perhaps as a reaction to complaints from readers. Renard was by no means the first writer of speculative fiction to become anxious about the potential discontentment of female readers—similar remarks can be found in Félix Bodin's *Le Roman de l'avenir* (1834; tr. in a Black Coat Press edition as *The Novel of the Future*)—nor was he the first feuilletonist to be forced to modify his text as he went along in response to external pressure, the latter being a problem that routinely troubled the works by Paul Féval that are consciously echoed in this one.

was in 1829, as everything that we have reported trickled through it.

Now, everything in old César's appearance indicated that he was making the final preparations for his departure. Much better placed than behind the little window in the loft, Charles could get as close to the plate as he desired. By that means, he could see the ridge-backed desk on which César had deposited his lamp as he came in.

The eccentric gentleman in green wrote a few pages with the aid of a goose-quill. At the foot of the fifth, he drew a line, in a rough manner. After which, adding the sheets he had just blackened to a whole stack of sheets, he placed all of them in a black-and-yellow-marbled cardboard box, whose three cords he knotted cleverly.

Getting up thereafter, he went to the bookcase, opened it, climbed on to a stool, took a considerable number of books off the highest shelf, and plunged his hand inside the item of furniture.

Charles, who was watching this in the lower pane of the window—the one which had been fixed beneath the other in the window-frame on the previous evening—changed plates and, in order to see better, continued his observation through the upper pane. He was thus placed on the same level as the top of the bookcase—which is to say, as comfortably as possible for seeing César's hand slide a portion of the back of the bookcase that was slotted in grooves sideways. The wall then appeared—or, to be precise, a little door set in the wall.

That door also slid sideways, obedient to César's hand, unmasking a cavity, a hiding-place hollowed out in the body of the wall. It was there that César deposited the box containing the manuscript.

He did not limit his actions to this placement, though. Having rummaged in the depths of the secret lodgment, he took something out.

What was it? A flat rectangular package wrapped in black cloth or black paper. It could have been a book, a volume in folio format…or a plate.

The sliding mechanism was brought into play; the cavity in the wall closed again—likewise the movable back of the bookcase. César replaced the books, and got down off the stool...

A few minutes later, he left the little top room, carrying the lamp and the black package...

Charles, in the darkness of his bedroom, in which the present crescent moon only spread a wan glow, could no longer see anything on the mantelpiece but two nocturnal scenes: on one side, the former grounds, whitened by the old Phoebe, who was silvering the bushes, its simple French pathways, its vineyard and its rustic summer-house; and on the other, the little top room, deserted and dormant.

Without losing a minute, in spite of the fatigue that was wearing him out, he took up a powerful lamp, lit it and rapidly went up to the second floor of the tower, to the doctored bookcase and the hiding-place in the wall.

It was quite natural that these secret dispositions had escaped him before, when he had undertaken the exploration and the rearrangement of the monumental item of furniture. The idea that a part of the back might be movable, capable of sliding laterally, supported by slots, had never occurred to him That characteristic had not been mentioned in any of the old papers that he had consulted; in particular, César Christiani's memoirs did not contain a single word to encourage the suspicion that the hiding-place existed. The ancestor had, however, known perfectly well that the removal of the bookcase would unmask the little door; one could therefore conclude that he had intended to return to Silaz before dying and to take less precarious measures relative to that secret.

Charles thought, judiciously, that reading the manuscript would clarify this point—and many others.

He had no difficulty recovering the black-and-yellow box, *whose cords were still cleverly knotted*. And after that, he brought out of the lodgment several more-or-less flat packages similar to the one César had taken away a century ago, each meticulously wrapped in black cloth. He weighed them in his hands and presumed that they were plates of luminite. Nevertheless, before making sure of that, he thought it best to read the manuscript, not knowing why these presumed plates had been so carefully sheltered from the light.

We have had this exceedingly interesting account in our hands, which reveals everything that César Christiani knew, in 1829, concerning the substance that his thrice-great-grandson was to call luminite, and which he called *optical glass*, in a spirit in conformity with the language of his era as well as, let us admit, his ignorance of scientific matters and the import of words.

The amplitude of this document prohibits us from publishing it here in its entirety. We shall summarize it as best we can, regrettably depriving it, in so doing, of the astonishing verve that the corsair captain deployed therein and the truculent bonhomie with which his work is imprinted, imparting to it such a southern warmth that one cannot help reading his narration in the accent of his native region.

Day was breaking for the second time, without Charles Christiani having obtained a wink of sleep, when he finished learning that which we are about to condense, in a paroxysm of overexcitement.

VII. The "Stone That Remembers"

On May 28, 1814, the three-master *Finette*, armed as a privateer, carrying 28 cannons, 130 crewmen and Captain César Christiani, was cruising in the Indian Ocean in order to impede English commerce by any means possible.

She was a pretty ship, sleek and slender in form, whose capacity for speed was as famous as the intrepidity of the coastal brethren who manned her. In the previous days, César had captured two important prizes and sent them to Port-Napoléon—the former Port-Louis—the capital of the Ile de France,[13] manning them with parts of his crew under the command of two of his lieutenants.

As dusk was falling, the lookout on the topmast spotted several sails in the wind. A convoy of eight East India Company ships was identified, sailing under the protection of three warships, one of which would not be long delayed in separating itself. Without waiting for it, César came about and fled away from it.

He was not worried about the approach of the English ship, a stout frigate with at least 50 guns and 600 men, which was heading straight for the *Finette* with all sails aloft. The chase, he thought, would not be prolonged. The frigate would be eager to link up with its convoy again.

Long after sunset, however, the night being clear, the enemy could be seen laboring the sea at a distance of two cannon-shots, and slowly gaining. César realized that only his skill could save him. To fight would be to race to his doom. Trickery seemed impossible—and in these distant waters, he could not count on any French rescue. He therefore set the course in which the wind was most favorable to his retreat and fled southwards in that fashion, with the Englishman in his wake.

---

[13] Mauritius.

The latter, a remarkable speedy vessel, seemed to be firmly resolved to extend the chase to the point of boarding. Had the *Finette* been recognized? César supposed so, in view of the other ship's obstinacy and the decision its master had taken to abandon the convoy. In response to the frigate's call to heave to, the *Finette* had not, of course, shown its colors on the mizzen mast, and certainly was not displaying César Christiani's guidon—a golden Christ on a red background—on the mainmast, but the corsair's lines and speed were not unknown to any officer in the British navy, and it was a good bet that the commander of the accursed vessel was already rejoicing at the prospect of sending César Christiani and his crew to the English hulks.

There was no alternative to augmenting the speed of the *Finette* and distancing her from the Englishman, in order to get out of sight. César, who knew his ship from stem to stern and from the keel to the tops of the masts, ordered the sails to be dampened in order to give them more purchase on the wind. The seamen deployed the studding-sails and the royals, which meant that the vessel was covered by all its canvas. That expectable ploy not being sufficient, César had four carronades that were overloading the Finette's decks thrown overboard. He ordered the trimming of the cargo, with the result that the ship was relieved of it; bales and packing-cases were thrown into the sea, six out of every dozen that had been lowered into the hold.

In spite of these efforts, the English frigate only lost a short distance—seeing which, César had recourse to drastic expedients. The carpenters unwedged the masts and removed the stanchions; the supercargoes emptied the reserve water-barrels. Thanks to these supreme measures, the lightened and more supple corsair, no longer offering any but feeble resistance to the swell and bending its flexible masts, bounded over the waves. Little by little, the Emperor's mariners saw the inclined silhouette of the large vessel—aboard which César, though his telescope, had already distinguished the cannoneers putting their forward guns in place—drawing away.

The pursuit was not over, though. Far from giving up, the enemy, sticking to its prey, was hoping that some hazard of the sea would put her at its mercy. And, indeed, in consequence of the extreme measures that the Englishman had doubtless also taken, the Sun rose on an uncertain situation. Admittedly, the distance between the *Finette*'s bow and the stubborn frigate's prow had increased further, but the latter, making as much speed as possible, did not seem to be despairing at all.

Even so tenacious an ardor, however, had to give way to the marine science of Captain César, stimulated by his love of liberty. By dusk, after 24 hours of exhausting flight, a vigorous "hurrah" went up from the *Finette*. On the horizon, now very tiny in the distance, the frigate came about. Its gleaming fireports were visible as it turned.

To imagine that César would immediately cease sailing at top speed would have been to underestimate him. He maintained his progress, and, in addition, "took a false route" in order to deceive the other vessel's possible return. Thus, veering further to the east, he plunged deeper into waters that are the deserts of the liquid world.

In the morning, while he was meditating on his misadventure and deploring the loss of all the drinkable water of which necessity had compelled him to disemburden himself, he took his bearings and his expression darkened.

We should note here that nowhere in his narrative, even though it was secret, did Captain César Christiani indicate the position in which he found himself at dawn on that May 30, 1814. In addition, it should be stated that in his non-secret memoirs, the episode of the English frigate is only mentioned in passing and excites no curiosity.

That point, the intersection of a meridian and a parallel, remains unknown. The location determined by the hypothetical encounter of a line of longitude and a line of latitude would have been able to serve as a basis for ulterior research. Quite apart from the fact that César suspected subsequently that he had not operated his sextant correctly, however, we believe that he retained until his death the hope of remaining the one and only *master of light*.

He was, therefore, reflecting joylessly upon the annoyance of being at the end of the earth, beneath a hot Sun, with 100 stout fellows of every color—great lovers of coffee, rum and bishop,[14] to be sure, but who, a week hence, would welcome drinking-water with loud acclamation. Now, he did not have much drinking water, and of wind, he had even less.

Meanwhile, the island appeared, so appropriately that César wondered whether he might be dreaming, or whether the man on watch might be dreaming in announcing the sight of land. The island, however, was no dream birthed by desire, and even though the ship's charts made no mention of it, it was there, verdant and mountainous, accompanied by half a dozen islets of more cheerful aspect.

The whole lot was no more than a hundredth of the size of Corsica, but the sight of it was as pleasant as that of a welcoming harbor. César, sniffing the fine odor of soil and foliage that was coming from the island, and seeing seagulls and coots flying around his masts, thanked Heaven for having steered him toward that little volcanic archipelago.

It was obviously volcanic. As the *Finette* drew closer, the captain's telescope clarified the ashen aspect of its mountainous heights and the nature of certain plumes of smoke— singularly numerous, it is true—which he had taken at first for evidence of habitation. They were only fumaroles, emerging from rocky crevices.

The isle was none the less inhabited; in the distance, the natives, who had no suspicion that they were being spied on through a telescope, were watching the *Finette* approach. They disappeared as if by magic when she moored in a hospitable bay, dropping anchor at a depths of nine fathoms on to a bed of smooth sand.

---

[14] A drink made from port, citrus fruit and sugar.

César immediately sent 15 armed sailors ashore to find provisions of water and wood. He leapt into the launch himself, equipped with his hunting-rifle and a game-bag.

The heat was intense. There was not a cloud in the blinding sky. The beach on which they landed seemed deserted. The little troop followed the course of a little stream that flowed into the sea; closer to its source, the water would be better.

The stream emerged from a forest, so they went into the woods. A place was soon found that was as propitious for the extraction of water as for the felling of a few trees—to which his men proceeded, under the authority of a junior officer. César moved away, drawn by his instinct as a hunter of woods and seas.

"There is nothing more beautiful," he says, "than that magnificent forest, in which the Sun's rays filtered through the most diverse foliage, playing among enormous and charming flowers, while a thousand songbirds flew forth from every direction, showing off their sumptuous plumage."

He killed a few of them, taking care not to wander so far that he could no longer hear the sound of the workers' axes striking the trees they were felling. But those noises and the detonations of his rifle had guided a band of indigenes to their vicinity, and just as César was taking aim at a multicolored bird on a branch, he was suddenly grabbed, tied up and gagged, and carried away on the shoulders of little yellow men who moved at a marvelously rapid trot.

They were akin to the Javanese, not at all barbaric although very primitive. Slender and delicately muscled, they wore dark blue sashes twisted around their loins. César soon made the acquaintance of their dwellings, which presented the particularity of being semi-subterranean. They were constructed from light, rather elegant straw, matched to cool cavities hollowed out in the ground.

It was into one of these caves that César was invited to descend. The indigenes treated him gently, even politely. His gag and his bonds had been removed. He went down the stairway that was indicated to him with a fairly good grace; its entrance was in a large, very orderly room in a large house of straw and bamboo.

Before going into this fragile edifice, César had had time to observe that the village was situated in a clearing at the foot of the principal mountain. At the foot of the stairway he was pushed, without rudeness, into a cavernous space and was surprised to find it very brightly lit.

The door, or rather the screen, was closed behind him. He was left alone. He took a few steps toward the center of his prison, vaguely doubting that it was a true prison, since there were openings to the exterior in several places.

Immediately, however, an inexplicable fact filled him with a sudden perplexity—which, given the circumstances, mingled anxiety with mistrust.

Those openings, in fact, which were similar to cave-entrances, were not barred; no obstacle appeared to oppose the passage of anyone entering or exiting—which had already surprised the prisoner. But there was more. César opened his eyes wide, fearful of a trap, and he looked at each of the sunlit openings in turn, beyond which landscapes extended…

Bizarre landscapes. Sunlit, yes, but nevertheless darkened in a strange manner. In addition, the trees and the plants that were framed therein gave César a surprising notion of the vegetation of the island. In these regions, there was nothing reminiscent of the first sight of the luxuriant forest in which the natives had just captured him. What he saw now formed a monstrous confusion of roots, green and hairy stems and vegetable tentacles. It was a forest of stout, baroque, giant, terrific and utterly abnormal plants.

"What does this signify?" César murmured.

He had no time to reflect any further. Something happened that deprived him momentarily of the capacity for discernment: an unimaginable thing, frightful and splendid, unparalleled and bewildering.

Outside, the gigantic green thicket became agitated. The tubers, hairy branches and thick leaves swollen with sap were violently parted, broken, split apart like a massive curtain—and an enormous animal emerged, suddenly standing still, moving its frightful head from side to side.

There was something dragon-like in it, and lizard-like; its head was that of a boa, its neck that of a tortoise, its tail that of a salamander, its posture that of a kangaroo, but from one end of its spine to the other it bore a formidable crest armed with spikes and its stature was not comparable to anything ordinary in the animal world. The tallest elephant would not have attained half its height by raising its trunk vertically.

The frightful creature retained its vigilant attitude for a few seconds, though. Then, heavily and slowly, it drew away, hopping on its tail and its colossal hind feet, touching the ground occasionally with its forepaws, excessively small but armed with menacing claws. César watched its interminable, slanted back rising and falling for some time, while the bristling crest undulated and the stupid but attentive head at its tip kept turning from side to side.

César only had extremely restricted notions of a science that had just been born at that time: paleontology. However, he could not doubt that the monster was a survivor of an epoch that he called "antediluvian" and he was certain that he had landed on an island where, by some extraordinary hazard, animals and plants that had disappeared everywhere else continued to exist—prodigiously.

He was in a cold sweat. Fear, just now, had made him shiver. He had regretted that the openings of his prison were not fitted with solid bars. For a second, he had wondered whether the indigenes might have intended him to make a meal for the titanic lizard.

He collected himself, and approached another opening to see whether the creature had veered off in that direction…and then made several observations that precipitated him into a cascade of astonishment.

The Sun was shining on one side, but in the other opening an abundant rain was streaming over a window.

Through a third lateral opening, birds of some sort, which resembled huge bats with horses' heads, were passing by in swift flight—but César could no longer see them in the sky by looking through the middle bay.

The landscapes in the various places were not concordant. Their heights were different. There was even one that was tilted, like a badly-hung picture. What they showed offered inconceivable dissimilarities; one might have thought that there were different seasons, different times of day, even different ages.

Those openings were not open at all, but—as the streaming rain had revealed—furnished with windows that had a slight darkening effect, without any supporting frames: huge single pieces of glass.

Finally, the prisoner's eyes having become accustomed to the obscurity of the cave, he discovered that the shadows on the walls, between the lighted views, were not absolutely dark, but that vague moving glimmers were retained there. There were, in fact, three new marvels there of the same kind as the others. They were three nocturnal scenes, three nights: two landscapes and a cloudy sky; a sky with nothing but clouds and pale stars—as if César had raised his eyes to the ceiling instead of looking straight ahead of him.

Our captain was beginning to understand certain things. He was no longer amazed to see, from underground, views of the surface in broad daylight, or nocturnal views of an open sky, or even perspectives on an infinitely distant past. His lively and sure intelligence had immediately grasped that all of this originated from the vitreous objects mounted on the walls of the subterranean room. When they were rapped with a hard object, such as a knife, each one rendered a dull sound, giving an impression of thickness, of an exceedingly dense and resistant mineral block.

These blocks, contrary to appearances, were not interposed in any fashion between the interior and the exterior, like the panes of a window. They were encased in the blind and insensible walls of earth that rimmed the cave.

But why had they been placed there? Why were these walls paved in this fashion with these huge pieces of some unknown quartz, which enclosed vertiginously ancient visions? The walls of a cave in which, moreover, the enclosed silence and space had helped César do justice to the illusion—was it, then, a sort of museum? A scarcely probable hypothesis.

César put his finger on the truth when dusk fell over some of the views, one after another, while day broke successively in the three nocturnal ones. The natives had simply found an economical and infallible system of lighting for their subterranean dwellings. It could even be supposed that the possession of such convenient luminous sources had provoked them to lodge themselves thus, partially underground, where they found a perpetually-illuminated refuge from the heat of their island.

In the days that followed, César became acquainted with the mores and customs of his hosts, and the ways in which they made use of the marvelous substance to which they had given the name *mong-tio*—which is to say, *the stone that remembers*.

They not only used the blocks to see clearly by night in their little lodgings, but to make signals from the summits of mountains and to scare away ferocious beasts; and they contrived something akin to thick curtains in order to veil their singular lamps—which, not content with illuminating them, showed them all sorts of incredible scenes—should the need arise.

As to how the corsair learned all this, and many other strange things that have no relevance to our story, it was quite simple.

When their captain did not return, the sailors in the landing party set out to search for him. Following the trail of the little troop of kidnappers, it did not take them long to discover the village at the foot of the mountain. They laid siege to it, being men familiar with that sort of amusement—but, fearing for César's life, they began with a thunderous demonstration of rifle shots fired into the air.

As they had foreseen, the indigenes took fright at that sustained fusillade, supported by appropriate howls, with which the coastal brethren habitually accompanied their boarding onslaughts when the grappling hooks had seized an enemy boat and the drums were bating in a sinister manner. César's few rifle shots had not prepared the natives for that diabolical charivari, evocative of lightning, thunder and volcanic eruptions. They thought they were doomed, and could think of nothing better to do than go in quest of César in his enchanted cave.

The captain understood immediately what was required of him. He calmed the racket without delay, and had his rifle returned to him along with his powder-horn and game-bag, which had been confiscated—and, immediately liberated, returned to the *Finette* with his saviors. He had not been in any great danger.

The thought of the mysterious material never left him, though. Once back on board, he reflected profoundly, still marveling at the sojourn he had spent underground, illuminated by the light of prehistoric days. His curiosity was still unsatisfied—and furthermore, he was certain that there was a fortune to be made by means of the secret of the unknown isle. That was why he had prevented his men from entering the enclosure of the village. That was why he reappeared before his attackers' eyes on the threshold of that enclosure on the following day, alone and unarmed, but with a provision of objects calculated to flatter the instincts of a simple and naïve population.

He was greeted with all the respect due to his honesty—and for several days he lived amid the indigenes, gradually gaining their friendship and winning their confidence. They allowed him to occupy himself as he wished, and informed him about everything, teaching him as best they could the elements of their language.

The blocks of *mong-tio* were found in a natural state on the island and the islets, on the surface of the ground, but especially in the earth. They quarried it and mined it. There were always masses that were more-or-less smooth, the rough and unequal edges of which clearly indicated its multilayered structure. It had many analogies with slate, but it was quite rare to disinter a block or a plate of *mong-tio* that was not "impressed"—which had not yet seen daylight. Many of them were exhumed without their smooth faces being illustrated with a moving image, but that did not mean that daylight had never struck them. Sometimes, an ancient image was secretly making its way through the plate in question, and an examination of the edge revealed the fact by permitting the sight of one or several luminous lines on the march, some toward one side and the others toward the other side. That was the light advancing slowly—very slowly—through the thickness of the substance.

Every evening, Captain Christiani went back to his ship, carrying a package wrapped in black cloth. The sailors who came to fetch in him in the launch in response to his signal counted 12 evenings and 12 packages. César thus transported a few virgin plates, extracted by feel from the darkness at the bottom of a mine, and a few others extracted from the surface of thick blocks—too voluminous to be carried away—and which restored the exciting spectacles of the eras of the giant saurians, flying lizards and, much later, the ape-men who were our first ancestors.

These latter plates, by the panoramas they exposed and the upheavals to which they testified, revealed a fact to which César attached little importance at the time, but which, a few years later, came back to his memory. That fact was that in ancient epochs, the island and the islets had been part of a vast land, perhaps a continent, and that, little by little, that continent had been swallowed up piecemeal. By 1814, a series of cataclysms had left only the sparse fragments visited by Captain Christiani: a few isles that were vestiges of an archipelago that had been a mere vestige itself.

On the 12th evening, César got ready to sail for the Ile de France. A party of indigenes had accompanied him to the beach. As the *Finette* put out to sea, he saw them waving spears that had been decorated with colored rags in order that they could be seen from a distance, and hurling them into the air as a gesture of farewell.

That evening, a dark cloud sprang forth from the mountain, and the fumaroles were powerful.

The crew of the *Finette* manifested the joy of their return in song. Among those rough men, there were usually some to be found to murmur protests against a port of call prolonged without reason or—which came to the same thing—for their captain's pleasure. They had grumbled all the more because he had forbidden anyone to go ashore. Some had permitted themselves observations contrary to discipline. César had had them put in irons or sentenced to receive a few vigorous strokes of the lash. It was always the same ones. The names of the same hotheads were to be cited frequently in the captain's memoirs of that campaign in the Indian Ocean.

We cannot insist too strongly on this point: the *Memoirs* make no mention of the adventures we have just related. In addition, the secret manuscript reveals the fever with which César Christiani envisaged the rewards that he anticipated obtaining from the *optical glass*, making a fortune worthy of Croesus. He projected several practical applications for it, and did not doubt that the substance would command fabulously high prices in Europe and the New World. He had a practical mind, and in his view, the most precious property of optical glass was not that of bring testimony to the century of Napoléon of the Age of Reptiles, the Ice Ages and the Stone Age; he saw it above all else as an instrument of everyday use, destined, in many circumstances of life, to serve as proof and to demonstrate how some event or other had occurred. Was not a piece of *optical glass* enough to ensure, in fact, that a scene could be recorded as durably as the thickness of the glass that contained it? And once that was done, it only required the plate to be split up, like a block of rigid sheets, to recover the living image of the scene in question, making its way slowly through the interior of the prodigious mica.

When we say "prodigious," though, it must be understood that were are putting ourselves in César's shoes and employing his own expression—for, to our modern eyes, accustomed to the marvels of photography and cinematography, the effects of *optical glass* are, after all, merely a sort of natural cinematography, which remains extremely curious for us but does not strike us with the amazement by which César remained flabbergasted.

The *Finette* had been at sea for two years. It had been agreed that its captain would head for Saint-Malo that year and undertake a sojourn in France necessitated by the management of his personal affairs. César did not think that he ought to modify his plans. He was fortunate enough to complete the long journey without any notable incident. His intention, relative to the optical glass, was to come back the following year and drop anchor off the island, with a carefully-chosen crew and a few reliable companions, in order discreetly to embark large quantities of the inestimable commodity. Until then, he had resolved to maintain silence.

The prizes that he had taken since the Emperor's enthronement ensured his wealth. He concluded his business with the bankers and the lawyers, converted his booty into investments and real estate, spent a few weeks in Paris, saw Napoléon beset with immense difficulties and foresaw nothing good coming therefrom, but went nevertheless to take a rest in Savoy. It was at that time that the plates, after several months at sea and transportation of every sort in a sealed crate, reached the little top room at Silaz and the hiding-place behind the bookcase that the suspicious César had personally contrived.

The Emperor's fall, the return of the Bourbons and the disgrace that followed for the captain upset all his plans. There could no longer be any question of setting out to sea again in a corsair ship. César did not hesitate to charter a seaworthy yacht, rigged as a schooner, at his own expense—and in spite of the expense of such an enterprise, he set off one morning from Bordeaux for an unmysterious destination: Madagascar.

You will have guessed that Madagascar had nothing to do with it, and that the island of the *optical glass* was the true goal of that so-called pleasure cruise—but whether an earthquake had completed the annihilation of the remains of the archipelago, or whether César had measured his position wrongly, that goal was not attained. The island and the islets could not be found. The yacht cruised in vain through the ocean region in which César expected to reach them. There was nothing there but the dismal and deserted expanse of the waves.

César was grievously disappointed. His sharp and honest temperament led him to accuse himself of incompetence. In his manuscript he returns incessantly to the error he might have made in taking his bearings. He prefers to attribute his distress to his own fault rather than to an earthquake, probably to preserve in his mind some hope of one day rediscovering that treasure island, which he called the Ile Christiani, and which he would have offered to France. Today, though, every inch of the surface of the globe is known, and the maps do not indicate anything resembling an island, however minuscule, in that zone of the Indian Ocean—so we must believe that the captain's sextant functioned correctly, that his calculations were accurate and that all the harm was done by a seismic cataclysm that was only to be expected sooner or later.

As for the lieutenants and sailors of the *Finette*, there is nothing surprising in the fact that they never said anything about the island. The first mate and the senior lieutenants had departed with the prizes sent by César to Port-Napoléon; the others trusted their leader when he assured them, deceptively, that the territories in question had already been discovered by obscure navigators. If one bears in mind that no one aboard the yacht had any suspicion of César's plans, he being as cunning as any good corsair, there is no difficulty in explaining how the mystery was perpetuated.

After various vicissitudes, the yacht was sold on its return to Bordeaux and César, disappointed and anxious about the sums he had spent, unwelcome at court and not very sociable, retired entirely to Silaz with his monkeys, his parrots and his exotic birds, of which he had a full aviary resonant with twittering and birdsong. It was 1816.

There was certainly a kind of miserliness in the care that he took to hide the existence of *optical glass*—a sort of egotistical enjoyment. He had to recognize, however, that if he wanted to reserve the privilege of using the material in his own interests, it was necessary for him to keep the secret. A witness as reliable, as mute and as above suspicion as optical glass might be a great help to him in many instances, especially if he were to judge it worthwhile to enter into one of the conspiracies in which the partisans of the exiled Emperor and the Duc de Reichstadt[15] unfailingly tried to involve him.

Was he waiting for the right moment to involve himself? Nothing indicates that—which did not prevent him from passing, in eyes of the Bourbons, for a passionate and dangerous Bonapartist.

The end of the manuscript reports a few relatively uninteresting experiments that he made with the *optical glass* during his years at Silaz, and some inconsequential considerations regarding an idea that he abandoned—to send specimens of the material to chemists in order that they might attempt to analyze it and then replicate it. Finally, he explains why, before going to Paris, he had thought of replacing two windowpanes in the little top room with two plates of virgin *optical glass*. It was simply to leave an invisible observer there. When he returned to Silaz, he would only have to take out the plates and split them up; by that means, everything that happened in his absence, in the grounds and in front of the château, would appear to him sequentially, and if any incident seemed worthy of examination, he would only have to observe its course in comfort.

---

[15] The title employed by Napoléon I's son after 1814.

He thought, however, that he might perhaps never return to Savoy, and it amused him to place two panes *a century thick* in plain sight, in order that, a hundred years later, someone might have the unparalleled surprise of perceiving the events of his own time through those plates. The window had no shutters, so no obstacle would mask the view or oppose the action of the light—at least for some time. The plates, being virginal, would remain opaque for 100 years; they would not attract any attention. César therefore fitted them into the frame of the casement, carefully sealing their edges to avoid the feeble glow of their cross-sections from betraying his stratagem.

He finally brought his confession—which he had written every evening in the little top room, where no one, to that late hour, could interrupt him—to an end. His penultimate sentence announces that he intends to take a plate of *optical glass* to Paris. The final one lets it be understood that he would leave three days later—and, returning to the subject of the plates that, from then on, would cover half of the window behind him, César gives his conclusion a mischievous turn.

When his thrice-great-grandson Charles Christiani read the final sentence of the memoir, that malice reminded him forcefully of the ironic glance that César—or, more accurately, César's shade—had darted at the window thus equipped: a glance that the young man and the chauffeur Julien had imagined to be directed at them.

As he closed the yellow-and-black lid upon the manuscript, Charles, his head buzzing, looked around, not longer quite knowing which century he was in. Feverishly excited, he was subconsciously subject to a puerile disillusionment, for the discovery of an unknown manuscript, the work of César Christiani, had made him hope vaguely for some sort of revelation concerning the relationship of the corsair and his murderer, Fabius Ortofieri. And however important what he had just learned might be, extraordinary as his wonderment was, it seemed to him that once again, deceptive Destiny—which might have been of service—was stubbornly refusing to do anything for him.

VIII. On the Brink of Misfortune [16]

The final tennis matches were being contested on the courts of Saint-Trojan. Outside the wire-netting, among the deflowered rose-bushes, groups of people were sitting on the benches and garden-chairs, watching the players.

They were the semi-finals and finals of the "men's singles." When the day was over, there would be a general dispersal. The following day, the ferry to Chapus would disgorge passengers who would be heading back from the pure autumnal light of Oléron to sterner skies.

Luc de Certeuil, who had already qualified for the final, was chatting with Marguerite Ortofieri. He was certain that he would win the cup and was not anxious to know which adversary the semi-final being played in front of him would determine as his final opponent. He was absorbed by a more serious preoccupation. He did not want the season to end without bringing a definitive precision to his situation with respect to Rita.

"In any case," he said to her, "I think that we might wait several years before knowing one another any better. This time tomorrow I shall have gone my way and you'll have gone yours. I'll only see you again at intervals. Don't you think it's time to put an end to these preliminaries? Your father and mother are here, and I have every reason to believe that they won't raise any opposition. Rita, will you authorize me to ask for your hand this evening?"

Rita remained silent for a moment, her eyes distracted by the contest of the two adversaries dancing back and forth on either side of the net. She was visibly troubled, though.

---

[16] Renard's chapter-title is "*Malheur moins cinq*," which relies on a pun linking the *heur* in *malheur* [misfortune] to *heure* [hour], "*moins cinq*" being the usual way of indicating "five [minutes] to" a particular hour.

"Forgive me," she said, effortfully. "I foresaw that you were going to speak to me, but not the effect it would have on me. Things don't happen as one expects them to. You find me very emotional and—how shall I put it?—devoid of bravery. I'm rather frightened."

"I shan't do anything without your permission," said Luc, with a great deal of softness and a certain understandable resentment.

"Naturally," said Rita, smiling momentarily.

"I understand your state of mind perfectly well, and I'd be a fool to be offended by it. It's a sufficiently solemn matter to require reflection. But permit me to insist that we no longer need, I hope, to reflect. Come on, decide whether I shall be happy!"

"Will you give me few minutes more?" implored the young woman. "Truly, I'm…I'm…"

She squeezed her handkerchief in the palms of her moist hands. In her bronzed face, further tanned by the sea air, there was a kind of snowy gleam, and her featured seemed to have lost the ability to relax.

"My dear Rita!" murmured Luc, in a tender voice.

She could no longer hear him more distinctly than the sportive words of the players—their calls of *play* and *ready*—mingled with the monotonous announcements of the umpire on his podium. It was only through a fog of anguish that she glimpsed the white or multicolored patches of the silent spectators of either sex. And yet…

And yet, since Charles Christiani's departure, she had told herself that it was necessary to settle things as soon as possible. The best thing to do was to finish it once and for all, without hesitation—not to linger, vainly and painfully, in superfluous regrets and dreams without foundation. To pass on to the next stage of existence, quickly, quickly, to heap life upon the impossible dream, to retreat precipitately into the depths of a past in which one irreparable event after another might be frantically accumulated to stun herself…

119

The request that Luc had just made of her, she had promised herself to prompt before their departure, if he had continued to hold back. It was the best solution, the most honest, the most courageous…and the most prudent. In addition, throughout the time she had been in Charles Christiani's company without making herself known to him, she had maintained a firm resolution to annul those romantic hours, fraudulently stolen, by necessity, immediately afterwards. She had sworn then to take up the thread of her interrupted destiny immediately and to become engaged to Luc de Certeuil the very next day, having made a concession to the dream and to love—the only one she would make in her entire life.

Geneviève Le Tourneur, consulted during the preceding days, had strongly approved of Rita's decision. Yes, all memory of Charles Christiani should certainly be erased as soon as possible; she encouraged her friend and congratulated her on her wisdom. Rita had felt very strong, stoical, almost content to accomplish a dutiful act of renunciation intrepidly. *Renunciation?* she had thought. *But what is it, then, that I'm renouncing. Nothing, alas, since it's impossible!* With respect to that, Geneviève had suggested that by getting engaged to Luc de Certeuil she would be working for the tranquility and appeasement of Charles Christiani, who was doubtless no happier than she was at present.

Rita, therefore, had *wanted* Luc to ask for her hand in marriage that day. She had prayed that he would take the initiative. Just now, as they had sat down on the bench, she had thought: *If only he will speak!* But now that he had spoken, a frightful distress gripped her heart. It seemed to her that the brutal proposition had been made that she should sacrifice the most beautiful chimera of all time. Until now, no action had been taken against her love. Now, she had been offered a dagger with which to stab it. The moment had come to be faithful or unfaithful, to renounce—oh, yes, to *renounce*—what? She did not know. She only knew that it was necessary to renounce something so beautiful and so great that there had never been a more atrocious sacrifice than that one.

It was necessary—but her distress was begging for a delay. She repeated, as firmly as she could: "A few minutes, all right?"

Geneviève Le Tourneur appeared then, very opportunely. Rita saw her coming toward them, with an indolent stride, and felt a sharp satisfaction. The young woman, suffering from a migraine, had made her excuses to Luc for not being able to watch the tournament; she had intended to spend the afternoon lying down in her room, as she often did. On seeing her, Rita experienced a pleasant surprise as well as joy. She had never been in greater need of having a female friend at her side, to console her and give her assurance in her struggle against the male of the species, the eternal war of the sexes. Geneviève was swinging her hips gently, with an amiable smile.

They made room for her between them, on the bench. Her fearfully pale skin reddened in the cheeks.

"Is your headache better?" asked Rita, affectionately.

"Not entirely," said Geneviève, placing a finger on her temple. "But sufficiently for me not to miss Monsieur de Certeuil's victory."

The said Monsieur de Certeuil did not flinch. Madame Le Tourneur brought out of an immense floral-patterned cretonne bag a sort of table-mat, and phlegmatically set about embroidering it with mauve and orange silk. She heard Rita say to Luc: "Go play your match. I promise to give you an answer immediately afterwards."

"But...come on...can't you just say yes?" he said, with a certain vivacity and a suspicion of anxiety.

Rita, reaching out her arm, had placed a hand on one of Geneviève's hands, which meekly fell idle. "Luc, you've asked me if you should speak to my parents now or later, haven't you? I don't think there's any question of anything else? What is there to be alarmed about?"

"Ah! Good, good..."

The activity of the spectacle that was taking place in front of them had just been modified. The players on the court had stopped, mingling with other tennis players who were coming into the wire-netting enclosure. Outside, the groups were on the move.

"It's Simpson who's won," said Luc de Certeuil. "Hey, Simpson! How long before we play?"

"I'd prefer to do it right away," the American replied.

"Okay." Luc got up and said to the young woman, laughing: "Chances are this game will be the quickest of my career."

"Oh…" Rita began, evasively.

"Come on!" Luc persisted, caressing the handle of his racket. "Say yes right now. It'll help me to win."

Rita looked at him uncertainly—but just at the moment when she might perhaps have uttered the desired word, the most unexpected, surprising and inconceivable sensation closed her mouth. With a sudden and brief pressure, Geneviève Le Tourneur's hand had just given her a secret but peremptory warning.

Nothing was visible; the two friends' hands had not even appeared to tremble. Their faces were impassive.

"After the game!" Rita confirmed. "What's decided is decided. Go on, my dear—I think Simpson's waiting for you."

He remained in front of her for one more second, looking at her profoundly, twisting and whirling his racket.

Two charming young girls approached. "We're going to study your skill," one of them proclaimed. Then, addressing herself to Geneviève, she added: "Madame, may we sit down beside you? By squeezing up a little…"

"All right." Geneviève and Rita cleared half the bench.

"Soon," said Luc. He drew away. The spectators were more numerous now. All the seats were occupied. Many of the men were standing or sitting on the ground.

Rita interrogated Geneviève with a supremely intrigued gaze, but their two neighbors, whom they knew, had started a general conversation in which it was necessary to take part. They could not think of quitting the spot. The descendant of the Ortofieris was seething with impatience. What had Geneviève wanted to tell her? Why had she asked her to be silent?

122

Her calmness was unbearable! What could she do, in order to find out before the end of the game—the game that it was necessary to follow until the end?

Meanwhile, Geneviève had not abandoned her embroidery. While talking, raising her eyes from time to time to look at Luc or Simpson, who were running madly around their cage, leaping and pirouetting, she never ceased to ply her needle.

Nevertheless, she suddenly declared: "I've had enough." And she opened her immense bag in order to put the table-mat away. "You haven't complimented me on my work," she said. "It's nice, though—how do you like my flowers?" She offered the canvas ornamented with orange flowers and mauve foliage to Rita's gaze.

"It's very pretty," Rita admitted. But she said no more, petrified by what she had just seen.

In large letters, around a flower, Geneviève had traced the seven letters of a name with a few needle-stokes: *CHARLES*. The name, which seemed from a distance to crown the marvelous flower with a capricious and purely decorative arabesque, burst forth for Rita in sunbeams.

"Bravo! Bravo!" cried one of the girls, because Luc de Certeuil had just retrieved a deep ball with a clever backhand.

Her eyes immeasurably widened, Rita stared at Geneviève. The latter, with a negligent gesture, buried the table-mat in the bag and remarked: "Lord! The things in this bag! It won't do! No, just look at this mess!"

She held out her huge gaping sack toward Rita. She had plunged a nonchalant and into it, and that delicate, ring-laden hand, as feminine as it could be, brandished the blue rectangle of a telegram for a tenth of a second within the dark depths of the vast pocket. Then, like a curtain falling at the end of a play, the floral cloth of the precious receptacle closed up, with a click of its clasp.

Applause went up in response to a cross-court shot by Luc de Certeuil. His adversary, precipitating himself forwards, could not return it.

123

"Game!" announced the umpire.

"Two love," said Geneviève's neighbor.

As he prepared to serve, Luc darted a glance at the bench. Elegant, mobile and precise, he offered, in the incomparable light of the clear sky, the fine form of a model human being. At a distance, his white silhouette enchanted the eyesight, nullifying what was sometimes displeasing about his overly pale features, his short snub nose and his enigmatic gaze.

Silent, turned into a statue, Rita stared into space, no longer seeing anything. She had run through all the imaginable possibilities, but the explanation of the telegram escaped her, cruelly and delightfully. Charles Christiani was however, back on the scene. Whatever had happened had influenced Geneviève to the point of making her revise her previous opinion. And that was intoxicating, delirious and divine! It carried away all the suppositions of her feverish curiosity on a magnificent wave of joy.

The final was completed in record time. Simpson did not win a single game. Luc de Certeuil had never played so brilliantly. Everything he tried had succeeded. He was, however, a long way from believing that his luck might be linked to the old proverb: "Unlucky in love..." And it was with the most self-satisfied expression in the world that he returned to Rita.

"My compliments!" she said to him.

He bowed, smiling. "The compliments are very welcome—but...the answer?"

"Later," said Rita, simply.

He was so disconcerted that for a moment, with his arms dangling and his mouth agape, he lost the greater part of his elegance. "Oh!" he said, reproachfully. "What!"

"Patience!" she advised him, softly.

"Oh well," he let slip, "you really are a woman!"

"Don't be annoyed. Patience, I tell you!"

"Ah!" proffered Luc, furious and consternated. But he controlled himself immediately. "I'm always obedient to your desires."

"With a smile?" she said, mischievously.

"With a smile, of course." And he contrived to put on a countenance so humble and touching, that Rita was able to give him credit for it and sympathize wholeheartedly with his disappointment.

Rita went into Madame La Tourneur's room behind her. "What's happened, then?" she asked her, avidly. "Who sent you that telegram?"

"He did, very foolishly!" Geneviève said, shrilly, in her weak and quavering voice. Deep down, she was excited. Things were taking a romantic turn, which could only please the majority of women. Furthermore, Charles's telegram made her think that the adventure might perhaps terminate in the fashion most in conformity with the laws of society and the dearest desires of her darling Rita. She therefore found it legitimate, and even praiseworthy, to serve the love of which she had previously disapproved, inasmuch as, divorced in the prime of life, she nourished—without being fully aware of it—that strange need which affects all human beings and consists of desiring for others the tribulations that have been inflicted on oneself...with the result that she was not displeased, fundamentally, to be working to break a marriage in the making.

Luc and Rita were not even engaged, but no matter! There is a hint of marriage in the vaguest of betrothals—which is to say that there is a hint of divorce in their rupture. And quite unconsciously, the gentle and blonde Madame Le Tourneur would have liked all her female friends to be lodged, as she was, under the sign of separation. That is the way of the world, and no one will ever change it. Thus, the most sincere friendships are sometimes subject to obscure penchants that influence them. This, Geneviève Le Tourneur, without being aware of it, took as much pleasure in burning Luc de Certeuil's cards as in spinning the wheel of fortune, which now seemed to favor Charles Christiani—according to his telegram.

Rita read and re-read that telegram, in inexpressible mental disorder.

Madame Geneviève Le Tourneur,
Hotel Floria Saint-Trojan (Ile d'Oléron)
(Charente-Inférieure)
Ruffieux, October 2, 1929.
Respectfully beg you to communicate to whoever has the
right to know that I envisage possible revision 1835 legal pro-
ceedings by virtue of new fact discovered this morning.
Thanks and respects.
Charles Christiani.

"A new fact!" Rita said, passionately. "A new fact! Naturally, it can only be something of capital importance! Something capable of demolishing everything that is known, everything that is imagined, about the murder of César Christiani! A new fact! What new fact? A document discovered among his papers? An unexpected revelation? Of what kind? Ruffieux—yes, I remember. He mentioned a journey to Savoy that he had to make. Is it in Savoy, then, that he has discovered…for *discovered* is the word…it certainly seems to be *him* who has *discovered* something. Oh, my God! But it's providential! It's too beautiful!"

"Yes—too beautiful. Don't get carried away so quickly, my darling. Weigh the terms of the telegram carefully. *He envisages a possible revision of the legal proceedings.* It's only a hope. It's evident that new perspectives have opened to him, because of a fact unknown until now—but there's no proof of the solidity of his conjectures. Remember that he must certainly have sent this telegram as soon as a glimmer of hope appeared to him, before having reflected overmuch—for the essential thing, in his eyes, was to warn you immediately, since he was not unaware of the imminence of your engagement. It's necessary to take account of his haste."

IX. The Declaration of Love

Charles, very knowledgeable about everything, was one of those people who only experience temporary astonishments. We may add that in these critical days he was not disposed to get enthusiastic about anything, except for that which concerned the inaccessible Rita. Any miracle unconnected with his love and unable to serve its cause held only a very limited interest for him.

To excite him to such a degree had required, in truth, that luminite should be, for him, at the outset, one of the most marvelous of marvels. He also recognized that the excitement would not have reached such a pitch if he had not thought, vaguely and fugitively, that the shade of César Christiani was about to reveal the secret of his death—and that that death had not been the work of Fabius Ortofieri.

In the confusion of his thoughts, he had, in spite of himself, gone over the whole story of that crime repeatedly, always coming back to one undeniable fact: Fabius had admitted nothing; he had died protesting his innocence! He forgot that the most overwhelming evidence had been united against Rita's grandfather. And, as a precocious dusk darkened his study, he had been overtaken, as he had that morning, by splenetic discouragement, a sort of stupid anger against the magnificence that he had found, but which was useless, since it cast no new light on the Ortofieri affair.

As one can see, his love had demanded a great deal of events—and it certainly appeared, at that twilight hour, that events had told him all they knew.

Passably taciturn, replying in monosyllables to the humble and respectful questions of Péronne, who served his evening meal, Charles ate rapidly and went back to his room. A large fire was blazing in the hearth, painting its vacillating reflections throughout the room.

He lit two stout lamps and, unable to sleep, examined the furniture and paintings that decorated the room. There were many old things, and many memories. Certain things attracted particular attention, in which he had previously taken only a slight interest.

Some of the furniture that César had bought in Paris to furnish his apartment in the Boulevard du Temple was there, along with some of the objects that he had taken with him from Silaz. On his death, his inheritance had been divided between the two branches of his posterity. Today, half of it now belonged to cousin Drouet; the other half was the property of Charles and Colomba—but in agreement with her husband, their mother had long ago sent the greater part of his furniture to Silaz, saying that it was cluttering up her home and would be better placed in the château in which César had lived for thirteen years. To that consignment, Madame Christiani had added all sorts of things that seemed to her to be undesirable in Paris, including a rather macabre but very valuable little painting that was, indeed, not a good thing to hang on the wall of a house that one desired to be cheerful, and in which there were children.

This painting, which Charles unhooked in order to examine it in the lamplight, was an "interior" drawn and painted in water-colors, enhanced with gouache, by the painter Lami,[17] to whom we owe so many invaluable documents regarding the reign of Louis-Philippe—including, among others, Fieschi's assassination attempt, of which he had reproduced the bloody spectacle.

The "interior" represents César Christiani's study in the Boulevard du Temple, with the cadaver of the former corsair lying on the floor in a pool of blood, with a bullet-hole in his breast. In the background, an open window overlooks the boulevard, where one can see the trees and houses opposite. On either side of the window, which has blue and green floral curtains, there are panoplies formed of axes and sabers, pistols

---

[17] Eugène Lami (1800-1890).

and daggers, mingled with primitive arrows. The right-hand wall is invisible, but the one on the left is garnished with portraits and marine charts, a pipe-rack, a framed cross of the *Legion d'honneur*, and a little glazed drawing that Lami's work does not permit the viewer to make out, but which Charles knew to be the image of César's cabin aboard the *Finette*—a drawing that was still in Paris. A large pastel portrait of Hélène de Silaz, César's late and lamented wife, also ornaments that wall, the paper of which—very First Empire—has a cream background and golden palm-leaves. Above a pretty roll-top desk in rosewood, there is a slate in a fir-wood frame, bearing a few figures traced in chalk. The roll-top desk is open, displaying three closed drawers and pigeon-holes containing papers and legers, neatly arranged. On the top of this desk there is a profusion of objects: a tobacco-jar, a copper chandelier, exotic trinkets, books and other items that cannot be identified, the artist's brush having indicated them sketchily.

César's cadaver is lying feet-forward, its head pointing toward the corner of the room, to the left of the widow—where, in the half-shadow, there is a terrestrial globe. He is dressed in a maroon frock-coat and iron-grey trousers. The head is lying on the unwaxed floorboards, the body on a Savonnerie carpet with a black border, which extends under the desk. One arm lies between one foot of the desk and those of a rounded Louis XV armchair with a rattan frame and green leather upholstery—evidently the chair in which César sat while writing. The other arm is just touching one of the three mahogany legs of one of those large circular occasional tables with a white marble top, supported by a frame of varnished wood, of which the Restoration has left us so many ponderous specimens. Between the open battens of the window, with small square panes, a marine telescope is balanced on its tall tripod.

Such was César Christiani's study when the murder was discovered; or very nearly, at least—for the painter Lami, who lived into our own era,[18] took care to note, on the back of his water-color, and to confirm orally many times over, that this reconstitution was not rigorously authentic. He had only gone into César Christiani's apartment on the day after the crime; at that moment, the body was no longer there; he had sketched it on his paper according to the indications of witnesses and policemen and the observations that he had just made in the morgue.

That note by the painter Lami is easily readable, for, in order to make it so, the work is glazed on both sides.

Charles re-read the note on the back distractedly. He remembered it, in fact. He had studied it all, taken his own *mementos* of it. Then again, the Musée Carnavalet had obtained his authorization to photograph Lami's work, which was precious with regard to the history of Paris—less, in truth, because it elated to the corsair's death than for the fact that it added a faithful testimony to all the known reproductions of the Boulevard du Temple at the moment of Fieschi's assassination attempt: an attempt characterized by such a singular coincidence with the murder of César Christiani.

Charles had often brought the photographic prints that the museum had given him out of his cardboard boxes. Fieschi's attempt was, for a historian of the Restoration and the reign of Louis-Philippe, an attractive subject: Charles had already been thinking about it for some time and had not neglected to compare the various documents, engravings, lithographs, drawings, etc., that represent for us the appearance of the boulevard in the month of July 1835. It ought to be said, moreover, that, until then, Lami's water-color had only interested him in that respect, the death of his ancestor appearing to

---

[18] Given the rather extensive interval of time between 1890 and 1929, when the story it set—and 1933, when it was published—it is possible that this sentence was left over from an earlier draft of this section of the story, perhaps made before the Great War, when 1890 still seemed to be part of "our own era."

be a settled issue, offering no more than a personal and, by now, rather feeble interest.

After all, the painter's note, written in a similar spirit, related as much to Fieschi's assassination attempt as to the murdered individual, and it was all the more natural that Lami had written that note on the morning of July 29, 1835, when the formidable assassination attempt had not only thrown all Paris into an unparalleled consternation, but the autopsy of César's body had not yet established the precise character of his wound. At that moment, it was still assumed that he had been killed by the ricochet of one of Fieschi's bullets, and that he was merely the 19th victim of the infernal machine—which, in reality, had left 18 dead and 22 wounded.

On the subject of the assassination attempt, the note said this:

The houses that can be seen through the window bear the numbers 54, 56 and 58. The one on the right, the tallest, contains a collection of wax figurines by Curtius. The middle one, the smallest, contains the restaurant and café Au Rendezvous des Théâtres. *The one on the left is the* Théâtre Lazari. *On approaching the window, one sees, further to the left, next to the Lazari, number 60, which is Madame Saqui's marionette theater; and on the right, next to number 54, one sees number 52: the* Estaminet Rustique; *then, next to the latter, which is low, the very narrow house that bears the number 50, which is the one from which Joseph Fieschi*[19] *fired at the King. He*

---

[19] Renard's narrative voice inserts a footnote here: "Fieschi's name was added later by the painter Lami. Initially, he wrote 'Gérard' the name under which Fieschi had just been arrested and which was only recognized to be false subsequently. The same remark, of course, pertains to what follows..." The Italian name Guiseppe was often rendered as Joseph by Frenchmen. The account of the other establishments visible from César's window takes some liberties with history and geography. Philippe Curtius (1737-94), a Swiss physician who gave up his profession in favour of his hobby as a sculptor in wax,

fired to his own right, as the head of the procession passed directly between his house and that in which I made the sketch, whose façade was peppered by grapeshot that had ricocheted from the pavement of the causeway. I have not given sufficient indication of the distance of the houses to the left. That is because the boulevard, in fact, broadens toward the Château d'Eau, and my perspective ought to give a better impression of the façades drawing away at an angle.

Relative to César's murder, the note adds the following indications to those that we already know:

I made the drawing by placing myself against the door that opens to the antechamber, which communicates with the landing. That door, as is evident, is on the right-hand side of the partition wall. In the wall that cannot be seen in my drawing, to the right of that door and very close to it, is another set at right-angles to it, which opens into the drawing-room. The captain's aviary and monkeys were in the drawing-room. Near to the drawing-room door, directly facing the roll-top desk, is the mantelpiece. On the mantelpiece is a bust of Napoléon and there are numerous objects of various sorts above it.

The apartment is on the first floor. The window is the second, counting from the right, when one looks at the house from outside; the first is on the landing. The house has three floors. It bears the number 53 and is only separated from the Jardin Turc by a little single-story building with a single window: the Bertin house. The terraced wall of the Jardin Turc

---

set up a Caverne des Grands Voleurs—the original "Chamber of Horrors"—in the Boulevard du Temple in 1782 but left his collection to his protégée, Madame Tussaud, who came within minutes of being guillotined during the Revolution and removed most of it to London long before 1835. "Madame Saqui" (Marguerite-Antoinette Lalanne, 1786-1866) was a famous tightrope-walker whose theater is cited as an item of local color in novels by Paul Féval, but not in connection with marionettes.

overlaps the front of Joseph Fieschi's house to a considerable degree.

Signed: Lami.

July 29, 1835, 10 a.m.

With a discouraged gesture, Charles hung the little picture on the wall again and started walking around the circular table, by the light of the fire and the two lamps. The table was the same one that featured in Lami's water color, with its marble top. That circular table had seen César Christiani fall on the Savonnerie carpet!

The rain continued to fall in the highland darkness, whispering its innumerable murmurs. The young man walked slowly around the chairs, pensively. As a logical consequence of the circumstances, his thoughts remained obstinately attached to César's death, and his imagination magnified all the mystery that death embodied. He could no longer see anything but the enigma.

A fortnight before, no doubt had assailed him in that regard; he had been firmly convinced that César had been murdered by Fabius Ortofieri, as everyone had always believed. Now, he doubted it. Knowing that the contrary would be favorable to him, he had begun to wish that the contrary might be the case; then, very rapidly, he had acquired the artificial conviction that public opinion was mistaken. An interior voice pleaded the case of the accused, the presumed murderer. In his mind, the arguments for Fabius Ortofieri's exoneration acquired an enormous amplitude. He would have been so insanely happy to prove that innocence that, progressively—according to the laws of a phenomenon well-known to advocates—he had ended up believing that the poor case was excellent and that Rita's grandfather had not been involved in the murder of his own. The magistrates commissioned to examine the case had taken too much account of the anxieties that César had revealed in his correspondence regarding his interminable disputes with the Ortofieris and the presence in Paris of his hereditary enemy Fabius. The latter had doubtless been the victim of terrible luck and fatal coincidences…for he had denied it, *until his last breath!*

All these reveries were good for nothing. Too much dust had settled on the events—an excess of dust that could not be swept away, being out of range.

Charles came to a halt in front of another painting: a pen-and-ink copy of a famous engraving by Mathieu, after Fragonard: *The Declaration of Love.*[20] It was a naïve copy, but not without charm—the patient work of Grandmother Estelle, who had set it simply and affectionately in a worthless old 18th century frame. Everyone is familiar with the grace of the charming composition, in which two enlaced lovers swear to be faithful before the altar of Eros in a luxurious boscage in which daylight plays upon the branches. The docile and patient pen of Grandmother Estelle—she of the broad shoulders—had not copied her model ineptly. The lovers' vivacity remained full of ardor, and the god of love bathed that verdant, allegorical and sensuous location with his inexpressible good fortune.

It is easy to understand why Charles did not pause for long before that triumphant symbol of felicitation by love. A trifle childishly, because the sight of it pained him, he turned grandmother Estelle's work to face the wall, then sat down in a winged armchair by the fireside and resumed his reverie.

Soon, all the ideas that had occupied him in the course of the day became entangled. He re-imagined the review of the National Guard of July 28, 1835. He heard the racket of the infernal machine. He saw the bloody tumult of its victims in the roadway of the Boulevard du Temple. At the same time,

---

[20] *Le Serment d'Amour*, an engraving by Jean Mathieu (1749-1815) of a painting by Jean-Honoré Fragonard (1732-1806), was one of the early best-sellers of a burgeoning late-18th century market in multiple reproductions of famous art-works. Numerous copies still survive in private hands as well as galleries; do-it-yourself versions like Grandmother Estelle's are probably rarer.

the phases of the criminal examination of the Ortofieri case returned to his memory, only to combine bizarrely with the departure of César in a post-chaise, his spectral apparition in the little top room, and a vision of Rita on the deck of the *Boyardville*, holding a book in her hand, with a parrot on her shoulder! Finally, he had the sensation of putting his arm around the young woman's supple figure, of extending his hand toward a boscage sanctuary in which smiling Love stood within a soft aura. On that note, his eyes closed as if he were rendering up his last sigh in a study decked out in Empire wallpaper and filled with disparate objects.

"Ah!" he murmured. "It's Fabius, alas! It's Fabius who has killed me!" And, plunging more profoundly into the tenebrous realm of nightmares, he went to sleep.

He slept so well that he woke up several hours later, without having heard Péronne knocking maternally on the door, come up to him on tiptoe, extinguish the two lamps and retire silently, like one of those individuals of whose actions the luminite made visible, without allowing the sounds they made—lost forever—to be heard.

But had he really "woken up"? Was it not, in fact, one of those false awakenings which, in the midst of the most stubborn dreams, give us the illusion of emerging from sleep while one, on the contrary, plunging us into it more deeply?

Charles thought that his eyes were open. He did not doubt it, for the moment. And he perceived, in the midst of the darkness, a light: a bright rectangle; a small window filled with diurnal clarity. It spread a little daylight through the room. The day, however, had not yet broken. The windows were black.

In the hearth there were a few dull embers, but no more fire. The night had to be very advanced.

Charles got up from the armchair—or imagined that he had got up—and, having taken two steps toward that tiny window, stood upright in front of it, bewildered and stupefied, surely asleep.

The dream continued to mix everything up insanely. That small window was not a window. It was Lami's painting brought to life, like a plate of luminite! Not Lami's painting as Charles had contemplated it before going to sleep, but the painting showing César's study from another angle, as if the indications of the manuscript note had been realized in the form of a drawing, water-color and gouache. But no! It was not the work of a painter! It was a *real image* of the study, the window, the floral curtains, the wall with its mantelpiece and the bust of Napoléon! And César was not lying dead on the Savonnerie carpet! César was sitting at the roll-top desk, writing a letter. He was moving! His hand, armed with a goose-quill, was moving over the paper. And he was seen from above, at an angle—from above and in front. *He was seen as if the viewer were perched on top of the roll-top desk!*

Ah! There is nothing more painful, more cruel than a nightmare! Charles, violently impressed by it all, took out his lighter, and with a click, ignited its minuscule yellow flame.

This time, he was *sure* that he was awake—but the absurd vision persisted, of Lami's painting metamorphosed into something else, still César's study, but a study seen from a different viewpoint and alive, like spectacle recorded by a plate of luminite!

The two lamps were feverishly relit. The downward view of César's cabinet was still there, in the same place: the same rectangle full of the light of a Parisian morning, the same small window pierced, so to speak, in the wall of time!

But Lami's painting was still exactly the same as it had been the previous evening. It could be seen hanging on the wall, not far from the vision in which it did not participate in any way—for that vision was painted naturally on the back of the frame that Charles had turned round in order not to see *The Declaration of Love* any longer.

Then, gripped by a great emotion, suddenly understanding how the facts were connected, Charles seized that frame and set about examining it—and then, very carefully, manipulating it.

It was a frame of varnished fir-wood with a black thread, something quite simple, which had been quite banal in its time—but those frames have a "good old times" charm that makes the collectible today. Immediately, under the pressure of the chain of events, Charles noticed the analogy between the frame and the piece of slate that the painter Lami had depicted above the roll-top desk. Evidently, it was the same. For some reason, César had taken it into his head to hang a plate of virgin luminite, which he had brought to Paris from Silaz, on the wall of his study—and in order that the plate, similar to a piece of slate, should pass unnoticed, he had, so to speak, "disguised" it as a real slate, placing it in a valueless frame and writing a few figures—which probably had no significance—in chalk in a corner of the fake blackboard.

These prudent measures on his part were indispensable. The presence above the desk of a frame containing nothing but a black surface would, in fact, have seemed quite strange. Thus made-up, the plate had not been able to provoke any curiosity or any indiscreet question.

Charles separated it from the fir-wood rectangle easily. It was precisely fitted, like the backboard of a painting or a mirror, but not secured by tacks. The customary tacks had been replaced by eight tiny flat copper latches, which pivoted, analogous to those that you see fitted to the back of photograph-frames to retain the cardboard backing. The exactitude of the framing prevented the luminosity of edges from being perceived from without.

It was easy to guess why César had wanted the plate to be removable and easily separable from its frame. He had made it into a *witness* and wanted to be able to split it easily every time he needed to know what had happened in his home while he was absent. Further evidence of that was that the plate did not constitute a compact sheet like those in the high window when Charles had removed them from their frames; over a certain small thickness it was divided into a large number of exceedingly thin leaves, exactly like an unbound book; it required careful manipulation to maintain these divisions in

137

juxtaposition and to prevent them from becoming disjointed, like a deck of playing-cards when the fingers holding them neglect to align them properly. César had, therefore, once done to this plate what Charles had done to the ones from the high window. He had *read them* many times.

Isolated, the plate was rid of Grandmother Estelle's ink drawing, and that side showed, in a softer light, blurred by a darkness that thickened toward the bottom, the wallpaper: the cream Empire paper with gilded palm-leaves. Without any possible doubt, the framed plate had become part of the inheritance handed on to Napoléon Christiani, who was to marry grandmother Estelle in 1842, seven years after César's death. Much later, Grandmother Estelle, searching for a frame for her copy of *The Declaration of Love*, had retrieved that fir-wood frame from some attic, doubtless thinking that it had once contained an engraving that had since disappeared. She had made use of it to frame her work, utilizing the luminite plate as a backboard. Then, later still, *The Declaration of Love* had ended up, along with many other family heirlooms, at the Château de Silaz, in this bedroom.

For years the frame, the drawing and the plate had remained there, a mysterious hybrid assembly. On all the occasions he had stayed in the room, Charles had not noticed anything. The dark plate, with the light that was slowly making it ay through it in both directions, had remained hidden from all eyes. The plate's thickness was almost identical to the thickness of those that Charles had removed from the high window; in consequence, it had required about a century for light to pass through it, finally emerging from each face; that had certainly occurred since Charles had last stayed at Silaz.

As he looked at the face on which, by some freak of chance, he had found old César in his study in Paris, he observed that the living image was obliterated in one corner by an opaque inscription that seemed to be traced on the plate itself: the chalk figures; the insidious chalk figures that had "disguised" the plate as a writing-slate. On the other face, examining the plate from the other side, he found slight traces of erasure, and having rubbed them with his finger he saw that his finger had been whitened by a slight residue of chalk. Grandmother Estelle, renowned for her shoulders and no less for her "artistic temperament," had not taken the trouble to wash the slate that she had used as a backboard for her *Declaration of Love*. The good lady, confused and distracted, had obviously paid no attention to the luminous streaks on the edge. To tell the truth, seen in broad daylight, those extremely fine lines might have been mistaken for reflections, and Grandmother Estelle had not cared overmuch whether there might be some slates that were not as dull as others.

How feverishly Charles Christiani's eyes devoured César's study, which was revealed to him as if through an opening pierced in the wall above the roll-top desk, like a secret spy-hole fabricated between the 19th and 20th centuries! And what fantastic hopes developed within him! For Lami's water-color testified to the presence of luminite in the study on the day after the crime, and on the very day of the crime! This plate, therefore, had witnessed César's death, had *filmed* all its phases *in color*! And, in consequence, he had only to divide it judiciously into sheets to proceed from one sheet to the next through the period preceding the murder to the day in July 1835 when the murder had been committed, to the very moment when the assassin had fired the mortal pistol-shot at his victim! César's murderer was *photographed* in the heart of the plate! Was it Fabius Ortofieri? Charles had the ability to ascertain that!

The day of July 28, 1835, marvelously conserved within the mass of the luminite, was advancing within it slowly toward one of the two surfaces, and one cut, one "cleavage" made at the required distance along the edge, would cause it to appear immediately.

Charles Christiani, as you can imagine, did nothing about it. He had immediately perceived all the precautions with which it was necessary to surround such an operation. Long reflection was necessary before attempting anything. Nothing must be neglected, from any point of view, and the points of view were numerous. He envisaged them, without quitting the incomparable observation-post that placed him in the past.

In the past, to be sure—but on what date?

He discovered that with a facility that enchanted him and revived in his mind the happy presumption that fate was on his side.

On the mantelpiece of César's study there was, as we know, a bust of the Emperor. There was no mirror there—a rather unfortunate circumstance, as we shall see later—but higher up, immense by comparison with the smallness of the room, and furled in order to take up less space, was the corsair's rutilant guidon: the red strip of muslin with the golden Christ. Beneath it, an Empire clock of the "bull's eye" variety, with an eight-part corolla, was fixed to the wall directly above the center of the mantelpiece, and below that, among a profusion of suspended weapons, between a sextant and a barometer, not far from colored engravings representing ships with all sails aloft, was a calendar, bordered by a ribbon of yellow paper, on which the six columns of a half-year were aligned.

This placard was too far away for Charles to be able to make out even the largest characters. He went down to the study on the ground floor of the tower to fetch a magnifying-glass and a pair of binoculars.

As he had expected, the magnifying glass produced no result, since the vision emitted by the luminite had nothing in common with an image drawn on a surface, but was, on the contrary, situated in space, like the reality that it was: a delayed reality; a reality similar to that of stars that disappeared a long time ago, whose image remains visible in the firmament because of the time required for light to cross the distance between their position and ours. In those conditions, however, the binoculars worked marvelously. They brought everything in the study in the Boulevard du Temple closer, as easily as if it had been a matter of ordinary vision.

Thus, Charles was able to read the year on the calendar: 1833.

He lowered his optical instrument toward the old corsair seated at his desk. He could have counted his wrinkles, and the hairs in his bushy eyebrows. He could see the nostrils moving imperceptibly with the breath of respiration. It was almost frightening: the life of that man of yesteryear, who, for nearly a century, had been no more than a corpse in a tomb in Père-Lachaise; that detailed life of which Charles sensed the rhythm and the warmth.

César was wearing horn-rimmed spectacles now. He leaned forward to write a new letter, which he had just dated at the top of the piece of paper: *May 12, 1833*. Charles deciphered that by placing the luminite plate upside-down, for, positioned as he was, facing César, he saw the letter that César was writing the wrong way up.

More than two years to live, my poor César!

May 12. Indeed, through the window with small panes, the four bushy rows of trees in the Boulevard du Temple had their young spring foliage.

At that moment, Charles experienced one of the strongest emotions of his life as a historian. The situation of the luminite plate was such that, from the place where César had suspended it like a painting or a mirror—as, we repeat, he had intended—it embraced a view of the boulevard toward the right, to the east. And by virtue of that, between the house of the *Estaminet Rustique* and the modest *Café des Mille Colonnes*, which displayed the enormous projection of the dropped roof of its four-floored hall at mezzanine height, a tall three-story building could be seen, each story of which had a single casement window, the first of which was painted—already—blood red, and the third of which, beneath an oblique roof like an arched eyebrow, opened a crafty eye upon a broad Parisian thoroughfare: a window crammed with panes, fitted with a Venetian blind.

With the aid of the binoculars, which trembled between his fingers, Charles read, on the right-hand sight of the first-floor window, on a white patch contrived in the scarlet paint, the figure 50. Higher up, above that same window, inscribed in white letters on the reed background, was: *WINE-*

141

MERCHANT. Further up, crowning the second-floor window, was a kind of painted sign:

Four francs per year
JOURNAL DES CONNAISSANCES UTILES
18 Rue des Moulins

The house of the infernal machine!

In two years' time—two years, two months and 16 days, to be exact—the murderous salvo would be fired from that window with the Venetian blind! And that paved thoroughfare would be littered with the dead and the wounded! And one of the most sadly celebrated assassination attempts in world history would have taken place!

No stranger sensation had ever overtaken the soul of a historian than that of standing behind his binoculars, visiting Fieschi's fatal, accused, abominable house with his eyes, at his leisure, stone by stone, in telescopically-enlarged detail, with its wooden shelter, its lantern, its three disparate windows, its tiles and the aggregated group of chimneys the loomed over it to the left.

There was a movement in César's study.

Emerging from the door to the right of the mantelpiece, which put that room in communication with the drawing-room, the monkey Coburg precipitated himself forward, waving his disproportionately long arms, chasing Pitt, the favorite parrot. He had presumably escaped; a fragment of chain hung from his leather belt.

The bicolored bird having regained César's shoulder, the latter scolded the chimpanzee roundly and dragged him into the drawing-room, which must have constituted a rather bizarre locale, given the guests that dwelt there. Charles, having moved to the left of the plate, was thus able to glimpse, in a mirror in the second room, the aviary filled with fluttering wings. By the same means, he discovered the study door giving access to the main entrance, against which Lami had sat to paint his water-color. That was, however, the limit of his visual field.

At any rate, the spectator had before him the very theater of the murder. That murder had been committed in broad daylight, the murderer certainly having not the slightest suspicion of any espionage. As the plate had definitely been in the study at the time of the murder, the conclusion that emerged in all evidence was admirably clear. It would be possible to remount, after 94 years, the examination of the Ortofieri case, with new means that would permit the interested parties to witness, in person, not a reconstruction of the crime but the crime itself. And that prodigious counter-inquiry would finally bring out the truth as to the innocence or guilt of Fabius Ortofieri.

There was, of course, no question of interesting the law in this new inquiry. It had made its decision a long time ago—and since no judgment had been reached, there could be no possibility of rehabilitation. Fabius, having died in prison, had not been convicted. It was, therefore, merely a matter of obtaining certainty by means of new information. If the result were favorable to Fabius, that could be loudly publicized; Charles, knowing his mother's rectitude, did not doubt that she would then extend her hand to Rita's father and express her sincere regrets regarding an ancient accusation, justified at the time by damning depositions. And if the result confirmed the opinion of the 1835 court, if Fabius' guilt were irrefutably established—and luminite was irrefutable!—there would be silence, in favor of Rita...in favor, alas, of the person who would then become Madame de Certeuil. The old affair would remain, for the public at large, a forgotten, distant and uncertain story.

Progressively, one by one, Charles perceived all the dispositions that the counter-inquiry would necessitate. He had immediately decided to ask Bertrand Valois for his close collaboration. He remembered the detective-story deductions that the young author had made, in his presence, with respect to the 17th century cane. Bertrand would be glad to participate in the extraordinary investigation, and Charles would have in him the most precious and most discreet of auxiliaries.

But all that was merely projects and cogitations; one action was immediately necessary, and Charles prayed to God that there was still time to do it without fear of serious complications. The most urgent thing to be done was to alert Rita.

She was due to leave Saint-Trojan the following day. Was her engagement to Luc de Certeuil an accomplished fact? It was necessary to hope that no firm promise had yet been exchanged. It might be, however, at any moment. Perhaps the next day's departure would be the occasion.

Get going! There's no time to lose!

Yes, but what means was there of communicating rapidly with Rita? Via the intermediary of Madame Le Tourneur? Hmm! Charles did not much like that sort of stratagem. He did not doubt, however, that it could be successfully employed. Geneviève Le Tourneur's friendship for Marguerite Ortofieri would ensure that his message would be transmitted to its intended recipient with the briefest delay. There was no embarrassment of choices, and urgency spurred him on.

Bah! he said to himself. *The end justifies the means!*

And from that resulted the telegram that had plunged Rita into great delight, mingled with ardent curiosity.

144

X. Telegraphic Response

Geneviève Le Tourneur had recovered the telegram in question from Rita's hands.

"Prudence is the mother of security," she said, professorially. "Let's burn this compromising evidence." She picked up a match-box, which she opened with the tips of her long manicured fingers.

"No," said Rita. "Give it to me, would you? It might be the first of a whole sequence of souvenirs…I'd like that very much! Who knows? Who knows how many other telegrams, how many letters, how many faded flowers and trivia of that sort might keep it company, wrapped in fine ribbons, in a drawer in my writing-desk? Don't burn it…"

"It's imprudent. If your mother or your father…"

"I'm free to do as I please!" the young woman retorted, proudly, raising her brunette head abruptly.

"Agreed, my child—but I confess to you quite frankly that I was thinking of myself. If your mother or your father learned of my complicity…"

"You've nothing to fear."

"Oh well! Here's your souvenir number one. I hope it inaugurates a brilliant collection! But please, don't let it go astray. Farewell, message of hope! There are times when telegrams ought to be green."

"No one will ever read it, and your reputation is in no danger," affirmed Rita, grabbing the thin piece of paper.

"I certainly hope so. Tell me—Luc de Certeuil will certainly give some thought to what has just happened. He's taken your answer to heart, and will certainly wonder why you've asked him to wait longer. Don't you think it will occur to him to make a connection between my arrival at the tennis game and the fashion in which you've modified your impatience to be his?"

"Certainly not. I'd already manifested a good deal of uncertainty before your arrival…"

"Hmm! Of course—but a good deal of emotional, fearful uncertainty; while, in the latter instance, you didn't have the same attitude at all! You seemed content, excited, with your eyes shining, beautiful Rita!"

"I tried to control myself—but it was so difficult!"

"I think, my dear, that the imminent future will provide you with more than one opportunity to master your pretty face," said Madame Le Tourneur, in a gently mocking fashion.

"We have to send him a reply!" Rita realized, suddenly. "We have to reassure him. The poor boy doesn't know how things stand here. At the very least, we should let him know that his telegram reached me. Please, Geneviève!"

She pleaded.

The match-box had not been opened needlessly. Geneviève smoked a slender cigarette of Turkish tobacco. She sat down, placing a notepad on her knees with affected docility. "Dictate," she said, taking the top off a mauve-enameled fountain-pen.

"Monsieur Charles Christiani…"

"That's quite a mouthful. Monsieur who? Say it again."

"Charles Christiani," Rita repeated, without any reluctance. The name, pronounced by her beautiful brazen voice, sounded in all its crystalline musicality, simultaneously pompous, ethereal and quasi-evangelical.

"I couldn't say it like that!" Geneviève admitted. "It's easy to see that you're Corsican, and in love."

"Shh! Not that word! Not yet!"

"I've added the address. What next?"

"Received and transmitted telegram. Nothing new. Any decision deferred. Our kindest regards. Le Tourneur."

"That's done. It's simple and in good taste. With those two lines in my handwriting, anyone could have me hanged high and short by our amiable father! Now, of course, I have to go and send it?"

"Of course. In fact…it's late."

"What a job!" lamented Madame le Tourneur, delightfully excited. She put a red beret over her pale blonde hair and went out of her room, gently pushing her friend in front of her. "Farewell, Juliet," she said. "Ours is the nightingale, the lark and the silken ladder with a little balcony at the end!"

They parted in the corridor, to which dusk was adding its darkness to the customary gloom.

"It will go this evening, won't it?" said Geneviève to the young woman at the counter, from whom she was separated by a grille.

"Yes, Madame; we'll send it immediately."

"Thank you."

With a gracious smile that took its time to fade away, she pivoted unhurriedly, in the manner of one of those nonchalant wisps of vapor that float above marshes in the moonlight.

On the threshold of the post office, Luc de Certeuil, who was coming in with letters in his hand, paused in order to greet her.

"Behold the conqueror!" she said, merrily, as she passed by.

"Excuse me," he said, very amiably. "I dread that my letters might miss the post." And he vanished into the office.

The man doesn't seem to have anything against me, Geneviève thought. *After all, it's quite probable that he has no suspicion. Even so, we must be jolly careful about taking chances. If he'd arrived a few minutes earlier, he'd have been able to dart a covert glance at my telegram—and it would only have required a little ill luck for the receptionist to repeat the name of the addressee: "Charles Chris...Christiani? Is that right, Madame?" A charming soirée! My god, I'm very grateful to have been spared that aria, as the nice people say. Rita's amours must be blessed, since a fortunate destiny is favoring them.*

While Madame Le Tourneur was saying all that to herself, however, confiding her tranquil steps to the slope of the terrain, Luc de Certeuil, standing at the post-office counter, was watching her from a distance. He had plenty of time to do so.

"How can I help you, Monsieur?" the young receptionist had asked him.

"Two registered letters."

"They won't go until tomorrow morning, by the first post. Would you permit me to attend to this telegram; I'm on my own at present…"

"Yes, of course—since it's too late for my letters."

At the back of the room, the *tap tap* of the Morse apparatus measured out the electrical transmission of the telegram.

Slowly, Madame Le Tourneur went down the hill. In the evening light, her red beret took on an extremely rare color against the whiteness of the walls that she was moving alongside. Luc de Certeuil did not appear to be interested in Geneviève, and if she had been able to see him she would have been fully reassured. Perhaps she might even have been shocked by an indifference that was hardly flattering and surpassed her wishes. It was not the woman he was looking at mechanically, but the red dot made by her beret as it was struck by the rays of the setting sun, blazing like a piece of stained glass amid the whiteness of its surroundings. His absent eyes were not those of a man who sees.

The calm of the evening was profound. There was nothing to be heard in the vicinity but confused and intermittent voices and the dry clicking of the telegraph-operator.

"I'm all yours, Monsieur," said the receptionist. She stuck the sheet of paper bearing the text on a long spike, and hurried to the counter. "Monsieur! Monsieur!"

"Ah! Yes, here! Two letters and two forms."

He seemed to be intensely absorbed. He was looking straight ahead, with his eyelids creased, etching two unequal slits were in his cheeks; his mouth was compressed on one side, which gave him a rather villainous expression.

"Three francs, Monsieur…Monsieur: three francs."

"Oh, I beg your pardon, Mademoiselle; I was distracted. I was distracted because I've thought of a reform, the necessity of which has just occurred to me—a reform in the operation of your services."

"Really?" The young woman, as she wrote out the receipt, looked at him kindly, not to say affectionately. He was known to be an intrepid sportsman and telegrams had been sent informing the newspapers in the region and in Paris of his victory.

"I'm told," he said, "that nothing is easier that to read a telegram by sound. Is it true that by listening to the noise of an apparatus, one can, with practice, understand the words that it is striking?"

"It's as easy as transmitting them, Monsieur."

"And yet, Mademoiselle, you don't have the right, as a functionary, to communicate the text of a telegram that a citizen has confided to you to anyone else?"

"Oh no!"

"Then why does the administration of the Telegraph Service permit telegrams to be transmitted by a loud series of clicks, Mademoiselle, in a public office, open to all comers? Suppose I were to give you a confidential dispatch, and, while you were sending it, there happened to be someone here very well acquainted with the Morse alphabet who was interested in knowing what I had had sent…?"

"My God, Monsieur, you're right…"

"Well, there you are!" said Luc, solemnly. "That's a necessary reform. Ah, there are reforms to be made in that respect!" Satisfied with the effect he had produced, he addressed a nice smile to the young woman, who visibly took a pleasant pride therein. "I might even mention it to the minister," he concluded, "if the opportunity arises."

And he wrote in his notebook, following a sporting reference:

Monsieur Charles Christiani,
Château de Silaz, via Ruffieux (Savoy)
Received and transmitted telegram. Nothing new. Any decision deferred. Our kindest regards. Le Tourneur.

149

XI. The Old Crime

In spite of the assurance that "any decision" had been "deferred," Charles Christiani continued to think that it was necessary to get to work quickly. In the matter of an engagement, the course of events cannot be maintained in suspense for very long, and Luc de Certeuil was not a man to let himself be played along. A resolution, one way or the other, was bound to be reached as soon as possible. The plan was to bring forward, as far as he could, the date at which, in the presence of witnesses and all precautions having been taken, he could proceed to the retrovision of César's murder.

That extraordinary séance could only take place in Paris. It was there that all the desirable commodities, all the advice and the maximum number of guarantees could be found. However, Charles restrained himself from taking precipitate action and fixed his departure for two days hence. In fact, he wanted to take with him everything that might be useful to his efforts—not only the most precious plate but the others, Lami's water-color, the secret manuscript, the corsair's memoirs and correspondence, and everyone other document, written or otherwise, relating to César. With that plan in mind he undertook to visit every room in the château from top to bottom, to search the furniture, and carefully to examine all the surfaces that might be plates of luminite clandestinely deposited there by César.

That is why he checked all the dark panels, wainscots, cupboard doors and dressers, desirous of verifying whether they might be plates that light had not yet traversed. He also took down all the glazed pictures to make sure that the painted or engraved images that were visible within were not images of yesteryear. It even occurred to him, as he took an old *Temptation of Saint Anthony* out of its frame, to reflect that, if the engraving had been taken out after once having spent time behind its plate, it would have continued to be visible for years when it was no longer there—and now, behind the glass, he would no longer find anything, even though the glass still displayed the engraving.

No mirror, glass or panel was suspect. In any case, if César had placed other plates of luminite elsewhere, his secret manuscript would probably have mentioned them. And besides, although luminite that was still dark could easily pass unnoticed, the same was not true of luminite that had begun to emit its light. The latter would have been revealed before Charles had become involved—there could be no doubt of that, especially if one considered that, entirely naturally, the substance sometimes showed daylight scenes, or night-time scenes well-lit by lamps, chandeliers, moonlight or stars, in pitch darkness. It was quite by chance that the mornings and evenings of 1829 displayed by the panes of the high window had coincided so exactly with mornings and evenings of 1929; otherwise, old Chalude and Péronne would have been able to see the nocturnal phantom of César moving his feeble light behind a near-dark window in the middle of the day, and by night, the little top room would have seemed to them to be bathed in inexplicable sunlight.

With the intelligent aid of the chauffeur Julien, these checking operations were conducted swiftly. The next day was not yet complete when the garaged automobile already contained, in tightly-wrapped packages, the principal elements of a counter-enquiry unprecedented in human memory. Charles would find the other elements in Paris, to wit: everything of César's conserved in the Rue de Tournon; the records of the Ortofieri case filed at the Palais de Justice, which Charles had already consulted; the 27 boxes of records of the Fieschi case in the National Archives, of which it would doubtless be important to make an accessory study; and, finally, certain documents that Rita Ortofieri would surely not refuse to lend him, concerning her ancestor.

The day after, very early, Charles said his goodbyes to the two servants. The dawn was grey and wan. The sky hung down in ragged clouds on the dull and ochreous mountains.

The damp roofs glistened bleakly. The road was shiny, littered with puddles of water. A winy odor emerged from the press, and a little four-wheeled cart laden with barrels, drawn by two oxen, emerged therefrom at a rapid pace with a noise of grinding wheels and creaking axles.

"Thank you very much, Monsieur Charles," said Claude.

"Oh, yes, thank you!" added Péronne, gratefully.

"Do you still believe in the *sarvant*?" Charles asked.

Claude, however, preferred another topic of conversation. "When shall we see you again, Monsieur Charles?"

He leaned out of the car widow, his hat in his hand. "I don't know. In the spring, at Easter…"

Easter! Between now and then, his destiny would be settled. How would he feel when he saw this sad rainy landscape, which was scented today by moist grass, dead leaves and new wine, when the chestnuts and lilacs were in flower? Would he be happy or unhappy?

"Come on, Julien, let's get going! *Au revoir*, Péronne, Claude!"

The polished, gleaming car, adorned by a thousand sparkles and as many reflections, moved off smoothly as the brake was released. Sprays of water sprang forth as the enormous tires moved through the cart-ruts.

Until Easter! Enigma! Mystery of the future!

And yet, thought Charles, *everything is written. I don't know how, but what is happening now is written, represented in advance, as if in a fantastic plate—a plate impossible to conceive in the physical domain!* And he tried to imagine what César's state of mind had been when he had left Silaz in a carriage a century before, to reach Paris ten days later, with his birds and his monkeys: Paris, where the assassin was lying in ambush with his pistol, at the future turning-point of July 28, 1835.

César would certainly have been more surprised to see his descendant moving along the roads of Savoy at 100 kph than Charles had been to see his ancestor climbing into a carriage at the end of a 100-year-old avenue!

152

Charles made sure that the movement of the car could not do any harm to the luminite plates. The fear of an accident, of a breakage, began to haunt him. He wondered whether there was a treasure in the world more precious than the sealed packet in which, by the effect of a natural prodigy—as rare, now, as the presence on Earth of one of those creatures whose ancient species is almost extinct—a century-old scene was on the move, retained in the same way that millenary ice sometimes retains entire mammoths intact, and prehistoric resins, gums and ambers similarly retain insects that seem to be still alive and merely sleeping. A bloody scene: a scene on which his happiness or distress depended, according to the face of the murderer who would appear in César's study.

Unless the murderer had concealed himself in order to shoot...

Unless things happened in a way that he had not been able to imagine—something absolutely unforeseeable, which would reduce all hopes of clarification to nothing!

And to think that, in order to find out, he had only to take hold of that plate, and dissociate its leaves! A mistake! Charles had a very imperfect memory of the features of Fabius Ortofieri—*the man that he had to recognize, or not.*

I've only ever seen him, he thought...

"I've only ever seen him, and not recently, in a poor portrait," Charles Christiani repeated, the following afternoon, to Bertrand Valois. "It was a mediocre lithograph that was hawked around at the time of the crime, of which the Ortofieri family bought up almost all of the prints—as, I presume, the author hoped!"

Bertrand Valois, with a bright gleam in his eyes and sniffing the air with his crafty nose, came to a halt in front of his future brother-in-law—for he had been striding back and forth in the latter's room in the Rue de Tournon. "Mademoiselle Ortofieri will entrust us with other portraits, won't she? That's the basis of our enterprise."

"I'm sure that she will do everything I ask of her."

153

The young dramatist had come to dine with the Christianis in response to a telephone call from Charles. Madame Christiani had not yet been put in the picture with respect to her son's plans; she did not know anything at all about his discovery and did not even bother to ask why Charles had called from Silaz asking for his friend's help. Colomba, however, had known the essentials since the morning of her brother's arrival, and Bertrand had just heard Charles's story in her presence, to which he had listened as the Sultan Schariar must have nourished himself on the stories of Scheherazade. He was dazzled, charmed, carried away by enthusiasm and impatient to act.

The packets were there, at the bottom of a vast open cupboard, which could be closed at the slightest alarm. And in that darkness, which they illuminated with a fabulous light, the unwrapped plates were pierced by the semblances of windows: one overlooking the grounds of Silaz, one into the little to room and the third, the *inestimable third*, into César's study in the Boulevard du Temple—and in that plate, César himself was smoking his pipe at his window, with his back turned, watching the pedestrians, the carriages and the crowds of spring 1833.

They saw him turn round, with a smile, at the entrance of a young woman who came into the study through the drawing-room door and began to speak to him. She was very pretty, no more than seventeen or eighteen years old, coquettishly clad in a printed cotton dress with flounced sleeves, with a black collar and a little apron, and a white underskirt. Her long shiny hair had been put up, in plaits rounded into large wings. She wore light shoes whose ribbons were wound around her slender ankles.

"Who is she?" asked Bertrand. "She's not a visitor."

"She's charming," said Colomba. "Who can she be, Charles? She seems very free-and-easy, for a servant..."

"She's not a relative, though," Charles replied. "At that time, César had no young woman in his immediate family. Why, of course—that's it! It's Henriette Delille!"

"Who's Henriette Delille?" asked Bertrand.

"An orphan that César took in at the end of 1832, if I remember rightly. She was the daughter of one of his former lieutenants, who had asked him to look after the girl before dying, and whose guardian he became. César detested domestics. Henriette supervised his household until the end. She looks eighteen, but I think that in 1833 she was only 16. She's very pretty!"

"Oho! Might our César have had some inclination toward his ward?"

"His memoirs, at any rate, offer no grounds for thinking so. He only left her a modest sum of money in his will. I don't know what became of her after her guardian's death. She was the one who discovered the corpse on the evening of July 28, 1835. Her deposition is in the files of the Ortofieri case."

"Could you give me a brief account the case?" Bertrand asked.

"Nothing simpler. In my bookcase, I have all the notes I took in the past, which summarize the examination. Give me two minutes—I'll be back."

Charles's study was next door to his bedroom. The two rooms, overlooking the gardens and the apse of the church of Saint-Sulpice, were immersed in the silence of a small provincial town. A worker could not have wished for a quieter retreat in the heart of Paris.

While Charles was rummaging through his archives, Bertrand and Colomba, holding hands, continued watching old César conversing with his ward.

He looked at her very tenderly, but also very paternally, and little Henriette, cheerfully respectful, seemed neither to fear him nor to be treating him in a familiar manner. Their moving lips were visible, as well as the gestures and expressions accompanying their speech—and, rather strikingly, there was an astonishing characteristic quality in their movements and the play of their features, the form of which was unexpected: something foreign, not of our country or our era. It was evident that they sometimes pronounced words that have since fallen into disuse, and gave an accent to others that would make us smile.

Bertrand remembered a very old gentleman he had known, who kept repeating: "*Louis-Flip, Louis Flip*; I once saw *Louis-Flip* pass by!" Like that gentleman, Henriette and César must have been saying "*Louis-Flip.*" Bertrand assured Colomba of that and, as everything is a pretext for lovers to caress one another, the immediately embraced, laughing, in honor of *Louis-Flip.*

Charles came back, carrying some notes tightly bound in a cardboard cover and a small card-index. He coughed twice.

"At your disposal!" said Bertrand, who set his fiancée aside, not without laughter.

The historian sat down at a table and began to inspect his papers. "Here," he said. "*On July 28, 1835, at 4 p.m., a young woman, declaring herself to be Henriette Delille, presented herself as the Château d'Eau police station, accompanied by a Monsieur Tripe. Before Commissaire de Police Dyonnet—the same man who had locked Fieschi in his cells four hours earlier—Henriette Delille explained herself. 'On going back into the house a little while ago," she said—or very nearly—'I found the cadaver of my guardian, Monsieur César Christiani, covered in his blood. I immediately went out on to the landing, to call for help. This Monsieur, who is named Tripe, heard me. He came running and assured me that my guardian was indeed dead, and that the only thing to do was to inform the police. I asked him to come with me.'*

"*Immediately, Commissaire Dyonnet went to the scene with a* sergent de ville *and Monsieur Joly, the municipal police chief, who was at his post in order to supervise certain consequences of Fieschi's assassination attempt and arrest. These functionaries, having reached the first floor of number 53, Boulevard du Temple, had no doubt that César Christiani had been struck by a bullet from the machine. The temperature of the body, which was already cold, and its rigidity, indicated that death had occurred about mid-day. The open window supported the hypothesis that seemed persuasive to begin*

156

with: that César was an additional victim of the infernal machine. It's true, though, that the cadaver was lying with its head toward the window and his feet toward the entrance door, and was lying on its back—a presentation that seemed to contradict the conjecture that a bullet or a piece of shrapnel had struck César Christiani, either directly or having richocheted of the pavement of the boulevard.

"The projectile had struck the old man from the front, full in the chest, and if César, thunderstruck, had fallen backwards, it therefore seemed evident that the shot had been fired from a point opposite the window. Monsieur Dyonnet and his superior, Monsieur Joly, did not take that into consideration immediately, and we would have reasoned as they did. In fact, nothing was simpler than to suppose that César had been standing in the center of the little room facing the window, doubtless approaching to see King Louis-Philippe and his magnificent general staff pass by, when Fieschi, on the upper floor of the red house opposite, committed his crime, and that a stray bullet had struck him down. Why should he not have turned as he fell? He might also have fallen face forward, in the direction of his motion, but, once on the ground, might then have turned on to his back in a convulsion of agony or in making a supreme effort."

"Perfectly correct!" Bertrand approved.

"In César's study," Charles continued, "in the presence of the body, Monsieur Dyonnet and Monsieur Joly completed the interrogation of Henriette Delille and Tripe—who only played a very minor role in the entire procedure. Tripe had been going past the door of number 53, examining the ravages of the infernal machine and the frightful debris, the red stains with which the boulevard was still soiled. He had heard cries for help. That was all he knew. For the rest, he could only confirm what Henriette Delille said.

"The latter testified that, after having breakfasted with her guardian that morning—I remind you that in those days the bourgeoisie ate breakfast at 10 a.m. and dinner no later than 6 p.m.—she had gone with friends to watch the review of

157

the National Guard in the Champs-Élysées, near the Carré Marigny. In fact, that review was a very impressive event. To celebrate the fifth anniversary of the Three Glorious Days and the advent of the July Monarchy, Louis-Philippe had ordered a vast deployment of troops. They extended to the right and left of the road from the Carré Marigny to the Bastille, passing via the Concorde, the Rue Royale and the boulevards—but the cavalry and the artillery were massed along the Champs Elysées, where the trees, moreover, formed a nicer background than the old houses in the Boulevard du Temple; and that's why Henriette Delille, yielding to a love of spurs and nature, had gone to the Carré Marigny.

"She said that her guardian had given her leave until that evening—which is to say, until 5 p.m. Even so, she had come back sooner because of the assassination attempt. She would have come back immediately after hearing about it if she had known the actual location of the catastrophe, but in astounded Paris the rumors agreed in situating Fieschi's house much closer to the Château d'Eau than it really was; it was said to be in the vicinity of the Ambigu-Comique. And, certain at the time that César had not been in any danger and that he could not be anxious about her safety, Henriette and her friends had continued walking along the Champs-Elysées after the dispersal of the troops. However, the general consternation having gradually taken hold of her, she had not taken advantage of the full extent of her liberty and had returned at about 4 p.m. Perhaps, too, 'a vague presentiment had slipped into her bosom', as the touching witness-statement that informs us of all this expresses it.

"Questioned at a later date on the state of the apartment when she went back in, Henriette Delille affirmed that the door to the landing was closed, as was the door between the antechamber and the study. The drawing-room door was open—the door to the study, at least, she specified, for all the other exits from the drawing-room were closed. She said nothing about the birds or the monkeys, which leads one to believe that order reigned in the bizarre menagerie, but we may assume that the thunderous noise of the infernal machine and the gunshot simultaneously fired in the apartment itself must have violently agitated Pitt, Coburg and their peers.

"*All the evidence suggests that the pistol shot was covered by the general racket, since no one heard it through the open window on the boulevard, which was full of soldiers and spectators at the moment when, unarguably, we are forced to admit that the pistol did its work. It is, therefore, absolutely understandable that Messieurs Joly and Dyonnet had no suspicion whatsoever that a forearm had been discharged independently of the explosion of the machine—an explosion which, moreover, was as prolonged as the firing of a platoon, decomposed into an uneven series of ongoing detonations that lasted longer than a second.*

"*The next day, they had to change their opinion, the medical examiners having delivered their verdict after the autopsy.*"

"Excuse me for interrupting," said Colomba, who had been following her brother's little lecture attentively, "but why couldn't the window have been closed at the time of the murder, then opened by the murderer?"

"It's doubtful, firstly because César would have opened it, given the fine weather of that magnificent July day, in order to get a better view of the parade. The proof is that, having a very poor view, he had installed a telescope by the sill in order to reveal the King, the Princes, the Marshals and the famous little Monsieur Thiers—a telescope that was found in the place I've just indicated, between the battens of the window, according to the testimony of Lami's water-color. Secondly, why would the murderer have opened the window? Why would he then have placed the telescope between the battens? That set-up could only have had one purpose, in my opinion: to create the belief that César had been killed by the infernal machine— for, if that had happened while the window was closed the latter would have been pierced by the projectile. But in that case…"

"In that case," Bertrand concluded, "the murderer would surely have completed his scene-setting…"

"Exactly!" said Charles. "That's what I was about to say."

"What do you mean?" asked Colomba.

"Of course!" Bertrand went on. "He would have completed it by placing the corpse in a position that left no shadow of doubt as to the provenance of the bullet—I mean that he would have placed the body facing the window."

"You should also bear in mind," Charles said to his sister, "that in 1835, the detonation of a pistol was very loud, and that, in consequence, had it not been masked by the machine, it would have been heard on the boulevard even though a closed window, especially if that window was on the first floor.

"Given that, I'll come back to the first opinion of Messieurs Joly and Dyonnet, and cannot absolve them of having made a mistake. At any rate, confronted with the report of the medical examiners, they hastened to yield to its evidence and recognize their error."

"It's lucky," Bertrand said, "that an autopsy was carried out. In the conditions you've just described, the affair might perfectly well have been shelved, the murder being purely and simply attributed to Fieschi and the autopsy judged unnecessary."

"No—for a superficial examination of the cadaver was obligatory in any case, and the medical reports say that the external appearance of the wound was sufficient to convince an expert of the truth. It was a matter of a bullet fired at close range and which, nevertheless, had remained within the victim's thorax. Indeed, the lead was found in a vertebra, which it had split after going through the heart.

"From July 29 on it was evident that César had been killed by a pistol-shot fired inside his study at close range—too close, undoubtedly, to admit that the assassin might have been in the antechamber. Death had been instantaneous; César had collapsed on the spot, unable to make the slightest movement on the floor, having been already dead before falling.

"It was at this point that the accusation was brought against Fabius Ortofieri by my family, represented by young Napoléon Christiani, the dead man's grandson, Lucile Leboulard, his daughter, and her husband the magistrate, César's son-in-law—and even their son Anselme, the future Councilor and future father of our cousin Drouet, who, it seems, was no less furious in spite of his 20 years at Fabius' escape. It is necessary to say, as well, that Napoléon Christiani himself had only just attained his majority.

"If anyone had had a reason to kill César, it was, let us admit, Fabius Ortofieri, his hereditary enemy, with whom he, personally, had had a few quarrels—petty quarrels, it's true, but which had been envenomed by the temperament and mutual rancor of the two men.

"The Christianis were immediately convinced that Fabius had fired the shot, that it was him who had got rid of César. Was the concomitance of the murder and Fieschi's assassination attempt solely due to chance? That seemed scarcely probable to our ancestors. Between Fieschi, a Corsican, and Fabius Ortofieri, a Corsican, there must be some mysterious connection that might perhaps be subsequently revealed. For the moment, the most important thing was Fabius's culpability.

"Lebouvard spoke to the court and to the Investigating Magistrate commissioned to examine both the murder and the matter of the infernal machine, Monsieur d'Archiac—but he did so with all the discretion of a magistrate well-versed in the customs of the Palais and who, knowing how delicate a matter it is to bring a accusation without evidence, only pointed the law in the right direction.

"Unfortunately for Fabius, a terrible witness stood up against him in the person of police officer Cartoux. Fabius, invited by the Investigating Magistrate to come forward voluntarily, as an enemy of César, to explain the relationship between the two, was recognized by this Jean Cartoux, who was present at his appearance. Cartoux, while on duty in the Boulevard du Temple on July 28, had seen…but I have a copy of his report here, written immediately after César's murder was separated from Fieschi's assassination attempt. The report is dated July 30:

"I have the honor of exposing the following facts. Although entitled to 48 hours leave that was granted to me at my request on the evening of the 28 last, in view of the great fatigue occasioned by work done on the night preceding the review, during which night we had carried out searches in the houses on the Boulevards Saint-Martin and du Crime…"

"He's rather long-winded," said Colomba. "But what's the Boulevard du Crime?"

"That was the Boulevard du Temple," Charles explained. "It was given that nickname because of the numerous theaters that were found here, in which dramas and melodramas were performed in which the characters were always killing one another at will."

"But to what searches is this Jean Cartoux alluding?" asked Bertrand Valois.

"There had been vague suspicions since the eve of the 28 that an assassination might be attempted as the King passed by. A man named Boireau, employed by Fieschi and his accomplices in certain preparations, having become belatedly and confusedly aware of their true purpose, boasted about it on July 27. One of his workmates, without being able to figure out whether or not Boireau was joking, was told by him that an infernal machine was going to explode in a cellar between the Ambigu and the Bastille. The comrade's father reported this conversation to the Commissaire de Police. The latter passed it on to Prefect Gisquet, who was probably incredulous, but who transmitted it through the hierarchy to Thiers. The latter, belatedly informed, could not warn the princes until they mounted up. The report that the minister had received with such regrettable slowness said that a cellar would blow up, level with the Ambigu. It was too late then to check the information, whose origin seemed, in any case, to be idle gos-

162

sip, and whose romantic allure was suggestive of a fantastic character.

"The police, however, had not remained inactive, and at three o'clock in the morning they had visited all the houses in the vicinity of the Ambigu. The unfortunate thing is that, although the information was correct, they got the wrong Ambigu, for there were two of them: the Ambigu-Comique, at 1828 Boulevard Saint-Martin, and the former Ambigu at 76 Boulevard du Temple, not far from Fieschi's house. They only thought about the Ambigu-Comique, because the former Ambigu had been replaced by the Délassements-Comique, and it was only out of habit that the people of the quarter still said 'Ambigu' to describe the theater at number 76. One might suppose that, without that error, The Fieschi house would have been searched from cellar to attic like the others, and that the attempt would have been averted. The Prefect of Police had, moreover, failed to have Boireau arrested—he was not apprehended until the evening of the 28, when the calamity had taken place.

"I shall continue, with your permission, to read the Cartoux report. Let's see: *Although entitled, etc. etc... on learning that a man had been found murdered in the house bearing the number 53 Boulevard du Temple, I thought it best to male known to my superior officer without delay that I believe I can offer certain indications on that subject.*

"*While on duty at mid-day on Tuesday July 28 on the Boulevard du Temple, on the side of the odd numbers, between the Rue Charlot and the Rue du Temple, which is the side on the His Majesty was due to pass as he went toward the Bastille before coming back along the other side, I observed a well-dressed individual who stood for some time in front of the door of number 53, and then decided abruptly to go into the house.*

"*I was a hundred paces away, behind the crowd, watching the façades of the houses, as I had been instructed to do. Even so, the actions of the gentleman attracted my attention. He seemed preoccupied. Instead of watching the roadway like*

163

everyone else, which was bordered on that side by the Nation-
al Guard and on the other by the infantry of the line, he was
moving back and forth, darting covert glances at the windows.
I must, however, admit that he did not inspire any anxiety in
me. He seemed to be on the lookout for someone at one of the
windows, the majority of which were garnished with specta-
tors.

"When he disappeared into the vestibule of number 53,
the drums were beating in the fields toward the Château
d'Eau, announcing the approach of His Majesty and his es-
cort. At the moment when the procession came level with me, I
redoubled my vigilance, observing, in accordance with my
orders, the houses and their vicinity. I was no longer thinking
about the man when the infernal machine suddenly inflicted
the ravages that are well-known. I immediately ran toward the
red house from which the smoke of the explosion was coming
and in order to do that, I had to pass through the butchery and
confusion of the boulevard.

"Until the evening, I was occupied with the consequences
of the assassination attempt. Then I went off duty, harassed by
fatigue. Yesterday, July 29, I enjoyed a well-earned rest. It
was only this morning that the thought of the man returned to
my memory when I learned the time and the circumstances of
Monsieur César Christiani's murder. I have every reason to
presume that his murderer is none other than the agitated in-
dividual that I saw hurrying into number 53 and who, at the
time, had not made any extraordinary impression on my im-
agination—from which it results that his appearance is not
precisely graven in my memory. I would, however, certainly
recognize him if he were presented to me.

"This report made a deep impression on Monsieur Duret
d'Archiac. Before having Fabius Ortofieri introduced into his
office, he installed the policeman Jean Cartoux close at hand,
in the place of his secretary, in order that he might examine
the witness at his leisure. When the latter had withdrawn, Cartoux affirmed that he was definitely the man from the boule-

vard. He recognized his bronzed complexion, his black side-whiskers, his July medal, his stature and his gait.

"The next day, Fabius was taken into custody. He denied it vehemently, claiming that he had never wanted César dead, and, furthermore, that he had been watching the review in the Place de la Bastille. No one, however, had seen him there. He could not produce an alibi. The declarations of a member of the police force accused him formally. The circumstances were such as to convince our ancestor and our great-aunt that Fabius Ortofieri had assassinated heir grandfather and father. They therefore added a civil suit to the legal case, and you can be certain that the accused would have been convicted by the assize court if his death had not spared him that shame."

"In sum," concluded Bertrand Valois, "the whole accusation rests on the word of this policeman."

"And on the fact that César had no known enemy apart from Fabius."

"They didn't wish him dead, though!"

"There's no evidence of that in the documents that we possess—but one thing has struck me since I've discovered the luminite plate that César hung in his study."

"What?"

"The simple fact that he had hung it there, and that he took it down it frequently to see what had been happening in his absence. Why should he have taken the trouble to install that undetectable spy on the wall if he were not experiencing some unknown anxiety? The first idea that came to mind in that regard was that he feared surreptitious visits…"

"Secret societies abounded at that time. Do you think that he was a member of one?"

"I don't think so. He was certainly not a partisan of any monarchy, constitutional or otherwise, but his memoirs show him to have been, to a certain extent, indulgent of Louis-Philippe—who, himself, did not hate the memory of Na-poléon, whose ashes he had returned to Paris. 1835 was a year in which the Bonapartists remained quite tranquil. After the Emperor, they had lost the Duc de Reichstadt; they gave scarcely any thought to Prince Louis-Napoléon, the future Napoléon III, of whom there was to be no real mention until 1836, in Strasbourg. I'm therefore convinced that César was not under suspicion by the government of the Citizen-King, and that even his disgrace was no more than indifference. In my opinion, there was nothing to prevent him being received at Court. A man who had displeased the Bourbons might easily have pleased the man who had just got rid of them. In essence, it was César who did not want to ask for anything, not Louis-Philippe who disdained his services."

"What worries me," Colomba said, "is the simultaneity of Fieschi's assassination attempt and César's murder. It's difficult to admit that hazard alone was the cause of it. Fieschi, Ortofieri and Christiani were all Corsicans—there's no getting away from that!"

"I should point out," said Charles, "that the Corsican origin of Fieschi had absolutely nothing to do with his crime. He too, of course, had loved Napoléon, whom he had served in uniform in Russia. I repeat, though, that in 1835, Bonapartism was temporarily devoid of an objective. Fieschi was the instrument of secret societies furious with Louis-Philippe because he had turned the revolution of July 1830, which had been designed to establish a republic, to his own advantage—but Fieschi hardly cared about the cause for which he was going to commit his crime. A murderer by nature, he surrendered himself to tenebrous masters without even knowing them well, or knowing them all, and he put to death at a single stroke a host of innocent people, less out of ambition than vanity, and most especially less out of conviction than ferocious cruelty and resentment against society."

"Don't you think, Monsieur Historian," said Bertrand, "that we're straying from the point…"

"No," said Charles, smiling. "All this is relevant. I sense it, like Colomba. And if I'm mistaken, there won't be much harm done. We're learning a little history, which is always good for something."

During this conversation, none of them had taken their eyes off the plate of luminite in which, marvelously, they saw the *future* environment of the *past* events that they had just been discussing. Henriette Delille had withdrawn now. César Christiani was smoking his clay pipe, sitting at the occasional table, reading *Le Moniteur*. Through the panes of the casement, in the distance, the so-called Fieschi house—or, rather, the house that would late be known as the Fieschi house—was visible.

Charles, armed with binoculars, could make out the profile of a young woman at the window furnished with the Venetian blind, which had served as an embrasure for the four-barreled cannon making up the infernal machine. She was sewing placidly. The Sun was shining into the room, on to a modest yellow-colored flowered wallpaper which was, indeed, already in the state described by the witnesses of 1835: torn in places, and crudely patched.

Charles had left the plate as he had found it, except that he had refitted it into the fir-wood frame, whose eight latches maintained its leaves, assuring the cohesion of the extremely thin tablets that César had once detached for the requirements of his mysterious surveillance. Since then, the light had continued on its way through the substance, the images of the past having advanced and all of the oldest aspects of the past being held within the intact thickness of the plate—a thickness that constituted, moreover, almost the totality of the depth of the whole, since the plate enclosed 93 years of retarded light and César had only searched two years and a few months.

At present, the fine plates that César had meticulously detached were showing the back of Grandmother Estelle's ink-drawing, *The Declaration of Love*, with a poor light filtering through its paper, probably from the bedroom in Silaz, whose shutters were almost always closed.

Charles had given Bertrand and Colomba a complete demonstration of the properties of luminite. Amazed at first by such a new phenomenon, they had quickly formed a very clear conception of it, in relation to the simplicity of its effects. And while they experienced delight in watching people, animals and things that had lived long ago live again—César with his pipe, passers-by, horses, swallows, flies landing on the plate, the houses on the boulevard, the quadruple row of elms in which sparrows were fluttering, a historical décor now vanished because of the reconstruction and the opening out of the Place de la République—they were no less dominated by the idea that soon, at a time Charles chose, the bloody day of July 28 would appear within that frame and they would be witnesses to the murder of César Christiani.

And Bertrand Valois, practical above all, as realistic as one can expect of a successful dramatist (which is not very), came back to what he justly considered to be the primary necessity: "Portraits of Fabius Ortofieri, old chap! That's what we need. As many portraits as possible! That's the key!"

"I'll do what's necessary," Charles said, smiling placidly. "Writing to Mademoiselle Ortofieri is out of the question, but I've found Madame Le Tourneur's address in the telephone directory. She'll return to Paris today or tomorrow, if she hasn't done so already—and as soon as I arrived, I sent her an explanatory letter, for which she was, I'm sure, waiting with impatient avidity. At the same time, I asked her to alert Rita with respect to portraits of her ancestor."

"Good work," judged Bertrand.

"I'm counting on you for a great deal," Charles said.

"To do what?"

"I deem it indispensable to know, hour by hour, what was happening in César's study for several days before the 28. Let's say a fortnight."

"That's perfectly sensible."

"My plan, therefore, consists of laying bare by progressive strokes, as soon as we've made all the preliminary dispositions, the surface the plate corresponding, on the day of the operation, to July 15, 1835. Afterwards, there must be an observer permanently in front of the plate. We'll have to do that sentry-duty in shifts—you, me, Colomba too, and other collaborators if need be—during the 12 days that the phase leading up to the crime lasts.

"During the entire day of July 28, 1835, apparatus for making cinematographic images in color will record the vision of that critical moment. I don't intend to film the 12 or 24 preceding hours, but that period too has to be recorded nevertheless, in order that we can look at it again if necessary."

"Recorded?" said the young woman. "Without the assistance of film cameras? How? Oh! Pardon me, I understand! By means of another plate of virginal luminite!"

"Why virginal?" queried Bertrand. "That doesn't matter. The power of luminite is inexhaustible, isn't it, Charles?"

"Of course. I can't re-emphasize sufficiently that the only advantage of a virginal plate is to seem completely dark, on its two surfaces as well as its edges."

"Evidently," Colomba admitted. "How stupid I am!"

"Permit me to contradict you!" said Bertrand. "All this is too new for anyone to be able to take it all in at once. What a marvel!" His quirky and voluptuous nose seemed to be sniffing a rare perfume in the air.

"Can I count on you—on both of you?"

"That goes without saying," said Bertrand, while his fiancée confirmed it. "When do you hope to begin?"

"When I have the portraits of Fabius and when I'm assured of the collaboration and attendance of certain individuals for the great day."

"Who?"

"Scientists, historians, magistrates, official witnesses *and representatives of the Ortofieri family*."

"Indeed," said Bertrand. "We can't do otherwise. It's indispensable to inform the banker about the counter-inquiry, and the secret is impossible to keep."

"Even so, we shall try to keep the family business—which is a criminal affair—private and confidential. As for luminite, it is included the inheritance of humankind, and we don't have the right to withhold it from science, any more than it is our prerogative to deprive History of a direct vision and a cinematographic film of Fieschi's assassination attempt. To begin with, I have to go about things stealthily, but…"

"You're right, my dear Charles," Bertrand declared. "All this is bigger than us; we don't own it."

Scarcely had he spoken than someone knocked deliberately on the door.

Charles closed the cupboard on the prodigious image that it contained. "Come in!"

The valet came in carrying a telegram on a tray. "For Monsieur!" he said.

The young man opened the telegram. "Ah!" he said. "It's from the worthy Madame Le Tourneur. Before even having received my letter she wants me to call on her."

"How amusing it is!" exclaimed Colomba, dazedly. "It would make a comedy, wouldn't it, Bertrand?"

"I see it more as a play for the Châtelet, personally," said Bertrand. "A modern fairy play…"

Charles, however, looked at them silently and reproachfully. His hope was not made for laughing at.

XII. Surprises in the Present and the Past

Before going to see Madame Le Tourneur, Charles realized that he could not leave his mother in ignorance any longer regarding his discovery and the project he had conceived to bring the circumstances of the 1835 murder to light. He even regretted not having spoken to her as soon as he had returned, and was annoyed to have let himself fall prey to a sentiment that was far from heroic.

Deep down, Madame Christiani inspired a certain dread in him: a vestige of the past, a relic of childhood. The good woman had ruled the education of her children with a rod of iron, and something of that still remained. Now, Charles knew that the initial shock would be rude…

He did it. Madame Christiani was not at all astonished. The existence of luminite did not surprise her at all. She said: "It's curious", devoted two minutes to the pleasure of knowing that such a bizarre thing was counted among physical phenomena, and, following her mental custom, stopped there, neglecting to think or speculate about that marvel or its effects. She cared little about the potential consequences of his discovery. The two minutes having gone by, Charles realized that his mother's thoughts had already resumed their quotidian course and that they would be occupied henceforth with the household accounts, the latest political article in *Le Temps* and the division of her contemporaries into worthy souls and bad lots—which is to say, into these of whom she thought well and the rest.

Everything changed when Madame Christiani was informed about the project of the counter-enquiry and that it might result in the revelation of the innocence of Fabius Ortofieri. That name made her shiver. For a long time, even before she had become a Christiani by marriage, she had known that Fabius had murdered César. She knew it as we all know that Ravaillac stabbed Henri IV. It was History, Gospel truth. To

171

revisit the question? She choked on the amazement and indignation.

Charles appealed to her sense of justice. Having pleaded the cause of impartiality for some time, he saw his mother calm down, but by closing her face, as she did when anyone tried to prove to her that Cousin Drouet had always behaved well toward Mélanie. Madame Christiani made an appearance of concession; she gave up arguing—but everything indicated that she was sticking to her position.

It was not a victory. Galileo had put on that face when declaring that the Earth did not rotate—so Charles did not look forward without apprehension to the consequences of his exposé.

"It's necessary," he said. "At the end of the day, it will be good, and even…necessary that Monsieur Ortofieri the banker can check the facts and verify…"

"What do you mean?" Madame Christiani exploded. "Do I understand that you have the intention of inviting that brigand to come here?"

"You know perfectly well that he won't come, Mother—that he'll delegate someone…"

"Never!" fulminated the terrible woman. "I forbid it. While I live, no Ortofieri will ever set foot in my house, even by proxy."

Charles could not help smiling.

"I'm not laughing!" his mother declared, dryly.

"Please," said Charles, in a serious voice. "You're much too good and too just to forbid anything whatsoever, from the moment that it's a matter of truth. We must do our duty in this regard."

"It's not for you to tell me mine!"

"You'll cause me infinite pain if you won't approve of all that I intend to do."

Madame Christiani fell silent. In the excess of her discontentment, she had turned her back to her son and was looking through the window into the depths of the garden that extended in front of her. Charles's last sentence, and the tone in which he had pronounced it, had awoken a sort of alarm in her of which she had given no sign—but the fit was doubtless difficult to hide, for she maintained her stance in front of the window.

Her silence, however, encouraged the young man, who said: "If you love me, trust me. Come on! I shall not do anything contrary to our dignity—but can a work of justice ever be less than noble?"

He had promised himself that he would only convince her with general arguments and not to get away from the question of justice. He did not doubt that his mother would give way on every point if she knew that the happiness of her child was at stake, once she had been made to envisage, astonishingly, the innocence of Fabius Ortofieri. But Charles foresaw the possibility that Fabius' guilt would be confirmed—in which case Rita might, in consequence, remain an impossible dream so far as he was concerned. Wanting to spare Madame Christiani from the great chagrin of seeing her son Charles unhappy, he would do anything rather than confess his love.

Madame Christiani turned around, unhurriedly. She had devoted herself, in the secrecy of her inner being, to observations, reflections and checks that had affirmed her immediate and initial assumption.

He saw immediately that he had won his argument—not that the hard face was at all suggestive of agreement. Only the eyes, having softened, were displaying contentment and capitulation. "All right," she sighed. "Do as you like."

"Thank you!" he cried, enthusiastically.

She sat down at her desk and calmly began to write. Charles wanted to put his arms around her; he did not resist, as he usually did, the need to shower her with tender kisses.

"Come on!" she said. "It's all right!" and, having pecked brusquely at her son's cheek, she gently drew away. "Let me work. There are serious matters needing my attention."

"I love you very much!" he said.

She shrugged her shoulders, and he went out.

173

Then Madame Christiani set her pen down and put her hands together. "No doubt about it," she murmured. "He kisses me, tells me he loves me! Come on! Just like all men! There's only one Ortofieri daughter on earth, and my Christiani has to fall in love with her! Now we have but one hope, and it's feeble. If that bandit Fabius remains guilty—and I'm convinced that he is—my son will be unhappy! For I know him! César's murderer will never enter into our family, even represented by his heir of the 20th generation! Never, while there are men among us like Charles and women like me!" She added, thoughtfully: "Poor boy! It's a stroke of luck that he's found those plates…"

But that seemed perfectly natural to her, while Charles' love for an Ortofieri seemed to her to be the most inconceivable thing in the world.

Madame Geneviève Le Tourneur had said to Charles, as he took his leave of her: "That's agreed, then. Come back to see me tomorrow. Let's avoid letters as much as possible. Tomorrow I'll have seen Rita and I'll tell you what she says about the portraits and the steps to follow."

And Charles had added: "Permit me to ask you to remain silent with regard to the luminite. I'd like to be completely finished with the Ortofieri affair before making the discovery public. If the newspapers get hold of it prematurely, it will put an end to our tranquility; we'll be besieged, and it's frightful to contemplate the rapidity with which the news that we want to keep secret will spread. Just now, when I came out of my house, my wonderstruck concierge didn't hesitate to ask me for details regarding 'the extraordinary trick that I brought back from Savoy.' The chauffeur must have talked, in spite of my instructions…."

"Don't worry," Geneviève had replied, in the jovial and slightly pedantic tone she sometimes adopted., by virtue of a little culture of which she was inordinately proud. "I shall imitate the prudent silence of Conrart."[21]

The next day, when Charles presented himself at the home of the blonde emulator of that obscure writer, he was powerfully moved to find himself in the company of Rita Ortofieri.

"Isn't this much simpler?" said Geneviève, with a little laugh.

"Indeed," Charles approved, mechanically.

There was then a terrible moment of disturbance and nausea, because of the immense effort those two hearts had to make to repress the explosion of their joy.

With common accord, Charles and Rita tacitly made a decision not to pronounce a word relating to their love. The slightest spark would have lit a fearful fire. They would therefore only speak about the enterprise that might soon permit them to let that passion, so painfully contained, off the bridle. And there again, as with Madame Christiani, there was no question of anything but searching for the truth and bringing about the triumph of justice. They seemed to interest themselves solely in the two old enemies, César and Fabius, and no longer to know that, beyond the ancient drama that it was necessary to clarify, it was their own destiny that they had to discover.

All a-tremble with a delightful fever whose assaults it was constantly necessary for them to overcome, they regulated the march to be followed with banal and cool phrases, avoiding meeting one another's eyes, devoured by the desire to look at one another recklessly and eternally.

---

[21] Valentin Conrart (1603-1675) left behind 42 manuscript volumes, and a set of memoirs, but published very little, which led the critic Boileau (Nicolas Boileau-Despréaux) to coin the phrase: "I shall imitate the prudent silence of Conrart." Conrart's house was the birthplace of the Academie Française, whose first permanent secretary he became.

"The best thing," Rita said, "is to approach my father with perfect frankness and clarity. He's a taciturn and surly character, but his conscience and his integrity are irreproachable. When he knows that a means is being offered to him to review the case against his ancestor, be certain that he won't hesitate for an instant."

"Should I ask to see him?"

"No—oh no!"

"Should I write to him, then?"

"It's preferable for someone else to write—your lawyer, for example. All this must remain, until the end, very cold and inexpressive. It's the best way to avoid any discord."

"Very well," said Charles. "What about the portraits."

"Ask him for them by way of the same intermediary, who must take responsibility for returning them intact."

"Are there many?"

"I know of three, no more. One portrait in oils, very large, showing the upper body. Another, smaller portrait in pastels. And a miniature—or, rather, two similar miniatures, painted by the same artist. One of them is hanging in the drawing-room; the other is in my bedroom. I've brought you that one. Look, here it is. Examine it at your leisure, but don't keep it; I want to take it back. We have to take every precaution and it's absolutely necessary that no one suspects me of any connivance with you."

"You've had an excellent idea," said Charles. "From now on, it might perhaps be useful to me to know what your ancestor looks like."

"I can't assure you that this miniature is the better resemblance of the two...."

Charles brought the little oval frame of waxed wood, equipped with a golden thread, into the light of a casement. The colors of Fabius Ortofieri's portrait were still vivid. The miniature was only vaguely reminiscent of the lithograph with which Charles was familiar. It depicted a robust man of mature years, with blue eyes and a dark complexion, and indeterminate nose and a mouth opening in a slightly pinched

176

smile. His hair formed a forelock and was brushed forward over his temples. Short side-whiskers of the sort known as "rabbit's-feet" striped his cheeks. The gentleman wore a white cravat wound several times around, a wide-open white waist-coat and a black frock-coat whose buttonhole was ornamented with a sky-blue ribbon with a red border.

"The July medal, isn't it?" said Rita.

"Exactly—and that tells us that the miniature must have been painted after 1830. It follows that Fabius Ortofieri must have looked very much the same in 1835."

"The big portrait is from 1834," said Rita, "and the pastel was painted during the trial, in prison."

"The same cut of the beard?"

"Always. The face entirely shaven, except for the side-whiskers."

"May I ask a question?" breathed Madame Le Tourneur, in a precious and faint voice. "What's the July medal?"

"A cross awarded by Louis-Philippe," Charles replied, "as a national recompense to all the citizens who distinguished themselves during the three July days and who, in conse-quence, put him on the throne."

"They gave away a lot of them, I believe?" said Rita.

"Yes. A few too many, it must be said. One finds all sorts of individuals among rabble-rousers, and the July cross isn't always worn worthily."

He continued looking at the miniature attentively, in or-der to commit it firmly to memory and to be able to recognize Fabius if the luminite gave him an unexpected opportunity. When he had done that he returned the object to the young woman—and the moment had come for them to separate.

Madame Le Tourneur sensed that they were so desolate at that necessity that she hastened to go in quest herself of a tray laden with small bottles and cakes that was fully prepared in the dining-room. Charles and Rita, however, made the same fearful movement at the same time. The sight of the tray and the prospect of the snack transformed the atmosphere of the meeting dangerously. It was about to lose its impersonal character. A lukewarm intimacy would be created, which would, as always, escape from the carafe of port or the fuming teapot. Charles immediately understood the peril and the impropriety. He pleaded the urgent necessity of talking to his notary that same day and excused himself for not being able to stay longer.

Rita's hand was so cold and so tremulous that he was desperate to abandon it.

"Whenever you have something to say," Geneviève declared, "you can always return here." She elongated her stride as she showed Charles out; he seemed to be fleeing, and did not reply.

"Pardon me," he said. "The notary, you see..."

"I understand perfectly," she said, softly, letting her voice descend in pitch from syllable to syllable.

Rita opened the window to watch him go.

The results of this clandestine conversation did not take long to manifest themselves. Two days later, in fact, Charles received a telephone call from the notary.

"Hello! Monsieur Ortofieri's reply reached me this morning, my dear Monsieur. I hope that you will be satisfied. Everything is proceeding as you wish, and Monsieur Ortofieri's letter is couched in the most exquisitely polite terms. He could not do otherwise, of course. As is only natural, Monsieur Ortofieri will not involve himself personally. The portraits will be confided to his delegate, who will present himself at your home directly. Monsieur Ortofieri has chosen this representative with a tact that you will doubtless appreciate. He preferred an acquaintance that you have in common to a business associate unknown to you. It is a certain Monsieur Luc de Certeuil, who is, it appears, your friend and lives in your building—a particularly fortunate circumstance...hello? Hello? Are you there?"

"Yes," said Charles. "That's perfect. Thank you."

Luc de Certeuil advanced toward Charles, his hand extended. His tread upon the drawing-room carpet was self-assured, and he accentuated his habitual stance—which consisted of further increasing his considerable height by throwing out his chest and raising his head, with a false familiarity. There is always an exaggeration in that sort of perpetual heartiness; one suspects it of being overly calculated, imposed by the soul on an actor on a body whose natural pose it is not. Luc gave the impression of mistrusting his body, of dreading that it might collapse at any moment, that he might lose an inch of stature or thoracial circumference.

Today, more than ever, he seemed not so much upstanding as hauling himself up, not so much tall as puffed up. His arm was excessively extended, the hand opened with a frankness that was too studied, but it was not uninteresting to see so thankless a face wearing so flattering an expression. That face and that expression were not in accord. The face was square, provided with powerful jaws, poorly illuminated by strangely colorless eyes; the short, large nose was reminiscent of the sinister muzzle of a hyena; the whole ensemble was pale and already fatigued, but the whole ensemble, carefully managed, powdered and perfumed, had never been displeasing to any woman. The wavy hair, combed back to reveal a broad and solid forehead, was a luxuriously well-groomed mane. A kind of manufactured superiority emanated from this individual, whose ugliness because it was virile, arrogant and athletic, made women say: "He's handsome"—while a few men said the same, because of the fellow's robust commanding appearance, his decisive manner and his affected friendliness.

Charles, on his guard, perplexed and malcontent, watched this tall and exceedingly affable gentleman coming toward him in his mother's drawing-room, wearing an archangelic expression on an essentially demonic face, attempting to spread throughout his being the light of the most elevated sentiments and the purest of intentions.

"My dear friend," Luc said, "I've come to place myself entirely at your disposition. Your notary has telephoned you,

179

hasn't he? You know, therefore, that Monsieur Ortofieri has done me the honor of…"

"If you are agreeable," Charles said, promptly, "we shall maintain silence regarding the mandate that you have been given by Monsieur Ortofieri. My mother, with whose opinions you are familiar, will only recant her prejudice in his regard if proof is produced of the innocence of old Fabius. I will take responsibility for telling my mother that I have selected you of my own accord to be my delegate to the banker, by reason of the relationship that you have with him—for if she knew that you were his representative, I fear that she would give you a frosty reception."

He had, indeed, understood that Madame Christiani would be incapable of going beyond the concessions that she had made to him. It was one thing to have convinced her to admit the involvement of the Ortofieris via an intermediate in an operation to be carried out under her roof, but to have her accept that the person granted that authority was Luc de Certeuil, whom she abominated, was something else entirely.

"As you wish," Luc replied. "I pray that you will see in me a friend disposed to do what is necessary in all conscience, without any other preoccupation than to fulfill impartially the mandate that he has entrusted to me. I understand that the situation is exceedingly delicate. I have not forgotten anything of the conversation we had the other day in Saint-Trojan, in the course of which we both, I believe, matched one another in frankness. Isn't that so?"

"Yes, admitted Charles, flagrantly insulted but replying with moderate softness nevertheless.

Luc continued, without emphasis: "I leave you to imagine how surprise I was when Monsieur Ortofieri brought me up to date with what's happening and ended up asking me to represent him with respect to you. My first impulse was to decline the honor, for reasons that you know—but I saw that it was impossible for me to refuse without revealing those very reasons, and it seemed to me that a gentleman did not have that right. I hope that you will approve."

Charles endured a few painful moments. The other was profiting from the circumstances to put on a show of chivalrous spirit, taking his stand on the terrain of generosity and elegance. Rather than approval, it was thanks of which he was in search, and to refuse them seemed impossible. However, his intervention in the counter-enquiry had something paradoxical and unsustainable about it, since—as he was not unaware—the result of the observations might ruin his most cherished hopes. On the other hand, was he telling the truth? Might he not have learned about the adventure of the luminite from the gossip that was running through the building from top to bottom? Had the concierge been any more discreet with him than anyone else? Might it not be him who had spontaneously offered the banker his collaboration when the latter had acquainted him with the contents of the notary's letter? Who could tell whether Luc de Certeuil might not have anticipated the letter by reporting to Monsieur Ortofieri the rumor that was making the rounds of the tenants in the Rue de Tournon? Charles's suspicions stopped there, however. He was intuitively certain that Rita's suitor would not have said anything to anyone that might harm the young woman in any fashion whatsoever. Rita would never have forgiven him for that, and it would have the immediate ruination of Luc's chances.

Meanwhile, the only course to take, for the time being, was to bow to necessity, however annoying it seemed. It was necessary to accept, while feigning a smile, that an enemy should enter the citadel, at the cost of his observing everything and involving himself in everything. There could be no question of sending Monsieur Ortofieri's ambassador away, and his declarations had to be accepted as honest and truthful. There was a game to be played in which bluff would be indispensable. An unprecedented vigilance was obligatory. That complicated matters awkwardly, but what he could do? Nothing, other than submit, while keeping his eyes open and his spine flexible.

"My dear Certeuil," Charles said, shaking his hand. "I can't tell you that I like the situation very much—but I'm sure that you don't like it any more than I do. Through you, I offer my compliments to the man whose delegate you are and, in the assurance of the sentiments that you have just expressed, I thank you and say: be welcome."

"I thank you in my turn," said Luc—and he put such perfect politeness into that sentence that Charles wondered, momentarily, whether the man in front of him might not be utterly dutiful, and entirely sincere. "These are the portraits you asked for."

Luc was, in fact, leaning on a large flat rectangle, parceled up with string. He unwrapped the light packaging and the four portraits of Fabius appeared, just as Rita had described them: the oil-painting, the pastel made in the prison and the two miniatures—which proved that Monsieur Ortofieri had asked his daughter for the loan of hers. A specimen of the lithograph previously mentioned was added to them.

At first, Charles experienced a certain satisfaction. He had wondered whether Luc de Certeuil had brought authentic portraits of Fabius Ortofieri. Trickery in this respect would have been very audacious, but the order of the day was to be watchful, and the password was "mistrust." Then, the improvised examining magistrate, reassured as to the authenticity of the portraits, felt a most unexpected disappointment—which a collector of old portraits would surely have foreseen.

The portraits bore no strict resemblance to one another; even the two miniatures, the works of a single artist and made simultaneously, were slightly different. There were, to be sure, in sum, four images of a correct, robust blue-eyed man with a swarthy face encased by "rabbit's-feet"—but, knowing one of the images, would one have recognized Fabius straight away in any of the others? Everyone who possesses ancestral portraits knows very well what we mean; even photographs do not always produce analogous impressions that make us see the same person within changing features.

"Let's hope that we won't require absolute precision," Charles said.

"Oh," said Luc, "the individual is strongly stereotypical. He doesn't recall any face out of all those I've seen in the world since I came into it."

"He obviously has character," said Charles, moving his gaze from the oil to the pastel and from the pastel to the miniatures. "That doesn't mean that we won't have to compensate, as far as is possible, for the inadequacy of the evidence. The dossier of the affair gives us very little. In 1835, there were none of the admirable means of identification that the law now has at its disposal. You won't find the slightest description of the accused in the file. We don't even know whether Fabius was tall or short."

As he finished speaking, Charles looked at Luc de Certeuil. He saw that he was inattentive—not indifferent, as one might have presumed, but exhibiting a state of mind quite distinct from interest, and even more so from detachment. He seemed to be dominated by a profound *astonishment*. He gave the impression—without being able to hide it—of returning in amazement from an idea that had occurred to him, a conviction that he had acquired. Readable in his eyes was something like: "Was all that true, then? It's not a stratagem? Is it possible?"

"Would you like to see the luminite?" Charles asked him, smiling.

"Is that what you call the extraordinary thing that…in essence, conserves the past?"

"That slows down light," Charles corrected. "It comes to the same thing, but it's more exact."

"Amazing!"

"No. Luminite exists, as mirrors, prisms and lenses exist, as water exists and all the other substances that affect the direction, intensity or speed of light. It exists like the air, through which sounds travel far more slowly than through the ground. It exists as naturally as your monocle and your eye. There has never been anything simpler, anything more logical. What would be illogical would be that it did not exist somewhere."

"Yes," said Luc. "All the same, it's startling!"

"Like everything that emerges unexpectedly. After an hour, there'll only be one thing that will still astonish you, and that's having been astonished. My plates of luminite, my poor Certeuil, no longer have any effect on me in themselves. It's like my phonograph, my telephone, my telegraph apparatus, which no longer hold any more interest for me than the use I might make of them."

He thought he saw a doubt floating in Luc's eyes: the idea, almost immediately effaced, of a possible subterfuge.

"Let's go, then," decided the historian.

The plates had been taken into a sort of studio illuminated by a large bay window, equipped with everything necessary for the eventual operation. Bertrand Valois and Colomba were conversing tenderly in the studio.

Luc had not expected to find Mademoiselle Christiani and her fiancé there, but on reflection, he told himself that he had, as required, informed Charles of the time when his visit was to be expected, and understood from then on that he would only ever be allowed to get close to the luminite in the presence of other people, who would be as polite as they were vigilant. He asked nonetheless, while expressing his admiration and uttering exclamations of delight, to examine all the faces of the plates. Charles hastened to authorize him to do so—and paid great attention to the facilitation of his task by maintaining a firm grip on the object of his curiosity. Accidents can so easily happen!

The plates that he was handling thus were those that had served the little top room as windows for such a long time. As for the illustrious plate from the Boulevard du Temple, it was already set up for observation. Standing on a solid support that held it vertical and framed it, it presented to the spectator the face that one is tempted to call the "front:" the one that showed César's study in 1833. The other face—the "back," if you like—which displayed the wall, was visible without the plate having to be turned round thanks to a mirror hung on the back wall of the studio, which reflected that "back."

In front of the plate, an apparatus for making cinematographic images (let us say a "camera") was set up, ready to function in response to a switch. Beneath that camera, another plate of luminite, suitably placed, was re-recording, for a further sequence of years, the successive images that the first delivered to the sight of men, after hatching them for 100 years. That silent and invisible transmission, that sort of incessant and surreptitious photography, could not help but be impressive, for it was as if one century were passing on that which it had seen to the following century.

In the plate, César, with his pipe clenched in his teeth and his parrot on his shoulder, seemed to be drawing nearer to it. He climbed on to a chair and reached out his arms; his face was magnified, like a close-up on a cinema screen. Then, everything within the perimeter of the image see-sawed. Evidently, César had taken the plate down in order to leaf through it. During the operation, the cloth and buttons of his waistcoat were visible, against which he pressed the object, while the other face, supported on the mobile desk-top, provided a downward-angled view of the top and bottom of the item of furniture—which was presently, in 1929, situated in Madame Christiani's bedroom.

Finally, César hung the plate up again, and his expression left no doubt as to his contentment. His "optical glass"— his secret agent—hand certainly not vouchsafed him any troublesome revelation. And that was even more manifest when, having taken Lord Pitt on his index finger, he engaged in a dialogue with him, which was, alas, impossible to grasp, but which made the old corsair laugh so much that he shed tears—whereupon he went in search of the money Coburg in the next room, and amused himself with his antics and grimaces.

"Quite an eccentric!" exclaimed Colomba.

Luc, gripped by the delight in which luminite always plunged its observers, forgot to maintain an aristocratic phlegmaticism and became as ecstatic as a country bumpkin— albeit a country bumpkin tormented by anxiety. Did he not

185

have proof, now, that no conjuring trick was involved? On this very spot, in a few days time, they would find out whether Fabius had murdered César. And what if, by chance, it was not Fabius? If the Ortofieris were innocent of the murder, what would then prevent Charles from marrying Rita, since they loved one another, since she loved him to the point of having spent an entire day with him on the Ile d'Aix and of having informed him telegraphically, via Geneviève Le Tourneur, that she had put off authorizing Luc to ask for her hand in marriage?

Charles thought he could read his comrade's thoughts and he discerned very clearly the dread that was mingled with surprise in those colorless eyes.

"For what are you waiting to commence your incredible and marvelous counter-enquiry?" Luc asked.

"I'm simply waiting for the cinematographers to be ready."

"What about this?" Luc said, pointing to the camera.

"Insufficient for the great solemn session of July 28, 1835. I intend, in fact, to conserve on film everything of which the luminite makes restitution for observers placed straight ahead, higher up, lower down and to either side. For that I need five cameras variously orientated: one in front, like this one, and the other four pointed at the four corners of the plate, two to the left and two to the right, the two upper ones pointing downwards, the two lower ones pointing upwards, all of them filming in color with the exception of the one in the center."

"Why the exception?"

"Because a color film is always dimmer than the other and I want to possess at least one strip that's as clear as possible.

"So when will you begin?"

"In a week's time. Next week we shall 'cleave' the plate as far as July 15, and then we shall not cease to watch it until the date of the murder, reserving for the entire day of July 28 the employment—intermittent, in any case—of the five cam-

186

eras and the access to this studio of the notable individuals I have invited and who have already promised me their collaboration. I've kept those invitations to a minimum. In spite of my precautions, the news has spread. I'm being assailed with solicitations; if I gave permission all those who have expressed a desire, the large amphitheater in the Sorbonne would be too small to contain the audience."

"Obviously!" remarked Bertrand Valois. "So many attractions rolled up into one! The demonstration of a hitherto-unknown marvel of nature, the retrovision of Fieschi's attempt to assassinate Louis-Philippe, and that of a murder whose mystery has been suddenly renewed!" And he it was who took the initiative of making a proposition that was to have certain curious and rather important consequences. "Why not start attacking the luminite today," he said to Charles, "in order to reach the days running up to July 15? Might not the glances that we dart at the period anterior to the 15 be useful to us, and perhaps tell us something? All your precautions have now been taken: Monsieur Ortofieri has been informed; Monsieur de Certeuil, who is representing him, knows what is going on; the camera is in position, along with the retransmission plate; you possess portraits of old Fabius. There's every reason to employ the week that separates us from the operation proper in taking a few soundings."

"I don't see any reason why not," said Charles, after due reflection. He took the plate out of its frame, asked Bertrand to hold it upright on a large table covered with a thick cloth, and, arming himself with an exceedingly fine blade, drive it into the thickness of the luminite with a few light taps of a mallet, almost at the edge of the month of October 1833—which was, at that moment, illuminating César Christiani's room at 53 Boulevard du Temple.

A tiny dry click was heard, and a first leaf of luminite was detached, so thin, in its sharp rigidity, that it had the semblance of a purely geometrical plane.

The light of distant days shone forth on all sides. The frightful thinness was set, with a thousand precautions, in a felt-lined rack prepared for that purpose.

"1834," Charles announced, having looked at the mantelpiece of the study through his binoculars. "There's the new calendar. And consider the trees on the boulevard—it's winter."

"Which winter?" Bertrand asked. "That of January or December?"

"January," Charles affirmed.

"Why?" asked Luc, at the same time as Colomba.

"Come on—I've guessed," Bertrand put in. "Because the new calendar, like the old one, only has half a year on each of its faces, and it's the first semester that is presently visible. César wouldn't have turned the current semester to the wall— that stands to reason."

"And there you are!" said Charles, merrily.

"In sum," Luc de Certeuil remarked, "At this moment, having left 1833, we're going into the future, towards 1835..."

"That's it exactly," said Charles. He was passionately absorbed by his resumed task, fearful of breaking or cracking the substance impressed with the invaluable images.

Chance and his skill favored him. He was able to continue his subtle work with as much precision as César had once brought to release these strange ephemerides from another part of the plate.

Having read with the aid of the binoculars the date of the copy of the satirical magazine—*Le Charivari*—that César, who was noticeably older, had left on the white marble top of the occasional table, Charles put down his knife rather excitedly.

"June 30, 1835. Let's stop there." Then he replaced the sunlit plate in its frame, on the easel.

César's study was relatively gloomy by comparison with the window, where magnificent daylight shone. The houses opposite were dazzling, above the tufted verdure of the elms.

The bull's-eye clock fixed to the wall beneath the corsair's guidon, marked 3 p.m.

Henriette Delille came in, finishing knotting the strings of her bonnet under her chin. César covered his head with a bizarre straw top-hat. They exchanged a few words. The former corsair was somber, seemingly peevish and complaining. The young woman, slimmer than in 1833 and still extremely pretty—perhaps more so—seemed sad, if not unhappy. With a touching grace, she put her hand on César's arm and, with an imploring gaze, seemed to be encouraging him or—as Bertrand put it—"rebuilding his morale." But they saw no more, for the two went out in that fashion: the one taciturn; the other gentle and filial.

The room remained empty, its casement open to the fine weather.

Charles raised the binoculars to his eyes, not without vivacity. He rotated the focusing-knob nervously.

"Fieschi!" he said. "With his mistress, Nina Lassave."

There were several similar instruments there, for all eventualities had been anticipated. Each of his companions picked one up.

In the distance, at the window on the third story of the red house, beneath the raised Venetian blind, a small, thin, bony and feverish individual was chatting with a much younger woman, modestly dressed in a drab dress. As he spoke, Fieschi gesticulated in an Italian manner; his black eyes gleamed within his dull complexion. He wore short side-whiskers. The windows framing the two of them had no supportive frame. They were gazing at the boulevard animatedly, leaning their hands directly on the stony rim.

Charles appointed himself the guide to this living Musée Grévin.[22]

---

[22] The Musée Grévin at 10 Boulevard Montmarte, founded in 1882 and named after its first artistic director, Alfred Grévin, is a wax museum—the Parisian equivalent of London's Madame Tussaud's.

"Fieschi has been renting that little apartment since March, under the name of Gérard, a mechanic. The house seemed to him favorable for the crime he intends to commit. Morey, his accomplice, selected it with him, but only came back to it on the eve of the assassination attempt, to load the 24 rifle-barrels of the infernal machine. Nina Lassave doesn't live with her lover; she's employed at the Saltpêtrière. Look— she's one-eyed; her left eye is closed and she lacks three fingers. She's a poor creature, whose childhood was abominably unhealthy."

"But charming, all the same," said Colomba. "The fresh face, the lovely hair, the rounded and flexible figure...."

"A grisette—a poor honest young woman who tried to commit suicide after Fieschi's crime."

"How marvelous and how horrible!" Colomba went on. "Look at the head on that terrible individual's shoulders, which will fall under the blade of the guillotine!"

"The camera!" said Bertrand! "We're forgetting it. This is what it's for, though. Filming that couple, so sadly celebrated!" He lowered his binoculars. "Look!" he exclaimed. "While we were watching Fieschi, someone has come into César's study. There's a man there!"

They all abandoned Fieschi and Nina in favor of the newcomer.

Charles had started the camera.

The man who had just come into sight, leaving the ante-chamber door ajar behind him, approached the mantelpiece like a thief. He held a key in his left hand, with which he had presumably released the lock on the door to the landing. Dressed without any luxury in a kind of black frock-coat, with his high white collar secured by a black cravat, coiffed in a heavy beaver hat in the form of a tube with a rounded top, he was hurrying furtively, giving an impression of mystery.

Who was he? A clandestine visitor, for sure, who had introduced himself into César's home in order to carry out some illicit task. That was obvious. His circumspect manner, the uncertain fashion in which he placed his muffled shoes on the

Savonnerie carpet, the jerky gait enforced by those careful steps—which he surely wanted to stifle in order not to be heard by the neighbors below—and the way in which he raised his shoulders by tightening his elbows, were all suggestive of intrusion, conspiracy, felonious enterprise, a preliminary lying-in-wait behind one of the trees on the boulevard or in a corner of the staircase, on the lookout for César and Henriette going out.

Was it Fabius? No. This man—whose face was now hidden by his shoulders, since they had missed his entrance—was surely much younger than Fabius Ortofieri. He put out his hand to the bust of Napoléon, and tilted it. It was difficult to see what he was doing. It was done rapidly. He turned round and proceeded to go back the way he had come.

They could see his face easily now.

"What!" said Luc de Certeuil. "Here's a fellow from another age who resembles you in a surprising manner. Have you, by chance, already lived in 1835?" He was talking to Bertrand Valois.

The latter did not know what to say. He had gone pale, struck by an inexpressible amazement. Colomba and Charles, holding their breath, strove to understand…

The furtive man was Bertrand's double. He was the same age; he had the same spirited face, the same rare and inestimable news, the same coppery blond hair. If he had been cheerful and light-hearted, instead of being beset by so much mysterious preoccupation, one would indeed have thought that Bertrand Valois, in costume, was playing a part in the luminite plate. The unknown man resembled him like a brother—*or a grandfather*.

Colomba had grabbed her fiancé's wrist and squeezed it convulsively.

The camera, still turning, hummed softly.

Luc studied the young playwright ironically. And the other three remained silent, nervously, secretly anguished— for the man of 1835, who had introduced himself into César's home in his absence, like a criminal, a month before his murder, was now displaying the right-hand side of his body. And on that side, clenched under his arm against his body, was a long rattan cane terminated by a silver pommel, exactly like the one that Bertrand Valois had inherited from his unknown ancestors: *too exactly similar to be any other cane but that one.*

XIII. The Man with the Cane

"That's an amusing coincidence!" said Bertrand, for Luc de Certeuil's benefit.

The latter had not failed to notice the shock that had just affected the young dramatist, his fiancée and his future brother-in-law so violently, but, completely ignorant of Bertrand Valois' origins, as well as the cane and the ring, he attributed their emotion to an unpleasant surprise, solely caused by the resemblance between Bertrand and the unknown man.

Now they were laughing, and Luc thought that they were right. *Isn't it natural that, in the course of the ages, many people should resemble one another? Resemble one another even more than Bertrand resembles the man of 1835? And aren't we all certain to have had numerous doubles, since the advent of humankind?* Thus thought Luc de Certeuil. He would not have reasoned in that fashion had he known that the cane—the cane he had just seen under the arm of the enigmatic man—gave a certain dramatic significance to Bernard's resemblance to that man.

In any case, Luc de Certeuil had more personal cares, and he cheered up along with the other three, feeling the need to do so even more than them. Like them, but for another reason that was not unknown to them, Luc feigned an amiable indifference.

How could he not have been slightly anxious? The appearance of the man with the cane threw an unexpected element into the matter of César's murder, and there had been no indication thus far of any connection between that element and Fabius Ortofieri—and that was not at all to Luc de Certeuil's liking. For him, for his success, it was necessary that Rita's ancestor had murdered Charles's ancestor. To see something, however trivial, that diminished his chances was an inconvenience that left him thoughtful behind his smile.

193

The study door had closed again softly. The stranger had disappeared. In César's home there was, once again, an emptiness and a relative silence that was easily imaginable, to which the rolling of carriages on the pavement below made a continual background, pierced by the shrill calls of the birds in the aviary.

Fieschi and Nina had left their window, over which the soon-to-be-historic blind had been lowered against the Sun.

Charles Christiani stopped the electrical movement of the camera. It ceased humming. Silence was also established in the present, more completely than in the past.

Half an hour went by, long for everyone. Everyone was ruminating painful thoughts. Luc's presence was no more agreeable now than at the outset; to Charles, it continued to be perfectly odious. We know what Luc, for his part, was thinking about; we can guess what Bertrand and Colomba were thinking about.

Madame Christiani's ideas were, in fact, familiar to them. Never, while she was alive, would a descendant of César's murderer enter the Christiani family. And now, by an unexpected caprice of fate, Bertrand Valois was threatened with the possibility of being that murderer's descendant! For one could not doubt for a moment that he was descended from the man with the cane; the luminite had recovered that ancestor.

What name the ancestor in question bore, they might perhaps have great difficulty finding out—it was possible that the luminite would remain mute on that question—but what was certain was that the damned substance would soon reveal whether the man with the cane had killed César. It would reveal it in the presence of Madame Christiani, who could not fail, with her piercing gaze and penetrating intelligence, to identify the ancestor of her future son-in-law.

If such a catastrophe were to occur, Bertrand's marriage would become impossible.

So, as soon as Luc de Certeuil had withdrawn, weary of seeing nothing more and finally embarrassed by the very embarrassment that had provoked his presence, the engaged couple, sensing that they might no longer be engaged in a month's time, collapsed.

"What a tile!" said Bertrand. "An entire roof!"[23]

"It's frightful! Frightful!" Colomba repeated.

"Oh, these ancestors!" said Charles. "What did I tell you, my dear Bertrand?"

Colomba started weeping.

"Come on!" her brother resumed. "Don't get depressed yet. All is not lost—far from it! Nothing's proven. The mysterious operation carried out by that man…."

"My great-grandfather!" Bernard rectified, with an ironic smile and a quiver of his unparalleled nose, which had betrayed him as much as the cane with the silver handle.

"All right," said Charles. "As I was saying: his mysterious handiwork doesn't tell us anything definite." And as his anxious sister's sobs redoubled, he added, softly: "Calm down, Colomba. Come on, there's no doubt about it—the murderer is Fabius!"

"But I don't want it to be Fabius either!" cried Colomba, weeping all the harder, like a little girl. "I want you to marry the person you love, so that you can be happy too! Oh, Charles, Charles, how I understand you now! A thousand times better than before! And yet, you know…I understood you before…"

The poor girl hiccupped. Charles embraced her tenderly.

"It's not definite that either of the two marriages will be wrecked," Bertrand observed. "Perhaps, after all, the murderer is neither Fabius nor my anonymous grandfather."

"Alas," said Colomba, as uncontrollable tremors shook her head and shoulders and her arms shivered," that man had a key to the apartment; he could get into César's home whenever he pleased."

---

[23] In French, *tuile* [tile] is used metaphorically to mean a stroke of misfortune. The pun is untranslatable.

"Don't excite yourself with suppositions," Bertrand begged. "Confidence! Patience! And tranquility! Why shouldn't the best surprises still be in store for us? See here, my dear Colomba, imagine this: that no one killed César."

"You're trying to amuse me to stop me crying. No one! You're joking!"

Bertrand examined the plate of luminite, taking an inventory with his eyes of everything that the now-vanished study contained: the furniture presently distributed in several locations; the objects now dispersed or destroyed. The calm of deserted rooms was still there, along with the external movement of passers-by and flying shadows cast from the drawing-room, amid which one could suddenly discern the leaping shadows of monkeys which were presumably quarrelling.

"Has anyone ever considered suicide?" asked Bertrand, making an abrupt about-turn without much regard for the plate's safety.

"The hypothesis was raised by Fabius's lawyer, but it was unsupported by any evidence, moral or material. César had no reason to kill himself..."

"Does one ever know?"

"And then there's the weapon—the pistol. What became of it, since he was killed instantly?"

"The open window, the trees...a branch retaining an object thrown through the window..."

"Killed instantly, I tell you, facing the entrance door...."

"Facing the door of the antechamber *or the drawing-room door*. Look, they're side by side, in the corner."

Colomba wiped her eyes and sighed.

"Better?" Charles asked her.

"Yes," she murmured, with a pretty smile.

"That's all I wanted," Bertrand admitted.

"How good you are, Bertrand," she said, "And how I love you!" Without letting go of Charles's hand she was about to lean gently upon her fiancé's breast when the latter stopped her.

"Look out! Here's César and his ward coming back in."

196

That announcement brought them back in front of the plate, observing, taking good care not to interpose themselves between it and the "photographic" equipment—not merely the camera, but also the other luminite plate, which was comparable to a natural and permanent camera.

Henriette Delille only stayed in her guardian's study briefly. She was carrying some little packages, encouraging the supposition that she had just been out shopping with César. The latter, seemingly distracted, gave her his tall straw hat and a green umbrella that he had in his hand, and the young woman, after having stood the umbrella in a corner and put the hat on a peg fixed on the door, went out via the drawing-room to attend to her household duties.

As soon as she had disappeared, César's features, without losing their somber and sullen expression, were animated by an excitement that he had obviously contained in Henriette's presence. They saw him take up a stance in the corner of the room, next to the two doors, visibly listening to see whether his ward really had gone away. Then he closed and locked both doors, and promptly headed for the plate of luminite—which, as we recall, was then suspended above the roll-top desk.

The plate was undoubtedly the object of his movement. He looked at it while he approached it rapidly.

Colomba, governed by her nerves, instinctively stepped backwards. César, of course, seemed to be looking at them rather than the plate. It was toward them that he seemed to be advancing so resolutely, his face set hard and his eyes gleaming. The illusion was impressive. One might have thought, in fact, that the old man was about to emerge from the frame and suddenly find himself in the midst of his great-grandchildren. They forgot that he was only an image transported by the eternal light: the image of a body that had turned to dust a long time ago; an image rigorously analogous to those of stars that were extinguished centuries ago, the light of which nevertheless reaches us because it has taken many centuries to reach our planet.

197

César took down the plate and grabbed a stiletto. The optical effects that we have previously described were replicated. The worker's fingers, or their shadow, moved along the edge of the luminite that he was about to split.

Ten minutes later, the plate had resumed its secret observation-post on the wall—and César, without any hesitation, marched to the mantelpiece, going around the circular table. They understood that he had witnessed for himself, retrospectively, the whole scene of the man with the cane, and knew what that individual had done in his home while he was not there.

In his turn, he lifted up the bust of Napoléon, took out a folded piece of paper that he found underneath it, quickly put on his horn-rimmed spectacles and went to the window in order to see it more clearly. There, his hands trembling and his face anxious, furrowing his bushy eyebrows, he read the note.

A few moments before, Charles had started the cinematographic apparatus again. Then he made use of his binoculars to attempt to read the text of the note, but he was frustrated, César having positioned himself facing him and no writing being visible on the reverse side of the sheet of paper.

As he read, a terrible rage took possession of the old man. He crumpled up the missive angrily, making a ball that he stuck into his pocket, and started walking around the table like a wild beast in a cage. As he went, passing close to the doors he turned the keys, opened the drawing-room door, which had not been closed before, and resumed his furious circling.

"What does all that signify?" Bertrand asked.

The man with the cane was either acting on his own behalf or for someone else," Charles reasoned. "Is he someone's messenger? In that case, why hesitate to believe that he works for Fabius Ortofieri?"

Bertrand took out his watch and got to his feet. "Don't go now, I beg you," said Charles. "Stay a while longer."

"Yes, stay!" begged Colomba, in an anxious tone.

He sat down without saying a word. He was expected at the Variétés for a rehearsal—but what about Colomba! What would he not have missed, for love of Colomba? Especially now.

He did well to stay. As Charles had anticipated, what followed was worth taking the trouble to see.

César was still circling, frantically. He suddenly stopped and reflected. He had had an idea and was plotting something. He nodded his head in approval. His decision was made. It was lucky that he was a southerner, for, even when he was alone, he was unsparing with his gestures, and his mime was expressive. However meagerly his thoughts were translated, it was much more than a man of the north would have allowed to appear in the same circumstances.

He picked up his umbrella and his hat, and hid them in his desk, lowering the rosewood roll-top in order to do so. Then he opened the door to the antechamber violently, went out, stamping hard on the floor-tiles and slammed the door— but reappeared almost immediately, closing the door carefully *without making any sound.*

Obviously he had just simulated a departure, and it was a good bet that he had also slammed the entrance door on the other side of the antechamber.

Quickly, he ran to one of the curtains at the window, and hid himself behind the green and blue flower-patterned cloth. There he was invisible.

He did not have to wait for long.

A shadow passes along the drawing-room wall, a color shows in the mirror—and the pretty Henriette appears on the threshold, leaning forward slightly, with one hand on the door-frame, her gaze anxious and interrogative.

Where does that gaze settle first?

The coat-peg. The straw hat is no longer there.

The corner where the umbrella had been placed. It is empty.

Lightly and swiftly, with her ears pricked, Henriette launches herself toward the bust of Napoléon and lifts it

199

up…then lifts it further, searches for something that she does not find, then, annoyed and disappointed, moves the objects surrounding the bust—in vain…

Ah! One would have sworn that she has cried out in alarm!

César is there, before her, having emerged from behind his curtain. He stands up straight, very pale, intimidating and authoritarian—and he is holding in his hand the uncrumpled note, which his other hand is striking furiously. He is speaking. What is he saying?

What he is saying, the facts have announced, and his pantomime does not give the lie to their prediction. "Ah! Ah, my beauty! You've just looked under that bust for a note that someone had come, during our absence, to deposit there for you! Well, it's me who has discovered your note! Look! Here it is, your note! A fine thing! So, Mademoiselle permits herself to enter into a relationship with a gentleman who comes into my house without my knowledge, who violates my home! You tolerate that: that a man should slip under my roof, thanks to your connivance, to hide a message here, in a place agreed between you!"

It would have been reckless to make César's gestures and expression say any more than that. Did he know the man with the cane? Had he already forbidden Henriette to see him and correspond with him? Did he mention the key and reproach his ward for having given it to an undesirable womanizer? Did he, in fact, consider the author of the note to be a womanizer? Did he list, in that case, all the reasons that led him to send him away? In relation to these various hypotheses, they could only speculate.

But César's fury did not abate. He thundered. He fulminated…

"He's in pain," said Bernard.

"I believe so," Charles confirmed.

The old corsair, standing as tall as his short stature permitted, solidly planted on his stocky legs, recovered the vigor and fire of his youth—and the unfortunate Henriette, submissive and prostrate, leaning on the mantelpiece in a despairing attitude, weathered the storm without trying to justify herself. From time to time, she raised her head fearfully, extending her hand in supplication—but the sight of the furious man robbed her of all courage, and she fell back limply.

"Poor girl!" said the kindly Colomba. "Oh, my God, what will he do? I wish it were all over!"

César, at the peak of his fury, had seized his ward's wrists and was shaking her cruelly, while hurling unknown insults in her face. She let herself fall to her knees, inert, offering no resistance to the rude shaking that was brutalizing her young body, so supple and graceful.

Finally, the irascible old fool shoved her away with one last violent thrust—and while she remained at his feet, in a state of collapse, but without any tears and showing no sign of repentance, he spoke to her like a master demanding that his orders are obeyed.

She got to her feet painfully, as if the divine lightness of her 18 years had suddenly become heavy. She stood up, pensive and mournful, facing her guardian, who was now looking at her silently, with a somber expression. Henriette's face was fully illuminated. Her lifeless eyes were staring into empty space. Mechanically, her fingers played with the cloth of her little apron.

César, apparently calm, his features contracted but no longer exhibiting any vehemence, resumed speaking in a different tone, betrayed by the shrugging of his shoulders, full of ponderous reprobation. Soothed, having given free rein to his fit of wrath, he devoted himself to a remonstrance tinged with sentiment. He was doubtless talking about wisdom and morality; he was appealing to the young woman's rationality and sensibility. Finally, standing directly in front of her, taking hold of her arms beneath the shoulder, amid the amplitude of her flared sleeves, he looked very paternally into the beautiful absent eyes, which were riveted elsewhere—and flash of anguish passed back and forth across his serious face as he slowly articulated a sentence that could only be an interrogation.

Henriette did not flinch. Nothing was visible in her but sadness and softness, resolution and perseverance. She replied simply by slowly shaking her head several times from right to left. Her decision was irrevocable.

Then César let her go, as if discouraged, took two steps back and, very coldly, without anger, with a firmness tempered with regret, pronounced a few words. His attitude signified: "Since that's the way it is…"

The young woman listened to him, rigid in her courageous sadness. With a wan, heart-broken smile, she said "yes" in such a way that she seemed to be yielding to an evil destiny rather than responding silently to an order. She did not withdraw until a word from César, accompanied by a disillusioned gesture, set her at liberty.

Left alone, César went to the window, leaned his forehead on one of the panes and did not move. He remained motionless for long minutes, his hands thoughtfully set behind his back. Abruptly, he turned round, lifted his head, shook himself, put his hands to his temples, and fluttered his eyelids, as if suffocated by the situation in which he unexpectedly found himself. *Come on!* he seemed to be thinking. *It's impossible! Me! Have I come to this? Get a grip, damn it!*

Suddenly, he let himself fall into an armchair, hiding his face in his trembling hands.

Dusk fell in the vision.

To satisfy the domestic requirements of Madame Christiani, Charles did not think it appropriate to delay dinner, of which Bertrand Valois partook.

When they returned to the studio, where the last glimmers of the October twilight had been extinguished for some time, the luminite plate was still emitting a feeble light.

The beautiful evening of June 30, 1835, one of the longest of the year, filled the image of César Christiani's study with its dying light. A few windows on the far side of the boulevard were lit up by mediocre yellow fire. A lantern suspended its miserable illumination over the boulevard itself.

The roofs and chimneys were bathed by the last redness of the dusk.

Old César was still there, huddled up in the shadows.

"Anything new?" asked Bertrand Valois, who did not attempt to hide his anxiety and the keen interest that he now took in the revelations of the luminite.

It was the day after César's anger and despair, early in the afternoon. Charles was in the studio.

"Just that your grandfather, in the form of the young man who has your nose and your cane, has 'got it in the neck' this morning, if I might express it thus," he told him.

"He's come back, then?"

"Yes. In my opinion, he was invited by César. I had the idea yesterday, at the conclusion of that heart-rending scene, that Henriette had received an order to invite her lover to come and explain himself to César as soon as possible—and he deferred to that imperative invitation immediately."

"What happened?"

"You'll see it on the cinema screen when the film is developed and shown. I turned the camera during the conversation, which was tempestuous. Or would you prefer that we separate the leaves of the second plate that recorded it immediately?"

"Bah! Tell me what happened first. Let's not complicate things. But tell me, did you get the impression that the interview augments the evidence accusing my ancestor?"

"That supposed ancestor might only be your great-uncle. Perhaps the man with the cane has a sister who resembles him, and it's her from whom you're descended…and everything's all right!"

"I've already thought of that. So long as no supplementary proof comes along to confirm my apprehensions, a feeble hope remains. I've also told myself that your mother might not perceive that accursed resemblance…"

"That's doubtful," said Charles, in an ambiguous tone.

"However," Bertrand objected, "suppose that, even if César was killed by the man with the cane, and Madame Christiani is fated to witness the murder via retrovision, the murderer *doesn't have his cane with him* on that day."

"Well?"

"Well, your mother won't be aware of one of the principal reasons for our believing that that man is my ancestor! For—let's be sincere between the two of us, and not nurse any false hopes—that is what we believe, and nothing else. It's 99% certain that I'm that I'm the grandson, not the great-nephew of the man with the cane!"

Charles looked glum. "All right," he said. "Let's suppose that my mother remains uncertain. Let's even suppose that she doesn't suspect anything at all—which is highly unlikely. What then?"

"Then we're saved, of course! Not only will you marry Mademoiselle Rita Ortofieri, since her grandfather will be innocent, but nothing will stand in the way of Colomba being my wife, since your mother won't know, according to this hypothesis, that my grandfather is guilty!"

Charles's silence and his disconcerting gaze gave rise to a certain anxiety in Bertrand's mind, and immediately reminded him that Madame Christiani was not the only member of the family who placed a fanatical respect for tradition and the grim memory of offences above all other considerations.

"That's true," he said. "*You too!*"

After that, there was an extremely heavy silence. Then Bertrand extended his hand and said: "I beg your pardon." He did not attempt to argue or beg in order to appeal to Charles's intelligence and modify his traditional sentiments. He knew full well that such sentiments are unshakable and that, although they seem extreme to those who do not share them, those who experience them, passed down from father to son for generations, hold them to be the very foundations of duty and bases of morality.

"Let's set hypotheses aside," said Charles. "*Ifs* won't get us anywhere. Let's stick to presumptions, which are a little less vain. You asked me just now whether the meeting be-tween César and the man with the cane reinforces the charges laid against him. I can give you a clear answer: yes."

"Ah!" said Bertrand, with a brief contraction of his entire face.

"The study clock marked 9 a.m.," Charles said. "9 a.m. on July 1, 1835—28 days from the murder. It was on that day, in close proximity to the crime, that César and our unknown man found themselves face to face, in the course of a conver-sation of rare violence. And when I say 'conversation,' it's a manner of speaking. César didn't allow his visitor much op-portunity to reply to his invective.

"He was sitting slantwise, writing on the tabletop of his roll-top desk—exactly as you see him at this moment, in fact."

Bertrand was, as always, gazing at the plate, unable to take his eyes off it; the extraordinary spectacle imposed itself on everyone's attention with incredible force.

"The door to the antechamber was open," Charles con-tinued. "Henriette Delille had shown the young man in and retired immediately. She was a sad sight: her pallor, her drawn features and her wretched expression would have wrung the hardest of hearts—but César would not even look at her. Per-haps he simply feared the sight of her grief, and felt that he was too likely to weaken. He pivoted in his armchair and looked the newcomer up and down. The other was standing before him, at a respectful distance, with his hat in his hand and his cane under his arm. He certainly didn't look too rosy either; his cheeks were bloodless, his nose was pinched…"

"To the extent that a nose like ours can be pinched!" said Bertrand Valois, with a mocking grimace.

"He was smiling, though," Charles went on, "and trying to put on a brave face. César looked at him for a few seconds—which the man found longer than others. Finally, there was a tirade such as you can imagine, of whose gist César's mime was able to give me some idea: the old man, still seated, vituperating and abusing, pale at first, then red-faced, gripping the arm of the chair and the edge of the desk, going mad, going to close the window to deaden his vocal outbursts, and standing up, firm, going from extreme to the other; the young man pale, letting the avalanche pass over him, phlegmatic at first, then playing negligently with his cane, while the old man, standing in front of him, with his hands in his pockets and his head in his shoulders, threatened him with I don't know what, as if he were a domestic.

"It seemed certain to me that César was demanding the key with the aid of which he had got into the apartment the day before. What followed convinced me. The unknown took the key from his inside pocket and held it out to the terrible old man, who grabbed it rudely and showed him the door.

"That significant gesture did not have the effect that he expected. The other didn't budge. César moved forward, menacingly. The man with the cane, in total control of himself, raised his hand placidly and was finally able to say a few words—in a very dignified and gentle manner, imprinted nevertheless with considerable energy.

"His little harangue appeared to make César pause for thought. He made no reply, and remained for some while in the pose of a man studying a problem, or examining a proposition...

"He came to a decision, opened the door, and called out, Henriette responded to his call.

"At that moment, it wasn't difficult to understand how much the young woman and her congenial accomplice loved one another. Their gazes told me.

"The scene was dramatic. I don't think I'm mistaken in saying that César had summoned Henriette, at the unknown's request, so that he might say goodbye to her. What I hadn't grasped until then is that the young man had not renounced the woman he loved in any sense—inasmuch as it seems to me that he bowed to the sovereign will of a guardian, but only for the period during which that will still had the right of exercise. Indeed, as soon as Henriette was beside him, he did something that César had certainly not anticipated, and which will also surprise you unpleasantly, Bertrand..."

"Me?"

"Yes, you. And it isn't without due reflection that I've decided to tell you everything—but if I didn't tell you now, you'd deduce it tomorrow when you see…"

"Oh, don't procrastinate!" cried Bertrand. "Don't hide anything from me!"

"You'll guess it when you see, on Henriette's finger, the black enamel ring that Colomba has been wearing since your engagement!"

"My ring!"

"Yes, your ring, my poor old fellow—the superabundant proof of what you dread so much!"

"But just now, you still seemed to doubt yourself…"

"I allowed myself to delude you…"

"Oh!" said Bertrand, unhesitating in his reproach. "But now, now, it's absolutely necessary that that man has nothing to do with the murder! That man is my ancestor—there's no longer any doubt about it! It's impossible that he killed César!"

"Nothing's proven yet," said Charles. "But everything is looking bad for the man with the cane."

"Oh—yes, that's true, you told me that the evidence is accumulating against him. How?"

"I told you that Henriette had come into César's study. Immediately, the unknown took her by the hand and, before the eyes of the old man—who seemed confounded by such audacity—he began to speak to her tenderly and solemnly. The ring was in his waistcoat pocket; he took it out and put it on the young woman's finger; she was both happy and frightened, on the point of fainting!"

"But what about César?"

"César, unfortunately, could not contain himself. I repeat that he certainly had not anticipated this passionate betrothal, celebrated against his will before his very eyes. He lost his temper again. The scene was frightful. A kind of cudgel was included among all the primitive weapons—look, the one you can see there, in the display, where César has since replaced it.

He took hold of that bludgeon and brandished it over the man's head, proffering insults that I regret not having heard.

"It was in that fashion that he threw him out, chasing him away under the threat of his stick."

"I'd like to think that the other didn't lack dignity!"

"No," said Charles, smiling in spite of himself. "He retreated very honorably, backwards, his cane still maintained under his arm, as if old César were already no more than an imponderable image. He addressed a glance charged with all his affection to Henriette—and she, half-dead, holding his black ring to her lips, watched him depart, pushed by that comedy guardian, and sent him that long kiss."

"It's pure Beaumarchais![24] In pantomime!"

"It's real life, alas! It's pain for three individuals—or, rather, it *was*. They're no longer suffering today."

"Today it's us—because of them. Here's an entire drama that no one has ever suspected."

"No one. History is made thus. We don't know the half of it."

"In conclusion," Bertrand said, "less than a month before his death, César made himself a mortal enemy—and that enemy was my ancestor."

"He no longer had the key..." Charles objected, obligingly.

"That's a detail, for such a shrewd fellow."

"Shrewd? What do you mean by that?"

"I think it very shrewd, on his part, to have hidden the note under the bust of Napoléon, in César's own study. He could have put it in a thousand places more easily accessible to the young woman—in her room, for example. At first glance, that seems simpler, more rational—but the old corsair might have discovered it there by prying. Would he ever have

---

[24] Pierre-Augustin Caron de Beaumarchais (1732-1799), the statesman and hobbyist playwright, best known as the author of the original versions of *The Barber of Seville* and *The Marriage of Figaro*.

had the idea of searching his own study if the luminite had not tipped him off on the sly?"

"But what if the idea was Henriette's, and not his?"

"It's all the same to me," said Bertrand, wrinkling his nose. "It's all the same to me."

"Because?"

"Because Henriette is my grandmother, of course! There's no doubt that she became the wife of the man with the cane…and the ring."

"Comtesse or Marquise!" Charles confirmed, laughing.

"Of course!" said Bertrand. "The man with the cane is an aristocrat—that's obvious. I've always said so! And a nobleman doesn't murder people!"

"God willing, my dear Bertrand! I hope so, for your sake, with all my heart!"

Was the guilty party the man with the cane, though? Was it Fabius Ortofieri? Would the luminite give the lie to History? Or was it someone else? Or, as had been suggested, no one at all?

XIV. The Great Day of the Prodigious Spectacle

We shall not think of detailing here the 16 days that preceded the moving and tragic retrovision of July 28, 1835 — which is to say, *in reality*, the period that extended from the October 30 to November 15, 1929.

In the Rue de Tournon, Charles and his friends had a very busy fortnight, a phase of preparations and continuous observation, which lent the circumstances an extraordinary interest. There was not a minute that did not contain a significant dose of attraction, due to the marvelous properties of luminite, the spectacle of the past that it restored, the formidable scenes of which the surprising vision was awaited on the appointed day, all the mysteries that would then be clarified, and the fortunes and misfortunes that would result therefrom.

During that interval, however, the surveillance of the famous plate did not give rise to general conclusions that made any essential difference to what they knew already, whether on the subject of César Christiani or that of his neighbor, Joseph Fieschi.

During the period preceding his death, César's study was not the theater of any indicative scene. The life of the former corsair and his ward went by monotonously and joylessly; all that could be deduced from what was seen was that, according to appearances, Henriette did not often go out alone, but mostly accompanied by her guardian. The visits received by César Christiani produced nothing remarkable. Among the visitors Charles was able to recognize relatives of his thrice-great-grandfather: his grandson Napoléon, aged, it will be remembered, 21; Lucile Leboulard and her husband, his daughter and son-in-law; their son, Anselme Leboulard, a young man of 20 who would become the father of Cousin Drouet. There was nothing but affection and deference in their conduct; they were earnest individuals who showed César great respect and Henriette a smiling and familiar consideration.

Of Fabius Ortofieri there was not the slightest sign.

As for the man with the cane, he had disappeared.

So much for matters relating to César Christiani; his last days were uneventful, dull, exempt from all anxiety, merely saddened by his disagreement with Henriette.

As for Fieschi, the surveillance only produced secondary results—very precious, it is true, for History, but which were not of a nature to modify the annals of the assassination attempt, nor to give any preliminary indication regarding the mystery of César's murder. Fieschi's appearances at his window, or smoking his pipe on the doorstep with the concierge Pierre, and those of Nina Lassave—their daily comings and goings—only held a mediocre interest. It was much more exciting to check, at close range, the assertions of History: to see, for example, on the eve of the crime, the tinsmith Boireau pass along the boulevard on horseback, in order to permit Fieschi to take proper aim with the diabolical organ of the 24 rifle-barrels, which could just about be distinguished behind the Venetian blind with the aid of binoculars; to see, moving in the shadows between the slats of that blind, the form of the man who was already lamentably ambitious to be a regicide; and to perceive, in the dusk, the old and massive Morey emerge from the red house to climb into a cab, after having loaded the infernal machine with powder, bullets and grape-shot.

It was not Charles who made these observations. To avoid the regrettable consequences of dividing his attention, he had assigned himself the particular task of tracking César, with the collaboration of Bertrand and Colomba. He had left the Fieschi affair to the care of a highly reputable historian, Monsieur Colas-Dunormand—who, as everyone knows, is also a specialist in the study of the Restoration and the reign of Louis-Philippe. Colas-Dunormand, or one of his own collaborators, only left the studio late at night to return at dawn, and every time a notable event occurred concerning Fieschi, he never failed to inform Charles—who came running, or, if he was already there, became attentive.

211

There was, in the studio in the Rue de Tournon and Madame Christiani's apartment, a visible effervescence that only ceased during the night, to give place to a less intense observation—but which never relaxed. Luc de Certeuil took part in it with a reserve that, strictly speaking, was imperative, but which Charles, aware of the fact that it was not the man's nature to push himself, knew to be voluntary too.

Orders of the strictest sort stopped at the door of the apartment those curiosity-seekers whom the concierge had been unable to discourage. A few, though, could not be evicted; they were people too important to be forbidden access to the luminite and the spectacle of the prologue to Fieschi's assassination attempt and César's murder.

In the final days, although the four differently-aimed cameras had been disposed around the plate, there were a dozen powerfully-captivated intruders continually in the studio. Their eyes grew wide, at varying distances, in the name of science, art or journalism, before the image, supported on its easel, in which the sky of the summer of 1835 lit a room and a boulevard of yesteryear. Meanwhile, the five cinema cameras were continually in play and gentlemen armed with binoculars, notepads and pens were keeping constant surveillance, relentlessly scrutinizing the progress of event happening a century ago.

It was necessary, from time to time, to ask these visitors to leave, for they never tired of savoring such a novel representation with their eyes. Others replaced them—but as November 15 drew nearer, their affluence increased and their insistence increased proportionately. Formal provision became necessary. At the door to the building there was an inexorable police officer, while inside the apartment itself, auxiliaries made sure that no reporter who was not invited to the great session had hidden himself anywhere until the moment came.

Madame Christiani took charge of ensuring that other measures were taken with a view to keeping everything safe. "Pathways" of strong canvas marked out the route from the antechamber to the studio through the successive rooms that it

212

was necessary to pass, and that trajectory was stripped of all the trinkets that, by virtue of their smallness, their portability and their charm, might have induced temptation in collectors of pretty trifles. An ill-informed passer-by might have wondered whether some great marriage or great funeral was in preparation there.

In fact, that is what Charles, Bertrand and Colomba were wondering. What was in preparation? Their marriage or the burial of their hopes? They had no idea—none at all, on the eve of the very day on which everything would be made known. But they, at least, always had something to do to distract them from their anxiety. They were perpetually in contact with the instrument of the revelation, plunged into the seething activity that surrounded it, occupied with a thousand concerns—and Charles thought about Rita, distant from that focus of attraction, deprived of any distraction, as alone as one can possibly be, who was spending all the time she could at Geneviève Le Tourneur's house, in order to keep track of the counter-enquiry as best she could. Charles had, in fact, taken to telephoning Geneviève at regular intervals and informing her of the historian's communications, for transmission to Rita. He knew that Mademoiselle Ortofieri would spend the entire day of November 15 at her friend's house, and he shivered in advance at the thought of the telephone call that he would make to Madame Le Tourneur, shortly after 11 a.m.

It was, in fact, at midday that César had been killed on July 28, 1835, since Fieschi's simultaneous assassination attempt had occurred at that time—but they had observed a certain temporal dislocation between present time and the time that the luminite plate was then unfolding. For the moment, taking account of the modifications made since 1835 to official French time, the plate was about 60 minutes in advance of the sun of 1929. As on every day, therefore, the hands of César's clock would be standing at noon when the clocks of the Rue de Tournon and the church of Saint-Sulpice were chiming 11.

213

On the evening of November 14, Charles Christiani, almost sure that he had not forgotten anything, only regretted one thing. That was that his cousin Drouet was not well enough to come and sit in the old armchair that had been reserved for her in front of the luminite plate at the hour of the double tragedy. By force of argument and obstinacy, he had persuaded his mother to make a gesture to the old lady, reckoning that on such an occasion, in spite of any more-or-less gratuitous prohibition, the place of Cesar's great-granddaughter—the last and only representative of the younger branch—was in the midst of the other members of the family. After all, while he had never believed that Cousin Drouet had "behaved badly toward Mélanie," he had reminded himself that the ancestor's heir might still have relevant documents and that, in consequence, to show her the deference that combined justice and utility was a course as judicious as it was commendable.

Madame Christiani had yielded eventually, finally vanquished by the spirit of race and family, which she placed so high in the scale of virtuous sentiments, telling herself, in addition, that since she would be obliged to invite the cousin to Colomba's wedding, she might as well see her again right away. So, accompanied by her daughter, Madame Christiani had gone to the Rue Rivoli, where Madame Drouet had given them a charming reception. Unfortunately, age having partly crippled her, she had expressed, with a politeness that was entirely Old School, her regret at being unable to go to the Rue Tournon on the fifteenth of November. She only hoped that her pains would give her leave to attend the dear child's wedding, at least for the mass.

While awaiting that still-problematic wedding, Charles had to dispense with Cousin Drouet. Let us admit that she was, in any case, far from his thoughts when he got up, at three o'clock in the morning, on the day that was to be *the great day*.

Bertrand Valois had been on watch until then. "Nothing new," he said, on seeing Charles come into the studio.

It was pitch dark. A fine drizzle was pattering on the large bay window. In the plate, however, the closed shutters of César's study filtered a dawn light clear enough to permit the dial of the octagonal clock to be made out. It marked a few minutes past four.

"So," Charles murmured, "on César's last night, nothing abnormal occurred in the room where he was soon to be assassinated. Good."

Colas-Dunormand and his secretary arrived at that moment, at the same time as the cinema camera-operators. The day's principal workers were punctual; other people followed them almost immediately, Luc de Certeuil among them. Thanks to Madame Christiani, the household servants were up and about. The studio gradually filled up with the 38 guests—a strictly limited number—that Charles had invited for that early hour. He excused himself for cutting short the greetings.

Light chairs had been disposed in a semicircle. Scientists and various technicians were seated therein, instinctively conversing in hushed voices, huddled around the celebrated chemist who had analyzed a specimen of luminite—which was, he said, "a sort of silico-aluminate of potassium." They had brought binoculars, on their host's advice. All of them having come previously to take account of the properties of luminite, there was no further explanation to give them. They even knew what the shadowy figures were that were visible in one corner of the plate, which recalled in an indelible fashion the stratagem employed by César to disguise it as a writing-slate. More than one was equipped with photographic apparatus as well as his binoculars.

Needless to say, all the important spectators were primarily interested in Fieschi's assassination attempt, and, without making it manifest, relegated the obscure tragedy of César Christiani's murder to the second rank.

Someone asked for the studio ceiling-light to be put out, in order that the great dawn of July 28, 1835 could be even more clearly seen. Someone else proposed that Colas-Dunormand or Charles Christiani should make a brief com-

215

mentary on the first light of the day that would go down in History.

Charles excused himself, wishing to confine himself to the role of observer, but Colas-Dunormand obliged with a good grace, and began by regretting that the shutters of César's study were closed. "For if they were open," he said, "we would doubtless be able to see something of Fieschi. He got up at daybreak after a very bad night. He will go out at five o'clock, not quite knowing which way to turn, hesitantly. He will go to the home of one of his compatriots, named Sorba…"

He suddenly stopped speaking, and the audience gave voice to a brief rumor compounded from little exclamations.

César had come into his study through the drawing-room door. He crossed the room, went to the window, and opened it, along with the shutters. They saw the old man, clad in a dressing-gown and slippers, lean on the sill to look out into the boulevard.

It was the beginning of a splendid morning. A multitude of tricolor flags, at the windows of the houses opposite, received a light that was already bright, coming from the right. It was noticeable that their blue and red were more vivid than in our time.

The four rows of elms had fine thick foliage, which the awakening of the sparrows caused to quiver in places. Shops and restaurants were visible through the branches and the trunks, decorated with sheets of cloth in the national colors. Multicolored streamers hung from the street-lanterns.

The paved causeway extended between verdant borders, separated from the contraflow by large stone blocks set at regular intervals. Blinds were opening almost everywhere. The Parisians were early risers that day. New flags were added to the others, brightening the windows whose shutters had been closed for the night.

"Need I remind you," said Colas-Dunormand, "that the Three Glorious Days of July 1930 were the 27, the 28 and the 29? Each was commemorated in its own way, and the festivals

216

of 1835 confirmed to that custom. Today is the 28; yesterday, the 27, was the festival commemorating the dead; several funereal ceremonies have been celebrated, not only in honor of the combatants killed in 1830, but the victims of the riots of 1832 and 1834; that's why you can already see so many flags—they've been there since yesterday.

"Today is no longer the day of *Requiem*; it's that of *Te Deum* and military solemnity: a great review of the National Guards of the Parisian region and the troops of the garrison. Tomorrow is to be the day of popular rejoicing, celebratory salvoes and jousting competitions, free theatrical performances, greasy poles, balls, street-lights, fireworks, the illumination of public monuments—but none of that will take place. Following the assassination attempt that you will soon witness, the festivities will come to an abrupt halt."

César left the window and went into the extraordinary "drawing-room" that was an aviary and a menagerie of monkeys. The play of the light permitted the belief that he had opened its window. A certain time went by, during which, via reflections in the mirror and the movements of shadows, it was deducible that he was occupied in taking care of his animals. That was, in any case, his habit; the observation of previous days had established that.

During this time, Colas-Dunormand watched the main door of number 50, surmounted by a placard bearing the name Paul. He hoped to see Fieschi going out, carrying the trunk that would subsequently be recovered, and which would doom him and his accomplices irredeemably—but that was not due to happen until later.

The animation in the Boulevard du Temple increased progressively. The carts of the market-gardeners were succeeded by urban carriages, tilburys and immense multi-stage fiacres furnished with steps. Little by little, the number of pedestrians in their Sunday best was augmented, some of them already sporting red carnations in their buttonholes, the recognition sign of members of secret societies. At 7 a.m., two National Guard drummers passed by, beating the call to order on

217

their drums. A gang of street-urchins followed them and flanked them, marching in step. From upstairs windows, several people waved to the drummers as they passed by, swaying rhythmically as the blue backs of their uniforms, striped with large white sashes, faded into the distance. Then the increasingly-numerous pedestrians mingled with the uniformed National Guardsmen who were hurrying to their legion's rallying-point, weapons in hand.

Henriette Delille brought César a little soup-dish, a bowl and a ladle on a tray. The former corsair ate his breakfast on the marble-topped table, and then disappeared, leaving his ward to sweep and tidy up the study, aided by a chambermaid.

At 9 a.m., the troops, raising a formidable cloud of dust, began to go by, heading for the positions that had been assigned to them for the parade. From then on, they saw the balconies fill up with spectators; the windows became crowded, and even the roofs were transformed into grandstands for the use of bold individuals gathered around the chimneys.

Fieschi came out then, with his trunk, in search of a porter. It was not without emotion that Colas-Dunormand pointed him out to the curiosity of the assembly. He was only visible momentarily, although he helped the porter, Meunier, to lift the package on to his hook.

The historian rapidly summarized the odyssey of that trunk, which the police ended up finding in the home of Nina Lassave, who was discovered at the moment when she had resolved to commit suicide.

Afterwards, the physiognomy of the boulevard was unmodified for quite a long time. The fifth legion of the National Guard took up position along the edge of the causeway, under the trees, in two ranks, their backs turned to the contraflow. Soon, on a command visibly pronounced by Lieutenant-Colonel Ladvocat, their arms were lowered and the men, at ease, gathered in the shade. Facing them, the soldiers of the fourteenth line regiment followed suit.

César Christiani reappeared at 10 a.m. He had got dressed and was wearing his brown jacket and grey trousers, the costume in which the painter Lami had depicted him 24 hours later, lying on the Savonnerie carpet. He had undoubtedly finished his breakfast in the dining-room, for his complexion was highly-colored, he was licking his lips and he lit his pipe in a certain fashion that indicated—although it is difficult to say how—that the smoker had just left the table. He had the parrot Pitt on his shoulder, with which he was amusing himself, and he made the monkey Coburg perform a few pirouettes.

The old man seemed more cheerful. His face cleared immediately when two genteel young women came in, ahead of Henriette. All three of them had simple brightly-colored dresses, large-brimmed hats whose ribbons were knotted under their chins, light shawls retained at the neck, and slender umbrellas whose taffeta was cut into lacy festoons.

"Ah!" said Charles. "There's Henriette, about to leave with her friends to watch the review in the Champs-Elysées!"

César displayed an extreme amiability with respect to his ward's companions; he embraced the latter very paternally. She seemed quite delighted with the little pleasure-trip that he had granted her, and accepted César's instructions without impatience.

The old man had put Coburg away. When the charming trio had departed, he set Pitt on a perch, with a small chain on his leg, on which the bird waddled to and fro. Then, extending the tubes of a marine telescope, he amused himself by watching the thickening crowd outside and the battalions that could be imagined lined up along either side of the boulevard, as far as the eye could see.

All this preamble to an imposing Parisian review required a majestic and peaceful brouhaha. Nothing, so far as could be seen, betrayed the fever and anxiety that—we are told—was vaguely present because the rumor that there might be an assassination attempt had been spreading for several days. For Madame Christiani's guests alone—who were there as if in a theater, or rather a cinema—the sinister scarlet-painted house took on an abject, hypocritical and treasonous

219

expression. The ambush was hidden there, in the third story, behind the Venetian blind. They felt ill by virtue of being unable to cry out to the people and the troopers: "It's up there that everything's prepared: 24 rifle-barrels on a framework. Warn those handsome *sergents de ville* who are ambling around in their blue coats and white trousers, with sheathed swords and cocked hats over their eyes. Tell them to go up…"

Grey smoke was escaping very abundantly from a chimney-stack on the roof of the red house.

"Fieschi's just lit the fire," averred Colas-Dunormand. "He must, therefore, have come back."

"And it won't be long before he goes out again," Charles added.

"What fire?" someone asked. "A fire, in this summer heat?"

"So that he has a brand within arm's reach," said Charles, "with which to set light to the trail of powder poured out in advance, leading to the rifle-barrels through the holes they've pierced in the 'thunderclap,' which are known as 'lights.' "

All the evidence, as usual, indicated that old César had not the slightest interest in Fieschi's house. The idea occurred to him of fitting his telescope to an improvised tripod, and he placidly set about securing the optical instrument to the wooden guttering with leather straps.

"There's a man who isn't expecting to be murdered," remarked Colas-Dunormand.

His words fell into the relative silence that the purr of cameras permitted to reign, for at least one of them was functioning incessantly, and most of the time, under Charles's orders each of the five instruments was recording the resplendent and terrible morning from a different angle.

As the morning advanced and they saw the hands of eight-leaved clock below the corsair's red guidon turning, an oppression tightened their chests. Colomba was as pale as candle-wax, wearied by having been up and about since 3 a.m. Bertrand and Luc were smiling too constantly for their expressions to be natural—but no one was untroubled by the deadly wait for the inevitable drama.

At 11:45 a.m., luminite time, the troops took up their weapons and lined up. The fateful moment was approaching.

Colomba, incapable of resisting the weakness that she felt invading her, had to withdraw. Her mother accompanied her but returned after a few minutes, to the great regret of Bertrand—who, in spite of everything, would have preferred the implacable Corsican to be absent.

In the plate, César, his pipe in his mouth, had pushed the widow aside and was meekly watching the spectacle.

Street-urchins climbed into the trees. The crowd became denser, massing together.

"I'm trying to locate Fieschi in the Café des Mille Colonnes," said Colas-Dunormand. "He's met up with Morey in the Rue des Fossés-du-Temple, who has reproached him for not still being at his post. In the Mille Colonnes, at this moment, he ought, by chance, to be facing Boireau, who is accompanying Martinault, the section-leader of the Societé des Droits de l'Homme…he'll only leave the café to race up the steps to his home at the moment when the drums start to beat in the distance. Then he'll hurriedly swallow a glass of brandy…ah! There's the movement of the troops that Maxime Du Camp describes in his book."[25]

Troops were, indeed moving off to the right. Others took their place.

"Now, Colas-Dunormand concluded, "it's the second battalion of the 8th legion that's in front of us…Colonel Rieussec, who will be killed. Watch."

---

[25] *Les Ancêtres de la Commune: l'attentat Fieschi* (1877) was a follow-up to Du Camp's successful book on the Commune, although his own memory of the event—he had only been 13 years old at the time—cannot have been much help. Du Camp is nowadays remembered primarily as a pioneer of photography, and as the "friend" who advised Gustave Flaubert to burn *Les Tentations de Saint-Antoine*.

It was 11:50 a.m.

A battery of drums from a regiment of the line took up position on the other side of the road, facing the window. The drummers held their sticks, removed from their sheaths. In front, the drum-major leaned on his cane, ornamented with tricolor tresses.

Colonel Rieussec brought his horse to a standstill with his spurs and dismounted. Two rows of shakos with red pompons, white trousers, white crossed harnesses, and metal buttons dotting the dark blue of long tunics extended through the foliage; the flashing streaks of bayonets split the shadows.

Suddenly, while the troopers were at ease, there was a vast leftward-orientated shudder in the crowd. Heads turned; upper bodies leaned forward. The soldiers and the national guardsmen craned their necks too, while the officers rectified the alignment. Colonel Rieussec, having swiftly remounted his horse, raised his sword. His men became immobile. Facing them, the soldiers of the line came to attention with a jerk.

César leaned out and looked to the left, like everyone else.

In the studio, Bertrand's voice was raised over the hum of the five cameras. "There must be an almighty drum-roll. Look through your binoculars at that crystal glass placed on the desk. *It's vibrating.*"

At that moment, Charles placed himself well to the left of the late, in order to look straight at the two study doors, since one of them was *certain* to give passage to César's murderer.

"The glass is vibrating more and more," said Bertrand.

In the plate, above and around the statuesque soldiers, the multitude, turned toward the approach of the King, became animated. Arms, hats, handkerchiefs and scarves were already waving in anticipation, like calls for help. Their motion accelerated and multiplied; the excited gesticulations took over the entire crowd, running along the upper floors and scaling the roofs.

César's clock marked noon.

222

The man who was about to die in a few seconds' time was looking out of the window interestedly, his soul evidently serene and his conscience tranquil.

Suddenly, the drum-major raised his garlanded cane and, behind him, his men immediately began to beat their drums.

"Look out!" said Charles, in a clipped tone. "Here come the municipal guardsmen of the escort."

A platoon of cavalry with copper helmets and red plumes advanced at pace, their sabers drawn. Two ranks of cavaliers. All of them were looking to the right, inspecting the houses and the spectators on the side of the troops that Louis-Philippe would pass in review. They were utterly neglectful of the other side, where Fieschi was posted, firebrand in hand, shielded by his Venetian blind.

The municipal guardsmen passed by very slowly. The junior officer bringing up the rear frequently looked behind, in order to adjust the speed of the platoon to the progress of the king, who was still invisible to the eyes of Charles and his guests.

Immediately after that advance-guard came a few men armed with cudgels who were marching hither and yon, easily recognizable as policemen in civilian dress. They too shamelessly ran their inquisitive eyes over the trees, the people and the façades located on their right.

The acclamations were visibly reaching their climax. The drummers beat their drum-skins in vigorous harmony, their white-gaitered feet marking time.

"The Maréchal Comte de Lobeau, Commander-in-Chief of the National Guard!" announced Colas-Dunormand, shivering from top to toe.

"Look out! Look out!" muttered Charles, clenching his teeth.

The Maréchal was riding alone. He wore his dress uniform open, with his right hand stuck into a waistcoat beneath the great sash of the Légion d'Honneur. It is quite true that he looked like a bulldog. He was frowning and, while examining the houses, made no attempt to hide his disquiet.

"Look how anxious he is!" observed Colas-Dunormand. And yet, he's less anxious than he was a little while ago, for they've now passed the Ambigu, where everyone thought that the assassination attempt might take place, and they're beginning to breathe easy. A false sense of security!"

Then, just as he finished, all of those to whom the words were addressed stood up, moved by a very singular sentiment—and several, under the influence of complex emotions, cried: "The King!"

Nothing, in fact, seemed more prodigious than seeing, with their own eyes, a King of France—the last one—on such a day of pageantry and blood.

At his window, César made acclamatory signals with his raised arms.

Louis-Philippe bowed deeply, holding tight to his large bicorn hat with white plumes and a tricolor cockade, set sideways. He was wearing the uniform of a general of the National Guard, with a blue coat embroidered in silver, the great sash of the Légion d'Honneur, silver epaulettes and white trousers that stood out against the crimson velvet of his saddle. The Ling was mounted on Le Régent, a magnificent dappled grey horse, which lifted his feet as he moved forward, prancing. The bridle was golden, with cockades at the front; the saddle-holsters and the saddle-cloth mingled gold and red.

Riding in single file to the monarch's left were Brigadier-General the Duc d'Orléans and the Duc de Nemours; to his right was the Prince de Joinville, uniformed as a naval captain, making his first public appearance.[26]

Colonel Rieussec, saluting with his sword, had come to place himself to the right of the King. The National Guardsmen brandished their rifles, cheering their sovereign. An officer—the Comte de Laborde—moved along their ranks

---

[26] Louis-Philippe's three eldest sons (he had five in all): Ferdinand-Philippe (1810-1842), Louis-Charles-Philippe (1814-1896) and François (1818-1900).

to collect petitions. Policemen in plain clothes moved along, level with Louis-Philippe.

Behind the King and the Princes, the imposing mounted procession began to appear: the maréchals and the generals decked out in gold braid, two ministers in no less brilliant coats, one of whom was Monsieur de Broglie and the other—very short, hoisted up on a gigantic horse and crushed beneath the weight of his plumed hat—Monsieur Thiers, with his hooked nose and spectacles.

"Ah!" Charles exclaimed, involuntarily.

César, at his window, had turned abruptly to the interior of the room, his face contracted in an expression of great surprise and alarm. He took three steps toward the doors. The one to the antechamber opened violently. César stopped in front of that door, displaying his back. A tall man with a dark complexion, sporting side-whiskers, was standing on the threshold of the room, with a top-hat on his head, his frock-coat buttoned all the way up to his chin, and a July ribbon knotted on his breast. His gaze went immediately to the window. He was panting, as if he had climbed the stairs in haste. He was seen to pronounce a few brief words, while standing very straight. His face was set hard, his eyes gleaming.

César, seen from behind, made a vague gesture that might have signified many vehement things: refusal, protest or surprise. His raised arms were all that could be seen of his reaction, and if he answered the other's remarks in any fashion, no one could tell.

The man had extended his arms with lightning speed. A short-barreled pistol elongated his arm like a monstrous index-finger.

There was a flash. César fell slowly backwards, his arms extended, face upwards, without any convulsion—but his murderer launched himself impetuously toward the window, for…

For, at the very instant when the pistol-shot had been fired, another instantaneous flash had sprung forth from behind the Venetian blind on the third floor of the red house.

Thick smoke rose up in front of the accursed window, and the brilliant general staff, ripped apart by the discharge of the infernal machine, was hollowed out obliquely by a swathe in which stricken horses and officers thrown to the ground, lying dead or writhing, wounded, in pools of blood.

In front, the King, pushing down his cocked hat, spurred his horse, which flinched, a bloodstain on its withers, Louis-Philippe passed his white-gloved hand over his forehead as if he were surprised not to bring it back soiled with blood.

The Princes were striking Le Régent with the flats of their swords, to force him to move forward. The Prince of Joinville's mount recoiled, though, its hocks giving way, its stifle torn open by a projectile. The maréchals and the generals were making a bloody gilded heap on the ground.

Maréchal Mortier was dead; Colonel Rieussec was dead; General Heymès, whose nose had been blown away, got up with his frightful mask. A horse bolted in the direction of the Château-d'Eau, mounted by a swaying cadaver. And the furrow of death continued among the National Guard and the crowd beneath the elms, where the carnage was swept away by a human hurricane, the pressure of frightened people in flight.

César's murderer, stepping over the corpse of his victim, considered all that momentarily, with his fists clenched on the window-sill. His face, which had gone grey, expressed an indescribable amazement—and immediately, he looked in bewilderment at the telescope on its stand, tapped it mechanically, then, suddenly coming to a decision, ran out, carefully closing the door behind him.

The smoke of the pistol-shot dissipated slowly, drifting toward the window, where it vanished.

"Ortofieri, wasn't it?" Charles asked his neighbors.

"That's certain," said Luc, firmly.

"I don't think it leaps to the eyes," said Bertrand. "All the citizens of 1835 have a period air about them that makes them curiously similar. *Perhaps* it was Fabius Ortofieri. I wouldn't swear to it."

"You can be reassured, at any rate" said Charles, shaking his hand. "It wasn't the man with the cane."

"Ah! That's certain! It's very good of you to have thought of it."

These words were exchanged rapidly, in low voices. The historic scene was coming to a conclusion in an atrocious disorder that was in complete contract to the solemn calm of the study in which César was lying dead, his eyes staring and his arms outstretched, almost exactly as Lami's water-color depicted him.

The King had succeeded in taking his horse forward. He addressed the national guardsmen, waving his hat, with signs of presence and amity, accompanied with comments that were obviously heated. The tumult reached its height.

While Louis-Philippe, taking the rest of his escort with him, set off ahead—still followed by more than 100 plumed officers followed by grooms and pikemen—the crowd flooding over the site of the outrage and around the massacre trampled a quantity of objects, vestiges of the panic: umbrellas, headscarves, shawls, rifles, shakos and bearskin hats. Civilians and military personnel lifted up the dead and the wounded, who were carried away on improvised stretchers. The dead horses were dragged to one side. The horrible task was carried out in consternation. White-faced women without hats went past at a slow pace, sustained by sympathetic people.

There had, however, from the very outset, been a stampede toward the red house; policemen and *sergents de ville*, brandishing their clubs and swords, had raced to do their duty. A mob suddenly gathered at the door of the Estaminet Rustique, in the house next to Fieschi's. It was there, in the rear courtyard, that the assassin had just been arrested.

Having remained on the spot, little Monsieur Thiers, circled by a large white belt, was gesticulating, giving orders, shouting to officers, soldiers and policemen. He leapt about, stamped his feet, went to the right and the left, his white casimir trousers spattered with Maréchal Mortier's blood. A livid gentleman, whom Colas Dunormand identified as the Prefect

227

of Police, Gisquet, spoke to him from time to time, looking utterly downcast.

"I know what he's saying," said Colas-Dunormand. "It's History! He's repeating: 'But they told me: *level with the Ambigu!*'"

"Yes," Charles agreed. "Always that confusion."

The attention of the audience relaxed slightly. The drama was played out. The moment of horror had passed.

It had not given the certain result on which Charles had been counting. They had looked César's murder full in the face, and it was impossible to be sure that it was Fabius Ortofieri. The man might have been the one whose portraits were there, but there was no certainty, because the portraits were not sufficiently similar and the man did not resemble any of them closely enough.

Charles, bitterly disappointed, clung to the hope that the comparison of cinematographic images with the portraits of Fabius might produce a better result. By proceeding thus, they would find themselves in infinitely preferable conditions. They could operate calmly and methodically, instead of being troubled by the emotion of the murder. No matter! The disappointment was considerable, and Charles felt heart-broken at only being able to convey such indecision to Geneviève Le Tourneur.

He did it, though, excusing himself to make a quick telephone call—because the day of July 28, 1835 continued to run by, and he had to track all its phases, not only by virtue of his duty as a historian, but also because César's murderer might return to the scene of his crime.

Guessing that Rita was standing beside Geneviève, listening to his words, he attached to the probable sequel of the operation an optimism that he scarcely felt.

"But who might it be if it wasn't Fabius," asked Geneviève, "since the man with the cane is now out of the picture?"

Of course! The very same thought had set a chill in Charles's heart. To doubt that it was Fabius was not reasona-

228

ble. "We shall see," he replied, however. "Perhaps the luminite hasn't said its final word."

"Oh!" said Geneviève. "We're in distress."

"No!" he exclaimed. "I beg you. While there still remains a small chance, we must cling to it. *Au revoir!*"

"Yes," said another voice, feebly. Grave and captivating, it caused him to shiver. "*Au revoir!*"

"Rita!" he murmured. "Rita!" But all he heard was someone gently hanging up the telephone.

When he went back into the studio, things were following their course. The audience was still passionately determined not to miss anything of the retrospective spectacle. The startling image of Paris in 1835 was still on its easel, with another audience at its windows, which had lost its joyful sparkle now, and down below, a crowd that had undergone a metamorphosis, struck by slowness and gravity, the sinister clearance of the causeway covered with debris and blood, the arrival of carriages into which officers covered with gilt and bandages were climbing painfully.

César's corpse inhabited the solitude of the study. Flies were invading the room.

A quarter of an hour later, Louis-Philippe and his escort, coming back from the Place de la Bastille, passed by in the opposite direction, this time looking down at the troops on the right. There was then an immediate reflux in the direction of the roadway, and the image displayed the mute agitation of passionately heated acclamations.

The octagonal clock marked 1 p.m. when the regiments formed up to march away. At the same time, a closed carriage brought Fieschi, who was to be interrogated in the very room of the infernal machine. A jostling crowd of curiosity-seekers, hurrying from both directions, assailed his re-entry to the scene of the crime. It was a wreck, a man half-dead, that they were carrying. Soon, through the slats of the sideways-displaced Venetian blind, they glimpsed moving forms.

Colomba, who had returned, fortified by a cordial, engaged in a whispered conversation with Charles and Bertrand.

Luc de Certeuil and Colas-Dunormand exchanged a few words. Madame Christiani supervised the provisioning of a large table that she had set up at the side of the studio, which constituted a buffet furnished with simple but succulent comestibles, to which everyone felt disposed to do honor—for it was mid-day by the clocks of the present day and the morning had been as long as it had been exciting.

The troops, in the meantime, filed from right to left, section by section, from the Bastille toward the Place Vendôme. The National Guardsmen and the foot-soldiers of the line, the sharpshooters and the sappers were moving along the contraflow on the far side of the road, in spite of which, as they came abreast of the field of the massacre, the left-hand section of their ranks had to be compressed in order to avoid marching through the bloody horror All of them, passing by with the slowness that was then standard, looked hither and yon and broke alignment, intrigued and alarmed, slowing down even further in order to see better.

The last of them disappeared. The façades were depopulated, no longer serving as grandstands.

In César's study, the flies were circling above the body, and the hands of the clock continued to mark the hours of the day.

Charles was hoping for some unexpected entry into the mortuary room, but the door of the antechamber only opened later, when the anticipated moment of Henriette Delille's return arrived.

She entered like a gust of wind, her face contracted by emotion, after having seen the funereal spectacle that was still displayed on the boulevard, perhaps including the stretchers emerging from the Jardin Turc, in which a sort of field-hospital had been installed. Immediately, her eyes went to the cadaver and filled with horror. Tottering, with one hand on her forehead and the other clawing at her mouth, which seemed to release a scream—a long scream of abomination—she moved a little closer to the corpse and leaned over from a distance, in dread and repulsion.

Being unable to bear any more, however, she turned round and went out in a hurry to call for help, as she was subsequently to say in the deposition she made in the presence of Commissaire Dyonnet.

"She'll cry for help on the stairway," Charles recalled, "and it's then that Monsieur Tripe will hear her."

Less than a minute later, in fact, Henriette Delille reappeared, halted, leaned on the door-frame, tragically, and beckoned someone to come in.

Monsieur Tripe—since it had to be him—advanced slowly.

"My God!" cried Colomba—to which Bertrand supplied a duller, but also more blasphemous, echo.

"That's funny," said Charles.

What was funny was that the aforementioned Tripe was by no means, as they had imagined, an unknown man—a banal corpulent passer-by, blowing out the rosy cheeks of some pork-butcher. Not at all. Monsieur Tripe, a slender young man tightly laced-up in his black coat, with his cane under his arm and his up-tilted nose, was none other than Henriette's lover and—for sure—Bertrand Valois' grandfather.

"That's women for you!" said Bertrand. "The scamp had sworn to César that she would be spending the day with her two friends, and…"

"And that's why she didn't come back sooner," Charles continued. "Henriette must have been with her boyfriend in some flowery riverside inn at Meudon or elsewhere, and not at the Carré Marigny on the Champs-Elysées, so she didn't find out about the assassination attempt until she returned to Paris. Tripe—since that's his name—escorted her back to the door of number 53…what am I saying?…as far as the first-floor landing! And if she came out again so precipitately, it's because she knew perfectly well that he wasn't far away and that she'd easily catch up with him."

"It's as clear as the water in a rock-pool," said Bertrand. "Except that she didn't think she ought to tell the Commissaire all that. She preferred to let him believe that she didn't know this Monsieur…hmm!...this Monsieur…"

"Tripe," Charles finished for him, maliciously.

Bertrand, disappointed and vexed, looked at Colomba with a calamitous expression.

"Baron Tripe, perhaps," Charles added.

"Oh, don't go on, I beg you!" Bertrand groaned.

"How naughty you are!" said Colomba.

"Bah!" said her fiancé, making his decision. "Whether my ancestor is named Tripe or not, he's a sound fellow, all the same. Look at him."

The newcomer, having deposited his cane and hat on the marble-topped table, was kneeling beside the dead man. A rapid examination was sufficient to assure him of the irreparable misfortune. He got to his feet, pale, letting his thin hands fall on to his thin legs, and enveloped the young woman with a sad gaze replete with tenderness and fidelity: the gaze of a good dog.

Henriette threw herself against him, sobbing. He touched his lips to the young woman's forehead, and they stood like that for a several long, gentle and profound minutes.

Henriette and Tripe, the man with the cane, came back a little later in the company of Monsieur Dyonnet, the Commissaire, Monsieur Joly, the chief of the municipal police, and a *sergent de ville*.

Tripe played his role as an unknown passer-by, a disinterested witness, quite well. The representatives of the law devoted themselves to the observations that were customary in 1835, using primitive and expedient methods, with known results.

Before nightfall, many others came in to perform their functions, and many auxiliaries also passed through the study. César Christiani's body was taken away for autopsy.

"It's amazing how much they resemble one another!" said Bertrand Valois. "They all have the appearance of being related."

"You're exaggerating," Charles retorted. "but I do recognize that, to our eyes, all these people dressed in an outdated
manner, almost all sporting the same side-whiskers, wearing
expressions corresponding to the tastes and sentiments of their
era—*in the psychological fashion of their time*—seem to me to
be much less dissimilar than my contemporaries. It's quite
bizarre, and, with respect to the case that concerns us, very
regrettable. Oh, why couldn't photography have been invented
a few years earlier? If we possessed a photograph—even
one!—of Fabius Ortofieri, I'm certain that by comparing it to
the images on the film yet to be developed, we'd know what
we need to know about the murderer's identity immediately.
We'd know whether it was Fabius or not. But with these hand-
made portraits, will we ever arrive at a decisive result?"

The portraits were lined up before him: the oil-painting,
the pastel and the two miniatures.

Night fell in the studio in the Rue de Tournon. Then the
twilight darkened in the study in the Boulevard du Temple,
now deprived of the likeable and eccentric man who had spent
his last years there. Henriette received César's relatives there,
with all the self-effacement and deference imposed by her
situation. Madame Leboulard wept copiously; young Napoléon Christiani looked for a long time, with a somber expression, at the large bloodstain that was now blackening the
Savonnerie carpet.

By the last light of that day of sinister fame, the animation at the foot of the Fieschi house persisted. Soldiers guarded
the vicinity. The Café des Mille Colonnes had been transformed into a guard-room. Up above, behind the celebrated
Venetian blind, opened crosswise, a vivid light that would not
be extinguished until dawn illuminated the interrogation
scene. Many arrests had been made, and it was easy to distinguish with binoculars the pale faces of the poor terrorized de-
vils who were protesting their innocence.

The next morning, there was a further descent of law officers upon the theater of César Christiani's murder, in the
presence of the Leboulard family, Napoléon and Henriette,

233

dressed in mourning. The former corsair's ward was interrogated scrupulously, but benevolently. The marble table-top served as a desk for the examining magistrate and his clerk. The roll-top desk, emptied of all its papers, was sealed. Policemen examined the room from top to bottom. They were rolling up the bloody carpet in order to take it away as an item of evidence when a man presented himself; he was still young, artistic in appearance, and carried painting equipment under his arm. There was not difficult in recognizing Eugène Lami, and it was understood that he was asking for authorization to make a sketch of the study as it was. He obtained permission and, while the actors in the judiciary scene continued their work by searching the room containing the monkeys, Eugène Lami installed himself in the corner between the two doors and set up a slender flexible easel—and his blue eyes took possession of the "interior" whose appearance he was about to record for posterity.

XV. Two Singular Auxiliaries

The studio in the Rue de Tournon had been subjected to a few modifications. A black curtain, sliding along a long rod, was able to mask the bay window and plunge the huge room into darkness. Against one wall, a blank screen stood in front of a cinematographic projector.

Positives had been made of the films taken during the great session. Several images of the murderer had been enlarged. Charles wasted no time in reproducing the rapid and violent event on the screen, nor in comparing the portraits of Fabius to the photographs of the man who had killed his thrice-great-grandfather.

That was disappointing. The resemblances were not sufficiently accentuated to convince anyone that Fabius was the murderer, but the dissimilarities were not sufficiently striking to prove the contrary. If the judges of 1835 had had the films in their possession, they would have been able to make a definite decision, having the ability to summon the flesh-and-blood Fabius Ortofieri into their presence, but today, the accused now being only represented by imperfect and diverse effigies, no conclusion could be reached either way. And the question arose of what the policeman Cartoux would have said, if one could have put him in the presence of such precise photographs of the murderer, even admitting that the murderer really was the man he had seen prowling on the boulevard— the man that he had, after all, only glimpsed. Confronted with the precision of the photographs, would Cartoux have persisted in maintaining that Fabius and that person were the same?

Only one person had formed a firm conviction: Luc de Certeuil. He persevered in his initial opinion. According to him—but was he sincere?—the evidence was incontestable. Fabius and the murderer were one and the same. He was persuaded, however, to be less affirmative. Charles consulted

235

specialists in anthropometry. They refused to commit themselves, because of the considerable variations between the different portraits of Fabius. The report of these experts shook Luc's faith—or, rather, confronted by so qualified an opinion, he *dared not* sustain with such stubbornness that one could not hesitate in recognizing Fabius Ortofieri in the sturdy, tall and swarthy individual with the July medal, who now killed the unfortunate César Christiani 20 times a day on the cinema screen, stepped over his inert body, ran to the window, remained bewildered for a few seconds on seeing the effect of the infernal machine, manipulated the telescope stupidly, and fled at top speed.

There was, in that terrible brief drama, one very particular moment that intrigued Charles and all those interested in the enigma of the detective film. That was—as you will already have guessed—the moment when the murderer, standing in front of his defenseless adversary, had addressed a few words to him in an abrupt, imperious manner.

What had he said? What insult, what challenge, what inflexible sentence had he pronounced?

Without any doubt, the words had emerged clearly from his mouth, forcefully articulated. The absence of a moustache permitted an admirable view of the movement of the lips—but alas, all that could be affirmed was that the man had spoken, and nothing more. Luminite had not been created to record sounds as it slowed down images. Mute had been the marvelous retrovision of July 28, mute remained the film of it that five cameras had preserved.

And yet, those words might be the key to the mystery! What a man says as he is about to commit murder cannot be banal. They were surely words heavy with meaning. If they did not explain everything, at least they would be of a nature to put a witness on the track of important discoveries.

Charles Christiani then had a rather good idea, which a professional detective might have envied him. He said nothing to anyone, but one afternoon, as he was chatting with Colomba and watching the plate of luminite—which no longer

236

showed them anything but an overly tidy locked room with its shutters closed, deprived of its carpet, wearing the well-known mourning-dress of all dead men's rooms—a domestic presented him with a visiting card.

"That's good," he said. "Show them in."

"I'll leave," said Colomba.

"On the contrary, stay!"

"But who is it?"

"Someone I've asked to come and for whom I've been waiting."

"You seem very satisfied. Is it a surprise?"

The domestic came back in, introducing a young boy, and then another, both dressed in the uniform of an institution. Behind them, a simple and correctly-dressed man came forward. He took the lead, and as he overtook his two companions his hands executed a series of movements that it was impossible to mistake—it was the language of deaf-mutes.

The visitor bowed to Colomba and Charles. "Here, Monsieur," he said, "are the young people whose assistance you asked for. I just spoke to them in sign-language, but they can pronounce a few words, thanks to the education that we now provide in our institutions, and they are first-rate lip-readers."

Colomba and Charles shook the hands of the two deaf-mute adolescents.

"If you would care to say something to them, Mademoiselle, you'll see how easily they can understand you."

Slightly anxious, Colomba smiled and said: "Good day, gentlemen, and be welcome."

Instead of speaking in gestures, the professor set himself before his pupils, who never ceased looking, with a sort of sharp vigilance, at the lips of the persons present. "Repeat what Mademoiselle has just said. You first, Emmanuel, then you, Martial." He expressed himself unhurriedly, without vocal force, in a low voice but emphasizing the movement of his mouth slightly, by virtue of professional habit.

237

Colomba had by no means done that; nevertheless, young Emmanuel, mute though he was,[27] started speaking in his turn—in a painfully hoarse and metallic voice, it is true, reminiscent of the voice of an automaton. The spaced-out syllables buzzed inhumanly, without any intonation.

"Mademoiselle said: Good-day, gen-tle-men, and be welcome."

And Martial, in an identical voice, repeated the same sentence.

"That's marvelous," said Colomba.

This emission of purely mechanical sounds seemed to cost the two disabled individuals a certain effort and to tire them. They were more accustomed to using the silent language of hands and fingers with their master.

Charles had closed the curtain over the bay window. The exploration of the past was about to continue by a new means.

The screen brightened. The workings of the cinematographic projector were set in motion, clicking away like a little factory. César's study appeared. The old corsair, leaning on the window-sill, looked at Colonel Rieussec, who, saluting with his sword, had just placed himself to the right of King Lois-Philippe.

In order to obtain the maximum clarity, Charles was showing the monochrome film obtained by the central camera, representing the scene stored by the luminite from head-on. The reel was perfect, the Sun not having struck the north-facing study window directly. When the murderer made his impressive entrance, he set himself in the light as completely as one might desire. As soon as he had spoken, at the very

---

[27] The boys are clearly not mute in the sense that they are physically incapable of speech, but it was rare in the 1920s for the deaf to be taught to use the voices they had, for lack of any established method of so doing, so they usually remained silent and were thus considered voiceless. The representation of the boys' feat might well seem more alien to the modern reader than that of the marvels of luminite.

moment when he raised his weapon to fire, Charles stopped the projection and restored daylight to the studio.

The two mutes immediately agitated their hands.

"Well?" Charles asked the professor.

"They both agree," the latter declared. "The man with the pistol pronounced the following sentence…"

The brother and sister were listening with an extraordinary excitement, gripped by a sort of bizarre fear, at the idea that they were about to attain, thanks to an admirably circumstantial assistance, the echo of words extinct for almost a century, and which, perhaps, might solve the most fascinating and teasing of mysteries.

The professor continued: "…'You recognize me, don't you. Captain?'"

"Is that all?" said Charles, disillusioned once more.

Colomba took on a sad expression. "No luck! That's nothing…"

"We're further forward than before," Charles recognized. "Fabius Ortofieri might well have hurled those words at César in presenting himself before him. It could well have been a long time since they had met."

"Can your pupils tell us anything about the *accent* in which that sentence was pronounced, Monsieur?" Colomba asked.

"That would be asking too much of them, Mademoiselle. "The grasp the form of words, but that's all. They would have to be considerable deformed to reveal an accent."

The boy called Martial made gestures. He had followed what the professor had just said with his eyes.

"Martial confirms that it is impossible for him to tell us more. He noticed nothing in particular. All that he can certify is that the elocution was precise and that there was no stammer blurring it. The man was speaking normally, without rolling his *r*s or lisping."

Charles explained: "My sister asked that question because, if the murderer had had a southern accent, the fact would have given us a precious clue. Certain people presume that the crime was committed by a Corsican—do you see?"

The professor expressed his helplessness with a gesture.

They were reduced, purely and simply, to deploring the fact that the murderer had been so laconic, and also that César had had his back turned throughout the very brief interval when the two enemies had been face to face—for it was probably that César too had spoken. Not only did that seem probable, given the circumstances of the event, but the old man's gestures—the movements of his head and his shoulders—clearly indicated that he had made some reply to that brusque interrogation: "*You recognize me, don't you, Captain?*" Admittedly César's last words might only have been an exclamation, and it was possible that they would not have thrown any light on the tenebrous matter of his death. A mirror reflecting the corsair's face might only have revealed a cry or a phrase as useless as the murderer's "*you recognize me...*"

They regretted, however, that no mirror had ornamented the mantelpiece, and searched the reels of film nevertheless, doggedly, in case some polished surface—the glass of a picture, the pane of an open window, or even the polished wood of an item of furniture, might have dimly reflected the face, and consequently the words, of the man who was about to die...

Nothing. They found nothing. Neither the eyes of Charles and Colomba, excited by their hearts' desire, nor those of the deaf-mutes, reinforced by a law of nature, could discover the shadow of a reflection.

Thinking at César's face must surely been reflected in the very pupils of his murderer, Charles employed a simple maneuver to enlarge the image of those wild eyes, which were staring into César's. As soon as the magnification attained the amplitude that would have permitted the tiny face of the old man in the round mirror of the pupil, however, the projection became confused, cloudy and pale; the magnification was effaced of its own accord, and Charles immediately had to renounce a hope that had not been lacking in a certain audacious and singular beauty.

Battle-weary, they abandoned the film of the murder and the operator showed some other reels: those that had been taken previous to July 28, 1835, including, among others, the dramatic scenes that had take place between César, Henriette and the man with the cane, whose name was Tripe.

By this means they reconstituted the entire dialogue of these altercations, which then appeared to be slightly different to the idea of them that they had originally been able to form. It emerged that César had never let slip a single word that might have revealed his profound sentiments in relation to Henriette. He opposed Tripe's assiduities, he said, because he was "a person of no account," without a penny to his name, who could "only make up silly rhymes"—but his amorous affection was never expressed; he had reserved its sufferings for his solitude and had always remained, in the young woman's eyes, a tyrannical guardian, violent but above reproach.

"I approve of that," said Charles, looking at his sister. "César was a worthy fellow, and I like him."

"And Tripe was a poet!" said Colomba. "Bertrand will be happy!"

"A nobility worth as much as many others!"

The deaf-mutes continued their work, not leaving unknown the least of the words visible in the films.

"And that's it!" Charles exclaimed. "Result: zero. '*You recognize me, don't you, Captain?*' Who did César recognize? There are thousands of people who would have been in a position to say that. Thousands! Among them, certainly, Fabius Ortofieri, whose portraits, in sum, *might* be those of the criminal, strictly speaking."

Colomba remained silent.

"I had higher hopes of today," her brother went on. "'*You recognize me…*' What do we do with that?"

"Set it alongside the other acquisitions we've made, with all that we've learned since the discovery of the luminite. And then…wait."

241

"Wait for what? What can the luminite tell us now? The hour of revelations is past, regarding this matter. Wait! I know who won't wait. The relatives of Rita and Luc de Certeuil, you may be sure, have no reason to delay…that we know of. Come on, it's finished!"

"You've said that before, Charles, and yet everything has begun again—don't you know that *nothing is ever finished?*"

XVI. The Approach of a Disastrous Denouement

The marriage of Colomba Christiani and Bertrand Valois had been fixed for Thursday, December 12. The preparations for that august ceremony did not hinder the researches in progress regarding the enigma of the Boulevard du Temple. On the contrary, they were conducted in a particularly active fashion during that period. Charles had recovered his courage with a new and determined ardor, like all those who, having perceived despair, escape with a sudden start. He felt, in any case, the increasing necessity of multiplying his efforts, for the imminent departure of the newlyweds would deprive him of his most valuable collaborators, and every morning he feared, more cruelly than the one before, that he might hear about the official engagement of Rita and Luc. He knew full well that Rita, pressed from every direction, would not be able to defer the hour of his conclusive renunciation indefinitely.

Bertrand, enraged by prejudices that he considered as fossils and were, he said, 200 years behind the times, worked no less wholeheartedly on the solution of the criminal mystery. "Since there's no other way of getting out of it," he said to Charles, "let's go! Let's search! Let's get to work! Word of honor, though, with your great principles and fine traditions, you break my heart!" He raised his mast-like nose and added: "Admittedly, a descendant of Monsieur Tripe has nothing to say on the matter. Silence, peasants! And to work!"

They worked. They proceeded scrupulously to make all the observations and all the cross-checks that the close study of the films suggested to them, in combination with the material in the dossiers, the vast heaps of various documents and even a relief-map found in the display-cases of the Musée Carnavalet, which reproduced the appearance of the Boulevard du Temple at the time of Fieschi's assassination attempt.

Why had the murder chosen the moment when the King was passing by to commit his crime? The evidence in the Ortofieri case offered an explanation of that. Everyone knew then that the passing of the sovereign before his troops was always accompanied by a great racket of military drums and bands, reinforced by a tempest of acclamations. The din offered a unique opportunity—and Bertrand had furnished the proof that the noise had indeed been considerable, since a crystal glass on the roll-top desk had vibrated. It was undeniable, on the one hand, that the noise could, in large measure, muffle a loud bang inside a room, all the more so if—a particularity of which Charles had not thought at first—the detonation might have been that of a pistol charged with very little powder, since it was designed to fire at point-blank range. It was no less evident, on the other hand, that the massed crowd on the boulevard offered a fugitive every opportunity to disappear promptly—was it not known that Fieschi had reasoned in the same fashion?

From these deductions, unfortunately, nothing resulted with respect to the identity of the criminal. Fabius Ortofieri, just like everyone else, had the right to be cunning in his premeditation.

They searched the case-files to see whether the pistol presumed to be "the weapon of the crime" in the investigation of 1835 was similar to the one that the luminite had shown in the hand of the gunman, and which the cameras had photographed. It was a waste of time; the searches carried out after July 30, 1835 at Fabius's home having only yielded an inconclusive result: that of several pistols of different forms, all well-cleaned, any one of which might have been fired recently without anything indicating that any of them had, in fact, been fired. Furthermore, none of these weapons was described in the reports.

These examples demonstrate how logically and how attentively the research was conducted. Many others might be accumulated, but that would have no other result than making our story longer.

It all came to nothing. And the news that Geneviève Le Tourneur received each day, coming from the studio, was as disappointing as that of which the young woman transmitted to Charles the dolorous echo. Rita, besieged by objurgations, alone against all her near relatives, walled up in the silence of her secret, found herself driven into a corner, heading for a capitulation that might happen at any moment, at the hazard of the assaults and her weakness. She sent desolate appeals to Charles through the intermediary of his friend. On the point of surrendering, she informed Geneviève sadly of the impossibility of further procrastination; Charles received the news in somber despair, translating everything that he had learned about that destiny into cries of alarm; "Quickly! Quickly! Find something! Tomorrow, it will be too late! I'm at the end of my tether!"

He had not seen Rita again and feared seeing her—but Madame Le Tourneur painted him a lamentable picture of the young woman. She feared that her health might be compromised by all the anxiety that was preying upon her and the torment that gnawed away at her incessantly.

Colomba's marriage took place in these circumstances. At that moment, Charles only glimpsed a tiny hope of salvation, so feeble that it scarcely existed. That chance resided in the documents that Cousin Drouet had inherited from her great-grandfather, César Christiani.

Charles knew that in 1835 the major part of the family papers had not been handed on to Lucile, the cousin's grandmother, but to Napoléon, as was appropriate, since Napoléon represented the elder branch and that males always have the advantage over females, by virtue of the fact that they preserve the family name and are responsible for perpetuating it. Meager as Cousin Drouet's family archives might be, however, they might by chance contain some unknown item which might, in some unforeseeable fashion, offer a clue relative to one vitally important question upon which nothing, thus far, had shed the slightest light: had César Christiani any enemies other than Fabius Ortofieri? More precisely: had he attracted the hatred of a man who was not Fabius?

One of two things had to be true: either the murderer was Fabius, or he was not an Ortofieri, for in 1835, no member of the Ortofieri family other than Fabius had been similar in age—which is to say, similar in age to the man who had been *seen* to murder César. If the murderer was not Fabius, therefore, it was necessary to search for him among the partisans of Ortofieri, no matter where they might be in the vast world.

Directed by this thought, Charles had attempted to discover—especially in César's correspondence—any trace of a dispute or disagreement, any revelation, however fleeting, of a quarrel or any kind of incident capable of engendering a mortal grudge against César. No allusion seemed to him to be worthy of being retained; even the most precise was too vague; his investigations had remained as fruitless on this point as on others. Might Cousin Drouet's papers be more informative than the documents held by the elder branch? It was doubtful, but it was necessary to check it out, and, while anything unknown remained fortified there, a little hope was in refuge there too.

Charles saw Cousin Drouet for the first time in his life on the very morning of the nuptial ceremony, in the drawing-room in the Rue de Tournon. The sight of that surprising old lady sensibly attenuated the melancholy caused to him by the obligation of participating in a celebration of that sort when everything seemed to be conspiring to postpone indefinitely the advent of his own happiness. He was attempting to overcome his affliction and to put on a brave face for the guests that flowed in—witnesses, relatives, ushers and maids of honor, black coats and decorations, exquisite dresses, youth, pomp and flowers—when Amélie Drouet advanced, in the midst of all that elegant society, like the charming ambassadress of a past that had unfortunately disappeared forever.

Why was that little old lady not ridiculous in her outdated finery? Why was there merely an exclamation to declare her adorable, with her 93 years, her wrinkles and her halting gait? It was because everything about her originated from an epoch whose forgotten grace had been made of imperishable seductions, handed down by forefathers. She might have been a shriveled antique Carabosse,[28] decked out in implausible furbelows, but she bore the indefinable mark of the politesse of yesteryear and an education without parallel. The young women could not comprehend why that caricature, instead of making them laugh, impressed them with such ease and surprising security. Great centuries in succession had dressed that little fragment of ancestry with an ungraspable elegance that generations had cultivated but which now astonishes people, as a marvel whose secret has been lost.

Charles literally launched himself toward her, so proudly did Cousin Drouet—who had never been more than a member of the upper bourgeoisie, not even the daughter of petty nobility—in her appearance, represent "the root and the branch."[29]

Her faded blue eyes looked like those of a pastel; they gave the impression of having been conceived by a La Tour or a Chardin,[30] then slightly effaced by the march of time. Suddenly, Charles Christiani realized fully why he found her so attractive; it was because of the incontestable resemblance she bore to César. The caprices of heredity had deprived the elder

---

[28] Carabosse was a "bad fairy" who bestowed malicious gifts. She made her first appearance in a story by Madame d'Aulnoy, but the name was then borrowed for application to the initially-nameless bad fairy in recycled versions of "Sleeping Beauty," and the name became most familiar in connection with Tchaikovsky's ballet; it is the costume of that character that is being evoked here.

[29] Renard has "*de la race et 'de la branche.*'" "Race" does not mean quite the same thing in French as it does in English, pertaining more narrowly to family, and specifically, to that element of family specified by the word's etymology—the ultimate meaning of "race" being "root." The wordplay is more brutal in English, but retains the double meaning well enough.

[30] Maurice Quentin de La Tour (1704-1788) and Jean-Baptiste-Siméon Chardin (1699-1779) were the two most celebrated French painters of pastel portraits.

branch, at least until now, of that carnal succession, but the face of the corsair lived again, softened, beneath the white hair of the old female cousin, and it was a and joy and a relief for Charles to find something of César still alive, since he had been contemplating the late corsair as if through the window of the beyond.

When the ceremony was completed with a magnificent deployment of religious pomp; all Paris filed into the sacristy of Saint-Sulpice, rubbing shoulders with the capital's notorious Corsicans, obscure actors or celebrated and able historians, biographers and other learned men who came to render homage to the bride's brother. The last-named took possession of Cousin Drouet and questioned her on the subject of papers that might be in her possession.

The good lady was hard, not of hearing, but of understanding. A light fog had begun to cloud her mind. Her older memories, however, retained a certain precision. She assured her great-nephew that she did not possess any document of importance. Furniture, yes, she had furniture that had come to her from César—but papers, next to none.

Charles persisted, in order to obtain permission to consult those few sheets. It was agreed that he would come to the Rue de Rivoli on the following day.

Without waiting for the ancient and amiable relative to open her home and her relic furniture to him, however, Charles begged her to open her memory. The lock was rusty, the hinges seized up, but if a few memories had crumbled into dust, others still held firm and could be manipulated to display all their faces, like fragile antiques on shelves.

Amélie Drouet had been born in 1846. She had already reached the age of 20 when her grandmother, born Lucile Christiani, had died, and was 37 when her father, the former Councilor Anselme Leboulard had quite this world in his turn. Those two witnesses to César's life, who had played an important role in the investigation of Fabius Ortofieri, had not failed to talk to Amélie about her great-grandfather and his tragic death. For them, however, Fabius's guilt was not in question—and Charles, confronted with such a deep-rooted belief, which Cousin Drouet had shared from the most tender age, judged it reckless to reveal that he was re-examining what she had considered throughout her life to be an indisputable truth. He preferred to let her believe that the retrovision to which she had recently been invited had had no other interest than perceiving, across the ages, an event of which no one had dreamed of contesting the principal facts.

Cousin Drouet talked about César willingly. She held his memory in reverence, knowing perfectly well that she resembled the corsair, although it had not been possible for her to lead an adventurous naval life rather than being a sedentary bourgeois lady, the daughter and wife of magistrates.

Had César had many enemies? Did she know?

She had no memory of that. She wandered off. She had been brought from Saint-Sulpice to the Rue de Tournon without having to be asked. Charles introduced her to the luminite. She only half-understood the marvel, attaching only a confused importance to it, and she withdrew in order to enter into civility competition with Madame Christiani. Both of them appeared to have forgotten the many years during which one of them had held the other at arm's length because of a hypothetical fault.

"What a pleasant dowager!" said Charles.

"Yes," replied his mother. "If only she had behaved better toward Mélanie…"

He laughed—but that was the moment when Bertrand Valois was about to bring in his young wife. They came in together, in their traveling costumes—and if our historian continued to laugh, it was certainly because he forced himself to do so,

With what surprise and emotion Charles Christiani found in his cousin's home so many objects that he had seen in César's study thanks to the effects of luminite, which he had thought to be lost!

Madame Drouet did not live in the most aristocratic part of the Rue de Rivoli. She occupied a beautiful apartment, slightly low-ceilinged, on the second floor of a building situated not far from the Châtelet. She had lived there for more than 20 years with two old chambermaids, with old furniture, in the midst of a quantity of souvenirs whose profusion was sufficient to recall César's character.

Today, age accentuated its owner's indifference to all that picturesque bric-à-brac, but it was easy to see that, ever since her youth, she had held the memory of the corsair captain in fantastic veneration. In her Louis-Philippe drawing-room, reached by the noise of a populous street through the railings of a narrow balcony, he recognized the octagonal clock, the map of the world, marine engravings, a little model corvette, the telescope and numerous weapons that had been illuminated by the daylight of July 28, 1835 in the Boulevard du Temple. All things considered, it had been sheer luck that, when César's possessions had been divided up, the plate of luminite disguised as a slate had gone to Napoléon Christiani rather than to his aunt Lucile.

Without dwelling on the thought of what the result of that transposition might have been, Charles surrendered to the singularly keen and mild pleasure of contemplating cherished things that he had thought extinct, and of feeling, in consequence, that the past was not as past as might have been supposed. Then again, in this environment, in her own home, Cousin Drouet reminded him even more of the most original of ancestors. She adored animals. For lack of monkeys, two stout little dogs were trotting over the carpet, yapping. Good Lord! That was the same Savonnerie carpet that César's death had stained with blood! Every macabre trace had vanished therefrom, and long wear had blanched the weave of its arabesques. In front of the windows, two large aviaries were agitated by flutterings and hoppings; their entire multicolored population was whistling and chirping, performing an incredible concert that would have delighted the ears of the late bird-lover. As she moved about amid this décor, Cousin Drouet's gestures and mannerisms had an abruptness that recalled, across the generations, the man from whom she was descended.

All of that formed a seductive ensemble, which charmed the historian. It seemed to him that César was determined to spin himself out, and was doing so by employing all the poor and petty means that the disposal of the dead—and, involuntarily, the dreamer that everyone harbors within himself was comforted thereby, thinking that the dead would not go to so much trouble for nothing.

Alas, although César Christiani had left his great-granddaughter a few facial features and something of his manner, a liking for animals and the ownership of a host of disparate objects, the benefits of his succession stopped there. The papers originating from the division of 1835 surpassed in their insignificance everything that Cousin Drouet had anticipated; they were bills and business letters. Ten minutes sufficed for Charles to convince himself that he had drawn a blank.

He hid his disappointment, not without effort, for he perceived now that, in the inmost depths of his being, he had founded much more hope than was reasonable on that last chance. He took his leave of Cousin Drouet, promising to come back to see her very soon.

As everyone knows, however, "man proposes, but God disposes," and seven months were to go by before the worthy old lady received the promise visit.

In fact, ominous incidents depleted Charles's morale in the following days. Madame Le Tourneur, for whom he had asked on the telephone, was not at home, and her chambermaid said that she would be away for some time. In addition, Luc de Certeuil, whom Charles now only encountered by chance, seemed bizarrely constrained and embarrassed when, on two occasions, he found himself in the presence of his neighbor at the door to the building. There was also a quite mysterious change in Madame Christiani's state of mind; she seemed suddenly preoccupied, sometimes treating her son more stiffly and sometimes more affectionately than usual.

Charles foresaw his imminent unhappiness; he had had confirmation of it in the form of indifferences. Rita Ortofieri was engaged to Luc de Certeuil. By the same token, he had understood that he mother was not unaware of his deplorable love.

He said nothing. He did not complain. Not a word was exchanged between Madame Christiani and him, but they came together more frequently, in a closer and warmer intimacy, which their pride led them to attribute entirely to Colomba's departure—and the mother, secretly tormented, prayed with all her heart for the alleviation of their mutual suffering.

Can one say that the alleviation in question was produced? It would doubtless be a very poor translation of their sentiments. However, when the news reached them that Monsieur de Certeuil's fiancée was gravely ill, was it not the case that their reaction, and even Charles's frightful anguish, was mixed with a certain release?

Charles wanted to believe that Rita would recover; he refused to admit any other outcome of that malady, whose causes he understood and which rendered the young woman as dear to him as a beloved martyr—but could he not see a truly providential intervention in that delay, a frightful surcease that would further postpone the event whose imminence he dreaded?

For the moment, he silenced the voices within him that cried: "All is not lost! Destiny is gaining time! Courage!" Furthermore, a week later, the health-bulletins that Geneviève Le Tourneur communicated to him daily became so menacing that anxiety alone reigned in his heart, and he reproached himself with abomination for allowing himself to be distracted by thoughts other than Rita's salvation. And for her to live, for nature to continue to count among the number of the living a woman blessed with so much grace and grandeur, he offered the world the sacrifice of his own life, provided that the world should not take hers.

Are such decisions, taken in the mystery of consciousness, capable of modifying the course of destiny? Are the forces that rule the future, direct its episodes and prepare its denouements sensitive—as we would wish them to be—to the reactions of souls? Do our attitudes have the power to determine the future in one way or another?

The time has not yet come to reveal to the reader how those forces would take account of Charles Christiani's vow, so pure and so elevated. Months passed, during which his thoughts, henceforth invariable, did not give the lie to his fine resolution. He was faithful to it at every moment, even when he was informed that Rita was out of danger and that, after a convalescence that was bound to be long, she would be able to take up her life where she had left off.

While the young woman had been in danger, Charles had not had to struggle against his instinct in order to persevere in his abnegation. That was more difficult when he knew that Rita had recovered her breath and her color, and that after having ceased, for weeks, to be anyone at all, she was now about to rejoin the march of time, and would soon give herself to someone else. It was then that the real sacrifice began. The wish having been granted, it was necessary to pay the price, by accepting with serenity whatever the future might bring.

It brought nothing during the entire first half of 1930—nothing but sadness, prolonged by the fact that everything remained in suspense and that, in the meantime, uncertainty authorized neither any new hope that might have chased the sadness away, nor the total abandonment that would have driven him to despair.

In February, Rita left for the Côte d'Azur in order to undertake her convalescence there. She returned at the end of May and discussion of the marriage was resumed. This time, Geneviève Le Tourneur did not think it necessary to avoid Charles Christiani's visits. One day, she told him, at the same time, that Rita's heart had not changed and that there was now much talk in the Ortofieri household of publishing banns and drawing up a contract.

It was in these circumstances that Cousin Drouet was to have the privilege of belatedly receiving the visit that she had being promised more than half a year before. Charles had learned, most inopportunely, that the banker Ortofieri had arranged a meeting between himself and his notary and Luc de Certeuil and his. He had to make great efforts that day—which was July 13—to hide his chagrin and remember his noble resolutions. Colomba and Bertrand, installed in their conjugal happiness, advised him strongly to undertake a long voyage.

At that moment, he was in their home; he was often there, for he was prey to a perpetual need to move around. No obligation retained him in Paris. There was no more hope. During the last seven months, the luminite had given him nothing but disappointments, without the slightest indication that might retain him. Destiny, thus far, was obstinate in frustrating him.

"I'd like that," he said. "I'll leave after the national festivities. I'll go…it doesn't matter where. Three of my friends are going to Sweden and Norway in a few days' time—I'll go with them. That's settled, then. Before then, though, I have to go see Cousin Drouet and bid her farewell. I've treated her lightly. She must be unable to understand my silence."

"I'll go with you," Colomba said. "She enchants me."

"Let's all go, tomorrow!" Bertrand proposed.

Charles objected that it was July 14,[31] which seemed inappropriate to him for a formal visit.

"You can make a 'formal visit' on the eve of your departure," Bertrand replied, "but tomorrow, she'll be delighted to offer us her balcony to watch the parade."

"That's true," said Charles. "The 1830 review."

"You wouldn't want to miss that, I imagine," said Colomba, "as a historian of that era."

"Oh, a few months ago we witnessed a much more exact and singularly moving review! And when my heart tells me to, I make entire armies file past in my imagination, whose reconstitution, I can assure you, is faultless. After all, though,

---

[31] Bastille Day.

it's not a bad idea. Shall I send a telegram to the cousin to warn her?"

"Of course!" said Bertrand "Come and collect us tomorrow morning."

The reader will certainly remember the military parade to which Bertrand Valois had just made allusion. On July 14, 1930, the traditional review of the troops of the Paris garrison was supplemented by a less common spectacle. The government of the Republic wanted to show Parisians the officers and soldiers wearing the uniforms of the ancient African army who had recently filed in front of Monsieur Doumergue[32] in Algeria, during the celebrations of the centenary of the conquest. The Bey of Tunis and the Prince of Monaco witnessed that curious and imposing manifestation, and 40 Arab chiefs on horseback took part in it. The review took place on the Esplanade des Invalides. Afterwards there was a march-past of the reconstituted troops, along the Concorde, the Rue Royale, the Boulevards de la Madeleine and des Capucines, the Avenue de l'Opéra and the Rue de Rivoli, all the way to the Place de l'Hôtel-de-Ville.

Cousin Drouet's apartment was, indeed, admirably situated to serve as the finest box for that vast military representation, which, without the assistance of luminite, would offer to the eyes of Charles, Bertrand and Colomba, in the heart of the 20th century, a spectacle distantly reminiscent of the famous review of July 28, 1835—but which, one could be certain, would not be disturbed by any infernal machine.

"Tomorrow, at least," Charles said, as he left his sister, "There's nothing to fear. Nothing unexpected!"

"Who knows?" said Bertrand, his nostrils flared.

Colomba embraced him tumultuously. "What a madman!" she said.

---

[32] Gaston Doumergue (1863-1937), President of the Republic from 1924-31.

255

XVII. Elegy

As Charles was bidding farewell to his sister and brother-in-law, two young women, one very dark and the other very blonde, their arms laden with a heap of roses, were going along a secluded pathway in Père-Lachaise Cemetery. Rita, thinner and lankier now, seemed to have grown taller since her convalescence. A remaining pallor further emphasized the rings around her eyes, which were brighter now and more profound. Now, beside Geneviève Le Tourneur, she no longer had the same gait, nor the same facial appearance, nor the indescribable evidences of an adolescence that was scarcely complete; there was no longer any of that to distinguish her from her friend. "Two young women," one would have said of them. Only their dresses and hats attempted to distinguish their status, but not everyone understands the language of dressmakers and milliners.

Things were no longer as they had been on the deck of the *Boyardville*. Mademoiselle Ortofieri's beauty had certainly lost none of its finesse by virtue of that grave pallor and that ardent melancholy, but her great pain and her long battle against death had permanently expelled the last traces of divine childhood from her being.

"It must be around here," she said.

The pathways were labyrinthine. That part of Père-Lachaise is shady and romantic; the monuments have an otherworldly appearance. The trees themselves are funereal, and the archaic mode of their foliage is tearful, like the poet's willow.

Geneviève and Rita were searching with their eyes among the steles, between the cypresses and the yews. Geneviève stopped. "There it is."

A tomb extended its mossy flagstone in a little enclosure bordered by chains linking a few boundary-markers. Beneath a tearful ask tree, the ogival stele stood up very straight, like the

256

head of a cold, hard bed of stone. On the flat tablet, engraved one beneath another, was a column of names.

The first was: *Paul Maximilien Horace Christiani, born at Silaz (Savoy), April 2, 1792; died in Paris, November 13, 1832*. The second was: *Louis Joseph César Christiani, ship's captain, born at Ajaccio, August 15, 1769; died in Paris, July 28, 1835*. The third was *Eugénie Christiani, 1844-1850*, then came *Lucile Christiani, later Leboulard, 1795-1866; Anselme Leboulard-Christiani, 1815-1883; Napoléon Christiani, 1814-1899; Achille Christiani, 1848-1923; Adrien Christiani, died for France, 1873-1915*.

They read in silence, motionless, Rita more piously, both rosy by virtue of the reflection of the flowers whose sumptuous masses they pressed to their bosoms.

Rita sighed profoundly. "Sad loves!" she said, with a fugitive smile full of bitterness.

Dusk was falling after a day devoid of sunshine. The setting sun blanched the branches in the funerary and archaic spinneys. The birds, on the point of disappearing for the night, were chirping competitively in the great silence of the garden of the dead, and it was infinitely sad.

All the roses were strewn on the stone, heaped against the stele, in a bright and magnificent bush.

Interrogating Geneviève with her eyes, Rita made a vague gesture.

"Yes, it's very good," her friend replied. "Since you were determined to express yourself, you couldn't have done it better."

"He'll never know anything about it..." she thought aloud. Then, with glacial irony, she added: "It's discreet, it's poetic, and, in sum, it's perfect."

"Shut up!" begged Geneviève.

"There!" said Rita, drawing away slowly, without taking her eyes off the tomb. "Here lies the love of Charles and Rita, 1929-1930."

Geneviève Le Tourneur made no comment. "Come on," she said. "Let's go."

"Oh, we have plenty of time! Remember that it's the last time that I'll permit myself to think about him. Nothing but this: bringing roses here, while thinking about him, in the guise of a farewell...nothing but this to give me joy...a joy without equal... So, as it's finished, isn't it...?"

"Come on," Geneviève repeated. She drew her away gently.

In the devout solitude in which the dusk seemed to be a prayer, the strewn roses were reminiscent of a young woman lying prostrate. Rita, turning round some distance away, was able to imagine that she had left behind the suave phantom of her dream, and that it was praying.

One never knows. Perhaps the roses' prayer was not without influence on the sequence of events—because there never was a vain prayer, nor a futile rose.

XVIII. The Review of July 1930

The birds were singing in the old-fashioned drawing-room. Cousin Drouet appeared before her visitors, executing an amiable little bow.

"Hey! Good-day, then!" she pronounced, in the most welcoming fashion imaginable.

She was decked out in black, in a loose silk skirt, a velvet spencer jacket with jet decorations, and an English lace bonnet whose strings hung down to either side of her wrinkled and shrunken but hairless face, in which her clouded eyes resembled two faded turquoises.

"Cousin!"

"Cousin!"

"Cousin!"

Colomba, Charles and Bertrand were enthusiastic. There was a delight in seeing that smiling and absurd antiquity once again, that picturesque example of good humor and good breeding—and then again, should they not honor the cousin to the same extent that Madame Christiani, née Bernardi, had neglected her?

"Ah!" she exclaimed, lowering the aged hands that she had abruptly attempted to raise. "How happy I am to see you, my dear children, and only the very day when we'll be able to watch the soldiers of my era march past! For, if I can believe the newspapers, there will be troopers disguised as Second Empire infantrymen."

"From 1830 to 1913, Cousin," said Bertrand. "But especially from 1830."

"That's before my time! But no matter. A Woman of my age is closer to Louis-Philippe than Monsieur Gaston Doumergue! You must think so, historian? Eh? A little pale, a little strained, the historian...you've been working too hard, I'll wager? Come on—I'll clear these windows..."

She rang. One of the housemaids came to take her orders.

"Open those for us, Delphine," said Madame Drouet, pointing to the casements." Then she pivoted on her heel with astonishing petulance and headed at a jerky pace for a fine table with tapering feet, on which stood a gleaming decanter and some tall crystal glasses.

"Do you like Muscat-Frontignan? This is the '83, which is said to be a good year..." She seized the decanter, which was ringed by a sort of breastplate secured to its neck by a little chain.

"Let me do that, Madame!" exclaimed the servant, hurrying over. She had just moved the aviaries aside, not without provoking a dazzling display of plumage and a frantic flutter of beating wings. The windows were now wide open on to the balcony, to which the little dogs raced as quickly as their stoutness allowed.

Delphine grabbed the handsome Charles X carafe from her mistress's hands. "Madame will break everything!" she said, with a conspicuous familiarity, in which respect moderated authority.

"Oh, that's true! Pour, my girl. Colomba, my dear, two fingers of Muscat-Frontignan?"

They were quite at ease with a hospitality that, providing a prelude to the review, already situated them in the past. Charles had not had his fill of contemplating, around him, so many witnesses—mute, unfortunately!—of the life and death of the eccentric César, who seemed determined to reappear, as best he could, in the amusing form of Cousin Drouet.

Meanwhile, that morning—as more than one person, we believe, will remember on reading these lines—the weather in Paris was the most favorable in the world for retrospection. The atmosphere, though merely warm, was a trifle heavy. There was a mist, intangibly, and an occasional stifling oppression. The air, as if powdered, dressed itself in a grey tone that tended towards mauve. There was something rather "close" about it. The streets did not give the impression of being exterior; the outside seemed to be inside. One could have imagined that the Rue de Rivoli was under a glass case in a museum, like the Boulevard du Temple at the Carnavalet. From time to time, though, haphazardly, a pale Sun shone through the greyness, the imponderable muslin, and that white sun was simultaneously so spectral and so delightful that one would willingly have take it for a sun contemporary with the conquest of Algeria, that of Constantine or Isly, a historic sun extracted for the occasion from a cupboard in the Invalides.

People were coming on to their balconies, including men. The flow was considerable, and increased incessantly. In front of the façades, abundantly garnished with blue, white and red flags, a very numerous crowd had wisely gathered, much cooler, more informed and blasé than that of 1835, with which Charles could not help comparing it. The sidewalks were swarming with a multitude whose density increased continuously. The circulation of traffic was interrupted.

How different it was from the royal review the appearance of which the luminite had brought back! What tranquility and civilian and military discipline there was today! But how many faces, too, expressed less ardor and more fatalism!

Meanwhile, a rumor spread, rising from the people aggregated in two parallel hosts. In the distance, the extremity of the Rue de Rivoli was traversed by a dark bar, speckled with colored dots and little flashes of gold and silver.

The racket swelled, then declined again, becoming nevertheless more animated than before.

The multicolored bar advanced, populated with movements. The noise of acclamations began to become perceptible. The troops were approaching. Trumpet-blasts and drumbeat were audible in gusts.

Holding a set of mother-of-pearl opera glasses by their long shaft, Cousin Drouet, flaring her nostrils and raising her eyebrows, watched the progressive approach of the marchpast. A concert of hurrahs accompanied it.

Finally, taking up almost all the width of the thoroughfare, a platoon of Republican Guardsmen marching in step made the wooden pavement resonate. Behind them, some distance away, a dream-like vision slowly advanced: the band, drums and clarions of the old fourteenth line regiment, preceded by a drum-major twirling his stick. And as these revenants came, the sun, functioning like a skillfully-handled searchlight, suddenly placed them in bright golden light, with the result that they seemed to be surging out of themselves, suddenly shaking off the last emblems of death. It was gripping, and the multitude, carried away, howled its enthusiasm, simultaneously applauding the trick of the light, the ingenious surprise of the weather, and the solemn bearing of the living mannequins passing by beneath the shakos of yesteryear, beating their drums and blowing their horns, playing the majestic *Marche de Moïse*—the one that had accompanied the victorious entry of the French army to Algiers.[33]

At that moment, entirely taken up as it was by the spectacle of ancient detachments following one another in columns at widely spaced intervals, Charles thought that this parade was giving him exactly what the luminite had been powerless to reproduce: the noise—the gigantic and diverse noise which, while Louis-Philippe had passed by on July 28, had combined the pitch of bands, the bass of drums and that extraordinary sonic firework display in which resounded all the cheers, shouts, greetings, appeals and joyful gibes of a population elevated by enthusiasm.

The bands, in particular, playing that august march, lent to the auditory representation a very marked impression of antiquity. By closing his eyes, listening to that measured melody beating its processional rhythm in the bosom of the immense clamor, he could easily imagine himself transported back to the Boulevard du Temple on July 28, 1835, by the

---

[33] I have left the title *Marche de Moïse* [Moses' March] in French because of the context. The music in question was added to a revised version of Gioachino Rossini's *Mosè in Egitto* [Moses in Egypt] in 1819, a year after the opera's first performance, and soon became a military favorite.

operation of a luminite that no longer slowed down light but sound.

It was then that something happened that choked, stupefied and maddened Charles Christiani more than anything else in the universe could have done, and his sister and Bertrand Valois no less: the most unbelievable, seemingly impossible thing; a thing, finally, that seemed worse than all that, even though we have announced it prudently. In brief, this:

While Charles closed his eyes momentarily, in order to savor the acoustic reconstitution of the review of King Louis-Philippe, placing himself imaginatively a few seconds before the frightful interruption caused by Fieschi, all of a sudden, behind him, in that apartment ornamented with César's mortal relics, partly decorated in the fashion of the study in which the old corsair had fallen to an assassin's bullet—yes, suddenly, from some unknown point in the gloom, a frightful voice resonated.

"*You recognize me, don't you, Captain?*"

Charles started. He turned round, with a single movement, to face the interior of the drawing-room. But that voice, surely, had only resonated within himself! It was…it was an auditory hallucination, complementary to his dream! He only thought he had heard it! His imagination had escaped, beyond the bands and the clamors!

But no! Bertrand and Colomba, both flabbergasted, petrified, were looking at him, wide-eyed and open-mouthed! What, then? Them too? Had they too heard that terrible voice launching that terrible question?

These reactions were triggered with lightning rapidity. Not three seconds had gone by following that prodigious statement when another voice—this one ringing with a clear and pronounced southern accent—cried, in a tone of fearful alarm: "*Good God! Jean Cartoux!*"

César's voice, of course. The pathetic voice of the Corsican, replying to that of his aggressor, pronouncing the words whose articulation they had not been able to see, because César's back had been turned as he pronounced them! But

263

what was this phenomenon, this sonic conjuring-trick? How had those words come to burst out there? By what miracle of the luminite genre had that dialogue been suddenly defrosted, in the midst of objects left by César—objects that had belonged to the victim?

With a common accord, Charles, Bertrand and Colomba rushed imperiously through the two windows into Cousin Drouet's drawing-room.

No one was there—just the furniture, the bust of Napoléon, the corvette with all sails aloft, the map of the world…

The cousin, in her turn, leaned into the room. She had wasted no time, but everything had happened so quickly! She, however, was smiling placidly.

And suddenly, once again, the vibrant Corsican voice intoned: "*Long live the Emperor!*"

"Well," said the cousin, "look who's awake. It's a long time since he's said as much! It's the Sun and all the drumming, no doubt!"

This time, Charles and the other two had localized the source of the voice; it came, not from a mouth, nor from the speaker of a machine, but from a beak. And that beak, remarkably hooked, belonged to a parrot that had lost so much of its plumage that it was necessary to look at it twice to recognize that its colors must once have been green and yellow.

Charles stared at his cousin, with an expression of illumination. "Pitt?" he asked. "César's parrot?"

"Naturally. He's not yet very old for a parrot. I believe he's no more than 140 years old, and I'm assured that he might live to be 200, with a little luck. Animal of that sort are better endowed than we are; their longevity is extraordinary. Didn't you know that? You seem amazed."

Pitt, almost motionless, like some venerable bonze, resumed speaking at the top of his voice, in the accent of his defunct master: "*Long live the Emperor!… Good God! Jean Cartoux!… Hurrah for Magna Carta!…. Ah! Ah!*"

Then, above the vast magnificent din of the street, the altercation of two voices resounded: *"You recognize me, don't you, Captain?... Good God! Jean Cartoux!"*

The three young people, dumbfounded, became ecstatic in silence.

Charles felt triumphant—and that triumph, so unexpected, so unusual, stifled him with joy.

"He very rarely speaks, for years now," said Cousin Drouet, from the balcony, on to which she had returned in order not to miss any of the costumed review. "Occasions such as this one are necessary to make him do it: faces that he's not used to seeing, unaccustomed sounds…"

"But Cousin, Cousin," said Charles, "you don't know…what he's just repeated…have you never suspected what it is? That name: Jean Cartoux…"

"Oh, he's always said that, along with a heap of other things we can no longer comprehend."

"And it never occurred to you to look for an explanation?"

"Certainly not! I've never attached any importance to it. Is it important? You're making me think so."

The parrot found its memory again, excited by the din of the people and the march-past. It was singing now, bobbing its little bald head:

"When I drink the claret wine,

"Everything goes round and round,

"When I drink the claret wine,

"The whole inn whirls around!"

"I should think that it is important!" Charles exclaimed. "Hold on to yourself, Cousin! It's the name of César's murderer that Pit has just revealed to us. Jean Cartoux!"

"It wasn't Fabius Ortofieri, then?"

"Eh? No. Fortunately, Cousin, fortunately."

The good lady, looking alternately at the exultantly joyful faces that were offered to her, seemed to be doubting many things, beginning with her own good sense.

"Jean Cartoux," said Bertrand. "Does that name remind you of anything?"

"Nothing at all."

"Come on! The Ortofieri case? Your father or your grandmother must have talked to you about the case. Don't you remember that a policeman played a crucial role in the investigation, by attesting that he recognized Fabius Ortofieri as a certain man?"

"Yes…I was told that a police inspector had formally accused Fabius. He affirmed that he had seen him lurking around the house in the Boulevard du Temple and going into it."

"Well, that inspector was named Jean Cartoux!"

"No one told me that."

"It's quite natural," Charles remarked, addressing himself to Bertrand. "When my cousin was old enough to understand the drama—a subject of conversation scarcely suitable for a child—she was doubtless about 16 or 18 years of age. That was in 1862, at the earliest; the case was already a matter of ancient history; nearly 30 years had gone by since the murder. The names of witnesses were no longer of any importance, especially the name of a functionary who had made his disposition in his capacity as a functionary."

"Indeed," said Colomba. "But Cousin, how is it that Pitt, in repeating the name 'Jean Cartoux,' didn't attract the attention of your parents? It seems to me that it ought to have done so, especially given that the bird pronounced the name in César's voice—which proves that he had heard it pronounced by is master, in response to a rather bizarre remark , and that…"

"Pardon me," said Cousin Drouet, "but couldn't you give me some explanation of what this is all about? My word, I'm utterly lost!"

"That's true," Charles admitted, cheerfully. "You won't be able to find your way through it if we neglect to tell you the whole story as we know it."

He did what was necessary in this regard—after which, Cousin Drouet clarified the matter that had troubled Colomba.

Immediately after César's death, the parrot Pitt had been entrusted to an old lady who did Madame Leboulard's sewing and darning, for Monsieur Leboulard had a horror of parrots. César's little comrade had remained with that woman's family until one day when, quite by chance, Amélie Drouet recalled its existence and succeeded in recovering it, in her passion for everything that had belonged to the old corsair, her great ancestor.

The excellent woman had not been able to get her fill of the spectacle of the review in peace. It was from the corner of her eye that she had admired the grenadiers and the fusiliers, then the zouaves, the turcos, the spahis and, to finish up, the oriental cavalcade of the agas and bachagas.[34] But she consoled herself, having understood that, thanks to the parrot, Charles had found an extraordinary joy under her roof, of which she discreetly awaited a more precise revelation.

She had positioned herself on a Restoration sofa and was caressing the two tubby dogs on her lap. Charles knew what it was she wanted to know, and was on the point of telling her that, now Pitt had proved the innocence of Fabius Ortofieri, his rehabilitation would authorize a certain marriage, when he realized disagreeably that his troubles were not over. For, even if the truth was obvious to him, and to Bertrand and Colomba, would Rita's parents be content with testimony as fragile as that...of a parrot?

In truth, the luminite was there to prove to anyone that Pitt had been in César's study at the moment of the murder; the cinematographic films had also, like the second plate, registered his presence and his emotion—which had appeared utterly irrelevant to the spectators of so terrible a drama, a parrot being an insignificant object, virtually non-existent, in a

---

[34] Zouaves, turcos and spahis were various kinds of French colonial soldiers; agas were, in this particular context, Algerian chiefs with whom the French colonial authorities had to deal, and bachagas were the latter's subordinates, who acted as diplomatic intermediates.

room in which a murder had been committed. But would that suffice? No. Certain minds, incredulous or finicky by nature, might refuse to admit the necessary relationship between the presence of the bird and the fact that he had cried today, 95 years later: "Jean Cartoux!" and "Long live the Emperor!" in a southern accent. A detractor might deny Pitt's authenticity.

No, no—the testimony of the centenarian animal was insufficient, or, at least, might be insufficient. It had revealed the truth, but *had not proved it* in a sufficiently irrefutable manner.

The road, however, had fortunately been traveled! The most important thing had been achieved. Charles knew. The doubt that had shackled him thus far had now dissipated completely. And since the truth was known to him—known with a remarkable precision—it ought to be relatively easy to trace its origins. Those origins were now in his possession. He was no longer wandering at hazard in the unknown immensity of the past and the human multitude. What he had was better than a trail; it was the murderer himself, indemnified by his victim among the millions of men of his time, in so many words! In words that a living phonograph had captured and conserved, and which it repeated from time to time, at the behest of its caprice!

Knowing the murderer's name, Charles now felt very well-equipped to seek, even after a century, proofs of his culpability attached to his memory. He had to work quickly, though. Were not the notaries of the banker Ortofieri and Luc de Certeuil conferring that very morning in the Avenue Hoche, in the presence of the interested parties?

Noon chimed. The housemaid poked an anxious face around the door.

"That's all right, Delphine," said Cousin Drouet. "I'll eat later."

Bertrand was striding back and forth with his hands in his pockets, his mind working hard. "Jean Cartoux!" he said. "Of all the people of yesteryear, of whose existence we're aware, he's the last one that I would have suspected! Why the

Devil did that man kill César? And why did he kill him at the exact moment when Fieschi set off his infernal machine? It's a real detective story, that business!"

"Hmm!" said Charles. "Take note that César knew Cartoux, since the other asked him if he 'recognized' him. Now, we know—or think we know—that César had never done anything that might legitimate the intervention of the law. It can't therefore, have been as a policeman that he knew Jean Cartoux…"

Colomba observed: "In addition, what strange sort of inspector must this Cartoux have been, not to baulk at the most abject of false testimony in order to mislead the investigation? He would have allowed an innocent man to be convicted in his stead! He would have had Fabius Ortofieri guillotined!"

And Bertrand added: "I understand why he asked for a leave on the evening of July 28. The real reason was not that he was fatigued, as he said, but that he dreaded being involved in the examinations in César's apartment. He was afraid of being brought face to face with his victim in that fashion. And that's why we didn't see the murderer again—it's because he wasn't among the policemen on duty in César's apartment!"

"I think that Jean Cartoux was taking revenge," said Charles. "His attitude when he came in seemed to indicate a cold, triumphant anger…"

"That's true," Bertrand went on. "But that expression was transformed immediately, when he realized that an assassination had just been attempted against the royal procession."

"That's understandable! Hadn't he neglected his duty and abandoned his post in order to climb the stairway of number 53 and shot César! Oh, the more I think about it, the more I believe that it was a premeditated vengeance. That duty, that obligation to be on the public highway at the moment when the king and the princes passed by—what an alibi for a policeman! Hang on, hang on… 'Jean Cartoux' Is that a matter of chance?"

The aged parrot, amid the cackles of parakeets and the deafening twittering of songbirds, was murmuring, to a well-known tune:

"Tack for tack, we've got them now,
"We'll attack them from the bow.
"With thrusts of the grappling hook..."

"Shut up, Pitt!" exclaimed the cousin. "Oh, there he goes again, singing that nasty song that finishes with a swear-word addressed to the King of England!"

Charles smiled. "The song isn't inappropriate, Cousin. I was just thinking about the mariners who made up the crew of the *Finette*, which César commanded. And I recall that his memoirs, as well as his secret memoir, mention the habitual insubordination of a small number of sailors who were aboard his ship during the famous voyage in which the unknown island was discovered..."

"Well?" Bertrand prompted.

"César had those diabolical fellows clapped in irons readily enough, or ordered that they receive a few vigorous strokes of the lash. Now, one of them was named, if I'm not mistaken, *Jean Carton*. At least, as he didn't write very legibly, I read it as Jean Carton. Today, though, everything leads me to believe that our corsair had formed a *u* like an *n*—a negligence quite frequent everywhere—and that, simplifying the orthography according to the custom of his time, he had simply ignored the x terminating the name *Cartoux*."

"And in time," said Cousin Drouet, "Jean Cartoux had become a policeman?"

"Nothing more plausible. Consider, Cousin, that Fieschi himself, a former sergeant in the Napoleonic army, had been a policeman after the revolution of 1830."

"How do we know, then," Colomba said, "that Jean Cartoux didn't know Fieschi, sine they had been colleagues?"

"My word, that's quite possible! But I confess that I can't see, for the moment, any connection between that possibility and what happened on July 28, 1835. On the other hand, it seems that we've established the origin of the hatred that directed Cartoux's pistol at César's breast. The former sailor wanted to pay his captain back for the harsh treatment to which he had been subjected aboard the *Finette*."

"All that's very well," said Bertrand, responding to his brother-in-law's preoccupation, "but we need confirmation of that, proof…"

"Yes, but how? That's what I'm asking myself. At the end of the day, what use are hypotheses relating to the motive for the crime? What we need, and what will suffice for our purpose, is to possess proof that Jean Cartoux is the murder: one proof, at least, that we can put forward without any possible contradiction. To carry out research on the subject of Jean Cartoux in the archives of the Sûreté, to know what became of him…yes. that's very good. But it's one more thing to do—and time's pressing!"

"And it's getting late," Colomba remarked. "We must let our cousin eat her meal."

"If I had been able to foresee this," she said, "I would have had places set for you."

They refused politely—but Charles, being anxious only deployed a distracted gallantry.

"Excuse him, Cousin," said Bertrand, good-humouredly. "He's in love—but he's wrong to be in a bad mood, for now, I'm sure, he's won his cause."

"Really?" murmured Charles, who smiled anyway.

"In love! A beautiful situation!" said Cousin Drouet, ecstatically. "And might one know…?"

The moon might have fallen on her head and left her less bewildered. The name of Ortofieri had the effect of a sledge-hammer blow. The two families had been enemies for so long that she could not imagine a reconciliation, even in the case that the ancient hatred lost all of its *raison d'être*. It seemed to her that they had hated one another for centuries, especially for the last hundred years. However, she soon yielded to the force of reason, and she was of a time when love had been too enthusiastically cultivated not to range herself willingly on the side of lovers.

271

"*Hurrah for Magna Carta!*" cried Pitt, mutedly. "*All hands on deck! Lower the topsail!*" A risible and yet troubling buffoonery! César's own voice, warm and musical, still surviving!

Bertrand approached the little creature, who moved from one end of his perch to the other, bobbing his head up and down. He spoke to the bird, prompting him with the sentence: "*You recognize me, don't you, Captain?* Come on, Pitt, what's next? *You recognize me…*"

The bird said no more. He gave voice to abominable inarticulate screeches, and that was all.

"Oh!" said the cousin. "When he doesn't want to talk, nothing will make him do it. Sometimes he goes for weeks now, without saying a word."

"Dash it!" said Bertrand, darting a glance at Charles.

XIX. Cartoux

As Charles left the house in which enlightenment had come in such a strangely unexpected fashion, he hailed a taxi. All three of them got into it. Bertrand and Colomba were deposited at their door. A little before 1 p.m., the historian got down from the car in the Rue de Tournon.

In the courtyard, on raising his eyes, he saw a valet who seemed to be stationed at an upstairs window, on the lookout for his return—a perfectly normal thing, at meal-times. But he found the servant on the threshold of the apartment, waiting for him with the door ajar. "Monsieur de Certeuil is in the drawing-room," he said in a low voice.

"What?" said Charles, sure that he had misheard.

"Monsieur de Certeuil had been there since noon. As I told him that Monsieur would surely be back for lunch, he decided to wait."

What does this mean? Charles wondered, extremely intrigued. *Certeuil here? Today? At this hour? Certeuil, who absolutely must see me? How is it that the Ortofieris have not retained him in the Avenue Hoche, for lunch with the notaries? Quite bizarre!*

He hurried to the drawing-room. Luc de Certeuil got up from his chair, smiling. Unusually, he was holding a leather briefcase in his hand, which gave him the new appearance of a businessman.

"Pardon me, my dear Christiani, for having myself introduced at an inappropriate hour, but I have a proposition to make that will certainly not fail to interest you."

The man was speaking with his customary straightforwardness, but that frankness, always artificial, was perhaps less skillfully contrived than usual.

Charles, very cold and distant, remained on his guard. "Please sit down," he said, tonelessly.

Still smiling and wan, with a chalky pallor that was even more obvious today, Luc sat down again and stood the large leather briefcase on his knees. His strong hand, sporting a signet-ring with his coat-of-arms and clutching cream-colored gloves, maintained it in position placidly. He sketched a gesture with the other hand, by way of introducing his subject. "This is what brought me here, my dear Christiani. I want to make you a business proposition. Can you imagine that I have had in my possession, for a long time, papers...documents...which, I presume, are of great value...historically? And, my God, I would gladly release them to you. I repeat, though, to avoid any misunderstanding from the start: it's a matter of business. One thing for another."

There was a brief silence. Charles, a trifle stunned, tried to overcome his amazement. "So," he said, "you're offering to sell me historical documents? That's it, isn't it? You—to me. I beg your pardon, Certeuil, if I insist. I confess to you that your offer is so unexpected, not to say...astonishing. For, after all, in order for you to take this step, you must be constrained by some imperious necessity. Let's be clear: you're in desperate need of money."

"That's right!" said Luc, with a sprightly familiarity. "And I thought...continuing to speak frankly...that you might give me a good price for my documents."

"But after all," Charles went on, nonplussed, "given the present circumstances—of which I don't have to remind you, Certeuil—I have to conclude that, in order to come to me, you must be in a situation that is not only very precarious, but also...special. For, even if you can't offer personal guarantees that might satisfy a money-lender....that hardly matters, damn it, when one considers you as the fiancé of Mademoiselle Ortofieri, the banker's daughter! That's a title that would open the doors of all the strongboxes of all the money-lenders in the world to you! Why not go knocking at the door of one of them? Have you not, among all your relatives and friends, a hundred people who would advance you any sum you care to name, against Mademoiselle Ortofieri' s dowry? Why do you prefer this petty commerce? There must be a reason?"

"The fact is," replied Luc, smiling even more broadly, "that I'm no longer the future husband of Mademoiselle Ortofieri."

"What? Your engagement has been broken off?"

"One couldn't put it better."

"Well, well!" said Charles, who could not help staring at Luc Certeuil with an investigative irony.

A suspicion of embarrassment was visible in the pale features of the young sportsman. "Since a little while ago," he said, "Mademoiselle Ortofieri is free. I recalled that she had the good fortune to please you. *Although*, I said to myself, *it's not sufficient for her to be free for that charming fellow to marry her. It's still necessary for certain obstacles, which oppose that union, to be removed...* Do you get my drift, my dear friend?"

"So what?" said Charles, his curiosity and his scorn increasing.

"Well, it's quite simple. The papers that I've brought you, which are here, in my briefcase, have the power to smooth away any difficulty..."

"You're fantastic, Certeuil, fantastic! Come on! What's all this about? I want to be clear! I need to know everything, and I pray you to authorize me to ask a few questions. Let's take things in order. What happened, this morning? Why are you no longer engaged?"

"Bah! Do you recall, my dear chap, that long conversation that we had, you and I, at Saint-Trojan last autumn? Didn't you notice, when you had confided to me—imprudently, as it happens—your admiration for Mademoiselle, how I hesitated before confiding to you, myself, that I was almost her fiancé?"

"Indeed, I remember it clearly."

"I was because I was extremely embarrassed. I was asking myself whether, rather than run the chance of an uncertain marriage, I might not do better to sell you immediately—at a

275

high price, naturally—the means of marrying the woman you loved. Your revelations had just opened new perspectives to me—less advantageous, it's true, than the marriage for which I had been scheming for months, but also far more certain. I feared that might nuptial hopes might, alas, run into a certain buffer at the last moment—which is what happened this morning. After having reflected avidly and weighed the fors and againsts—cruel alternatives!—I decided to attempt the marriage, and to fall back on the other solution if the marriage fell through. It has fallen through, so I'm following my plan, falling back on the sale of my papers. Obviously, if I'd known, I would have spared you these months of waiting. You'll excuse me for that; business is business, and, after all, present mores being what they are, it could perfectly well have been the case that the Ortofieri family would accept that which, the morning, inflamed them to noble indignation..."

"But, after all, what was that?"

"It's my name, more than anything else, as you know, that permitted me to conquer the sympathy of Monsieur and Madame Ortofieri—my name and my noble titles, of which I had never made any ostentatious display. Unfortunately, that name isn't mine and I have no titles at all, which was revealed before the notary no later than today. These days, when one encounters so many people who wear false names and are received everywhere, I hoped that it might pass...but it didn't. So be it! And that's why Luc de Certeuil, whose real name is Lucien Cartoux..."

Charles started. "Cartoux!" he cried. "Your name is Cartoux?"

"I understand your surprise," said Luc. "'Cartoux,' you will recall—don't you?—was the brave police officer who made a statement against Fabius Ortofieri in 1835. He was, in fact, my ancestor. I don't hide that, and I admitted it quite frankly a little while ago, in the presence of the banker Ortofieri, who was unable to make me regret it. My grandfather was only doing his duty, wasn't he?"

"Well, well!" sniggered Charles Christiani. "Your name is Cartoux, your ancestor was the Jean Cartoux of the Ortofieri case, and you've come to sell me papers that are, in all probability, related to the case. Papers originating I presume, from the policeman in question?"

"You've said it—and I had no intention of making a mystery of something so easy to guess."

"Oh, what a sorry lord you are! What! It's in order to arrive at this abject negotiation that for ten months, you've let us suffer—*her and me*—martyrdom! What! While *she* was within an inch of death, you could have saved her with a word, and you said nothing!"

"I make no claim to virtue," Luc said, slyly steadfast.

"Let's set that aside," said Charles. "It's not for me to judge you. Let's talk business, as you say. These documents are, of course, conclusive and indisputable?"

"I give you my word of honor!"

"Permit me to laugh."

"All right. Well, I assure you, more modestly, that these papers contain undeniable proof that Fabius Ortofieri was not the murderer of César Christiani."

"I suppose, therefore, that—doubtless many years after Fabius's death, which over took him during his preventive detention—your grandfather, the policeman Cartoux, was informed of certain new facts related to the murder?"

"Not exactly, but it comes to the same thing. You'll be settled when I've put you in possession of the document."

"So there's only one of them?"

"Only one, indeed."

"How much?" Charles asked.

"A million."

"Damn! A million! That's rather overdoing things, my dear chap! A million for the confession of Jean Cartoux, seaman aboard the *Finette*, commanded by César Christiani! Jean Cartoux, inspector of the Sûreté, on duty in the Boulevard du Temple on July 28, 1835! *Jean Cartoux, the murderer of his former captain!*"

"How do you know that?" Luc screeched, almost howling.

"Your calculations were false, my poor Certeuil. You've waited too long. This morning, I too learned something. It's the day of revelations, it seems! Before dying, César Christiani formally recognized and denounced his murderer, and there are several of us who now know that!"

"Hard luck!" sighed Luc, who had collected himself with remarkable rapidity. "Say, rather, that it's the day of failures. I've lost everything. I've I'd had any inkling of what would happen, it's me who wouldn't have hesitated, at Saint-Trojan. At the end of the day, though, there's no point wishing things had gone differently. *Au revoir*, Christiani. Since you know everything, and the document is of no value to anyone but you…"

"I beg your pardon," said Charles, negligently, "but as a historian, I'm curious about everything related to History, and I'll wager that Jean Cartoux's confession includes some interesting details. I'll consent, for that reason alone to buy it from you."

"How much?" said Luc, in his turn.

"At my discretion."

"That's not worth much," said the former Certeuil, disdainfully. "Go on, I trust you. Take it. I'll accept whatever you give me."

"Thank you, said Charles, accepting a notebook tied up with humble string. He threw them into a drawer, which he locked and whose key he put in his pocket. "Now, let's settle up."

"No less than 500 francs, though?"

"Wait." Charles took out his pen and a check-book. "Tell me—you're 'on the rocks' aren't you?"

"Well…"

"No vanity. Answer me frankly."

"Yes," said Luc. "Even worse: sunk."

"If I help you to get afloat again, will you swear to me to change your ways?"

"Of course!" cried Luc. "I ask no more than that!"

"Swear."

"I swear it, with all my heart."

"Good. To start with, then, I'll give you a check made out to Lucien Cartoux, right?"

"But 'Cartoux' is the name of a murderer."

"Of a murderer that you aren't! While 'Certeuil' is the name of a crook that…that you have been."

"Thanks for the past perfect tense of the verb 'to be.' Come on! It's settled. Certeuil—Luc de Certeuil—is dead. Put: *Lucien Cartoux*."

"We're beginning to understand one another. Here's the check."

Luc, dazzled, passed his hand over his forehead. "You're a generous fellow!"

"Not as much as all that," replied Charles, taking him by the shoulder. "To begin with, a promise like the one you've just made is beyond price. And then…"

"It's too much! All the same, it's too much!"

"And then," Charles continued, "it's right and necessary that your victim should take his small revenge. The document that you've just given me has more value to me that I let you believe. I didn't have incontestable proof. Thanks to you, I no longer lack anything now."

"Oh well! I'm delighted by it, on my honor as a Certeuil—hold on!—on my honor as a Cartoux!"

"Well done!"

"Nothing remains but for me to take my leave…"

The valet advanced discreetly. "Madame asked me to tell Monsieur that lunch…"

"I'm saved!" said Luc, confusedly.[35]

---

[35] When Luc says "Je me sauve," he is using a conventional formula to express an obligatory refusal of a potential invitation to stay for lunch, but I have given a crudely literal translation [I'm saved] because Charles' retort and Luc's next remark both refer to the double meaning, just as Charles' final *adieu*

279

"Save yourself, then," Charles said, "and in both senses of the term!"

"*Au revoir*, my savior!"

Charles took the hand that was offered to him, a trifle lightly, without affectation, but said very clearly: "*Adieu.*"

---

does not merely counter Luc's *au revoir*/"until the next time" with a conclusive "goodbye forever" but carries a specific implication that the scoundrel must now fulfil the obligation to God incurred by his sworn oath.

XX. All the Light

The apartment in the Avenue Hoche was a sort of palace. The banker Ortofieri got up from an admirable armchair and extended his hand across the immense Louis XV table in his gigantic study toward the old manuscript that Charles Christiani was holding out to him, saying: "To conclude, Monsieur, here is the wretch's confession. Gripped by remorse, he wrote it in his old age—without, however, having the courage to surrender himself to the law. The notebook, in isolation, could not be considered absolute proof of the truth. Any written document might be a forgery—but if we combine this evidence with those that I have just described, we are in the presence of a set of proofs rigorously distinct from one another, whose ensemble is one hundred per cent decisive. There is no longer any doubt. Read this."

"I think," said the banker, with charming courtesy, "that we ought not to waste any more time. For nearly a century, a grievous error has separated our two families. Now that the error is dissipated, every minute that prolongs that separation constitutes a denial of justice, for which we are responsible. Can you not, Monsieur, summarize the contents of this memoir in a few words? Everything that you have told me about the reconstitutions obtained by the luminite and the delightful episode of the parrot has prepared me to comprehend what you are about to tell me, even briefly, and in which I hope—need I confess it—to find the clarification of a supreme enigma."

Charles, marvelously happy with the welcome he had received, and astonished to have "tamed" the "bear" that had been described to him, suspected that a third influence had prepared the way for his visit. Madame Le Tourneur having been informed, by telephone, of the morning's events, it was not very difficult to divine what kind of enchantment had turned the "bear" into a businessman of the most affable sort.

281

It was, therefore, heatedly, and coloring his tale with all the force of enthusiasm, that he sketched out the biography of Jean Cartoux in a matter of minutes.

"This morning," he said, "my sister, my brother-in-law and myself made deductions on the subject of this policeman, which, I am proud to say, are verified by the manuscript that you have in your hand. Jean Cartoux was, as we presumed, a sailor aboard the Finette—an able seaman, to be exact. César's severity, undoubtedly justified, galled him, filled him with rancor and caused him to abandon the sea. How the mariner became a policeman, after having manned the barricades during the Three Glorious Days is what I am about to tell you.

"At the end of 1830, the Prefect of Police, who was named Baude, resolved to purge Paris of a host of vagabonds who had inundated the capital since the July Revolution. In order to carry out the necessary sweeps, he recruited men capable of lending a strong hand to the regular police. Fieschi was one of them, as was Cartoux."

"Ah!" said the banker. "There we are!"

"Illusion!" said Charles. "We're not there yet. Listen to this. While Fieschi ceased to figure in Monsieur Baude's lists and was named, on the latter's recommendation, to work as a supervisor on the project to rectify the course of the Bièvre, Jean Cartoux, by contrast, having given proof of the requisite qualities, passed from temporary to permanent status and took his place among the 32 agents of the Sûreté.[36] He was, there-

---

[36] The figure of 32 is derived from the notorious *Mémoires* of Françis-Eugène Vidocq, published in 1828, whose author gave a highly fanciful and almost entirely fictitious account of his career as a police agent and founder of the unit that eventually became the Sûreté—the equivalent of the English C.I.D. (Criminal Investigation Division)—whose staff gradually increased under his supervision to reach that number. In fact, Vidocq's unit consisted entirely of ex-convicts recruited as informers, who were widely suspected of using their police activities as a cover for their own criminal activities, on which

fore, an inspector in the Sûreté in the era when Fieschi pre-pared his assassination attempt.

"You will recall, Monsieur, that a certain accomplice of Fieschi, named Boireau, had talked imprudently on the eve of the event. The police were informed that an assassination at-tempt would take place in the course of the review, in the vi-cinity of the Ambigu. Now, if the prefect, who was then Mon-sieur Gisquet, had done his job better, and if one of his inspec-tors had not kept to himself a clue that the man came across by chance, Monsieur Gisquet would have known, firstly, that the Ambigu in question was not the new Ambigu but the old one, and secondly, that the potential author of the assassination attempt was a Corsican.

"The inspector concerned was Jean Cartoux. Why, in keeping quiet, did he commit such a serious failure of duty? Out of ambition and vengeance. He had known for some time that César Christiani lived at number 53, Boulevard du Tem-ple. He kept watch hatefully on his former captain, the corsair who had so often punished him by clapping him in irons, and of whom he conserved an infallible souvenir, in the form of stripes on his back. He suspected him of all sorts of crimes and conspiracies, and was on the lookout for any opportunity to harm him—if possible, to ruin him.

"César Christiani was a Corsican. Number 53, Boulevard du Temple was in the vicinity of the old Ambigu. Thus, for Jean Cartoux, the man designated by the denunciation was César Christiani.

"Everyone feared a legitimist plot—everyone else, that is! Jean Cartoux, personally, was convinced that it was a mat-ter of an imperialist plot, for he was sure that the conspirator was named César Christiani, and he knew full well that César Christiani could be nothing other than a Bonapartist. However unlikely it might seem, the old servant of Napoléon had to be

---

basis Vidocq was fired. Cartoux would not have been a misfit therein; his title of "inspector" signifies that he operated in plain clothes, not that he held a superior rank.

in secret communication with the great emperor's nephew, the young Louis-Napoléon, about whom very feeble rumors of ambition were circulating. Finally, it had to be César who had been denounced without being named, since there were no other Corsicans in the indicated vicinity but him and Fieschi, whom Jean Cartoux could not suspect, because he too had been a policeman, performing his duty meekly and humanely, and had subsequently been provided with official employment on Prefect Baude's personal recommendation. It's true that Fieschi was living under a false name—Gérard—but such was the fury of Jean Cartoux's rancor, and such was the force of his preconceived idea, the certainty that he was not mistaken, and the blinding effect of the possibility of obtaining his vengeance and making his fortune at a single stroke, that he did not attach any importance to Fieschi's false name.

"I said: making his fortune. In fact, Jean Cartoux had resolved to be the hero who would save the king single-handed. He did not breathe a word of what he had learned to anyone, in order to reserve all the glory of the act for himself. He had himself assigned by his superiors to surveillance duty in César's neighborhood. At the moment when the king was to pass by, he would get into his enemy's house with a false key, and he would exact justice at the very moment when the regicide was preparing to commit his crime. Nothing would be easier than never to mention the denunciation, and to attribute his prowess to a providential intuition. Then there would be renown, promotion, the august recognition of Their Majesties.

"Unfortunately, just as the police had got the wrong Ambigu, Jean Cartoux had got the wrong Corsican. Instead of running toward Fieschi, he went into Christiani's home, killed him, and immediately realized his mistake on seeing what had happened on the boulevard: the terrifying effect of the infernal machine and the cloud of smoke that, almost directly opposite, was escaping from his ex-colleague's window. The telescope aimed through César's window was not fake, as he had thought at first; the long copper tube did not enclose anything like a rifle-barrel. Bitter disappointment—and sudden terror.

Jean Cartoux had just murdered a man. His crime had no excuse. To cap it all, he had abandoned his post at the moment of an unprecedented assassination attempt. What would become of him if he were found there, next to his victim, a murderer and traitor to his duty? If arrested, he would be lost; perhaps it would also come out that he had known but concealed the truth about the Ambigu, about the Corsican…

"He fled. The disorder on the boulevard was his accomplice. No one noticed him. Throughout the rest of the day he displayed, without pause, a particular zeal, which certainly contributed to his being given the leave that he requested that evening. That leave, as we suspected, had but one aim: to spare his the possible ordeal of having to go back up the stairs of number 53—which filled him with dread. The idea of seeing his victim's corpse again was intolerable.

"Meanwhile, your ancestor, Monsieur Fabius Ortofieri, was incarcerated. It was then that Jean Cartoux committed his second crime, by swearing that he recognized him."

"And it was to the grandson of that scoundrel that I was about to give my daughter!" said Monsieur Ortofieri, sketching a rictus of commiseration. He picked up the manuscript and threw it back across the table with disdainful pity. "I'd like to introduce you to my wife now," he continued. "And…hmm…hmm…to my daughter as well. I assume that they're in the house…"

Charles, very embarrassed, hastened to reply: "My mother will be happy, Monsieur, to pay her respects to Madame Ortofieri. She would like, moreover, in the name of the Christianis, to offer you the homage of our apologies. We owe them to the heir of Fabius Ortofieri."

"May the dead rest in peace," said the banker. "Let's forget these old matters. The essential thing is that there has never been bloodshed between us, nor anything that justified bloodshed. Apologies! You have no need of them!"

"In any case," Charles went on, "my mother is most desirous…"

"Come, Monsieur Christiani!"

Why is he laughing? Charles wondered, as he obeyed the very cordial push that directed him toward a door at the rear of the vast and sumptuous study. He was not long delayed in finding out.

"My dear," said the banker, opening that door, "let me introduce Monsieur Charles Christiani, the distinguished historian."

In the middle of the drawing-room, several familiar individuals grouped around a tea-table turned toward the door were momentarily immobilized by Charles's appearance, which held them, as it were, suspended in their attitudes and their smiles. That momentary immobility was simultaneously reminiscent of a dream and a wax museum. Charles automatically thought of the Monsieur Curtius who had once set up an establishment of that sort in the reign of Louis-Philippe at 54, Boulevard du Temple, opposite César's house. He had to ask himself whether these individuals whom he had discovered unexpectedly might be insensible effigies rather than, in actuality, Madame Ortofieri, Madame Christiani, née Bernardi, Cousin Drouet, flanked by the shade of Mélanie, Bertrand, with his nose, the brunette Colomba, Geneviève Le Tourneur, so blonde and plaintive, and, finally, the incomparable Rita. By that reckoning, he might have been astonished not to see among them simulacra of the master of light, his famous great-great-great-grandfather, Fabius, the invisible accused, pretty Henriette Delille, Monsieur Tripe, the man with the cane, and the sinister Jean Cartoux...

But in the center of the drawing room, at least, there were only people of 1930 there, living and very congenial. Charles, who had not really had any doubt about it, saw that perfectly well when all that affectionate company resumed moving, when Madame Ortofieri started walking toward him, her hands reaching out...and when she was set aside by the irresistible surge of a swiftly-flying little divinity, mad with joy and emotion, running toward him as if borne by the zephyrs of the god of Love: Rita, the diligent enchantress who, in connivance with Colomba, had worked the magic of that assembly.

That child! Passion had carried her away. It was, as they say, stronger than she was. And Charles, incapable of speech, received her in his bosom, where she collapsed, weeping with joy. She hugged him so forcefully that he choked.

"Rita!" groaned Madame Ortofieri, without conviction, making praiseworthy efforts to hold back her tears. But all the relatives in the world would not have been able to prevent Charles and Rita from finally joining their lips together. They would have embraced one another under the fire of a hundred thousand gazes, in front of all of humankind, past, present and future.

Half laughing, half weeping, Charles, in an attempt to restore gaiety, said to Bertrand: "It's a pity no one thought of bringing the luminite! It's a member of the family—and a plate, here and now, would find an occasion worthy of it!"

"What do you take me for?" Bertrand Valois said, feigning indignation. "Would a playwright miss such a denouement? Look!"

Charles turned round.

The plate called "secondary" was there, hanging on the wall. A prodigious window, it had silently absorbed the light of the entire scene. Now it would keep, for many long years, the image of the first kiss that Charles and Rita had exchanged: the image of the tender reconciliation of the Christianis and the Ortofieris.

And because Bertrand, the skillful scene-setter, had split it ingeniously, that plate, like a window to the past, showed the old corsair César Christiani, with his pipe in his mouth, gently caressing the yellow and green parrot on his shoulder, smiling softly at the young lovers.

Afterword

Although it is wrapped in a historical mystery story that is itself wrapped in a love story, the aspect of *Le Maître de la lumière* that remains most interesting to modern readers is the scientific marvel with the aid of which the mystery is solved and the love story brought to a conventional conclusion in the wake of the customary tribulations. It turns out, in the end, that the mystery could have been solved and the love story concluded satisfactorily, even if the scientific marvel had never existed, but the novel would certainly have been much less satisfactory without it, and the story so uncomplicated as to have been hardly worthy of being told.

The text conscientiously explains that the idea of "luminite" was obtained by analogy with the years, or centuries required for light to pass between the stars. It does not, however, make any reference to the previous French scientific romances in which much had been made of the ability of handily-placed observers to see events that had transpired on the Earth's surface long before.

The first work of fiction to do that in any elaborate fashion was Camille Flammarion's *Lumen*, initially published in the collection *Récits de l'infini* (1872), and subsequently expanded for separate publication in 1887. The most significant subsequent work inspired by that aspect of *Lumen* was Eugène Mouton's comedy "L'Historioscope" (1883; tr. as "The Historioscope" in the Black Coat Press anthology *News from the Moon and Other French Scientific Romances*), which features a device akin to a telescope that is capable of picking up cosmically-refracted light preserving images of Earth's past. It seems likely that Renard had read the former work, if not the latter, although—as the introduction to the present volume notes—he might well have come up with the notion of luminite independently, as a result of his attempts to rationalize the

289

"mirage" to which he had subjected the characters in his own account "Le Brouillard du 26 Octobre."

Like most of Renard's pioneering notions, luminite was eventually replicated—quite independently—by a subsequent science fiction writer, Bob Shaw, who termed it "slow glass."

A comparison of the two developments of the idea is interesting in more than one way. Shaw first introduced the notion in the deliberately understated "Light of Other Days" (1966), regarded by many people as one of the classic short stories in its genre, which assumes that the glass in question is marketed in the form of windows, to provide houses with better views than their actual situation permits, but reveals a corollary of that notion in a small mystery whose solution turns out to be a love story. Shaw then went on to write two short "sequels" exploring further applications of the technology, one of which focuses on a plate of slow glass that is the sole "witness" to a crime. In writing that story, Shaw was not only ignorant of Renard's similar use of a similar notion, but also of a not-dissimilar use of a more straightforwardly quasi-cinematic technology in *The Bell Street Murders* (1931) by "Sydney Fowler" (the pseudonym under which Sydney Fowler Wright, a notable writer of British scientific romances, produced hack crime fiction).

Shaw subsequently went on to embed all three of his slow glass short stories within the text of a novel, *Other Days, Other Eyes* (1972), whose main narrative describes the invention of slow glass and the gradual realization by members of the society exploiting it that it has the potential to change that society completely. In the concluding part of the novel, entire nations are "dusted" with particles of slow glass, which, in spite of their smallness, preserve images of everything that happens in their vicinity, making secrecy impossible and ensuring that all future crimes and misdemeanors can be retrospectively observed. That is, of course, exactly what Renard did not go on to do—and, indeed, could not do, within the constraints of the literary marketplace in which he was operating.

In a mystery wrapped in a love story, packaged as a *feuilleton* soap opera, there was no elbow room for Renard to do anything with his own scientific marvel but use it as an instrument of his plot. He could not even indulge in the kind of philosophical rhapsody about its larger implications and possibilities that he had earlier felt able to append to *Le Docteur Lerne* and *Le Péril bleu*, but which had given him such extraordinary difficulty when he made such elaborate extrapolation central to the narrative scheme of *Un Homme chez les microbes*.

Bob Shaw's invention of slow glass was, inevitably, subject to criticism by picky science fiction fans, who did not take long to point out rationally suspect corollaries of the notion—including the inconvenience that, by storing so much energy in the form of retarded photons, slow glass might be more effective as a high explosive than in any other application, and could not plausibly maintain its integrity as a solid. Another awkward objection, which is particularly pertinent to luminite, because Renard makes such an issue out of the ability of observers to look through it at an angle, is that light rays passing through retardant glass at an oblique angle would presumably take longer to pass though it than rays striking it at a right angle, and would thus preserve an image of a more distant past. An observer looking through a retardant window would not, therefore, see an image of a single past but an image of a whole series of pasts melting into one another, with the most recent along the most direct line of slight and the most distant at the periphery of vision.

Since Renard was so proud of having discovered a flaw in the optical logic of *The Invisible Man*, he would presumably have been annoyed with himself for missing the latter point— or if he had thought of it, slightly ashamed of himself for keeping quiet about it. It is conceivable, however, that luminite (unlike slow glass) might be protected from the latter criticism by virtue of the emphasis that Renard places on its laminar structure. If the retardant effect is proportional to the number of lamina that a light ray passes through, and not to

291

the thickness of the material *per se*, then differently slanted rays might be able to preserve images of the same past rather than a sequence of pasts. Perhaps Renard thought of that too, but felt it unnecessary to add such a complication to his narrative.

If that were the case, it would imply that the photons progress through layers of luminite in a discontinuous series of "delayed quantum jumps" rather than propagating in a manner analogous to a continuous wave—a phenomenon not entirely out of keeping with the peculiar ideas of modern theoretical physics, the imaginative extrapolation of which might lead to some intriguing cosmic possibilities. On the other hand, the notion might be an unnecessary over-sophistication of a speculative motif that writhes rather discontentedly within its own externally-imposed limitations.

Like many feuilleton serials, especially those by Paul Féval to which *Le Maître de la lumière* appears to be paying homage, Renard's novel is content to leave some narrative threats hanging loose, as well as wrapping others up with an exceedingly casual swiftness. The "cardboard baby" motif is not really taken to its full extent; Charles and Bertrand make no attempt to investigate the history of the unfortunately-named Monsieur Tripe, although one would surely have expected them to find out whether he actually ever published any of his poetry, and to make some attempt to track his descendants in the hope of finding out who abandoned his father as a baby, and why it was necessary to do so. A more interesting loose end, however, concerns the bargain that Charles offers to what is identified at that point in the text as "*le monde*" [the world], although it is identified elsewhere as Fate, Destiny or God: the offer to sacrifice his own life if Rita's is spared.

Given that there was no need to introduce that notion into the plot at all, let alone to emphasize it with teasing hints that the offer might have been heard and the bargain accepted, the fact that it is subsequently forgotten seems a trifle odd—unless we are expected to believe that the prayer subsequently offered by Rita's rosy *alter ego* has somehow superseded it and cancelled it out. Is it possible that Charles's offer is a hangover from an earlier draft of the work, which ended in a markedly different manner from the extant version? There is no doubt that the present ending—in which the sly enmity of Luc de Certeuil fades away into an unconvincingly abrupt *deus ex machina* and a ridiculously unsatisfactory promise to mend his ways, before Charles's subsequent interview with the banker hurriedly melts away into saccharine schmaltz—contrasts very sharply with the *conte cruel* tendencies and jaundiced view of romantic love expressed in Renard's earlier scientific marvel stories.

If he really had written, or even planed, a version of *Le Maître de la lumière* before the Great War, one would not have expected the besotted Charles to meet a kinder fate than poor Fléchambeau in *Un Homme chez les microbes* or the wretched Robert Collin in *Le Péril bleu*, either of whom might have made a similar bargain with fate (and, indeed, made their own bargains on poorer terms).

As a conscientious and chastened *feuilletoniste,* Renard was, of course, working under conventional obligations that had to be respected, but if the serial was, as one is free to suspect, the second—or even the third, fourth or fifth—"edition" of a text first envisaged in very different circumstances, perhaps the reference to Charles's proffered sacrifice is a deliberate tantalizing reminder of an ending-that-might-have-been, and a consummation deliberately withheld.

In the interests of aiming at a very different effect on the reader, that alternative climax would presumably have endeavored to reduce the petty infatuations of human beings to their true insignificance, within a cosmic scheme that could contain such marvels as luminite.

Is that likely? On balance, probably not; but we are free, nevertheless, to think that it might have been the case—just as we are free to wonder what Maurice Renard might have achieved and become, as a virtuoso of scientific marvel fiction, had he not been so direly fettered by the crass and pusillanimous demands of the literary marketplace of his time and place, thus becoming a Prometheus bound, condemned to await an enlightenment that never did contrive to penetrate the dull grey walls, whether of mist or of slate, that surrounded him.

SF & FANTASY

Guy d'Armen. *Doc Ardan: The City of Gold and Lepers*
G.-J. Arnaud. *The Ice Company*
Aloysius Bertrand. *Gaspard de la Nuit*
Félix Bodin. *The Novel of the Future*
André Caroff. *The Terror of Madame Atomos*
Didier de Chousy. *Ignis*
C. I. Defontenay. *Star (Psi Cassiopeia)*
Charles Derennes. *The People of the Pole*
Harry Dickson. *The Heir of Dracula*
Sâr Dubnotal *vs. Jack the Ripper*
Alexandre Dumas. *The Return of Lord Ruthven*
J.-C. Dunyach. *The Night Orchid. The Thieves of Silence*
Win Scott Eckert. *Crossovers* (non-fiction)
Paul Féval. *Anne of the Isles. Knightshade. Revenants. Vampire City. The Vampire Countess. The Wandering Jew's Daughter*
Paul Féval, *fils. Felifax, the Tiger-Man*
Arnould Galopin. *Doctor Omega*
V. Hugo, Foucher & Meurice. *The Hunchback of Notre-Dame*
O. Joncquel & Theo Varlet. *The Martian Epic*
Jean de La Hire. *Enter the Nyctalope. The Nyctalope on Mars. The Nyctalope vs. Lucifer*
G. Le Faure & H. de Graffigny. *The Extraordinary Adventures of a Russian Scientist Across the Solar System* (2 vols.)
Gustave Le Rouge. *The Vampires of Mars*
Jules Lermina. *Mysteryville. Panic in Paris. To-Ho and the Gold Destroyers*
Jean-Marc & Randy Lofficier. *Edgar Allan Poe on Mars. The Katrina Protocol. Pacifica. Robonocchio. Tales of the Shadowmen* (anthos.; 6 vols.) *Shadowmen* (non-fiction; 2 vols.)
Xavier Mauméjean. *The League of Heroes*
Marie Nizet. *Captain Vampire*
C. Nodier, Beraud & Toussaint-Merle. *Frankenstein*
Henri de Parville. *An Inhabitant of the Planet Mars*
Polidori, C. Nodier, E. Scribe. *Lord Ruthven the Vampire*

P.-A. Ponson du Terrail. *The Vampire and the Devil's Son*
Maurice Renard. *Doctor Lerne. A Man Among the Microbes.*
The Blue Peril. The Doctored Man. The Master of Light
Albert Robida. *The Clock of the Centuries. The Adventures of*
Saturnin Farandoul
J.-H. Rosny Aîné. *The Navigators of Space. The World of the*
Variants. The Mysterious Force. Vamireh
Brian Stableford. *The Shadow of Frankenstein. Frankenstein*
and the Vampire Countess. The New Faust at the Tragicomi-
que. Sherlock Holmes & The Vampires of Eternity. The Stones
of Camelot. The Wayward Muse. (anthologist) *The Germans*
on Venus. News from the Moon
Kurt Steiner. *Ortog*
Villiers de l'Isle-Adam. *The Scaffold. The Vampire Soul*
Philippe Ward. *Artahe*

MYSTERIES & THRILLERS

M. Allain & P. Souvestre. *The Daughter of Fantômas*
Anicet-Bourgeois, Lucien Dabril. *Rocambole*
A. Bisson & G. Livet. *Nick Carter vs. Fantômas*
V. Darlay & H. de Gorsse. *Lupin vs. Holmes: The Stage Play*
Paul Féval. *Gentlemen of the Night. John Devil. The Black*
Coats: The Companions of the Treasure. Heart of Steel. The
Invisible Weapon. The Parisian Jungle. 'Salem Street
Emile Gaboriau. *Monsieur Lecoq*
Steve Leadley. *Sherlock Holmes: The Circle of Blood*
Maurice Leblanc. *Arsène Lupin: The Blonde Phantom. The*
Hollow Needle. Countess Cagliostro
Gaston Leroux. *Chéri-Bibi. The Phantom of the Opera. Roule-*
tabille & the Mystery of the Yellow Room
William Patrick Maynard. *The Terror of Fu Manchu*
Frank J. Morlock. *Sherlock Holmes: The Grand Horizontals*
P. de Wattyne & Y. Walter. *Sherlock Holmes vs. Fantômas*
David White. *Fantômas in America*

SCREENPLAYS

Mike Baron. *The Iron Triangle*
Emma Bull & Will Shetterly. *Nightspeeder. War for the Oaks*
Gerry Conway & Roy Thomas. *Doc Dynamo*
Steve Englehart. *Majorca*
James Hudnall. *The Devastator*
Jean-Marc & Randy Lofficier. *Royal Flush*
J.-M. & R. Lofficier & Marc Agapit. *Despair*
Andrew Paquette. *Peripheral Vision*
R. Thomas, J. Hendler & L. Sprague de Camp. *Rivers of Time*

CINEMA

Stephen R. Bissette. *Blur 1-5* (non-fiction) *Green Mountain Cinema 1* (non-fiction)

HEXAGON COMICS

Franco Frescura & Luciano Bernasconi. *Wampus 1*
Franco Frescura & Giorgio Trevisan. *CLASH*
 Luciano Bernasconi, Jean-Marc Lofficier & Juan Roncagliolo Berger. *Phenix 1*
Claude Legrand, Jean-Marc Lofficier & Luciano Bernasconi. *Kabur 1*
Franco Oneta. *Zembla 1*
Lina Buffolente, Jean-Marc Lofficier & Jean-Jacques Dzialowski. *Stangers 1: Homicron*
Danilo Grossi. *Strangers 2: Jaydee*
Claude Legrand & Luciano Bernasconi. *Strangers 3: Starlock*

ART BOOKS

Jean-Pierre Normand. *Science Fiction Illustrations*
Raven Okeefe. *Raven's L'il Critters*
Randy Lofficier & Raven OKeefe. *If Your Possum Go Daylight...*
Daniele Serra. *Illusions*